NINE DAYS

JOELINA FALK
Unfrozen Four #1

Nine Days
Copyright © 2023 Joelina Falk

All rights reserved. No part of this publication may be reproduced, distribute, or transmitted in any form without written permission of the publisher, except for brief passages by a reviewer for review purpose only.

This is a work of fiction. All names, characters, locations, and incidents are a product of the author's imagination and used fictitiously. Any resemblance to actual persons, events, or things—living or dead—is entirely coincidental.

Updated Version April 2023

You can find me here:

https://www.instagram.com/authorjoelinafalk/
https://twitter.com/joelinafalk

To my mother because not only will she drown me in holy water after this, but she will also provide me with ten therapists.
I love you though, so that's okay.

Note to reader:

This book discusses mental health, more specifically depression, and suicidal thoughts.

The female main character thinks and writes about death *a lot* and glorifies it in her inner monologue slash letters.

Should this be triggering for you, I do not recommend reading this book.

To see the full list of triggers, please head over to my website.

Also please note that just because you might have a different experience with depression, doesn't mean Lily's is depicted as unrealistic. Every individual has a different experience, with different factors that are triggering or tolerable. And just because Lily's doesn't align with your own personal experience doesn't make hers any less real.
Most of these letters, as well as certain thoughts throughout the book, are written from experience.

Playlist

all the kids are depressed — Jeremy Zucker ♡

In My Blood — Shawn Mendes ♡

sex — EDEN ♡

It's You — Henry ♡

comethru — Jeremy Zucker ♡

Roxanne — Chase Atlantic ♡

Dandelions — Ruth B ♡

Little Things — One Direction ♡

Empty Space — James Arthur ♡

this is how you fall in love — Jeremy Zucker ♡

Chapter 1

"wouldn't it be nice to live inside a world that isn't black and white?" –Wonder by Shawn Mendes

Lily Reyes

Dear whoever reads this,

they say time heals all wounds...

they were wrong.

It's been exactly 5840 days and I'm still hurting.

Oh, I should start this off with more information than that. Although I'm sure you are someone who's supposed to be close to me, otherwise you wouldn't have found this book.

I'm Lily Heaven Reyes... and I live in fucking hell.

Not actually, but it feels like it, which is quite ironic given my middle name.

Whatever happens after death can't be much worse than this. I'll be finding out soon enough.

It's too bad that I can't tell you about my experience with death, but I can tell you about my journey toward it.

Anyway, this is my goodbye book, I suppose. So please, make sure to send the letters in this book to everyone mentioned. Or burn the entire thing, it's not like I will ever find out if you did. Is that enough of an introduction?

I only have two more weeks left. Well, that's the time I grant myself. I wouldn't know how much time on earth I have left if I didn't decide it myself, and I'm not here to find out. My life will end in two weeks because I want it to.

"Jesus, Lily!" Winter calls from my bedroom door, interrupting my precious time writing my goodbyes.

If only I could be mad at her for it. Winter has been my best friend since freshman year of college. More or less a good one. We happened to be roommates, and we remained roommates up until senior year. We no longer share one room though. We have separate ones, with one living space, a shared kitchen, and one bathroom. It's not too bad.

Unfortunately, Winter is a self-centered person. She only cares about herself. And if she does *care* about someone else, it's only up until she can turn the topic to herself again.

"Have you been in bed all day?" she asks, staring at me with wide eyes. My room is dark since I never bothered to open the blinds, I also never quite bothered to get up to get dressed.

"I have." Not that it's any of her business. "Is that a problem?"

"You're twenty years old, a senior in college. You shouldn't spend all day, especially not all Friday lying in bed," she tells me. "We're going to a hockey game in an hour. Our school's team is playing against Yale!" Winter flips on my ceiling light, causing my eyes to squint close for a moment. *Perhaps it is darker than I had realized.* "You look horrible, Lils."

"*Gee*, thanks, Winter."

When I manage to open my eyes, I'm greeted by a pair of blue ones staring back at me. Winter is standing at the foot of my bed, her red hair curled into beach waves. She even put on makeup. It doesn't surprise me. Winter is *always* ready to get out of the house. Or dorms for that matter.

"Please don't tell me you forgot." She's staring right into my soul, it's unbearable. Seriously, if Winter lays eyes on someone when she's mad, you'd wish you were dead. But then again, I do wish I was dead. Maybe that's why I don't mind it.

I don't think I'm in any position to judge Winter's eyes too much; I have always had some kind of hatred for blue eyes. It doesn't have a reason, I simply never trusted blue-eyed people as much as I could trust brown-eyed ones. Could be because dark eyes

Joelina Falk

are more interesting to me than lighter ones.

It sort of makes sense that dark eyes seem more trustworthy to me when all I've known my whole life was the dark. The mystery it brings and, as weird as it sounds, it brings me comfort.

"I didn't forget," I lie. "I just don't feel like going anymore."

Despite my wish to die and my incapability to stay happy for longer than an hour, I used to love going out. Every now and then, that is.

It's nothing compared to Winter. She's attending parties every other day. Go her for being social.

But it's not for me.

"Then why aren't you dressed up already? It's Aaron's big day! Scouts will be there, and God knows, maybe he will get an offer to go pro after graduation!" She's way too excited about that.

Though, it's nice knowing one of Aaron's ex-girlfriends still truly cares about him. She always has, but I understand why Aaron got sick of her.

Winter knows I struggle with depression, but she doesn't know how deep it goes. She thinks I take some medication that plasters a smile onto my face and makes me happy again, and that's about it.

"I just lost track of time. But I will get ready right away."

Winter nods in approval and leaves my room.

I will continue this later. Winter urges me to go to a hockey game.
I love hockey though, so that's fine.
    Lily

As promised—*kind of*—I force myself off my comfortable bed and walk over to my dresser. It's all I could fit into this tiny room with a bed and a desk.

I grab a pair of blue jeans, a white, long-sleeved blouse, and a beige sweater vest.

After changing into something more suitable for a hockey game, I walk over to my desk and take a seat. Since Winter takes way too long in the bathroom each morning, I converted my desk into a half vanity and half desk.

I rush to cover up the dark circles under my eyes and add some concealer to areas that need covering up.

At last, I'm adding some mascara and I'm ready to go.

I don't want to leave my bedroom, but I don't have much of a choice. If I don't go to this game, Winter will never forgive me. And neither will Aaron.

"Look at you!" Her mouth stands wide open as her eyes scan my body. "You're so beautiful!"

I know she is lying. Ever since she found out I'm depressed, Winter made it her responsibility to remind me I'm beautiful. Daily. Even when I look like a truck ran me over. Sometimes her lies sound like she believes I think I'm too ugly for this world.

I'm aware that I'm not. I'm depressed, not insecure about my facial features.

"Thank you," I say and give her a small smile. It's a fake smile.

"I do hope I get to go down on Aaron again. Jesus, I miss him so much, Lils." I cringe at her statement.

"I'm sure he would let you in a heartbeat."

"I don't know. He's been pretty cold with me today, and he refuses to talk about it." Her usual happiness now darkens the room. I hate when she's upset, takes me down right with her.

"Well, you two aren't together anymore. Maybe he doesn't feel like talking to his ex about possible struggles," I remind her. It also reminds me that Aaron has as much of a shitty day as I do.

She lets out a long sigh as she walks up to me, wrapping her arms around my neck.

"I wish I could help him through his heartbreak," she cries out in a thick voice.

Somebody have mercy on me, please. I can't deal with tears. Not with my own. Not with anyone else's.

"His parents split up, and according to him, they're still fighting over it."

"It's not that unusual for parents to split up, you know," I say.

"I know, Lils. Your parents separated as well, and they do fight, too. But it's Aaron we're talking about. He is perfect. His life should be perfect." I roll my eyes. Luckily, she can't see it because we're still hugging.

For a short moment, I want to remind Winter that life sucks and everyone's problems matter. But in Winter, there are differences. She doesn't want to see that no matter how deep the water someone's drowning in, drowning stays drowning.

To Winter it has steps. If someone has "bigger" problems than the other, the one with less severe ones shouldn't whine about them. Not in front of the other person at least.

But then, Winter does speak to me about her boy problems. More specifically, Aaron problems. The ones I don't want to hear.

"We should get going. I don't want to miss a second of Aaron's sweet ass." A sort of gagging sound leaves me right after those words leave her mouth. And she laughs. "Ah, maybe we'll see Colin. I'll make sure to set you up for a date with him. He's ridiculously hot, not as hot as Aaron, obviously. But he's single, inked, and just as dark-humored as you are."

Dark-humored. I'm a depressed being, making jokes about my death to cope. Maybe they're not too much of jokes since I do want to die.

Her arms leave my body, and she walks over to our coat rack, getting out jackets for tonight. We're in desperate need of one, for very obvious reasons. Ice rinks are cold unless you're the one on the ice.

For some reason, the cold just disappears when you're on it. Probably because of the movements. No, definitely because of the movements.

I have no idea why that is. I'm not much of a physics girl. I don't understand most of it, so I ignore it.

Chapter 2

"well now I know that I'm the fuel and she's the spark" – Wildfire by Seafret

Colin Carter

"FIRST GAME OF THE SEASON," I ANNOUNCE to my teammates. It's not like they're not aware of it, of course they know. But I guess it's my job as the team captain to say a few words before every game.

The room quiets down. The only sounds filling this locker room are heavy breathing and my voice.

"It's the last season for this year's seniors. It would be a shame if they graduated without a last win." I look around the locker room. Everyone's staring at me. Most of the guys are still half-naked from being mid-changing, but neither of us cares. "This game will determine how good this season will turn out for us." Not really, but you know, everyone has their superstitions. "After last season's defeat at the Frozen Four finals, I think we all have enough rage to rock this one."

A loud roar comes from my teammates. God, they're so annoying sometimes. They couldn't even think of anything better. Other teams cheer or have a special saying, but no, my team roars like a lion.

Come to think a catchphrase such as *"Nine, Nine"* from that TV show *Brooklyn nine-nine* would be great. Maybe like a *"Trews!"*

Okay, no, that's just as stupid as roaring.

"And to all of our new freshmen," I continue, looking directly at the handful of newcomers. "Best of luck proving yourselves worthy for the St. Trewery hockey team."

The St. Trewery ice hockey team has been one of the best college ice hockey teams in the State of New York for as long as anyone can remember, so it won't be easy for them.

"Now that we have a new coach, I think you guys have a pretty good chance to impress him."

"Or not," one of my teammates laughs. I immediately shoot him a death glare. One of our many unspoken rules is and will forever be: *Never make fun of your teammates. And never doubt they can make it.*

Teammates should respect one another, and I find it important to keep that up. I don't need my team hating on each other. Every single one here should know that we've got each other's backs. If one falls, we all do.

"I'm just saying, man. Coach Carter is a hard nut to crack. He's only coaching us because he isn't coaching the pros at the moment. Why ever that is."

I roll my eyes at Aaron Marsh's comment. Aaron is my closest friend of all those douchebags. He's been stuck with me ever since freshman year. We somehow ended up renting a house together.

And the house right across from ours, two of our teammates decided to move in. We share one backyard. Neither of us minds, and neither of us cares that the other two guys hang around Aaron and my house more than they do at their own. Still, we're all referring to the other as "roommate", though technically we're not. Just Aaron and me, and Grey and Miles. The four of us are inseparable.

Aaron is a fit guy. Not only fit, but he also has a brain. He is ridiculously smart, and we all hate it. Not that I don't refer to myself as smart, but this guy, *damn*. I think he's majoring in Architecture. No, I *know* he is. Pretty impressive to me.

Most athletes choose an easier major.

"Yeah, Coach Carter is going to be the death of us," another teammate says. *Miles*. He is one of those filthy-rich kids who get anything they want.

Miles is a lot to take in, and a lot to deal with. Lucky for my father, he knows his way around an arrogant hockey player.

"Enough now. Coach Carter will push us all to our limits, we all know that. But it's what the team needs," I tell them. "He will pity some of your asses though." Laughter erupts.

"You mean, he will pity *your* ass," Miles corrects, raising his eyebrows at me. Of course, they all know Coach Carter is my father.

Under different circumstances, my father would be coaching the New York Rangers. He had recently decided to take a break as he doesn't want to be away from his family, more specifically, from Eira, my younger sister. Eira is sick and before he would regret traveling the world with his team instead of being with his daughter, he decided to take a step back for a while. Hence why he coaches us this year.

However, my father coaching us doesn't mean he will go easy on me.

I ignore Miles's comment. "Now," I speak again, "Get your asses dressed and let's crush Yale!"

Another round of roars echoes through the room. But this time, it's a great spirit. Maybe a roar isn't so bad after all.

♥ ♥ ♥ ♥ ♥ ♥ ♥ ♥

We crushed Yale. 5-0, that's what the huge scoreboard reads when the last second of the timer runs out and a loud, deafening tone shrills through the arena. People jump off their seats and cheer for my team. Other people, probably Yale fans, have their heads hanging low.

I'd be lying if I said winning isn't one of the best feelings ever.

As the team captain, I feel obligated to skate over to the Yale hockey team, their team captain more precisely, and have a quick word with him.

I go tap Anderson on his shoulder blades as I approach him. "Good game," I say, he nods in agreement. At least they're good losers. Before I know it, his team skates off the ice and leaves for interviews, I guess.

"DUDE! FIVE TO FUCKING ZERO!!" Miles cheers, yelling

through the arena. Loud cheers stream through my ears, followed by a ton of "TREWERY!" cheers over and over again. Damned if that doesn't boost my ego.

"Off to the locker room!" Coach Carter claps his hands to get our attention.

He slaps everyone on their backs as they pass him, telling us how good of a game this was. He also adds we could've done better. I'm the last one to leave the ice, the last one to approach my father.

"You've done a great job there, son," he speaks, giving me a fatherly hug. "You make me proud." *Yeah, right.*

I do have a great relationship with my father. He has never been anything but nice to me. He has always supported me and celebrated every victory, but he pushes me over my limits. That's not a bad thing, I don't think, it's just *too* much sometimes.

One time, I was about sixteen years old, he pushed me so far, I vomited on the ice during practice. He made me practice with his team. It was an honor to be there, but since I was only sixteen, not even close to those guys' age. They had way more experience, more intense practice than what I was used to. And sure enough, my stomach couldn't take it anymore and I was emptying my guts on the ice.

Being mortified after *that* would be an understatement. I wanted to sink into the floor, and die right there on the spot.

I'm sure my father is proud of me. I mean, what kind of jackass father wouldn't be proud of their child's victory? But hell, he lives his life through me. He could never go pro himself thanks to an injury, but I can. Unless I fuck up and get an injury like he did. I want to go pro, it's always been a dream of mine. I was maybe three years old when I was on the ice for the first time. Of course, I couldn't do much then, but my father insisted to take me with him. I loved it.

When I step into the locker room, my team is out of control, roaring like they don't care if they lose their voices, singing, dancing in victory. I can't help but laugh at these dorks, but then I join them because to hell with silliness, we fucking won.

I strip off of my hockey gear and quickly throw on some sweatpants and a T-shirt. We've got some interviews to get to, so I'll be showering afterward.

The interviews are as boring as ever, they ask the same old questions and receive the same answers. Vague and without any depth to it.

When we get back to the locker room to *finally* take a shower, I still don't.

I will be going back out there. I want to work on my speed on the ice, and now is my only free time to do so.

"Where are you going?" Aaron asks when I head toward the exit of the locker room, clearly not having my stuff with me.

"Just going to skate for a while. You know, getting some extra practice in," I tell him. He nods slowly, then shrugs and waves me off. I don't owe him an explanation, but I also know he thinks I'm off to fuck someone. "Seriously, just some skating." I point at my feet.

"Didn't say you weren't." He laughs. "Don't stink up the whole rink. We've got early practice tomorrow."

I flip Aaron off with a grin on my lips and walk out of the locker room, heading out with my back first. The second the door closes, I turn around and walk toward the ice.

I'm pleased to find the arena empty. It's an oddly calming silence, one that's good for improving skills. I grab the AirPods case from my sweatpants pocket and stick the buds into my ears, opening my music app right after. I press play on my favorite playlist, only to find out that my sister added some songs when I last visited.

My ears are filled with *Get Into It (Yuh)* by *Doja Cat*. I don't bother skipping the song though. Eira loves her, and whomever Eira loves, I shall love, too. My sixteen-year-old sister would be mocking me right now if she heard the song I'm listening to. Fortunately, she isn't here right now.

Only seconds after I step on the ice, I come to realize that I'm not alone. Sure, my teammates are still in the locker room, shower room, or anywhere back there. But I'm not alone *here*.

Blond hair catches my attention. Someone's sitting right on the opposite side of where I'm standing. Their head is lowered and doesn't look above the boards, which makes it pretty hard for me to identify that someone. I skate closer. So close that I'm now standing in front of *her*, still on the other side of the tempered glass.

I knock on the glass, hoping that will catch her attention. It doesn't, she's in her little bubble. Usually, I would just shrug it off and go back to do my thing, but her body is shaking. I think she might be crying.

The blonde is holding a notebook in her hands, writing something into it. Judging by the few wet stains on the paper, she most definitely *is* crying. *Someone can't take the loss of their hockey team very well.*

Being raised to care for vulnerable people, I tug back my ego and get off the ice. Fortunately, there's an exit right next to where she sits. At least I don't have to make an extra effort to walk all around the rink in skates to get to a crying girl.

She doesn't even notice me when I walk up to her, nor when I sit down beside her. I remove my AirPods from my ears and put them back into the case, then go to take hers out of her ears. Well, one of them.

Green eyes meet mine. Jesus, her eyes are the most beautiful shade of green I've ever seen. She has a few freckles on her nose, spreading over her cheeks and forehead. It suits her and reminds me a lot of someone else I know.

Her eyebrows find together. She frowns at me in confusion. Can't blame her though.

"Are you okay?" I ask. Clearly, she's not. Her face is tear-stained, which means my assumption about her crying was correct. She nods but doesn't use her voice to confirm. "I don't think you are, sweetheart."

She doesn't say anything.

"What are you writing about?" Maybe that's a bit forward, and obviously private as she slams the notebook shut and sets it down on the seat beside her.

"Congratulations on your victory," she speaks. Her voice is sweet and calm, I think I just fell in love with it. That sounds stupid, I admit. Doesn't keep me from wanting her to talk more.

I thank her wholeheartedly, though I'm not sure *she* means it. "Sorry your team lost."

Blondie chuckles quietly, but I'm not sure if it's an ironic chuckle or a "*great, now leave*" one. Perhaps both. "I'm attending St. Trewery, Colin. I wasn't here for Yale." *Oh, fuck me.*

"You know my name," I notice, somewhat bobbing my head.

"You're kind of Trewery's big star, you know." She shrugs unapologetically, giving me a slim smile. Not even a genuine one that reaches her eyes. No. It's a pity smile.

"So, who's your favorite?" I don't think talking to her about what I saw would be such a great idea. So, hockey it is.

"Aaron Marsh," she answers with no hesitation. I must look like I've seen a ghost because she starts to laugh, looking at me with an awfully intense stare that would make me want to back off if she didn't seem all nice.

My hand finds the spot over my heart, my mouth opens as I pretend to be butt-hurt by her favorite hockey player choice.

Aaron is good. He has mad skills; I can't blame her for liking him. And it's not even that, Aaron is *fine*. Even I can say this guy doesn't have issues getting it. Not only because of the tons of girls he brings home every week.

"Sorry, sweetheart, but Aaron doesn't do girlfriends, otherwise I would link you up."

She freezes, but shortly after, she gags.

"I'm good, thank you very much."

"Not into ice hockey players then, huh?"

"I'm not into Aaron specifically." I don't miss the disgusted tone in her voice, but I don't dare ask her about it. "He dated my best friend for a while before breaking her heart." At least she offers me an explanation anyway. I don't believe her.

Nine Days

"Aaron isn't the dating type. So, I call bullshit."

"Aaron totally is the dating type. He just doesn't date anymore because Winter and Aaron have this on-again-off-again thing going since freshman year. But I bet he told you all about it. Aaron adores you." I wonder how she knows. I mean, Aaron and I are pretty damn close, but there's no way she knows that for sure.

He did tell me about Winter and their relationship though. Roughly.

"So, what's the deal with you and Aaron?"

"There's none. I hear a lot about him from my best friend." Again, I don't believe her. But I don't have any other choice, this girl won't talk.

"You know my name, so it's only fair if I get yours," I demand, but she shrugs and gets up from her seat. Without saying another word, she walks away. She. Walks. Away. From me. *Ouch*.

I watch her leave, and when she's around the corner, I notice a mint green notebook lying on the seat. She forgot her notebook, *dammit*.

Maybe I should go after her. Only so she gets her book back, but she's too far away already. I can't possibly catch up with her while wearing skates. I could yell out her name, but I don't know it. Let's pray I will find her on campus, that way I can give it back to her.

The mint green notebook is staring at me, screaming *read me*. I know I shouldn't, but c'mon, as if I could keep this book with me for what? Days? And not look inside at least once.

I allow myself a quick glance, just trying to see if I find any indications as to who she might be, but then I'm hooked.

Dear whoever reads this,

I have no idea how I'm supposed to talk about me. Maybe this will just be a way of me expressing what I felt while writing. Maybe not.

You see, I don't ever speak about my past. Come to think it's a habit of my mother's that I picked up along the way. She never speaks about what happened, but I think it's what I needed back then.

I.

Want.

To.

Die.

I'm not afraid of death. In fact, I think it will be quite peaceful. For me anyway.

I won't have to deal with all these feelings anymore.

I won't have to deal with the pain anymore.

I won't have to deal with the people causing the pain anymore.

I won't have to deal with the constant cries and long nights anymore.

It'll be over. Nothing could be better than that.

I used to be afraid of death, but I can't be afraid of it anymore. How awful could it possibly be?

I could be dead. But that's the whole point, isn't it?

Maybe I will remember my life on earth, have an afterlife, or continue to live as a spirit. But even if that's not the case, it's the best-case scenario.

I don't want to remember me.

    Lily

I stare at those two pages. Two whole pages of the girl I found crying. *Lily*. Two pages on which she talks about death as if she's been fantasizing about it for way too long already.

Two weeks. *God dammit*. This girl is giving herself two weeks left to live. I hope she's joking. Though it'd be a really bad joke.

When I first found the book still lying on the seat, I thought she left it on purpose, I highly doubt that now. There's no way that she ever wanted anyone to find this before she… what? left?

I turn the page to see if she wrote more. She did. I want to read it, but I know I shouldn't. This is her battle, her thoughts. But how am I supposed to ignore a cry for help like this?

I remind myself that this isn't a cry for help. It's a goodbye.

If only I knew more about her. Where is she from? Does she have any other family members who care about her? Who are her closest friends? Literally, anyone I could inform about her situation.

She needs help. But if she wanted it, she would ask for it, right?

Does she know she needs help? Of course, she does. Someone doesn't just want to die for funsies, right?

The next page is the beginning of a letter. One of the letters she mentioned before. It reads *"Dear Ana"*. I wonder who Ana is. Maybe her roommate. Does she live in the dorms? Maybe Ana is her best friend. No, that was Summer. Or Winter? I don't care, it was a season.

Maybe Ana is her sister. I have no idea who Ana is, but she must be close if she's getting a letter.

I try to stop myself from reading any further. This is private. I shouldn't read it. It's not meant for my eyes.

But Lily needs help.

Instead of reading it myself, perhaps I should hand this notebook over to the counselor, the Dean, or anyone. *What do I do?*

Dear Ana,

I'm so sorry.

I'm sorry that I never gave you a chance to be more to me.

Dad told me you always wanted a big sister. You always wanted a sister who would help you out, and give you great advice when it comes to boys. Teach you how to do makeup when you're old enough. You wanted me.

But I didn't want you.

That sounds awful, I know.

I have to be honest with you, Ana. I hated you. For as long as I can remember I wanted you gone because you had what I didn't:

My father.

Joelina Falk

You got to see him daily. You got to have a loving father who would protect you, love you, be there for you. But he was my father, too, you know.

My brother got to experience it along with you. But I didn't.

I couldn't hate him for that, but I could hate you because you weren't my family.

Dad isn't your father, not biologically anyway. But he is mine. And yet, you still got more of him than I ever did.

I was jealous. I think I still am.

But it's time I forgive you for getting what was mine. It's not like you had any say in it anyway.

Ana, I want you to know that all my hatred never had anything to do with you. I feel awful for letting it out on you.

Whenever I would visit, I never paid you any attention because you got enough from the man who was supposed to be there for me, not for someone else's kid.

You were so young when you came to this family, you could not have known what it did to me. I knew I shouldn't have hated you for it. But I did.

And I'm so endlessly sorry for it, Ana.

Maybe we get to be sisters in another life. Despite what I told myself all these years, I like you.

You are a part of my life. Maybe not a huge part, but you are. And I love you, Ana. I really do.

I loved you from the first second I saw you.

I'm sorry I couldn't be a better sister to you, but I will make it up to you in another life. I promise.

And Ana, please don't ever give up on your dreams. I know you can make it far. I will watch over you and protect you from this day forth. I will smile with you, laugh with you, cry with you. Be the big sister you've always wanted.

Nine Days

Even though I may not be there with you physically, I will be there. Every step you take, I will be there.

Lily

Yeah, I shouldn't have read this.

Lily Reyes is writing her goodbyes in a notebook. In. A. Notebook. The one that she forgot here. In an arena for just about *any*one to find.

I jump off my seat, quickly skate over the ice to the other side to get back into the locker room. I have to find her. I have to give this notebook back to her and find someone who can help her.

Standing outside of the locker room, I hear laughter coming from inside, which means some of my teammates are still around. Honestly, I thought they'd be gone by now. I have no idea how long I've been gone, but I assumed long enough for everyone to have left.

"Yo! That was a short skate," Miles says while he's struggling to put on some pants. His hair is still damp from his shower, and I bet he didn't bother enough to dry off his skin before trying to slip into his pants.

Fuck it, right? Miles knows everyone. "Do you know someone called Lily Reyes?" I ask him. Miles shrugs and shakes his head.

"Never heard of her. Is she hot, though?" I roll my eyes at his question. I'm not up for this talk right now.

"Reyes? I've heard that last name before," Grey Davis—the last guy I more or less reside with—informs me. "I think she's in one of my classes."

"Which one?"

"Not sure. I don't pay much attention to people, you know that." That's true, at least in some ways. Grey isn't a people person. He doesn't mind being around people, but he tries to avoid them as much as possible.

"Nah, you don't pay much attention to *girls*," Miles mocks, winking at his best friend. He slaps Grey on his back, then goes to stand on the bench.

It's not even true. Grey *does* pay attention to women, but he tends to pay even more attention to men.

I let out a deep sigh. Whatever is about to come out of Miles's mouth can't be anything good.

Miles mocks people. He's an arrogant ass and uses anything to make stupid jokes at all times. But that's the thing with Miles. No matter how silly and immature he may be, he's the most loyal friend anyone could have. And he would never use anything that's a no-go topic against someone.

I get it though, he was forced to grow up from one day to another.

"I have an announcement to make." Miles holds his hand up, pretending to hold a glass when he says, "I think our team captain has a little crush. That would be a first."

Grey pulls Miles off of the bench, shaking his head disapprovingly.

"I need more information than a name, Princess," Grey says. He raises his brows in anticipation, waiting for the ultimate description on my part.

Okay, maybe Miles is the one hoping for the greatest description, not Grey.

"Uh, she's blond and has green eyes," I tell him. "A few freckles, and she's cute, I guess."

"Ah, now that narrows it down." Grey laughs. "We need a little more than that, Colin. Why don't you just call her and ask for a date already?" Just when I thought Grey would be more mature than Miles.

I wish I could do that. But I don't do dates. "I don't want her that way." I shrug. "She forgot her notebook in the arena, I want to give it back to her."

"Who even still writes in notebooks?" Miles asks, walking away from Grey and me. He's back by his cubby, gathering his stuff.

"What are we talking about?" Aaron comes walking into the locker room with just a towel around his hips. He's always the last one to exit the shower room. For some reason, he has a hard time showering with anyone else in there. Okay, anyone who isn't Grey, Miles, or me. But the other guys, he prefers to stay away from them.

I get that. Some of the guys are assholes. Kaiden Callahan once took a picture of a teammate's dick and sent it to our team group chat... and possible girlfriends. It was a dick move, but Zachery didn't take it too badly. Zac winked at Kaiden and proceeded to pose, making Kaiden take even more pictures.

As I mentioned before, this team is... different.

"Lily Reyes," Grey fills Aaron in. "Forgot her notebook in the arena. Our princess here wants to give it back."

"I can do it if you want," Aaron offers. That's weird. Aaron never does anything for a girl, not since his ex-girlfriend fiasco anyway. Winter was it. God, of course. Aaron knows Lily. He was dating her best friend after all.

"It's fine. Do you have her number so I can text her or something?"

Aaron furrows his eyebrows. Something about his expression screams "*discomfort*". He doesn't like the idea of me texting her. Maybe their relationship goes deeper than I thought. "Don't think she would want you to have it."

"Look, she mentioned you in our short conversation. If y'all are dating, then you can gladly give the notebook back to her, and I promise I won't try to start things. But then you should know something," I tell him.

To my surprise, Aaron does the very same fake gagging sound as Lily did. *That's interesting*. So something did happen between them already, and neither of them is proud of it. But he also doesn't jump on the opportunity to find out what he's supposed to know.

"I take that as you guys aren't dating?" Grey speaks for me. "So what's the deal then? Having a crush? Long lost enemy?" That gets a snicker from me. Lily seems like she has a few of those. I mean, her not-really-sister seems to be one of those. Then again, Lily did apologize for treating her wrongly, so maybe Lily isn't the type to make enemies.

"Nah, neither. Just not my type."

"Marsh, if Carter thinks she's cute, she's totally your type," says Miles, chuckling.

Aaron eyes me. Disgust is written all over his face, but there's more. Something he doesn't want to talk about. Clearly Lily is a topic he doesn't like to discuss, and I respect that. But if there is some kind of relationship between them, maybe he should know about her situation. "Is she an ex-girlfriend? Someone important to you?" I ask. Aaron shakes his head and walks away from us.

He stays in the room, but I suppose he is getting cold.

"Can't tell you guys the deal with her. But we're not a thing, nor will we ever be, trust me on that. But if you touch her…" His voice is strict but still has the slightest amount of discomfort in it.

I shouldn't push him any further, but Aaron Marsh just openly admitted to not being with her, yet he doesn't want me touching this girl.

Something is off, and I will find out what it is.

Chapter 3

"there's just too much that time cannot erase" – My Immortal by Evanescence

Lily Reyes

I can't believe I forgot my notebook in the arena. I must've left it on the seat when I put it as far away from Colin Carter as possible.

I checked every corner of my room already, it's not there. And it's not in the living room either. *Because it's in the hockey arena.* This can't be happening. Fuck that damn goodbye book.

It's only a matter of time before the school's counselor comes marching in here, forcing me to see yet another shrink. Or worse, sends me off to a mental hospital. Can he do that? I mean, he's just a school counselor after all, and I'm twenty years old, I have a say in what's happening to me, right?

My phone chimes. I'm not up for company right now.

Aaron: You forgot your notebook. What did you need a notebook for at a hockey game?

Oh, God. Of course. I should've known Colin wouldn't be able to keep his mouth shut. Does Aaron know what I wrote? No, he would've called me, stopped by personally only to push me off a building himself.

Lily: Homework. Do you have it?

I couldn't possibly tell him the truth. I'm praying he won't open the book and read what's inside. He would tell Dad, or worse, call the counselor and get me into a mental hospital. *Dammit.*

Aaron: Carter has it. What's going on between the two of you anyway?

Lily: Nothing, Ron. We talked for a moment, then I left. Forgot the book, apparently.

Aaron: Mkay. You up for coffee? We should catch up. I don't have the notebook, but maybe I can get Colin to tag along.

I consider it for a second, but Colin most definitely looked inside. He even asked me about what I was writing before, so there's no way he didn't read it when he got the chance to. This means, if he comes, Aaron will find out.
Though, why would Colin even care? He doesn't know me.

Lily: Coffee sounds good. Colin not so much. Just take the notebook with you, will you? And don't look inside, please. It's private.

Maybe telling the only guy who ever truly cared about me not to look into something private is the wrong thing to say. But I know for sure Aaron would not invalidate my privacy unless it's one hundred percent necessary.
If he's smart enough, he will look inside. It wouldn't change anything about the way I feel about life, but it could potentially force me to stay alive a bit longer.

Aaron: Kk. Meet me at Claire's in ten.

Claire's is the only place he shouldn't have chosen. It's always crowded with tons of college students, granted, it's the only coffee shop close to campus. There are a few up in the city, but why would anyone go there when Claire's is a five-minute walk from campus?
I didn't plan on leaving my room again today, but I guess meeting up with Aaron won't be too bad. I've always loved

catching up with him. And I always have a good time whenever we're together. It's like I forget all my pain for a moment. He makes me happy, so why wouldn't I grab a coffee with him?

Okay, maybe Winter wouldn't like knowing I meet up with her on-again, off-again boyfriend. But she doesn't know half the truth, so I don't care.

♥ ♥ ♥ ♥ ♥ ♥ ♥ ♥

But I can't blame him. I'm not sure if he's still at the arena or went home. If he did go home, it will take him at least fifteen minutes to drive down here.

He lives on a college-student street. Well, it's not really a street for college students, other people used to live there, too, but every year the overpriced houses were rented out to college students. Eventually, the families got tired of the noises, the constant parties, and fights, and moved away.

"Can I get you anything, Lily?" Mia, a friend of mine asks. She works here.

"Yes, uh, could I get a Chai Latte and a black coffee, please?"

"Coming right up." Mia writes down my order, smiles at me before walking away.

Good thing I know Aaron's order by heart. Literally anywhere. I know what he will order, even if we have never been there before. It's not only coffee shops, but also any Café or restaurant we go to.

"I'm so sorry, Lily. Carter refused to give me the notebook, so I had to fight for it." Aaron sounds out of breath. He takes a seat across from me and slides the notebook over the table. "I won."

"Thank you, Ron." I take the book and slip it into my purse. "You didn't read it, did you?"

"What? You think I want to read about your sexual fantasies? No thanks."

Relief instantly sweeps through my body. I give Aaron a weak smile, but eventually, this weak smile turns into a genuine one. I don't know how he does it, but his presence makes me feel so much lighter, so much happier.

"How are you, Lils?"

"Stressed, I think. You know, tons of assignments and stuff." I allow a chuckle to cross my lips. I don't feel like talking about me, I never do. Fortunately for me, Aaron loves talking about himself. "Oh, Winter mentioned scouts watching you today."

"Yeah." At first, he tries to hold back his smile, but I know Aaron. I can read him like an open book, and he knows it. The corners of his mouth twitch, and soon enough he's grinning like a toddler. "I'm not supposed to talk about it, but I got an offer from the New York Rangers." He sighs. "Nothing *too* official yet cause… well, NHL rules and such but…"

"Seriously?!" I'm so proud of him. He worked so hard for this, for most of his life. "That's huge!"

"I suppose."

"Quit the modesty, Ron." He laughs and shakes his head at me. "You're never modest about anything. Then this happens and suddenly you don't want to rub it in my face?"

"It doesn't feel the same anymore." *What?*

"What do you mean?"

Before he can elaborate, Mia is back with our drinks. She sets them down on the table and glances at me with jealousy. Yes, jealousy. I know that look on her face. On any face, actually.

I'm surprised Mia is jealous. She usually stays as far away from any jock as humanly possible.

Aaron isn't bad looking. I, however, never fell and never will fall under his spell, for *very* obvious reasons. He's my twin brother.

Mia turns on her heel and leaves as fast as she came. She's going to tell Winter.

"Skating just doesn't feel the same anymore when we don't do it together." *Here we go again.*

I used to skate a lot. I was a figure skater, even did competitions. I loved it more than anything. Aaron and I used to meet up every Sunday to race one another. I've always been faster than him, and I can do more tricks than he can. It was refreshing, playfully competing with the guy you wish nothing but the best.

For most of my life, I was excited to meet him Sundays. I loved our skate dates. Though they were never dates, and it's kind of weird that I refer to them as such. *They're not dates. Never were.*

Eventually, my depression got the better of me and I gave up on skating. I made up excuses as to why I couldn't show up. I never told him the real reason. I know he would have understood, he would have dropped everything to be with me and make me feel better, but I didn't want him to feel bad for me.

So I lied. Told him Mom wouldn't allow me to skate anymore. She was too afraid I could get seriously injured and dic. He didn't question it.

"Aaron," I say quietly. I hate that he's affecting my feelings this much, by being upset only.

He feels bad because skating was both of our passion since forever. Skating was an escape to me until it wasn't. "You know Mom wouldn't be happy to know I started again."

"I can't believe she would do that to you. I mean, she knows how much skating means to you. She knows how much you love it." And now I feel guilty. I hate lying to him, but I can't tell him the truth. Maybe I will tell him someday. *In his letter*.

"She doesn't know we're still in touch. Actually, she doesn't know we've ever been in touch. I think she would officially replace me with another daughter," I say, he chuckles but agrees with me. "I can't believe she never even tried to reach out to you."

"Well, no offense, but I don't want her in my life anymore anyway. Liz has been *my* mother for as long as I can remember." Yeah, Liz Marsh, Aaron's new mother. The very same who broke off my parents' marriage. But, hey, my father loves her, and she loves him, so I'm happy for them. And for Aaron.

"You had Mom up until you were five," I remind him.

"Almost five," he corrects. "But yeah, I guess. And then she pushed me away like I never mattered in the first place."

Sixteen years ago, our parents decided to split up. And as it is, everything gets split in half when a divorce doesn't go through peacefully. The house had to be sold, the money for it got split in half. Every single one of our belongings; sold and the money was split in half.

Their children; split in half.

They thought, *good thing we have two kids, twins even. Makes it easier.* My father got one, and my mother one.

"Lily stays with me. She's a girl. She needs her mother. You can take the boy," she said. I was only five, but I remember her words as she said them yesterday. *"I don't allow her any contact with you or Aaron. And Aaron may never get in touch with me either. This is your half now, your commitment. No going back."* I think I've hated her for years after that.

But I was five, well four but soon to be five. I didn't understand what was going on. All I knew was, I would never see my brother ever again.

Jokes on my mother, my dad's a decent guy. He wanted me in his life, and he wanted to be part of mine. So before he left, we made a deal. Aaron and I would meet up every Sunday at the ice rink in town. I told my mom I had new skating lessons every Sunday. It was my first ever big lie. And I regret nothing.

So every Sunday, Dad, and Aaron would meet me there. We would skate for a while, then grab some food before he took me back to the rink so my mom could come to pick me up.

When I grew older, I used to lie to my mother about where I would spend the nights. I would tell her I was going to a friend's house when in reality, I went to stay with my father and Aaron for the weekend. These were the most fun weekends I ever had.

And my mother never found out about it.

I have no clue why my mother never questioned my new skating lessons, or why she never wanted to come inside to see if I was meeting my coach. But I'm not mad about it.

If she did figure it out, I wouldn't want to know what she would've done to my father.

"Do you think she ever regrets not keeping me in her life?" Aaron asks. A small number of words, yet they break my heart. The answer is no. Mom never regretted turning her back to her son. She never even gave him one more thought after that day. She didn't keep pictures, didn't speak about him to me, didn't even mention him to other people.

When someone asked how many children she had, she had no more than one daughter. Aaron wasn't even worth mentioning.

"No." I know this will hurt him, but I can't keep lying to my brother. He's got a kind soul, he shouldn't hold on to her when she has no intentions to see him or invite him into her life. He deserves better. Liz is better... to him.

The doors to Claire's open. Usually, I wouldn't pay attention to who's entering but when the same muscular figure from the ice rink enters, I can't help but stare.

He's here. What in the world is he doing here?

"Marsh!" Colin yells out. Aaron's back is turned to Colin, so Colin has a great view of me. And he uses it. His eyes are locked with mine. He doesn't seem like he knows anything. Colin Carter just gives me the very same smile he gives everyone else. The star-smile. The I'm-oh-so-much-better smile.

Colin walks up to our table, his eyes still on me before he takes a seat next to Aaron. His hand finds the back of Aaron's neck, grabbing it, and squeezing it before he lets go.

"What's up Lilybug?" Colin nods his head at me. *He read it.* I just know he did. Colin didn't know my name before, so he checked if there was one inside the notebook. Hence how he figured out my name, read the rest, ratted me out to Aaron, and now... what now? He's here. Why is he here? And why isn't my brother yelling at me for wanting to die?

"Lilybug?" I raise my eyebrows at him. He nods. "Seriously?" Another nod. Aaron laughs, of course he's laughing, as is Colin.

"Should I call you *little lady* instead?" he asks.

"How about Lily?"

"No can do, Lilybug."

I let out a sigh. To avoid his intense stare, I'm now looking at my fingers underneath the table, playing with the ring on my left ring finger, though that only ever happens when I get nervous. Why am I getting nervous?

"Hope I'm not interrupting your little coffee date," he speaks, annoying me.

Aaron groans, closing his eyes to calm down, taking a few deep breaths. I just know he's trying his hardest not to grab a knife and stab Colin with it.

"No date, dude. She's like a sister to me."

I *am* his sister.

"So what's the deal then?"

"What's there to be?" Aaron asks in return.

We both agreed on never mentioning that we're siblings. Though, if someone looked at the both of us a little longer than just one second, I'm sure it's obvious that we're twins. We look ridiculously alike. But I'm way shorter than Aaron, probably by a whole foot. Not a clue how that happened.

Aaron and I only agreed to never say a word because we don't want to risk our mother finding out we're at the same college. We did the same back in high school, and elementary. My father made sure my mother never found out.

"Are you an item?"

"For fuck's sake, Carter," Aaron cusses. "Lily and I are not together, and we won't ever be a thing."

"So then what the hell is going on between the two of you? You told me I can't touch her, so there must be something."

Oh yeah, that's the big brother I remember. Aaron never wanted any of his teammates to *"get in my pants"*—his words, not mine—at least not after that one disaster back in high school.

He has always been protective of me, always made sure the guys I've been with weren't some criminals.

It used to be difficult for me to even be with someone because whomever I was interested in, he was never putting up with Aaron's expectations for me.

Which is why the only guys I've ever dated were fictional.

"Just leave it, would you?" I demand.

Colin's eyes meet mine. He looks bemused. I know he's got something against me that could ruin my life or my way out of life. Maybe I should watch my mouth around this dick.

"Fine. Then I don't see a point why I can't fuck her," Colin speaks, his eyes never leaving mine. Aaron presses the palms of his hands to his face, stroking them down with another groan.

He's so gross.

"All right then. No girlfriend shit you have with her, but exclusivity got it. I will stay away." Colin winks at me and gets up from his seat. He makes his way over to another table and sits.

I'm not even surprised when that the table wasn't an empty one. Colin Carter now sits with two brunettes. *Maybe brunette is his type.*

"Your friend is gross," I tell Aaron. He bobs his head in agreement, watching Colin flirt with yet another girl. "But so are you. You do the same thing."

His head whips around, wide offended eyes lay on me. "We're not going to discuss my sex life, Lils."

"Not discussing it. I'm stating a fact."

"Whatever. Tell Winter to come over later tonight." Aaron gets up. He pulls out some money from his back pocket and places it on the table. "I need a good fuck after this."

"*Ew*, Aaron!" He laughs as he walks away.

♥ ♥ ♥ ♥ ♥ ♥ ♥ ♥ ♥

"Lily, I mean it, Aaron hates me!" Winter complains, frustrated. And like the dramatic person she is, she does a perfectly dramatic fall onto my bed, with the back of her hand pressed to her forehead and everything. *She is such a drama queen.*

"Aaron doesn't hate you. He's having a bad day," I reassure her. I'm not sure if Aaron ever truly loved her. I wouldn't blame him if he didn't.

And I'm pretty sure the only person Aaron ever truly loved lives in Germany.

"But I should be the one he wants to talk to, Lils." *Yeah, if they were dating, perhaps.* "He never talks about himself. He doesn't even want me to meet his parents. It's so tiring."

"Then why do you stick around?" I ask. "You're always jumping on the next opportunity to fuck him. He calls, and you run. That's a fuck-buddy arrangement."

"I love him. You wouldn't get that, but I do think he loves me too." Tears roll down her cheeks.

"Love shouldn't be that much work, Winter. If you have to fight for his love, then maybe it's not supposed to be."

She stays quiet. The only sounds coming from Winter Varley are the sobs from all the crying.

Winter ends up falling asleep on my bed. I don't mind it though. My bed is big enough for two people, and to be honest, I could use some company for once.

Chapter 4

"breathe in, breathe deep, you know that's all you need"—Chariot by Jacob Lee

Lily Reyes

It's been two days since I last ran into Colin.

It could have happened yesterday, but I refused to go out with Winter, which was a good decision because Winter ended up in—*surprise*—Aaron's bed.

At least I had the dorm room to myself. I could fill my notebook without any interruptions.

To my surprise, Colin didn't inform the counselor or Dean about me, at least no one tried to reach out to me yet. Maybe he didn't read the entries after all and just looked for a name. Or maybe he asked his friends if they knew whom this notebook belonged to. But that can't be the case, I just recently bought it. No one would have known.

"Twelve more days," I mumble to myself as I write another entry. "Twelve more days and this will all be over."

Today is another one of my down days. That's the case on most Sundays. I would much rather be at the ice rink and skate with my brother, but I can't. Not because my mother wouldn't allow it. Hell, she wouldn't even have a say in it if my lie were to be true, but I haven't been on the ice in three years.

I'm sure I still know how to skate, but I don't want to start loving something again. Not right before my life comes to an end. It's just not worth it.

Dear whoever reads this,

I can't stop thinking about skating.

Ever since Aaron mentioned it on Friday, I can't stop thinking about how good

Nine Days

it felt.

I can't stop wondering if it would still feel this good.

Would I still feel like floating when I step on the ice?

Would I still lose track of all my surroundings when the sound of classical music streams through my ears as I go through my program?

Would I still feel as light as a feather when my skates glide over the frozen surface?

Would it be the same?

Aaron got an offer from an ice hockey team. He doesn't seem too happy, but I know he is. It's what he has always dreamed of.

I'm so proud of him, but some part of me wishes I could see him rank up with every new season. Unfortunately, I will not make it this far.

You should have seen the sadness overpowered him when I told him I will not return to skating.

Let me tell you this:

Aaron and I had this dream. It's silly and unrealistic, but we were determined to make it come true.

Aaron Marsh, the superstar hockey player. He's on the ice, playing against whatever team they're up against. And then, it's one of the breaks. I would get on the ice and entertain the hockey fans while they wait for the game to continue.

I would skate and have fun.

I would have loved this.

We both would have.

It's such a shame that it won't be happening, especially because it's very unrealistic, to begin with.

But, hey, at least I'm determined to go through with my suicide plan.

Okay, this needs a better name.

Joelina Falk

My unalive journey 101.
Sounds just as stupid.
   Lily

"Does this need reasons why I want to die?" I ask myself. "Probably," I answer myself. Yeah, I talk to myself, so sue me.

What if Aaron finds me first and reads this book? He would want to know the reasons behind all of this.

I rest my head in my hands. I can't imagine how devastated my brother will be when he finds out that this notebook was the beginning of my ending, and he held it in his hands before. When he finds out that with just one look into this book, he could have saved my life.

But it wouldn't have saved me. I would find a way to die, even if he found out in advance. This whole thing here, breathing, it's getting too much for me. My body doesn't want to be here anymore, neither does my soul. I'm tired. *Oh, that's a good thing to mention.*

So I start to write again. And after that, I start another entry. And another. And another. Until it's time for the second letter.

The next letter will be even harder on me than Ana's was. I was never close to Ana, but the next person, I owe my life to.

Dad,
If you're reading this, I've died.

Jesus, that's the lamest way to start a letter. Ever.

Don't worry though, I'm not suffering anymore. (I hope)
I used to… when I was still alive. Right in the moment when I'm writing this letter to you.
Dad, I need you to know something.
I'm thankful for you. Truly, I am.

Nine Days

You gave me a family when I needed it.

You didn't give up on me when Mom wanted you to. You know, at the same time she gave up on my brother.

I'm so grateful that you gave Aaron a better mother. Liz is perfect. She's everything Aaron needs to be happy.

So, thank you. Thank you for giving my brother a chance to see me. Thank you for giving him a chance to have a better family than I did.

But most importantly, thank you for sticking around.

You know, it's usually the dads that leave the family. According to some of the "hilarious" internet users. But that wasn't you. You, Dad, you were my hero. You are my hero.

You stuck around when you shouldn't have, at least that's what Mom wanted: you gone.

But you stayed. You stayed for me. You made me happy. You made my childhood less gray.

There's no other way to say this, Dad.

You are my hero.

You were my chariot, urging me to become courageous and determined to take life into my own hands.

You were my savior when I needed you the most.

It's ironic, I know. You couldn't save me from my pain.

You couldn't save me from my suffering. You couldn't save me from committing. But Dad, that's not your fault.

You did nothing wrong. You were always there for me. You always cared.

This is a battle I lost. A battle against myself. There was nothing you could have done to prevent it.

I love you, Dad.

    Lily

Just when I finish writing the letter to my father, the door to the dorm room opens. I hear giggles coming from the living room. It sounds like Winter's, but she's not alone.

"LILS!" *Yup, I can now confirm, it's Winter.* "COME GET DRUNK WITH US!" The hell I will. It's Sunday. I have classes tomorrow. I won't get drunk on a Sunday night with my best friend and whomever her company is. She knows better than to ask me such a thing.

The door to my room swings open in a swift move. It's so fast, I barely even see it until I hear the *thud* it creates when the door slams into my desk. Let's pray my door didn't get any damage from that.

"Mia told me she saw you with Aaron last Friday." A completely drunk Winter stumbles into my room and takes a seat on my bed. Her makeup is smudged all over her face. It's everywhere but where it's supposed to be. She looks awful.

That's a new thing to say because Winter Varley always looks flawless.

"We ran into each other at Claire's," I lie. "Told him to stop playing with you."

"I call bullshit, Lily." Of course she does. Just like everyone else at this college, Winter has no idea that Aaron and I are related. "He's totally cheating on me with *you*. My best friend. You're not supposed to screw guys I'm in love with."

I debate telling her the truth, but Winter has a big mouth. She talks. She loves listening to gossip, and she loves gossiping. If I told her Aaron is my twin brother, she would lose her shit and tell the whole school. Actually, she would probably print it on a banner and hang it up by the main entrance.

Truth is, sometimes I wish people knew. Whenever someone sees us together, they immediately assume we're dating. The disgusted looks I get from that are painful. It's not like it should bother me much, but it does. Either they see me as the biggest whore in history or some bitch that stole their man. Though, Aaron doesn't do dates, and they should know that.

Either way, looks can hurt. And I think people seem to forget that. Not only do words cut deep, looks do too.

"Believe what you want, Winter. I'm not up to discussing this. Aaron and I are *friends*, not ever going to be more than that. If you think your *ex*-boyfriend is cheating on you, then maybe that's a you-problem."

Winter lets out a gasp, covering her mouth with her hand. She looks at me as if I just told her to kill herself.

"You know what, Lily Reyes"—she shoots up from my bed, crossing her arms over her chest—"go fuck yourself!" I don't bother reacting to that. She doesn't give me a chance to either.

The next thing I know, Winter is storming toward my door. She grabs the door handle, pulling it after her as she leaves my room.

But right before she leaves the room completely, she turns around and looks at me one more time. "I liked you, Lily. But you're such a bitch, maybe you are better off dead."

Ironic, isn't it? I believe the same thing. I'm better off dead, and here's proof that not only I believe it.

But the worst bit, even if Winter, my best friend, is mad at me. As a friend, you don't tell the other person they're better off dead. In fact, you don't ever say those words to *anyone*.

Wishing someone to die is not okay. Not ever. No matter how deep your hatred goes.

Who knows, maybe they're like me and wish the same thing.

And who knows, maybe they will go through with it.

Like me.

And oh so suddenly, I feel like I'm *Hannah Baker*, and Winter is my thirteenth reason why.

Chapter 5

"if love is what you need, a soldier I will be" – Angel With a Shotgun by The Cab

Lily Reyes

My film directing class started twenty minutes ago. For some reason, my alarm decided not to go off this morning, which now makes me late for class.

A great way to start my Tuesday.

I've always hated being late for class. Back in high school, I would skip the entire day if I was late.

The looks when you walk into the classroom when you're late scream far more than *judgment*. They're filled with arrogance like any person who was there on time thinks they're something better.

People will pay attention to me. Attention that I don't want or need.

I know the second I open that door and walk inside; people will look at me.

They will look at me and think I'm trouble. They will think that I'm some wrack that can't even set an alarm to be on time.

It shouldn't even matter to me, not right now, *not ever*.

I'm late, so I shouldn't waste any more time thinking about being late. Instead, I should just walk right into the classroom.

Fortunately for me, someone else is late as well.

Unfortunately, that someone is Colin Carter.

He smiles at me as he stands beside me, looks down at me, grinning like the smug superstar he is. The grin he keeps on his lips is disgustingly charming. He has a beautiful smile, so much I can admit.

"Hey there, Lilybug," he greets me. "Since when are you in film directing?"

"Since forever. You would know that if you paid more attention to your surroundings, Carter."

Colin snickers and grabs ahold of the door handle. I inhale a sharp breath. *Yup, this is totally going to be the death of me, emotionally.*

"You okay?"

Why does he care?

Probably because he wants to make fun of you for wanting to die, I tell myself.

But the real reason shows soon enough.

My breath is out of control. It's quick, and I feel as though my lungs don't fill up with air. It's painful. My lungs start to hurt. I'm hyperventilating, aren't I?

Of course I am.

I place my hand over my heart as I stumble backward until my back hits one of the walls. I slide down to the floor. My chest rises and falls so quickly, I can't even see it. But fuck, it hurts. Every breath hurts and yet I don't feel the air coming into my lungs.

"Jesus, Lily," Colin says, a hint of worry sounding through his voice. He approaches me again, kneels. He takes my hand in his. "Breathe," he tells me. *No seriously? Thanks.* "You're okay, nothing is going to happen."

"Would you—" air gets caught in my lungs, but it still doesn't feel like I have enough oxygen in my body to breathe properly "—shut up."

The feeling of death is streaming through my veins. Not that it's something bad, I want to die after all. But not like this. Not at school with superstar Colin Carter watching me.

I feel tears run down my cheeks. Great, now I'm crying in front of the asshole who stole my notebook. Or somehow gave it back to me. Either way, he read it.

My whole body is shaking. My mouth is dry, and I can feel a headache coming. For a moment I'm praying death won't actually feel this way.

No, Lily. It's going to be peaceful. Remember that.

Nope, fear takes over my body. Not the fear of death, fear of the pain. I don't want any more pain, *please*.

"Lily, try to calm down." He speaks calmly as he lays my hand down on his chest. I can feel his chest rise and fall under my palm, taking slow and deep breaths that I try to mimic.

His hand covers mine. Our gazes locked as he counts from one to eight, inhaling. Not once does he break eye contact.

We hold our breaths for a short moment, then he counts again as we exhale. Colin is repeating this exercise for a little while until I find it easier to keep up and my body begins to relax.

Only when my body stops shaking does he release my hand. I immediately pull it away from his chest. For the first time, I acknowledge the worry in his eyes.

Is Colin Carter worried about me? Why would he? He doesn't even know me.

Even though my body's slowly calming, I still find it hard to breathe, hard to feel the air fill my lungs.

"Thank you," I mumble weakly.

"Wait here, don't move, okay?" I nod. Like I was going to do anything else. And just like that, Colin leaves and disappears into Professor Meisner's classroom.

By the time Colin returns, my breathing is almost back to normal, but I still feel drained and more than exhausted. Every muscle in my body feels sore like I've worked out for hours.

My head spins, throbs in pain. There is no way I will make it through the day without breaking down again.

And that's just another reason for me to leave. My own body hates me. I can't fight this any longer.

"We're partnered up for a project," Colin informs me. He grabs my hands and helps me up on my feet. "You're off for the day, Lilybug. No way in hell will I let you attend classes in this condition."

I chuckle at his phrasing. "No way in *hell*," I repeat to myself, but he hears it. "You do know I will be there soon, right?" I know he knows.

"You won't." I'm not sure why *he* is so convinced of that. "If anything, you will get send straight to heaven for fighting against whatever makes you want to die."

"Colin," I say in a whisper. He's still holding me up, but I'm glad he is because I doubt I could stand on my own. My panic attacks aren't normally this bad, but for some reason, they chose today to intensify. "You know we can't be partners."

"Nonsense, Lilybug." There it is again, the smug grin on his. "Even if you decide to kill yourself, it will only benefit me."

"We aim to please, Carter." I offer him a weak smile. I know he's joking. Well, it would benefit him. When I die, our assignment will automatically be graded with an A. "But there is no 'even if' and 'decide', Carter. It will happen. I've made my mind up already."

Colin doesn't respond, he does, however, walk us out of the building, leads me right toward his car. Of course he owns a Tesla. I knew he was rich. I mean, his father coaches an NHL team. His family is probably bathing in money.

"I assumed you'd be more into sports cars. Saw you owning an Audi R8 or some Lamborghini."

Colin snorts, then presses his lips together. "I am. The Tesla is my father's. It's just that my hockey bag barely fits into my BMW, the Tesla has more room for it."

I nod, suddenly feeling like an ass for assuming, even though I was right after all.

"Got my BMW for my twentieth birthday last year, didn't even buy it myself. I feel like a spoiled Frat for never using it."

I hold on to his arm a little tighter, trying to keep myself up.

"Where are you taking me?" I clear my throat. "I live in the dorms."

"I know, Aaron told me. But you're coming with me." The hell I am. This guy can't just kidnap me and take me home with him. I'm not one of his puck bunnies.

"Aaron will chop off your head if you touch me," I say with confidence.

"Aaron will also murder me when I tell him I knew you wanted to kill yourself and I didn't let him know what was going on with you. So either way, I will die." He's not wrong. I can see Aaron throwing Colin out of the house they share because of it. "Gives me a chance to haunt you in the afterlife."

"Fuck you, Carter."

"You want to?" He looks at me with lust, maybe? No one has ever really looked at me like he does. It's like he's staring into my soul but with this desire to undress me. Or he's already undressing me, mentally.

"No, thank you."

"Fine with me." He chuckles. "Now get in the car." Colin opens the passenger door for me and helps me inside. It's not like I need help. Maybe I do. I can't even stand without feeling like I'm tipping over.

Once I'm seated, Colin closes the door and jogs over to the other side. Though, once he's inside the car, he doesn't start the engine yet. He just stares at me for a moment as if he's trying to get me to talk. But I'm not speaking.

He takes the lead. "Do you actually want to die, Lilybug?"

I look out of the window, hoping to come up with words to say. I end up nodding an answer.

There is no way I could explain what he read otherwise. It was as clear as a clean window. The words "I want to die" are unmistakable. There's no way anyone could interpret them differently from what they say.

"Why?"

"That doesn't concern you, Colin."

Colin's lips form a straight line. He knows he shouldn't get involved in my business, and I'm sure he regrets every second of him reading what I wrote. But he did. He read it, all of it. I'm sure once he started, he couldn't stop. And now here he is; stuck with his best friend's suicidal sister.

I've never referred to myself as "suicidal", though it's obvious that's just what I am. A suicidal wrack.

"How come Aaron never mentioned you before?" he asks, changing the topic. Another topic I would gladly stop talking about altogether. Not just with him, with anyone. Aaron and my relationship is nobody's business.

"There's nothing to mention. We're friends. I'm sure you, too, have friends you don't talk about."

"Sure, but they're all dudes, mostly. And I don't care about either of them as much as Aaron cares about you. I mean, Lilybug, he forbids me to touch you, and I never even wanted to. That's not exactly 'we're friends' kind of behavior." He is right. It's not. Aaron is my overprotective, by two minutes older *twin* brother. But Colin doesn't know that.

He starts to drive, accepting my lack of enthusiasm to answer his questionnaire about my family tree. Just that he doesn't start driving toward his house. I know where he lives, and I know how to get there. The direction he's taking is not the one.

"This is not the way to your house," I let him know. He snickers. "Where the hell are you taking me?"

"Relax, Lilybug. You're coming home with me." What does that mean? His *home* is in the other direction. "I need to see my sister. And since I can't leave you by yourself, you're coming with me."

"I'm not going to meet your family, Colin!" Now I'm furious. Is he sick or something? I won't meet his family, it's weird.

"Too bad, you are. My father isn't home because he's coaching *my* hockey team in a bit. My mother is probably at work as well. So it will only be Eira, Reece, you, and me."

"Still. It's weird."

"Why is that? Friends can meet the other's parents, right? And my siblings aren't even my parents, so it's not weird at all." He smirks. Thank God he's looking at the road because I know this smirk is to die for. I've seen it in pictures and videos on Instagram before, even on the college website.

Colin Carter is everywhere. He takes everyone's breath away in a heartbeat.

I bet it's doing his already rock-hard ego nothing but good. The guy who breathes off of others' breaths.

♥ ♥ ♥ ♥ ♥ ♥ ♥ ♥ ♥

An hour passed and we're finally in NYC. Lucky for us, St. Trewery is only a one-and-a-half-hour ride away from Manhattan.

I have never been here before. Never had the chance to go. Dad always promised that he would take me to Manhattan someday, but we never got to do that. My mother would have somehow figured out where I was at. I couldn't possibly tell her I was going there with friends. She's a control freak, she would have asked all of my friends if that was true.

I'm surprised she never questioned my sleepovers back then. Glad she didn't, still surprised though.

I want to get out of the car as soon as it comes to a halt, but Colin stops me. We didn't talk for the majority of the time during the car ride, which is why I'm quite surprised when he chooses now to speak.

"Lilybug," he says in the softest tone I've ever heard him speak in. It's almost flattering.

Looking at him, I feel as though my breath gets caught in my lungs. It should be illegal to look this good.

He's about six foot three, I guess. Colin is a tad taller than Aaron, and Aaron is six foot two.

Colin's hair is long, but not too long. The top half of his hair is rather long and fluffy. Truthfully, I was never a fan of his haircut, but it suits him. A lot.

Colin has blue eyes, the color I don't trust, but for whatever reason, I couldn't picture him with dark eyes.

Don't even get me started on his body. He's muscular. I think that's what most of these hockey players are. Colin's jawline is literally as sharp as a knife. I'm sure if I touched it, it would cut me, despite it being physically impossible.

On top of that, he looks good in a suit. I've seen a couple of pictures before.

Though to be fair, other than the suit, Colin only ever wears black and white, maybe some dark blue if he feels silly. Mostly some black cargo pants and a wider shirt.

The only color I've ever seen on him is red, but only because of his hockey clothes.

It suits him. It suits his body, even when his muscles go lost under his baggy shirts.

Colin has quite a few tattoos decorating his arms. I'm not sure, but I would say his chest is tattooed as well. Assuming, because he has a tattoo on his neck going down to his chest, I haven't actually seen his naked torso before.

I'm also not planning on doing that.

Anyway, his seemingly dark and broody appearance doesn't suit his bubbly personality all too well. Another assumption. I can't judge his personality yet. For me to be able to do so, I would have to know him a little better. But he seems... okay?

What's there not to like about Colin Carter? He's pretty handsome, and apparently, he cares about suicidal girls he doesn't even know one bit.

"I have to warn you about my sister." He sounds serious, sad even if I'm being honest.

"Why would you have to do that?"

"My sister has been diagnosed with..." he trails off. I can see the gloomy cloud rising over him. "She's sick at the moment. She has a fever, but that's not what I have to warn you about."

The cloud vanishes as fast as it came.

"Eira is talkative and cheerful, way too happy sometimes. I don't think you will like that much." Although he doesn't seem upset anymore, his voice says differently.

Colin may be good with plastering model-like smiles onto his face, but he certainly can't hide pain in his voice. I wonder why it's there.

"She talks about death a lot. In a good way, as you do," he tells me. "It's scary."

"I don't think death is scary."

"It is for everyone who doesn't want to die."

"Your sister wants to die?"

There's a twitch on his face like I just hit some kind of nerve that I shouldn't have.

Why would he phrase his sentence like this when he doesn't want me thinking it? What else am I supposed to think?

Perhaps he just wants me to talk to another suicidal person in hopes that it will change my mind.

As if he could hear my actual unspoken question out loud, he answers. "I took you here because I want you to be here, Lily. Eira isn't suicidal. She just doesn't see death as something worth crying over."

He continues, "Just, please don't talk about it. I really don't like this topic. It makes me uncomfortable."

"Colin, in case you didn't notice. I don't talk about wanting to die. Neither do I talk about the pain I feel." I have never said this out loud either, not even to myself. It has always just been on paper.

The pain I feel, four simple words that make it real.

"I didn't think you would. I also want you to know that I didn't take you here to reconsider. Death is off-topic today, for you and Eira."

I have known Colin for four days. Knew of his existence long before that, but we only started talking on Friday.

That's not necessarily true either as we had like three conversations. And for some reason, I come to think he's anything but the asshole I imagined he would be.

♥ ♥ ♥ ♥ ♥ ♥ ♥ ♥

Colin leads me inside the huge house or mansion. It's definitely a mansion. Everything looks so much cleaner than back at my house, although I wouldn't consider my childhood home "dirty". Maybe this house just appears cleaner because of the marble flooring this one has. It's so shiny, bright, and reflective in here, I might need sunglasses.

"Don't worry, not every room looks like this," Colin utters with a slight chuckle.

This entryway is bigger than my bedroom back at home. Of course I'm amazed.

I feel like a celebrity walking the red carpet here, only without the red carpet and paparazzi taking my picture.

Colin gets ahold of my hand, interlaces his fingers with mine, and leads me upstairs.

My heart beats a little bit faster as I come to realize that this floor doesn't just *look* like I could slip on it; it is a whole ass slipping trap.

But, hey, at least if I do slip, fall down the stairs and die, I would have died on expensive flooring.

"What, you don't have an elevator?" I tease jokingly.

"Don't get ahead of yourself, Lilybug. You haven't seen half of this house." He squeezes my hand lightly. "Eira is in her room, and this is the fastest way to get there." There are more ways than one to get to her room? I'm officially blown away.

Though, I'm wondering why Colin only comes here to see his sister. He mentioned someone named Reece possibly being here. Assuming it's his brother, why wouldn't he want to see him?

Colin leads me down the hall once we reach the first floor. He doesn't even give me a second to breathe, and I could use that intake of oxygen.

He approaches a white door, lets out a heavy sigh before forcing a smile onto his face. And for some reason, he's still holding my hand.

His grip tightens as though he's nervous, kind of like he could use some comfort.

Why is he acting this way?

"Sweet chicken nuggets, COLIN!" A brunette girl screams in excitement. She looks just like him, I have to admit. Eira is utterly stunning.

She holds her arms out for him, and finally, he releases my hand

and walks right over to his sister's bed. He picks her up, twirls her around a couple of times before laying her back down. She giggles.

I shouldn't be here. I don't even know this girl. Colin took me here without asking if that was okay with me.

It's not okay with me. This is his family. I shouldn't meet his family. I'm not his girlfriend, and I'm sure that's one of the first questions we will get asked by his parents.

It always is.

"Colin." Eira inhales a sharp breath. "*¡Dios mío!* Is that your *girlfriend*?" She asks excitedly, pointing at me. *Even his sister assumes we're together.*

I press my lips together into a thin line, trying my best not to roll my eyes. I'd die before I'd ever develop feelings for Colin Carter.

When Colin's eyes meet mine, there's something odd in his gaze. Like he's trying to tell me he has to lie to his sister for her own good.

Or maybe I'm overanalyzing it and he just knows that I won't ever have a boyfriend.

He looks at me with sympathy, he does it a lot when he lays his eyes on me.

If *I* were to answer, I would say no. I would tell her the truth. And maybe she should know nothing but the truth.

When the opposite words of my answer leave Colin's mouth—"She is"—a sudden rush of anger bolts through me like fire, burning on my skin.

Colin is as much of a liar as I am. Only that I lie about my happiness, and he lies to his sister about his relationship status.

But when Eira lets out an almost unbearable shrill shriek, I start to believe that she wished for him to be in a relationship. For whatever reasons that might be.

Even if she wants Colin to be in a happy relationship, he shouldn't lie about it. Colin and I are neither happy together nor in a relationship.

"Don't just stand there. Come over here," Eira says to me. She's so energetic, I can barely wrap my head around it. But I suppose Colin did warn me about it.

With as much respect as I could say this, Eira looks awful. She's pale and appears to break any second. She's still beautiful with no doubt, but her, what I assume is the flu that she has, clearly rules over her body, and it shows. Yet, she still has energy left to be happy and cheerful.

I admire that about her.

As she wished, I walk over to her bed and take a seat. The space right next to Colin will have to do. And if it couldn't get any worse, Colin takes my hand in his once again, stroking his thumb over the back of it.

"Tell me everything about you," Eira demands. She wears a huge grin on her lips. It's the same one Colin shows most of the time.

Eira is such a copy of him, which makes me wonder what their mother looks like.

I know for a fact that Colin doesn't look much like his father. Sure, he has some features, like the same nose, same hair color. I'm not sure if he got the eye color from his father though. To be fair, I don't pay much attention to the new hockey coach.

"I wouldn't know what to tell you," I reply in all honesty. It's the truth. Even if I wanted to open up to her, I wouldn't know what to say.

"What's your name? Let's start there."

Colin chuckles at his sister's eagerness.

"Well," I begin, "my name is Lily." *This is awkward.*

"I love it. I'm Eira, but I'm sure Colin mentioned that before." He has, but I don't say that out loud. I prefer to let her do the talking. "When did you two meet? Are you also a senior at Trewery? Do you have a favorite color? What's your favorite animal? Do you like hockey?"

Why is she asking so many questions?

Since my brain consists of two brain cells when it comes to social situations, I only remember two questions. "I do like hockey, and, yes, I'm a senior at St. Trewery."

To my luck, Eira doesn't repeat the other questions she asked before and just moves on.

I listen to Eira babble about literally everything and nothing at all. For the next thirty minutes, she tells me all about how Colin used to take her skating when their mother wasn't around. She mentions something about their mother never liking the idea of Eira being on the ice because her bones have always been pretty breakable.

Somehow we're all laughing at that, but I'm not sure why. It's not necessarily funny.

I also find out Eira is sixteen years old. She spent her birthday at the hospital, it was also the day she decided to go home and spend the rest of her life where she thought she belonged.

I don't question her words. Teenagers talk a lot of nonsense; I know I did back when I was sixteen. I figure going with Eira being a bit overdramatic is the safer option.

"Eira?" A voice shouts from down the hall, only moments before a knock appears on the door and it swings open.

"Ay, Colin. I had no idea you were stopping by this early." A woman, I would assume around forty-five, steps into the room, looking a bit startled. Her hair is blond, but it's obvious it has been bleached before. Okay, it would not be too visible if her roots weren't dark. I'm assuming she had no time to get a touch-up.

Mrs. Carter has a heavy and distinct accent when she speaks.

"I didn't know I was coming until I was," Colin answers.

"Mamá!" Eira does a little excited dance. "This is Lily, Colin's *girlfriend*." Just when I think this couldn't get any worse with the fake-dating scenario that I've never agreed to, it does.

"*¿Novia?*" Mrs. Carter is surprised, but I can't blame her. Colin could never have mentioned me before, and judging by what his mother said, I'm sure he visits a lot. "When did that happen?"

Without opening his mouth, Colin is conveying to his mother the message he should've told his sister. And how do I know that Colin is telling his mother that he isn't dating me? She nods and drops the question like she has never even uttered it.

I'm unsure of how this is even possible. Does mentally conveying a message require a special bond with the other person? If so, I certainly don't have this with my mother.

"It's nice to meet you, Lily." Mrs. Carter holds her hand out to me. I shake it carefully. She offers me a smile, which I return. Good thing I mastered the fake-smile skill a long time ago. "Are you guys staying for lunch?" she asks Colin.

"We would love to, Mamá," Colin answers immediately. I'm not even hungry.

"*Eso es adorable*. I will start cooking then. Do you have any allergies I should know of, Lily?"

Humans, I almost blurt out, but I manage to hold myself back. "I don't, but thank you for asking," I say, giving Mrs. Carter a sweet smile. "Actually, Mrs. Carter, can I help you cook?"

She seems stunned for a moment, but then a huge grin appears on her lips. *They get their smiles from her*. "I would be delighted."

And so I follow her out.

"So, what are you getting in exchange for playing Colin's girlfriend?" Mrs. Carter asks as we walk into the enormous kitchen.

I swallow a giggle, not wanting to be rude by laughing about her question. My answer would most definitely be "*a headache*".

"Nothing. I didn't even know I was playing his girlfriend up until he declared me as such," I answer. Figured the truth is always a great way to go.

"I can't believe this boy sometimes." I can tell she wants to laugh, but just like I did, she holds it back. "Colin never brought someone home." *Just great. Now there are expectations.*

"Really?" I do hope I don't sound disinterested.

"Really. I never thought he ever would. Figured ice hockey would always be more important than meeting someone."

"Well, if it makes you feel any better, Colin and I are just friends, and I'm not sure there would ever be anything more between us." I can't possibly tell her Colin and I would never be a thing because I will be dead in the next ten days. But regardless of my death, I don't think I'm Colin's type. And without my *unalive journey 101,* we would have never even gotten in touch in the first place.

"He's a good guy, you know." She rests her hands on the countertop. "I know, every mother says this about their sons"—*not mine*—"but Colin truly is. He comes to visit Eira every single day. Colin and she were always really close. When she got sick, he even refused to go back to college. He wanted to drop out only so he could be around more often."

That's weird. I assumed it's just the flu. Colin never confirmed Eira has the flu, though he did say she is sick with a fever. It will be over in a few weeks at most.

And once again I'm proving myself that talking to mothers is not for me. I never know what to say, especially to Mrs. Carter.

I offer Mrs. Carter a weak smile. Not because I don't know what to say, I sure don't, but because I believe I shouldn't have anything to say.

"I thought you wanted to start cooking and not tell Lilybug all about your awesome son." Colin's voice echoes through the kitchen. He makes his way to the refrigerator, opens it, and takes out a small orange juice box.

Correction, he takes out *two* of them. After closing the refrigerator again, he walks over to me and hands me one of the orange juice boxes. "Hope you like orange juice," he says with a smile.

"And I thought you were staying with Eira," his mother replies. She's searching through some cabinets until she finds a pot and fills it with water.

"She got tired and wanted to sleep for a while."

Mrs. Carter doesn't reply, but I suppose it's nothing new for Eira to get tired easily. But even though Mrs. Carter doesn't say a word, her face speaks for her. She's in pain, but why? There's no way Eira would walk around dancing while having the flu.

"Lily, *cariño*, would you be so nice and grab me some pasta from the pantry?" If I knew where their pantry was, sure. "Colin can show you where it is." Seems like Mrs. Carter is great at mind-reading as well.

"Sure." Just like that, Colin leads me out of the kitchen and to their pantry.

I'm not surprised to see that everything is so organized in here, with nametags and all the fancy mason jars. They have probably ten to fifteen different kinds of pasta in here, all tagged with their names.

"Now, which ones?" I ask Colin. He laughs like he has no idea either. "Well, I can't just take spaghetti when your mother cooks lasagna."

"She's making lasagna?" he asks.

"Not a clue, and that's what I'm talking about." *Point proven.* "Well, she did take out a pot, so I think it won't be lasagna."

"Lilybug, I have no idea how to make lasagna. Do you really think I gave that pot even one thought?"

"I always thought everyone knew how to make lasagna," I tell him. All I get in response are a few fast blinks as if he's trying to make sense of what I just said. Maybe he feels like I called him stupid. If so, he can gladly feel that way, because I did. "What's your favorite kind of pasta?"

"I don't know, Lilybug. The normal ones?"

I'm laughing. I'm actually and genuinely laughing. I'm wondering how he does that. It's as though Colin Carter is naturally funny even though what he said wasn't even supposed to be.

Does stupidity come with a clown costume?

"Please tell me you know pasta varies in taste depending on their kind." But to my horror, he shrugs.

"They all taste the same. They're all made of the same ingredients, so there's no way they taste differently." Now it's my turn to stand there just blinking at him. He can't be serious, can he?

Not willing to continue this conversation, I decide on Penne. They're one of the more basic ones, can't do anything wrong with them. Taking them from the shelf, I walk past Colin and make my way back to the huge kitchen.

Colin follows, but before I can enter the kitchen, Colin reached for my free hand. "Give me two weeks, Reyes."

"Two weeks for what?"

"To show you that life isn't as bad as it may seem at the moment." *This can't be happening right now, can it?* "Give me two weeks to show you that there is more to live for, more to be alive for. Give me two weeks to make you fall back in love with life."

Chapter 6

"but if you never try, you'll never know just what you're worth"—Fix You by Coldplay

Colin Carter

Lily doesn't exchange a single word with me. Not at my parents' house, not when I drive us back to campus either.

I get Lily doesn't want someone to save her. She made up her mind, but that's just one more reason to let me try, right? She could spend her last days drowning in assignments and emotional pain, or she could give me a chance to make her last days bearable. I just want to try to bring a smile to her face.

Even when her world has been painted gray, she should never stop believing that there is more to life than pain and sorrow.

I'm sure she used to believe it, at least I hope she did, but clearly, she's never gotten the chance to see it.

Eira always talks about how the universe will rip you out of your current life because you're no longer needed. But in exchange, it will give you another adventure.

I never believed in all that. I never believed in the theory of a soul being infinite, immortal, and just wandering into other bodies to collect as much experience as possible.

Technically it makes sense because a body contains energy, and since energy doesn't get lost, it'll have to go somewhere after death, right?

Maybe this whole theory is more common to believe than I could imagine. At least that would be one of the less horrible ways to think about death.

I think Lily wants that, too, leave this life to start another one because she thinks what her current life has to offer is too much to take.

Nine Days

If we go with that theory, then Lily is forgetting something.

She would not have been put in this life, into her situation if the universe didn't know she would be able to take it.

Lily needs to start believing in herself. But most importantly, she needs to see that beyond all the pain lies beauty.

Not one beautiful thing comes without a bad part. It's what *yin and yang* taught us. Bad comes with good, and good comes with bad. It's just a matter of time for the good to shine through, or the bad to fog up the place. Nothing ever comes for free, but nothing ever stays unrewarded either.

Lily is *yin* in this scenario. She's in the dark, fighting through pain. She can't see that *yang* is about to come. She can't see because her world is gray and foggy.

So if there is a chance that I can be her light shining through the darkness, that I can be the *yang* to her *yin*, I have to try.

But I will not accept someone throwing their life away just like that. Not without trying to help.

Lily might not want my help. Fuck, she might even think I'm crazy for caring. I know it's not any of my business, but I can't just let her go through with it. Someone needs to show her what she'll miss out on.

I was lucky enough to never have to deal with anything Lily is dealing with. I will never understand what it's like to feel the way she does. What it's like to look forward to the day they die.

But I can try to give her a helping hand out of her misery.

I roll up at the dorm parking lots and turn off the engine from my car. Even if Lily doesn't want to speak to me, there is no way I would let her be by herself today. Or any day until she agrees to my offer. Or at all for that matter.

"Unlock the door," she demands, trying to get out. The doors stay locked until she agrees. "For God's sake, Colin. Open it."

"Fourteen days, Lily. Give me fourteen days. That's all I'm asking for."

Lily lets out a heavy sigh and falls back in her seat. She doesn't look at me, doesn't speak either. She just stares ahead toward the building entrance in front of us.

She is fidgeting with her fingers. I'm assuming that means that she is getting either uncomfortable or nervous. I've seen her do the same back at my parents' house whenever my mother asked her a question.

"What do you have to lose?" I ask. "You want to die. So what does it matter if you give me two weeks to try, make you reconsider? Either I will convince you, or you will die. But when your mind stays the same, you at least had a good time before death." She won't die, because even if I won't manage to convince her, I'll just get her professional help on the last day.

"Who says I will have a good time?" Her hands turn into fists. "I'm not the type to go big, Colin. I don't have the energy to go out every single day. And besides, I gave myself two weeks left to live. That was four days ago."

"Give me ten days then. I can work with that."

Beautiful green eyes look back at me with something mad in them. Something that screams for me to leave her alone. But I can't.

"I need my off days, Colin. Sometimes even attending classes gets too much for me. Imagine what ten days of constant going out with someone I don't even like would do to me," she says. "That wouldn't be a good time, it would be torture."

"Give me nine days then. You will have an extra day to do all the drowning in self-sorrow on your last day." *Plus it gives me an extra day to get her some help.*

Lily looks out of the window, her head leaning against the glass as she lets out a heavy breath.

"I don't even know you, Colin," she speaks after a good minute of silence. "How would I know that you don't want to murder me?"

"Well, if I did want to murder you, I don't think you would be mad at me. After all, you want to die, don't you?" That gets me an ironic chuckle, easing into sweet, innocent laughter.

Lily has a beautiful laughter. Probably one of the most sincere and sweet ones I've ever heard. It's not too high-pitched, not too low, and it's not fake either. When she laughs, then she does because it's genuine.

Sure, Lily fakes smiles, but who doesn't? No matter how hard she tries to fake a smile, she can't fake a genuine laughter.

And this was hers. Sweet and adorable.

"And besides, when you get on a plane, you don't know the pilot either, yet you trust them with your life, don't you?" She nods. "When you take the bus to go somewhere, you don't know the driver, yet you place your life in their hands and hope you get to your destination without getting into an accident, right?" Another nod. "You don't have to know me to trust me."

"Colin," she breathes out. "Why would you want to do this?"

"I'll even volunteer to make sure everyone gets their letters when you do end up dead," I offer, ignoring her question. "Just give me those nine days, Lilybug. You have nothing to lose."

"I have nine days of my life to lose."

"Wrong," I disagree wholeheartedly. "You wouldn't do anything but finish writing your suicide bo—"

"I named it my *unalive journey 101*," she corrects, interrupting me.

"Fine. You would only finish writing your *unalive journey 101*, stupid name by the way, and cry to some sleazy rom-com."

"Wrong," she mocks. "I would cry to dramas and eat pints of ice cream."

"Same thing."

Lily narrows her eyes at me. She takes a short moment to think before letting out a groan.

"Fine. You have nine days. Eight, because I count today as day one."

"I can work with that." I unlock the car and step out of it. Lily does the same.

In all honesty, I would've liked it if I had opened the door for her, but we're taking it one step at a time.

Now all I need is to find awesome activities to do with Lily in just nine days. That shouldn't be too difficult.

I do, however, hope my father doesn't decide to add even more ice time to my schedule. If it were up to him, he would have the team at the arena from Mondays to Sundays during all of their free time. Luckily, the school says no to that.

I follow Lily into her dorm room. She isn't too happy about me sticking around, but I also don't care.

"What do you even want here?" Lily plops down on her bed, frees some space for me by simply throwing books and papers to the floor. "Sorry, no energy to tidy that up."

Although she claims for her room to be a complete mess, it's not too bad in here, aside from the books and papers she just threw on the floor. Or her desk that's crowded with brushes, makeup stuff, and more books, and her chair that's overflowing with clothes.

Sure, there's a little bit of a mess in some corners, but whose room is ever a hundred percent clean?

I feel the urge to pick the stuff off the floor and lay them on her desk, but I don't want to upset Lily, so I don't. Instead, I take a seat on her bed and make myself comfortable.

And with comfortable I mean, lie down with my head on her mountain of pillows. I rest the palms of my hands on the back of my head and just relax.

Her bed is actually pretty damn cozy. I never thought the number of pillows and stuffed animals—*mostly frogs*—Lily owns would be anywhere near comfortable, but they are.

I might stay here forever.

"We have a film directing project to work on," I remind her. "Told you about it."

"Right. When is it due?" She picks up a notebook from the floor, then grabs a few pens from the nightstand and lays them on her bed.

"We should be done filming by October 7th. It has to be completely done, with cutting, voiceover et cetera by October 15th," I let her know.

"Great, so I will still be alive for finishing the filming part. Sorry to dump the cutting and voiceover onto you."

Nine Days

I did the math as well. Today is September 28th, which means ten days from today would be October 8th, meaning she will still be alive by October 7th to finish the filming.

I can work with that.

What she doesn't know, I will cut the video while filming. I want it to be done early enough so that she can watch it. Because what she isn't aware of, I picked the topic *"Life and its beauty"* for us.

I plan on filming her process. The process of Lily Heaven Reyes falling back in love with life. How she goes from misery to seeing the beautiful parts.

Perhaps it doesn't exactly hit the topic I chose, but then again, it does.

Not one assignment sheet states that we can't portray the bad side and turn it into something beautiful. Not one sentence in the requirements *or* tips section for our project states that beauty is only within flowers and sunshine.

Beauty is also within the darkness. It's within misery and solitude, even if it's masked.

And I will not only show our film directing class that life's beauty is found in everything, but I will also prove to Lily that there is beauty within *her*, and her life.

"Just let me do all the work. I'm a video production major after all. I just need you to be the actress, okay?"

"You are? Because so am I." She looks stunned for a second, but she shakes it off flawlessly a second later. "But if you do all the filming, what am I doing? I can't just act. I'm not an actress. And I'm certainly not a drama major."

"Just trust me on this one. You have no dialogue. Nothing to act out. I will just record you randomly throughout our nine days and maybe ask you to send me some voice notes for a voiceover." She doesn't seem convinced. It appears Lily doesn't like sitting back, and she doesn't like working on a partner project when the parties' work isn't equal.

"Lilybug, it's just a video project. And besides, you'll be dead before this project is officially due. So relax, it's not that deep."

But it is. Because this project could either show that Lily Reyes fell in love with life again or lost the battle. Either way though, this video book will end with a moral to learn from. Which would check off point one from the assignment checklist.

♥ ♥ ♥ ♥ ♥ ♥ ♥ ♥

Lily and I are sitting on the couch in the living room when the front door suddenly opens, and a young woman tumbles into the room.

I pause the TV, not wanting to miss even a second of what's playing. Lily made me watch Grey's Anatomy with her. I've always hated this TV show. There was never a real reason behind my hatred, it's a great show, but it's just not for me. Or so I thought.

Now that Lily makes me watch it, I come to realize that I might actually like it.

"Lily, I'm so sorry," the redhead speaks as she walks into the living room. The living room is the first room that's coming into view when opening the front door, but for some reason, Lily's roommate still takes a bit of time to find her way in.

"Jesus, Winter. Are you drunk?" Lily raises from the couch and walks over to Winter. *So that's Winter.* "It's 4 p.m., your classes just ended, how are you drunk?"

Winter starts to cry. I consider leaving. I shouldn't be here when Lily's best friend walks into their dorm, crying like someone just ripped her heart out. Maybe someone did.

Yeah, I definitely shouldn't be here for that.

But I don't want to leave Lily.

"Come here, sit down," Lily says, leading Winter over to the couch where I'm still seated. I don't dare move. Truth be told, I'm afraid I might get yelled at for being here. So if I don't move, maybe Winter won't see me. *Yeah, right. Because this is some action movie featuring dinosaurs.*

"Aaron broke up with me," Winter cries and falls back against the couch.

"You weren't even dating, Winter. He can't break up with you when you're not a couple." Lily speaks in a soft tone, trying not to sound as though she was making fun of her best friend.

I'm most definitely not welcome here right now. I should leave.
Yet I stay seated.

"He said he loved someone else," Winter speaks through gritted teeth. Suddenly, she sits up straight. Her attention is focused on Lily, so I assume she doesn't even notice me. "We both know this *someone* is you."

I don't agree with random girls most of the time, but Winter does have a point. The way Aaron cares about Lily, there has to be something going on between them.

Aaron never insisted on giving anything back to any woman, unless it would get him sex in return. He also never told me to keep my hands off of someone unless he had a soft spot for her. So clearly, Aaron and Lily are hiding something.

But then why wouldn't Aaron try to stop Lily from committing suicide? Does he even know Lily is suicidal?

"For the millionth time, Winter. Aaron and I are not dating. And to think you believe we are shows your trust in both of us. I told you so, and I know Aaron did too." She lets out a soft breath. "And it's Sofia he's in love with, not me."

Who the hell is Sofia?

I finally decide to leave. This is a conversation they should have in private and not with me, the best friend of the guy in question, being around to hear their conversation.

As soon as I get up from the couch, a hand grabs mine. I turn around for a second as I did not expect anyone to try and keep me from leaving. But I'm even more surprised when I see that it's Lily who's holding my hand.

She looks up at me with brooding eyes, anxiety gleaming on her face. Her grip on my hand tightens.

Lily doesn't want me to leave.

"Stay," she mouths, followed by a pleading expression.

Certainly can't say no to this.

"Oh, my God." Winter spots me right next to Lily. She is still holding onto my hand. "You've got to be kidding me. Now you're cheating on Aaron!?"

"I'm not. Jesus, Winter. You really think I'm some kind of home-wrecker, don't you?" So much to best friends. I doubt a best friend should act the way Winter does.

"I don't, Lils," Winter says. "You're my best friend. You know I would never think of you like that."

"You just did."

"I didn't mean it." She sure did though. "Why is Colin here then?"

"We're friends," I speak for Lily. "Friendships between boys and girls are a thing, you know."

"Is this why you keep seeing Aaron? So you can see Colin?"

Lily's eyes move from mine to Winter's and back. "Yes," she lies. "Aaron is helping me get close to Colin." She lets out a quiet groan, rolling her eyes when Winter isn't looking at her since she's looking at me now.

"I totally got her to confess her feelings for you, Colin. Now you will have to confess yours too."

"I didn't hear any 'I love you's' so that was not a confession," I say, praying Winter will drop it. This situation just got really awkward, and I have no idea where this is going to go if it doesn't stop soon. "I can give you some advice, though, Winter."

"That would be?" Of course that catches her attention. She looks at me with anticipation.

"Drop those feelings for Marsh. He's not into you. And I'm pretty sure he would have mentioned having feelings for Lily to me. He doesn't have the time for commitment at the moment. Just leave it, move on, and be happy."

To my luck, I no longer have to participate in this conversation after that because my phone chimes. I don't care who texted me because whoever did, they just saved my ass from girl talk.

Nine Days

Aaron: Celebrating my birthday this Sat. so drop any other plans you might have, bro.

Speaking of the devil.

Colin: What makes you think I would drop my plans for you?

Aaron: We're going to Vegas to get married, dude. No way you won't attend your wedding.

Sometimes I don't understand this guy. He has the weirdest fantasies. I'm honestly afraid to even question whatever he just texted. I don't think I want it to make sense.

It doesn't even matter. I do have plans this Saturday, and there is no way I would drop them.

I don't think Lily would like to tag along with whatever Aaron is planning. There is no way that Aaron didn't plan something stupid, but I'm certainly not going to let Lily be all by herself watching some boring rom-com all day and night long.

But I could ask her if she's doing anything, maybe that would solve things.

"Lily?" She's in the middle of arguing with Winter. I wonder how I didn't hear them. I'm standing right beside them, and yet I heard nothing.

"I'm leaving!" Winter shouts as she storms off. "You're the worst best friend ever!" *What happened?*

"Don't get pregnant," Lily shouts after Winter.

Winter stops and looks back into the room. Shortly before she would shut the door behind her, she starts to laugh, flipping Lily off.

Unexpectedly for me, Winter comes running back toward Lily, hugs her, and then disappears.

I don't understand women. I don't think there is ever going to be a time I will.

"You said my name," Lily states. "My actual name. You didn't call me Lilybug."

"It's weird for me, too," I admit, though, I know I did it before. "But Lilybug, I have a question."

"And I suppose even if I don't want you to ask, you will ask anyway." She sits back down on the couch, pulling on my arm so I would do the same.

She has a point. Even if she didn't want to hear my question, I would ask. "What are you doing on Saturday?"

"You tell me. It falls into your nine days schedule." She shrugs like she truly thinks I'm planning out her entire days now.

"Lilybug, I don't make decisions for you. You can have plans. I will only ever take a couple of hours from your days. Mostly evenings because I have hockey practice. And believe it or not, I do have plans myself."

"Alright. I planned to visit my mom for a little while. Probably go see my dad, too, but that's unlikely."

"Why would that be?"

"Why did you ask me what I was doing for my birthday, Colin?" She is dodging my question, but I'm okay with that.

There's no other way around this. "It's Aaron's birthday, so would you mind if I took you to his party with me?"

"I know it is." She sighs heavily. "As your date?"

"Sweetheart, we're basically a couple now," I utter. "You will be my date, Lilybug."

"Aaron wouldn't like that."

But sweetheart, I don't care what Aaron thinks, I want to voice, but instead I say, "I will talk to him." She snorts in disbelief. "Here, I will shoot him a text right now."

I hold my phone visible for Lily as I open the chat with Aaron, shooting him a text message.

Colin: Have plans to marry Lilybug instead. Can I bring her?

I figured Lily wouldn't be too happy about the way I phrased it, but I did not think she would beat the hell out of me. But that's exactly what she's doing.

Lily slaps me. Once. Twice. I lose count of how many times her palms come into contact with my arm before I eventually stop her. I grab her wrists and hold her steady to the point where she can no longer slap me.

Her face is so close to mine, I can feel her hot breath roll off my skin. Her lips are so close, it would only take me a slight leaning forward to touch them with mine.

She stares into my eyes, then down to my lips. I smirk when I notice where her eyes keep wandering to.

But that's when she snaps back to reality. "He will murder you, Carter," Lily informs me. "And he will kill me right with you."

"Aw, so you do want us to haunt Earth together as spirits." She rolls her eyes, yet a smile tugs at her lips. I think I'm growing on her. She's growing on me.

Man, today's our first official day of hanging out together. The first day we've truly talked, exchanged more words than five and she's already got me wrapped around her finger.

What the…?

"Fuck you, Colin." Now if that's not an invitation.

"I think we should get to know one another a little bit better first. But you could kiss me."

Her jaw drops. I can tell she's trying to find words to say, but somehow can't articulate herself properly. So she just stares at me in shock, blinking.

"I'm not kissing you, dumbass." I guess she found her voice after all.

I can't help the laughter that follows.

The way her eyes are trying to express rage, but she's too confused by what I've said is the most adorable view I have ever seen. No, the most adorable confusion I've ever witnessed.

Her nose scrunches up when she processes information she didn't expect; that much I learned about her. And she's speechless a lot, Or maybe she just never expected me to tag alongside her, so that's why she has a hard time processing *my* words.

"Did you just give me a really cute pet name?" I pout at her.
"I called you a dumbass."
"Like I said, a cute pet name."
Lily shakes her head regrettably, speechless once more.
That's a 1:0 for me, Lilybug.

Aaron: Fuck off, dude. I told you to stay away from Lily.

Looks like Aaron truly doesn't want me hanging around Lily. Should I listen to him? *Totally.*
Do I care? *I certainly should.*
Am I going to continue to speak to my Lilybug despite his demands, and risk my best friend chopping off my head for betraying the bro-code? *Most definitely.*
"I told you Aaron wouldn't be too happy about it," Miss Know-it-all says. I forgot she could look at my screen and read my texts.
"Maybe I would back off if I knew why he wants me to stay away. You two aren't dating, the both of you made that pretty clear. Tell me what the deal is, Lilybug, so I can ogle you without feeling guilty." All this is getting totally weird.
Not a single guy acts like that unless he thinks the dude wanting to be with the girl is a total dick. And even then, most guys don't even care. Unless there's a way deeper meaning behind all of it.
"Tell me, Lilybug." I give her the most hopeful and pleading eyes I have to offer. "*Please.*"

Aaron: You can bring her, but if I see you touching her just once, I will have to chop off your hands.

Doesn't that just prove my point?
Lily's silent treatment tells me that she won't budge, so I'll have to find another way to get the information out of her. "When did Aaron and you meet?"
"A long time ago." *Seriously?*
"Alright. Who was your first boyfriend?"

"First grade, he was fictional. Just like every other guy. Why's that relevant?" Her eyes narrow at me. "Who was your first girlfriend?" Lily asks in return.

"I've never had one." I shrug. I'm not ashamed of it. I could've had some before, but I didn't want one.

None of the girls who were throwing themselves at me piqued my interest. I did other things, but I never wanted to go any further with it.

I was kind of telling myself that I would know if she was the right one. That it would click right away. We would get along right when we meet, and that would have nothing to do with sexual tension.

Aiden used to tell me that's how it works.

Kind of like with Lily.

"That's boring," she says.

"Did you know Aaron in high school?" I ask, she nods slowly. "Was he your first boyfriend? Fuck, maybe even your first time? No wonder he's so protective of you."

Lily sighs, but it turns into a groan. "As I said, I've never had one." Her head falls back into her neck for a moment before she turns her attention back to me. "He's my brother, Colin."

Now, that's my time to be speechless. I blink at Lily as I try to wrap my mind around her words. *He's my brother, Colin.*

That can't be. They don't even share the same last name.

Aaron never even mentioned her. I know his siblings, even met them. Well, Ana, I met her. Aaron did mention having another sister, he said she attends some college on the west coast, which is why she's never around.

I remember her letter. Lily was talking about a sister that isn't her sister. The one that "stole her father". *Ana.* Lily mentioned a brother. She said he had their father, but she never did.

Oh, God. Did their parents split them up? Who does that?

"My parents," Lily says. Was I thinking out loud? "They split us up. Aaron lived with my father, I had to stay with our mom. We weren't allowed to see each other, but my dad kept in touch with me anyway. He gave me a chance to keep my brother in my life, our mom never found out."

"I'm sorry, Lilybug." My mind is running marathons. How didn't I notice the similarities? "Aaron and you, you're twins?"

"Did you look at Aaron and me?" She chuckles. "We look identical. Almost."

"Why the hell didn't you just say so right away? No, instead you let me babble all about how you fucked your *brother*."

As I said, I knew Aaron had another sister, other than Ana. Though, whenever I went home with Aaron and the topic of his other sister came up, all they ever told me about her were basic information. Like she attends some college outside of the state of New York, somewhere in Los Angeles. Or that she's two years younger than Aaron.

So basically, they dished me some bullshit. Unless it's true, there's another sister and Lily is a third lost one. One that happens to never have been mentioned before.

Emerson Marsh wouldn't neglect his children like that, I hope. He never appeared to me as the type of father who'd disappear from his children's lives.

"Yeah, that's a nasty thought," she agrees. "Aaron and I refuse to tell anyone. The more people know, the higher the chances our mom finds out."

"God, that means it's also *your* birthday this Saturday!" I make a mental note to buy a present for her. "You guys are almost twenty-one years old. I don't think she can do much about it."

How am I only now registering this information? She mentioned it like five minutes ago.

"Colin, it's always just been me and my mom. Sure, I had my dad every Sunday, and when I was older, I stayed for a weekend once every six months. She pushed her son away because my parents are both egoistic. Neither of them wanted the other to have one tiny bit more. So splitting up the children it was. My dad wasn't supposed to be in touch with me, and my mom was denied any contact with Aaron," she tries to explain. "She thinks my dad kept

Nine Days

his promise, but he didn't. Imagine what she'd do if she finds out my father had both me and Aaron, and she only had me."

I don't dare say anything. I don't think I can.

What Aaron and Lily's parents did is awful. How could anyone separate their children like that and then refuse to stay in touch with the other?

I'm wondering if that's where Lily's depression started. I mean, a divorce can be traumatizing for children, and Lily certainly didn't just lose her home that belonged to both of her parents. She lost her brother as well.

I've always been close to my sister, and ever since Reece was born four years ago, I have quite the bond with that little guy as well. Sure, it's not as deep as it is with Eira, probably due to the age gap, but I couldn't imagine what it'd be like losing that bond.

And to be completely honest, I always thought twins have an even deeper bond than "*normal*" siblings. Which, in my world, means Lily Reyes lost the other half of her the day her parents decided to start a war.

"Carter," Lily speaks quietly. "You cannot tell Aaron about this, about me. You need to promise you won't say a word."

Chapter 7

"if only you saw what I could see, you'll understand why I want you so desperately"-
What Makes you Beautiful by One Direction

Colin Carter

I manage to record a few videos of Lily.

We spend all evening long talking, mostly about the fun times she's had with Aaron and her father without her mother's knowledge.

She calls these Sundays their skate dates and also admits that it sounds inappropriate, but she doesn't really care about it too much.

While she's talking all about her memories, it's quite easy to catch a few shots of her expressions. Mostly sad ones, but not *only* sad ones. They're just what I need.

The happy ones will come soon.

Before I can portray the happy side of life, I have to make sure I capture the ugliness. That being sadness.

Though, even sadness has its glory.

Lily's face lights up like hundreds of lanterns in the dark when she speaks about skating and how she was supposed to take her competitions seriously but never did.

As it appears, figure skating might've been her passion, but she'd much rather do it for fun than be bound to contracts and such.

I love listening to her talk, love watching when she smiles at memories, and laughs when she remembers how she felt in these moments. She looks so… carefree. So calm. Even when a tear rolls down her cheeks every now and then as though these memories are painful.

When I get home around 10 p.m., I'm lucky enough not to bump into Aaron. I'm not mad at him for not telling me about Lily, but I sure do love to pretend I am.

♥ ♥ ♥ ♥ ♥ ♥ ♥ ♥

It's only 5 in the morning when I come downstairs to get some water from the kitchen. As surprising as it is, Aaron is sitting on a barstool, his elbows propped on the island counter and his head rests in his hands.

"You good, Ron?" I ask as I enter the kitchen.

His head immediately shoots up and he looks at me. I grab a new bottle of water and lean against the closed refrigerator, waiting for an answer.

"Lily told you." *She did.*

"Yeah, I kind of pressured her into telling me. I'm sorry." I really am. If I had known the background behind their we're-going-to-keep-being-twins-a-secret pact, I wouldn't have disgusted her into telling me. But I couldn't have known. "I won't say a word. You know I wouldn't."

"I know." Just like Lily, Aaron lets out a heavy sigh. Ever since I know they're related; I began to see it in their habits as well.

Aaron sighs a lot when he's frustrated. So does Lily.

Lily has this one special stare that leaves you feeling intimidated. Aaron has the same one.

And don't even get me started on their facial features. Their eye colors? The same shade of green. They have the same nose. Their hair color is identical as well. Both of them have freckles.

The only major difference is that Lily has a bigger bottom lip and it's more curved than Aaron's. Her cupid's bow is more defined than his. Aaron's lips are slim.

And perhaps the fact that Aaron has a *way* bigger ego.

Now I do want to kiss Lily though. I was joking yesterday but thinking about her lips makes me want to try them.

"Now I get why you don't want me to touch her," I say, hoping it would somehow get the dark cloud over Aaron's head to disappear.

"Look, Colin," Aaron starts, "if you're genuinely interested in my sister, go for it. I know you wouldn't treat her like shit. But I don't want you using her for sex, okay? She's my sister. I don't want her sleeping with half the team like some puck bunny."

"Was that the okay for me to get in her pants when I want a relationship with her as well?" I tease.

Since it's still dark—and I didn't bother turning on the ceiling lights—I don't see the cloth Aaron throws at me coming. As luck would have it, it's just a cloth, could've been something worse—a lamp, for instance.

"You disgust me." He laughs. "Why are you up so early anyway?"

"Taking your sister out on a date."

"Dumbass. You completely ignored all of my '*keep your hands off of Lily*'s."

"Funny. Your sister calls me the same name. Just sounds way cuter when she says it." Did I mention that I love teasing Aaron?

"It's five in the morning. Where are you taking her?" I doubt it's a question. He's demanding an answer.

So Aaron *is* the overprotective kind of brother, all right.

"Not sure yet," I lie. Of course, I know where I'm taking her, but I wouldn't want him to spoil it for my Lilybug.

I wonder if she's awake. Probably not. Wouldn't hurt to shoot her a text though, right?

"Can you send me her number?"

He snorts. "You're taking her out on a date, and she didn't even give you her number?"

Technically it's not a date, but I can't tell him that.

Perhaps I should tell him about her *unalive journey 101*.

But she made me promise I wouldn't.

But she's suicidal. That's enough of a reason to break a promise, no?

I'll tell him... in a few days.

"In my defense, I was out for sex"—I wasn't—"Apparently, I can't have that without declaring her as my girlfriend. So, send me her number, please?"

The ceiling lights turn on as footsteps approach us. Aaron and I both turn toward the sliding glass door that leads to the porch of our backyard.

"What the hell are you guys doing up this early?" A perplexed Grey leans against the wall of our kitchen.

Aaron crosses his arms in front of his chest, lifting his eyebrows. "We could ask you the same."

"I have a visitor," he answers with no hesitation.

"Oh, who is it?"

"Some guy from my psychology class. Don't think you know him." *Sure.*

Aaron narrows his eyes as he analyses our best friend's face and body language.

That's something he does a lot. He analyses people when they don't provide him with exactly the kind of information he expects. "So then, if you have a guy over, why are you here and not over in your house, in your bedroom, cuddling up to Mr. Psychology class guy?"

"Because he's asleep, and I'm hungry." Right. The house across from ours lacks groceries. Not because they don't have enough money to buy some, but because they're twenty-something-year-old guys, busy with assignments, Hockey, and sex.

And, well, one's barely at home.

It's not like Aaron or I go grocery shopping regularly, but we at least have something to eat here at all times.

A wrinkle appears on Aaron's forehead, he licks his lips then lies his hands flat on the island countertop. "Are you guys like, just friends? Friends with benefits? Exclusive? In a relationship?"

Grey chuckles. He shakes his head slowly, then looks away from Aaron and me. His cheeks are slightly flushed.

"So it's serious, huh?" I note, bemused by Grey's reaction.

"I think so, yeah."

"That's awesome, dude! We got to celebrate," Aaron throws in with a cheer, clapping his hands before jumping off his seat. He walks over to Grey and takes him into a very manly embrace.

And with manly I mean he hugs him like a guy would hug his girlfriend. With the butt cheek squeeze and everything.

"You're so weird, Marsh." Grey somehow gets out of Aaron's embrace and takes a few steps back. "By the way, you could've told us you have a twin sister."

Aaron freezes. His voice vanishes as if he never even had one in the first place. And the color is draining from his face.

It's obvious Aaron doesn't like talking about Lily, or their relationship, but from what Lily told me, I think I understand.

I bite my tongue, not wanting the laughter that's lingering in the back of my throat to come through. Although Aaron tried to hide Lily from us for three years, even having a great reason for it, it's still hilarious how his ass just got busted.

"I should go," I say, walking out of the kitchen to go find my car keys.

"You're not off the hook, Carter." Grey stops me. "You have a thing for Aaron's sister. Good luck with that. If she's only a tiny bit like him, you will definitely need it."

Even if she wasn't anything like him, I'd need it.

"Got to get going, assholes. See you later at practice." To Grey, I only reply with a lopsided smile, followed by a lazy wink.

Five minutes later I'm out of the house, sitting in my car when my phone chimes. It's a message from Aaron, I know because he has a special notification tone. He actually sent me Lily's number.

Thank God he did. I thought I might have to fight him for it.

I click on her contact info and decide to shoot her a text right away. If I'm lucky, she's awake. If not, I will have to call her to wake her up.

Colin: Hey, Lilybug. Your favorite boyfriend here. You awake?

I can hear her groan in my head. I just know a groan will be the first sound she makes after reading my message.

And the thought alone makes it worth it.

Lily: I am now. Thank you, dumbass.

Lily: And you're not my boyfriend, Carter. You're my unalive delayer.

Suddenly I'm really glad I waited a couple of minutes to see if she would respond. I like her energy. I like that she doesn't admire me as all these other girls do at Trewery.

It's refreshing. Such a shame that she doesn't see how much of an awesome person she is. And I mean, even I can see it after knowing her for only five days.

Colin: I'm not a plane that comes with delays. I'm making the rest of your days better. I don't add time to it.

Though I wish I did.

Lily: Why did you ask if I'm awake?

Colin: We're going out. Get dressed. I'll be there in about fifteen minutes.

Fifteen minutes later I arrive at the dorms. Lily told me I should wait outside but I don't like listening to what she says when it comes to spending time with her.

I fear she might trick me. If I wait outside, she'll probably never even come out, which leads to me knocking at her door until she opens it. And when she does, I wish she didn't.

Lily didn't get dressed. In fact, she's still in pajama shorts and a thin tank top. I assume she went to sleep like that. She's also not wearing a bra, which brings up fantasies I don't need at the moment.

"I told you to wait in the car," she snaps.

"You aren't even dressed yet. I said I would be here in fifteen minutes. It's been twenty and you're still half naked."

"I'm tired, Colin. I don't want to go out. It's not even six in the morning yet." She lets out a quiet groan as she opens the door wider, allowing me to come in.

"Don't kill the mood, Lilybug. You'll love today." I walk inside, following Lily into her room. She takes a seat at her desk—the clothes that laid there just yesterday now spread all over her floor—while I lie on her bed.

"I won't kill the mood. I'd kill myself instead."

I sit up in a heartbeat. A sigh escapes me as I look into Lily's eyes through the mirror. "You have to stop saying things like that."

"Why? It's the truth."

"I don't want to hear you talking about your death. The one that most likely won't happen," I tell her. I'm pretty convinced that she'll end up wanting to stay alive after these nine days.

Okay, I'm not convinced. I'm hoping she'll want to give life a second chance. Being positive is the key.

"I will most likely be dead by October 8th."

"Lilybug, you're underestimating my power to make you fall in love with me first."

She snorts and drops the brush she was holding. "You wanted to make me fall in love with life, not you," she reminds me.

"But if I'm your life, it's two in one." I'm joking. I don't plan on making Lily fall in love with me.

Yet.

Making her feel loved will be enough for now.

"Keep on dreaming, Carter." Lily continues to freshen up her face. She looks beautiful, but she also did before she put on some makeup.

"Gladly." I lean back on her pillows, relaxing. "Your brother told me I can get in your pants. He gave me the go for it."

"He did not. Stop kidding yourself."

"He did. Aaron loves me," I argue.

"Whatever. We won't ever go there. Now close your eyes so I can get dressed."

"Or I leave my eyes open and watch you," I suggest, but before she could beat me up again, I grab the next best thing to keep my eyes busy with.

The next best thing is her suicide book. Correction, her *unalive journey 101*.

"Do you mind if I read this?" I ask. "After all, I promised I would make sure your people here get their letters after your death. I will read it no matter what."

"Go ahead. But don't you dare comment on it."

Like I would ever do that.

Actually, I could see myself doing just that. Comment on every single phrase I don't agree with. Phrases like "*I want to die*" or "*This is my goodbye*" or "*I will be dead*".

Dear whoever reads this,

I begin to read, but I can't help myself.

"Why do you always write 'Dear whoever reads this,'?" I ask. "You should exchange it with 'Dear Colin Baby'."

"That sounds awful. I will just leave it." Of course, she would ignore my question, though I guess I can imagine why she wouldn't address this to one specific person.

Colin Carter is an asshole.
I planned on spending my two remaining weeks writing my goodbyes, and my thoughts on the way toward death, but instead, I'm stuck with an ignorant and stubborn jock.

"I'm not sure what I'm supposed to think of that," I comment, despite Lily's command not to. "I'm *not* an asshole."

"You so totally are."

"Am not." I tsk. "I'm an amazing guy with only the best qualities."

He won't even accept a simple no.
He demanded to show me that there is more to live for.
Now guess what?
I'll have to spend the next couple of days at his mercy.
Nine days, to be exact.
I caved in and gave him nine days to prove me wrong.
He won't manage to do that.
My mind is set on dying.
He can show me whatever he wants, it won't change a thing.
But I guess he's right.
Why would I spend my last days on my own when I can spend them with some stranger who offers me a good time for free?
I certainly hope he won't make me pay for anything.
I mean, I don't even want to be there in the first place, so he might as well pay.

I start to laugh.

I wonder if these days count as dates.
Isn't that what dates are all about?
Two people go out, go on adventures, eat in a way too expensive restaurant, do stupid things. And just have a great time.
But if that counts as such, does spending time with a friend count as a date as well?
A friend date perhaps?

"Lilybug, you're my girlfriend now. These are dates," I inform her, joking.

Only a second later I'm getting beat up by Lily's stuffed

animals.

Well, she's beating me up with one of them, but it's the same thing.

"I'm not your girlfriend, dumbass."

"That's too bad. I planned a few dates. Stargazing for instance, or wine painting. Maybe even take a swim course together," I joke.

"*Aw*, Trewery's superstar doesn't know how to swim." She pouts at me with big eyes. "Does he only know how to skate?"

"Oh, I thought you didn't know how to swim." And once again she beats me with that frog stuffed animal. I think I'll be naming him *Sergeant Froggo*. He wears an Army outfit, so might as well go big or go home with the name. "Stop beating me. You're hurting Sergeant Froggo."

"Sergeant-who-now?" She bursts into laughter and falls on the bed beside me. "That's not his name."

"I'm pretty sure it is. He looks like one."

"His name is Kermit."

"Way too basic. It's Sergeant Froggo now," I say. "Now let me continue to read. It's getting interesting, sweetheart."

I wouldn't know. I've never been on a date before. Not a real one anyway.

The next letter will be addressed to Winter.

I know, Winter is a lot. She isn't very nice most of the time. And yes, she's a drama queen.

Oh God, Winter, if you're reading this right now, I'm sorry. But you know it's the truth.

But despite her urge to cause drama, she has been my best friend for a while now. I couldn't live with myself if she didn't get a goodbye letter.

That's ironic, I won't even be alive to witness her reading it.

Lily

You're so wrong, Lilybug. You will be alive. You will be happy again. I promise.

Chapter 8

"don't worry, I promise you'll be fine"-Fee Time by Ruel

Lily Reyes

After a fifteen-minute drive, we find ourselves on Long Clove Rd, currently hiking up a hill.

If I had known I'd be hiking this early in the morning, I would've stayed in bed. Though, I doubt Colin would've given me a choice.

Who am I kidding? I don't have a choice but to follow him wherever he wants to take me. I agreed on these nine days, it would be a bitch move to bail.

And besides, Colin doesn't seem to be half as bad. Maybe he'll be great company for my last days.

I'm just worried I might grow on him like he's starting to grow on me… kind of.

Colin is still an arrogant ass. One I'd much rather punch in the face than have as my wannabe savior. But it would be unnecessarily cruel if I grew on him, and he lost me to death.

Then again, he kind of put himself in this position. I didn't ask for his help. I don't need his saving.

"Great, so it's six in the morning and we're sitting on a blanket on top of a hill, and now what?" I speak in a sort of annoyed tone.

"You're so anti-romantic." He laughs to himself. "We'll be watching the sunrise."

"I always hated them," I tell him. "I never understood what was so magical. It's just the sun that rises. Nothing special."

"Wrong." He nudges me with his elbow, then hands me a cookie in the shape of a goddamn frog. I almost have to smile. "Sunrises are beautiful. A new day arrives. It's a new beginning. With every sunrise, you get the chance to start all over again. It's like a reset button."

"I'm not superstitious."

"Lilybug, this has nothing to do with superstitions. It's simply a new beginning. View the sunrise as whatever you please. See it as a moment of carelessness. The second you can see the sun rise and the sky starts to show itself in all its glory, close your eyes and wish for something you truly desire. For instance, a painless day."

"That doesn't make any sense."

He takes my hand in his and strokes his thumb over my knuckles, still being cautious of my reactions. "Fine, let's just wait until the sun is rising, then you can stand by the edge and scream from the top of your lungs. Release all of your anger from the past years. Let the pain from yesterday leave your body. Grant yourself a pause, just until the sun is up and then you can come back to reality," he offers, I think?

Our fingers link together before he lays them down on his lap.

"This is so ridiculous, you know that, right?"

"Feel free to give feedback once the sun is up." Colin flicks me that perfect grin of his, then turns his face away to look over the dark city.

I have no idea when the sun would start to rise, I never paid attention to it before, and yet I'm somewhat excited.

Honestly, I've always viewed sunrises as something stupid. Sure, it's the beginning of a new day, but I never understood what would be so interesting to see.

People watch sunrises and sunsets every single day and enjoy it. It's just a huge fireball showing on the other side of the globe. Nothing spectacular.

"Lilybug?" Colin's soft voice streams through my ears.

"Yeah?"

"Tell me something about you, you've never told anyone before."

"I want to die," I answer with no hesitation. It's true. I've never told anyone about it, nor have I ever really said it out loud before.

"Something I didn't already know."

"I have a weirdly shaped birthmark."

His eyebrows rise, lips press together as he waits for me to elaborate, but I don't. "Well, if you're not going to tell me what it is, don't bother mentioning it."

"It's too embarrassing."

His eyes roll. "Fine. I'll find out eventually. Give me something else then."

"You go first," I say.

Let's be honest, I have no idea what I'm supposed to tell him.

"Okay." He exhales heavily, and although it's still dark, I can see the fog in front of his face rise into the air. "Two years ago, when Eira had been diagnosed with leukemia, I tried to bribe the doctor into taking extra care of her."

"You were nineteen when you tried to bribe a doctor to find a better cure for cancer?" I question. Then suddenly I realize: *His sister had cancer?*

"To be fair, I'm not a doctor. And I never really had to care about all that. I've always been healthy. I've never broken a bone, not even had a sprained ankle, and I play hockey, always have. So that's quite the miracle. I never put too much thought into anything medical. I was so stupid. I was still eighteen, by the way."

"I'm so sorry about Eira, Colin. She doesn't deserve this."

He shrugs. "Yeah. It's alright though. She's Eira. I mean, Eira thinks beyond everything. She's excited to die because she believes that the universe wants her to start a new adventure. No, *needs* her to go on a new one."

That's a really beautiful way of thinking about death.

"She's dying?"

"Nah." He dismisses my question. "She's cancer free now."

"Did you think she was going to die?" *Why am I even asking?*

"Sure did, for a while. I never wanted to accept it. I mean, she's my sister, of course, I don't want her to die, but I learned to accept that I can't do anything about it. And crying about it now won't give her more time either if she were to die." He lets out a painful sigh. Something is off. "Good thing, she's cancer free and won't die yet."

I need to change the topic. I doubt Colin wants to continue speaking of his sister's death. And I'm not sure if I should be wanting to carry on this conversation either. "I used to think the moon is made out of cheese."

Colin snickers. "Everyone thought that as a child. Give me something deeper."

I think about my life for a second, letting every event run through my mind before admitting, "There was a time Aaron hated me."

"I don't believe you." His head snaps toward me, his eyes landing on mine. He isn't expressing any kind of anticipation, but at the same time, it looks a lot like he's desperate for me to enlighten him.

So I do.

"Our dad got married to another woman. Her name is Liz, but I'm sure you know that already. I didn't take it very well. But I took it even worse when I found out that Liz has a daughter. Ana. She was only three when she became part of our family. Aaron and I were eight. I was so jealous of her."

"I can't believe you're Ana's stepsister. I mean, that kid is like a sister to *me*." Then he chuckles. "And I read the jealous part, sweetheart."

"Yeah, I know you did," I say, rolling my eyes. "Aaron loved Ana right from the start. He played with her all the time. And well, I only had my mom. She never gave me any other siblings. When I went to see my dad and Aaron, Aaron only ever wanted us to play with Ana, which led to me getting mad at him. Eventually, my jealousy got so bad that I didn't want to look at Ana anymore. I would do cruel things to get attention. I even cut Aaron's cuddle blankie in half."

Colin gasps. "No way, Lilybug. You can't just do that. That's some real trauma you caused Aaron! No wonder he's the way he is. You quite literally *tortured* him, ripped his heart right out of his chest at such a young age."

I laugh. The kind of laughter I didn't allow myself to let out for years. It gets so much, I start grunting like a pig while inhaling. And those piggy grunts only make me laugh even more.

I don't pay much attention to what's around me. But when I catch Colin smiling at me, I feel this weird tingle in my stomach. Probably a sign I'm about to vomit.

Colin Carter has smiled at me before, but it was never like this. Never with admiration. I think he's proud of himself for making me laugh like that. Even if I was overanalyzing this whole smile right now, I don't care.

I don't care because laughing feels good.

Feeling a hand come in touch with mine again, I immediately stop to laugh and look down at Colin and my hands. He's intertwining them, holding mine closely to his as our fingers interlock. His thumb brushes over my skin in soft strokes.

Colin isn't looking at me, but I'm watching his side profile while he stares straight ahead over the city.

He's handsome, but that wouldn't even matter to me. Colin has a loving soul, even if I'm still convinced Colin Carter is a complete asshole and is good at hiding it from me.

He cares about people he doesn't even know. And I come to believe that maybe if I wasn't going to die, I could see him in my life as someone more than just a friend.

I can't think like this.

My time is almost over. I have only eight days left. I can't fall in love now. Not that I was going to fall in love with Colin. We've only known each other for six days, and our relationship didn't start too great.

Colin could potentially be a great friend. Maybe even turn into my best friend if we had more time.

That's what I'm talking about. A great, deep friendship.

The only reason Colin is here with me right now is because I want to die. And he wants to show me I don't.

I do want to die, and no matter what adventures he takes me, my mind won't change.

"Look," he says and points toward the horizon.

Only a few lights in New City are turned on. It's not as bright as I thought it would be at six-thirty in the morning. I expected more people to be awake, more lights would light up the city, guess I was wrong.

And I was even more wrong to say that sunrises are nothing but a waste of time.

The sky turns into all the colors I could only ever imagine it could turn into once the sun starts to rise.

The darkness diminishes, and it's as if the ocean could catch on fire and turn into something completely new. As if a pool with the deepest blue water cleans up and appears golden from a source of light shining on it.

Something completely odd and yet something everyone needs to see.

There is no sign of darkness left as the sun slowly rises on the horizon, spreading warming gold and purple color throughout the sky in every direction. The clouds gleam like dusty pink cotton candy in front of a work of art.

It's breathtaking.

Colin gets up from the floor, helping me up once he stands. He walks us to the edge so we're just standing there, watching the sunrise.

I wonder what he'd do if I tried to jump.

"Do it," he whispers. "Scream, shout, let out your anger and frustrations."

I allow myself to look at Colin in shock. He said I could do that, but I didn't think he would actually want me to.

"Think of the sky as your pain and scream."

"You're crazy."

"I can live with that." He turns and lifts my face to the sky. "Now, Lilybug. Scream." He takes a few steps back, giving me more space.

And then it comes over me. The anger I feel for never being

good enough. The frustration I feel for longing for a better life that will never come. The pain I have felt for years from my parents' divorce.

So I scream.

I scream at the top of my lungs, letting all the anger and agony from my past leave my body.

He was right. It's refreshing. It feels good to finally let it all out.

It's like being at the gym and lifting 220 pounds at the bench, then finally getting rid of the weight. The satisfaction that comes through when you realize you carried so much weight like it was a feather. You feel lighter when it's gone and only then do you realize how heavy it was on you.

The weight is lighter on me. I know it's not gone, will never be gone, yet it feels good to get rid of it for a moment.

Tears escape from the corner of my eyes as I calm and stop screaming. I'm not crying, but I kind of am.

I always thought crying only happens when your heart is aching from all of the pain you feel, never did I think you could cry from relief.

When I look at Colin, I see him pocketing his phone.

I think he just recorded my entire outbreak of anger. I wonder what our project is all about, he won't tell me anything.

Despite the unwell feeling of assuming that Colin Carter has a video of me screaming on his phone, I don't really care much.

"Thank you." I thank him wholeheartedly, walking closer to him.

Colin opens his arms for me, allowing me in for a hug.

I hate hugs. Or I used to until I'm in Colin's embrace. His arms wrap around me so gently, yet firm enough, accompanied by so much protection, I feel like he's trying to convince me that he's my armor now.

And boy do I feel safe in his arms.

The side of my face presses against the front of his shoulder as my arms wrap around his torso. I feel Colin's hand glide through my hair, and his other hand draws circles over my back.

It's soothing.

A few more tears roll down my face as I realize that I won't get to experience moments like these anymore. At least not many.

But that's all right. I'll save them and if I do remember my life before death, I'll think back to these moments with a smile on my face.

Suddenly I'm way more excited for the next seven days with Colin. I can't count today anymore, he's chosen the early morning as his time of the day, so I don't think I will see him much for the rest of it.

We're just standing here, hugging for a whole while until I eventually pull away.

Colin cups my face with his hands, caressing my cheeks ever so lightly by sliding his thumbs over my skin. It sends shivers down my spine.

For a moment I believe he wants to kiss me, but I know that's not the case. So, as quickly as the thought enters my brain, it vanishes from it.

His eyes are staring into mine. A gentle smile is tugging on his lips as he watches me.

"You're really beautiful, did you know that?" He speaks softly. Something in his voice seems odd. Usually, he's all cheerful and chirpy, but this time he's gentle.

If I read Colin correctly, he doesn't like being vulnerable, so telling me about his sister, about how he felt when he thought she was dying—and acting like anything but Mr. tough-guy—must have been pretty difficult for him.

"Thank you," I say, offering him a small smile.

Colin tilts my head up, his index finger under my chin as he does. His face moves closer to mine until his lips brush over my skin.

He places a kiss to my forehead, slowly.

My heart beats faster. So fast, I can feel it beating inside of my chest. My stomach seems to be turning upside-down, but this time it's not from feeling sick. Maybe I do feel sick, but a different kind of sick.

It's like a flutter in my stomach, like someone is tickling me from the inside.

It's nerve-wracking, a feeling I have never felt before.

Please remember this when you're dead, Lily.

When he pulls away and goes to collect the blanket he brought, I feel empty again. Like something inside of me feels lost without Colin by my side. I hate that I feel this way.

I shouldn't feel this way. I shouldn't want Colin. I shouldn't because it's not fair to him.

But I do anyway. I want Colin, even just for one night. I want to feel his lips on mine as much as I hate the thought as well.

I hate wanting him.

How did this happen anyway?

Colin was nothing to me when we met. Actually, he was a pain in the ass. I didn't want him around. I didn't want him to show me the beauty of life.

Yet here I'm, longing for his lips.

I think it's because he's the only guy who ever truly paid attention to me. He's the only person who's trying to save me. The only one who noticed me. Of course, my mind goes crazy and gives me wrong signals.

Colin isn't nice. Not once did I hear someone refer to him as a good person. He's an asshole. He's still the same superstar that so much as nods in a girl's direction and has her undressed a second later.

But despite all that, he seems nice enough for my brain to mistake his newfound kindness for something else.

♥ ♥ ♥ ♥ ♥ ♥ ♥ ♥

"No, I swear Miles was staring at me throughout all of finance," Carina tells us. With us I mean my friends and me.

As I do every day, I spend my lunch break with my friends in the cafeteria. The four of us are sitting at a table, currently listening to Carina Rico's fantasies about Miles King.

After attending St. Trewery for a while, I figured that a lot of women at this school have a thing for the hockey guys.

They're all ridiculously hot, I give them that much. I used to think being hot is a requirement to start playing hockey here. Obviously, that's not the case.

Still, Miles King seems to be getting the most attention.

Miles has a couple of tattoos, not as many as Colin (I think). I'm actually not sure how many Colin has. I've only ever seen his arms and neck covered in patchwork.

Miles, however, I know he does have a lot.

Simply for having tattoos and a pretty face, Miles is getting quite the attention. For no reason, so I believe.

Okay, maybe for a reason. His abs are more defined than any I have ever seen before. And then in combination with the tattoos on his body, he's to die for. If you're someone who likes tattoos. But he's missing the dark hair.

I wonder if girls are just as crazy about Colin as they are about Miles. The thought irks me, but it's not my business anyway. I shouldn't care.

"He was just looking for the next girl to fuck," Mia says unfazed. She's one of very few women here that wouldn't sell their soul to the devil for Miles King's existence. "Honestly, Miles is disgusting. Just like the rest of them."

"He's not disgusting just because he has a more active sex life than you do," Carina defends her beloved Miles.

"Sure not. But do you see me fucking two different women in a time span of five hours?" Mia asks.

"Stop trying to make him the bad guy, Mia. Just accept that he's ridiculously hot."

"Sure, I can do that. Doesn't mean I want to ride him."

"I don't want that either. Well, I do, but I want him as my boyfriend as well," Carina cries out quietly.

Carina is as much of an emotional wreck as me. It's just that she's emotional when it comes to people, more specifically guys.

She gets attached to a guy because he gave her two seconds of attention.

Before anyone can save her from it, Carina has planned her wedding, then gets frustrated when said guy doesn't even want to be with her.

"Now shut up, he's here!" She squeaks, staring as Miles and three of his teammates walk right into the cafeteria.

Every single voice in this room mutes. If a pin were to drop, everyone would be able to hear it. That's how quiet the room goes once the jocks make their entrance.

Aaron walks in next to Miles, followed by a black-haired guy. He's very tall. I would guess about six foot four or five, taller than Aaron and Colin.

Since Colin is the last of the four jocks to enter, I assume the black-haired guy is Grey, the other not-really-roommate.

Thanks to Aaron, I know that he lives in a house with Colin, yet Grey and Miles sort of live there too but not really. At least they get their food from my brother's house.

Aaron didn't stop talking about Colin for the first two months of freshman year. He mentioned Miles a couple of times before as well. And it's not too surprising to know who Miles is.

But Grey? He's been mentioned, I just never saw him around before. I don't think he's around a lot.

My friends—*and I*—watch the guys walk over to the queue to buy some food. They're goofing around, ignoring the eyes that are solely on them.

I always thought stuff like this only happens in teen movies, but being here right now, witnessing it myself makes it pretty realistic.

Trying to get my friends back to talking, I ask a question, but it stays unheard. Clearly, they're too focused on the hot guys who are buying food, the same way every single other person in this cafeteria did before. Apparently, when jocks buy food it's automatically more interesting.

"Miles looks so good in his clothes," Carina swoons. If my eyes aren't playing any tricks on me, I could swear she's drooling.

"He's wearing jeans and a shirt just like ninety-eight percent of the other guys here," Mia points out. She's right, Miles doesn't stand out too much, aside from his height.

"What do you think they're talking about?" Carina questions, still watching as Colin starts to laugh and Aaron shakes his head after an obvious eye-roll.

Then Colin slaps his hand on Aaron's shoulder blade before he starts to walk away. Toward the tables.

"I think Colin found himself another victim," Mia jokes, taking a sip from her orange juice.

Winter and I turn back around to face Mia and Carina, turning our backs to the guys. I'm glad the fascination about the hockey guys only ever lasts a couple of minutes before life continues to go on. I wouldn't be able to sit through this until they eventually leave again.

"You're partnered up with Colin for your film directing class, aren't you, Lily?" Mia asks. I manage to nod a reply. "Poor you. You probably have to do all the work."

I don't. In fact, I'm the one doing nothing, but I can't say that aloud. Fortunately for me, I don't have to. The second I try to speak, Carina gasps seconds before I feel arms wrap carefully around my neck.

"Hey there, Lilybug," Colin whispers into my ear, then I feel his lips brush my skin. This time he plants a kiss to my cheek and not my forehead.

His arms loosen around my body, then disappear completely. My friend all look as equally shocked as I feel.

Thinking Colin left, I'm dumbstruck when he suddenly takes a seat right next to me. Or more half under me.

The second he's seated, Colin tugs on my leg and places it over his so that the bottom half of my leg dangles between his. At this point, he might as well have pulled me right on his lap.

"You didn't eat," he says, pointing toward my full tray. I'm not hungry, but I promised Winter I would try to get something down. It just never happened. I was hoping that maybe if I let it sit in front of me, I would grab something eventually.

"I'm not hungry," I tell him. "What are you doing here?"

"Keeping an eye on you." He shrugs like there's nothing wrong with the way he said this so casually in front of my friends. "The guys are coming as well. Hope you girls don't mind," he says to my friends.

Of course they don't, it's good for their campus reputation.

Plus their presence will give Carina a chance to speak to Miles.

I'm not so sure about Mia. She believes they're all arrogant assholes who only care about themselves.

Winter probably won't like it too much either. I got her to block Aaron's phone number as she needs to heal and stop dreaming about a perfect relationship with him. It won't happen.

"Of course not," Carina replies with excitement.

Only a few moments later the other three guys approach our table. Luckily, the table's big enough to sit a group of eight. Well, it gets a little tight, but it fits.

Aaron sits next to Colin. Miles and Grey are on the opposite side of their teammates.

Unfortunately for Carina, Miles doesn't sit next to her, but that's good for him. Poor guy wouldn't be able to eat in peace otherwise.

"So, you got not only one but four hockey players wrapped around your finger now?" Mia snorts bemused.

Mia isn't the only one snorting, Aaron does the same thing, but I bet for a whole other reason.

"Just me," Colin answers. "We are a package deal though, so they will have to do some good deeds for her too." I wish I was faster with answering questions. "That sounded dirtier than intended."

My friends laugh, as so does Miles. Grey looks a little like he wants to disappear. Aaron, Colin, and I stay quiet.

"Stop taking so much space for yourself," Aaron says and pushes Colin closer to me, if it gets any closer, that is.

Bemused, Colin presses his lips into a thin line, then grabs my other leg—the one that's still free from his body—and pulls it over his leg as well. Shortly after that, I'm seated on one of his thighs.

He moves a bit closer to Winter, giving Aaron a bit more space. He seems grateful for the space but annoyed that his twin sister is currently sitting on his best friend's lap.

Colin seats me sideways because if I sat with my back against his front, it would get super uncomfortable in a short while.

Colin holds me close to him, one of his hands rests on my hip, his thumb traces the outlines of my panties through the thin layer of my leggings.

Since I don't know where else to place my hands, I decide to rest them on my thighs. Just that that's exactly where Colin's other hand rests. *How did I not even notice that?*

Aaron almost gags. I only have to look at his face to know exactly what he's thinking.

"No way, you're an actual thing then?" Miles looks Colin and me up and down.

"Don't think so, love. Carter isn't even trying to eat her face right now," the guy, whom I'm still assuming is Grey, speaks. His voice is deeper than I thought it would be.

"Is this what guys do in private?" Mia asks. "Do you guys watch your friends make out?"

"Make out?" Miles laughs. "I have full-on sex tapes of these guys on my phone. I watch them every evening before going to sleep." He's trying too hard to appear serious, forcing his face to stay expressionless. It only makes the mocking joke more obvious. And maybe because he won't stop laughing at himself for his hilarious lie.

"He's joking," Grey confirms.

"So? Do I get an answer?"

"We don't watch the other make out," Miles says. "But at some point, you just know your best friends. That includes knowing how they act around—and with—girls they want to fuck, and girls they want for more than a quick thing."

"Yeah," Aaron agrees. "You can't tell me you don't know when, let's say, Winter wants to bang, or when she wants a relationship." He eyes her, she looks back at him with fury.

If looks could kill… Aaron would be six feet under right now.

They continue to talk, but I can no longer concentrate because Colin slides his hand up my body. So high that it's eventually crawling under my sweatshirt and trails over my skin.

Chapter 9

"you kept breathing but stopped living" – Birthday Cake by Dylan Conrique

Lily Reyes

Dear whoever reads this,

I've had another panic attack today.

It was worse in comparison to the one I had yesterday.

They're getting worse with every day, but I don't know why.

I've occasionally had panic attacks since I was younger, but recently they're so much worse.

They're so much more intense.

Maybe it's fear? But I wouldn't know where that would come from.

I'm not afraid.

Okay, I'm afraid that I won't want to die anymore. I do, as of now, but what if Colin manages to convince me to stay?

I don't see it happening, but what if?

When he touched me today, my body reacted in a way I never thought it could.

I felt warmer. I felt like the ache in my heart got less because he was around.

But that's not right. It can't be right.

Colin is Colin. (Sorry because I know you will read this, Colin).

Perhaps I'm afraid of feeling altogether.

I didn't plan my life further than October 8th of this year.

I don't have plans for my future.

Nine Days

I don't know what I want to do after I graduate college.
I don't know how to live.
I don't know how to smile, how to laugh, how to be happy.
But Colin makes it all look so easy.
He knows what he wants to do after college.
He knows how to be happy.
He knows how to live.
But I don't.
I will never know.
And it scares me.
I'm scared that if I stay, I will only continue to live in misery.
That's why I can't stay.
I don't want to stay.
I can't feel the pain anymore, it's getting unbearable.
I can't fall asleep with dry eyes, and I can't wake up with them either.
I'm always crying.
Always, except when I'm with people.
But even when I'm with people I cry sometimes.
And now I'm crying again. Perfect.
The pain is back.
I don't want it to come back.
Make it go away, please.
I can't do this anymore.
I keep telling myself that it's only nine more days. Eight if you don't count the couple of hours I will be alive on day nine.
It's way too far in the future.
I should have just done it right away instead of giving myself more time for this stupid book.

Joelina Falk

Fucking ridiculous.
I'm so fucking ridiculous.
My chest hurts, Colin.
My heart's in pain.
I can't take this anymore.
I want to leave, but I want to stay.
I want to stay so we can have more of these fun days together.
It's only been two days.
But it's been two days I have enjoyed more than the twenty years I've been alive.
We didn't even experience anything exciting, just spent time at his parents' house, then watched TV in my dorm room.
But he made me enjoy it.
And today was amazing.
I like sunrises now.
They're beautiful and a new beginning.
Today was a new beginning.
But it won't last forever.
Things aren't meant to last forever, that's why I'm okay with saying goodbye to Colin soon.
He'll continue to live happily.
I know he will.
He's Colin.
But I wouldn't.
I would cry. And cry. And cry some more.
Colin would leave me when he convinced me to live.
I won't fall for his trap. Or his marvelous blue eyes. God, I hate blue eyes.
My heart's still hurting.

Nine Days

It's painful.

I'm so tired of fighting.

Isn't it funny how people look into your eyes every day, and yet they never see that you're about to cry? That you're holding back tears?

Can you imagine how exhausting that is?

Can you imagine how painful it is to be feeling drained and pretending to be the most cheerful person all day? Until you're on your own, lying in bed, finally able to break?

Whoever reads this, please know I'm hurting.

I'm not feeling the kind of pain that goes away with some Advil.

It's not some kind of pain a doctor can make disappear.

Sure, I have my medication to help. If only they were helping.

Every single one of my days feels like I'm falling apart.

I spend every day picking up the pieces that fall throughout the day and glue them back together. But what's once broken can't be whole anymore.

No matter how much glue I put on my broken pieces, I will never feel whole again.

Every single day I'm begging the crying creature staring back at me in the mirror to just hold on for a little while longer.

Begging myself to stay strong.

I keep telling myself that it will get better.

I've been telling myself that for years.

It's never gotten better.

So you tell me, what do I do?

Do I continue to live in pain? Continue to feel like nothing makes sense anymore? Continue to shatter my own heart by allowing myself to have hope, only to get disappointed again?

Or do I give up?

Do I end my pain, my suffering and move on to another dimension?
A dimension where I don't have to feel this way.
Where I don't have to cry myself to sleep.
One where people don't tell you "Well, if you're upset, you have to know what it's about."
That's another thing I hate.
When I do say I don't feel well... I don't always know why. Actually, I rarely know why I don't feel okay. I just don't feel okay, accept it.
But people tell me I need to have a reason.
I don't.
But it's hurting when they say this. It makes me feel unworthy, stupid... as though something's seriously wrong with me.
They don't understand me.
They don't want to understand me.
No one does.
So, tell me:
Do I stay, and continue to feel worthless, or do I leave and pray to God I will be happier wherever I end up?
    Lily

Chapter 10

"I'd do anything for my bippity-boppity-boo?"–Find My Way To You by Miles Parrish, Shalom Margaret

Colin Carter

Once the last class for today is over, I head home. I can't wait to take a good nap. Today has been exhausting, all this studying and thinking about Lily is exhausting.

I'm not even too sure if I'm more worried about Lily killing herself any moment, or her staying alive and cutting me off.

It's definitely odd.

But I try not to think too much about it. Lily's a great friend to me. Maybe I would even consider her my best friend at this point. Which is weird because I already have three of those. One being her twin brother, who—*if I'm being honest*—is my favorite of those three dorks I call my best friends.

Something about Lily is refreshing, and it irks me that she believes that I won't have her around for too much longer anymore. That is if I "fail" to convince her.

The second I arrive at home, I make my way to my bedroom. I don't have much time before I have to leave again.

My father forces the team to come to the arena for practice at four p.m. if I'm late, he will probably force me to stay another hour. He wasn't all too happy that I skipped yesterday's practice. Luckily, when I told him I was visiting Eira, he seemed less mad.

I know I shouldn't use my sister as an excuse to skip practice, but it wasn't even a lie. I did see her.

But to be honest, despite what I told Lily, I did want her to meet Eira. I was kind of hoping it would mess with Lily's head.

I'm aware of how shitty that sounds.

I have no idea what suicidal people go through. I don't know what makes them happy, or even reconsider wanting to commit for just a second.

It was a selfish and dumb thing to do, I admit.

Telling her the crap about Eira and her fascination with death, if it brought just a tiny bit of doubt to Lily, I will be pleased.

Unfortunately, I can't read Lily's mind, so I won't ever know if she thought about it. I won't ever know if she doubted her decision, even if it was just for a second. Apart from my wishful thinking, Lily doesn't even know half of the truth.

We haven't spoken ever since we bumped into one another at the cafeteria. Okay, "bumped into one another" might be an understatement.

Lily ended up sitting on my lap for a good hour before she had to leave for her next class. Not even going to lie, I was pretty disappointed when she left.

Thinking of her reminds me of something. I have this other *thing* planned for today. I'm aware that I took her out this morning already, but she technically only gave me eight days instead of nine, so I get an extra date today.

Who am I kidding? I don't have anything else planned, I just want to make sure Lily doesn't kill herself.

Colin: Meet me at the arena at 6. I'm taking you out.

Lily: You already did. Your time is over for today, whatever you want to do will have to wait.

Colin: I had less time yesterday, meaning I have more today.

Lily: I'm not stepping on the ice.

I chuckle. She's so adorable, thinking I wouldn't get her back on the ice eventually. Lucky for Lily, that's not my plan for tonight.

Colin: Why? Can't skate?

I know she can skate. I've read it in her journal.

Lily: You hit the nail right on the head there, dumbass.

Colin: Well, don't worry then, Lilybug. I'm an excellent skater. And so are you, liar.

Lily: Seriously, I don't skate anymore. I have evolved a rational fear of ice skating.

Colin: Liar. I'll let it slide for now if you come to the arena at 6.

Lily: Fine, whatever. Do I need to dress up?

Colin: Hm... Yes. Wear my jersey.

Lily: Nude, got it. Don't forget protection. x

I need a moment to remember that I have to breathe. Not for a minute have I imagined Lily being this bold. Like, I knew Lily could be... different. But bold like this? Never did I see that coming.

♥ ♥ ♥ ♥ ♥ ♥ ♥ ♥

"Carter, we have a surprise for you!" Zachery yells with as much enthusiasm as he can offer the second when I enter the locker room.

A surprise from this team can't be good. They don't do surprises. And if *we* do plan on a surprise, it's never something good.

This means I'm positive whatever they've planned to surprise me with, it's more likely going to be a punishment. *Oh, sweet baby Jesus.*

"Take a seat, Cap," Parker Griffin, our goalie, says. I choose to obey for my own good. These guys are capable of anything, and I mean *any*thing.

"We spoke to Coach, he's in on this, so there's no need to play the dad card," Aaron informs me, speaking loud enough for the entire team to hear. It wouldn't even make a difference if they hear a thing or not, they're all in on this.

Judging by the grins on their faces, I'm even more certain now that this is more of a punishment. I've suspected it before, but now I'm one hundred percent convinced I will end up losing a body part after this.

"You didn't show up for practice yesterday," he continues. "What was so important?"

I don't hesitate to answer. "My sister."

My team knows about Eira and that she used to have cancer.

This team is like a second family to me. We're all a little crazy and do call the other out for dumb shit. Sometimes we even throw insults into conversations, but we stick together like chewing gum sticks to the bottom of a shoe.

That said, it's either all of us or none of us at all. As I said, we're a package deal. The whole team.

Sure all of us have our little groups. I have mine, but that doesn't mean the rest of the team doesn't belong to the package.

"You skipped practice for your sister?" Aaron makes sure he got that right. "Not mine?"

The team starts to laugh.

Ever been seated in front of twenty-one other guys and they're just laughing at you? Me neither. Up until now.

"Ana isn't exactly the age-appropriate girl for me. She's only sixteen."

"But Lily is age appropriate. She's almost twenty-one." Kaiden winks at me with a nasty grin on his face. I'm just going to assume Aaron finally admitted to them having a twin sister. I suppose it was long overdue anyway.

I also assume that Aaron threatened to cut off the guys' junk if any of them let the word out to any other student.

I clear my throat, not knowing how to say anything back to Kaiden.

"You remember the unspoken rules, right?" Aaron takes over again. "Unspoken rule number one: Skipping practice for a girl will not stay unpunished."

"It's an unspoken rule. How would I remember it?" I question. "And I didn't skip for Lily. I actually went to see Eira."

Of course, I know how I'm supposed to remember a rule that has never been mentioned before.

These "unspoken rules" aren't too unspoken.

I made them up. And they're all written down in a notebook. Twenty-five *unspoken* rules in total.

They're not getting talked about, but everyone knows them. When I first got voted as captain, I made sure we had some rules. I figured we needed them because the captain before me didn't care one bit about the team. It was all about him and winning.

I wanted a team that actually sticks together. One that would take care of the other, be there for one another.

So I made up some rules.

Every teammate got a list to learn by heart. They called them the "teammate requirements". Most of the rules were jokes at first. Rules such as "don't ever jump into a pool at a party on your own" weren't meant to be taken seriously. But the team did anyway. Meaning, we'll go by them.

"Oh, I know," Aaron says, chuckling. He undoubtedly spoke to Lily before all of this, to get proof that I was with her. But that means he also knows we were with Eira. "What about rule number ten?"

Unspoken rule #10: Teammates' siblings are off-limits.

"Oh, fuck you, Marsh," I snap. "You gave me the go, remember?" And besides, I'm not even dating Lily. We're not a couple, nor will we ever be one. I just want her to stay alive and realize life is worth living.

The problem is, I can't tell him that just yet.

"You're a complete asshole, but I know you will be good to her." Aaron offers me a slim smile before he turns back to grinning like the devil. "But you will have to face a punishment either way."

"Alright, beat me up already."

Another round of laughter erupts.

Whatever they think my punishment should be, clearly beating me up doesn't measure up to their expectations.

"We figured you could use a wardrobe change." The grin on Aaron's face widens, so do the ones on the other guys' faces.

This can't be good at all.

"Remember, Coach signed in on this."

Only moments later, two of my teammates hand me a piece of clothing each. Grey hands me a white cropped top that looks like it's going to be way too small on me. Zac hands me a fitting tutu. A white tutu that'll freeze my ass off.

But these aren't the highlights yet.

When Grey and Zac step back, Aaron comes into vision. He's holding a pair of white fairy costume wings in his hands. I know they're from a fairy costume because these belong to my sister.

"You guys know I'll most definitely break a few bones or die from the cold, right?"

They shrug. All of them. They're just shrugging and then burst into laughter like this costume is the most hilarious thing ever.

It is. If I wasn't the one in the hot seat.

"Come on, Princess Fairytale, get dressed," Aaron says, swinging a wand around before bopping it to the tip of my nose. After that, he makes his way to his cubby as quick as possible.

The laughter never dies. In fact, with every piece of clothing, I strip off of, my teammates find it more and more hilarious. And by the time I'm only in my boxers and have to put on the *great* costume, they're all dying of laughter.

But I don't back away from a challenge, so I squeeze myself into way too tight clothes and try to present them as manly as possible. When that doesn't work, I decide to unleash my inner princess. Or fairy for that matter.

Does that make me the Fairy Godmother?

I mean, I'm the team captain in a fairy costume. That definitely makes me the Fairy Godmother. Now, where's my Cinderella?

Just when I think this couldn't get any worse, it happens.

"Someone take a picture of this!" Grey yells, bringing his hands to his mouth to mimic a megaphone.

I give Grey the finger but embrace my photogenic genes and pose for some great ass pictures, being fully aware that these dumbasses will post them all over the internet later today.

But, hey, what's a team without some fun shit like this, right?

"Since we don't want you to get hurt," Kaiden begins. He walks over to me, his hands hiding behind his back. "We made sure you have a helmet." Kaiden brings his hands upfront, showing me the helmet they prepared for me.

It's a plain white helmet, a usual hockey one, but what's new is the paper crown glued right to the top of it.

"Why, thank you, guys. This is awesome!" I take the helmet with pride and put it on, continuing to pose for more pictures. "Wait, did I get some awesome new skates as well?"

"Do we look rich or something?" Aaron asks.

"You do, actually." It's sort of the truth. Aaron doesn't look too rich, but what even defines *looking rich*?

What I do know, his family has money. His father is a medical lawyer. And his mother, what I know now is his stepmother, is a cardiothoracic surgeon, like mine.

"Fuck you, man."

"I would, but I have your sister for that."

Aaron tenses, his hands ball into fists. For a second I think I've gone too far, I probably have, but he doesn't act out. His lips form into a thin line like he's thinking about what to do next.

"She's not sleeping with you," he ends up saying. "I would know, Winter would rat you out."

"Not unless Lily doesn't talk to her."

"Winter would have to unblock you first, bro," Miles throws in. The other guys stay quiet, choosing to chuckle every now and then, instead of getting themselves some ass-whooping.

"Yeah," I agree, "what's going on between you two anyway? Is it officially over?"

"It's been for a while. She just didn't get the memo." Aaron rips off his shirt, completely unbothered by this conversation. "She's a great fuck, but nothing for long-term. She's too giggly and dramatic."

Or he's just in love with Sofia, whoever that might be.

"I saw the dramatic part," I admit. "Did you know she's driving Lily nuts?"

"Well, Lily is twenty years old, she can handle Winter."

"I doubt that," I mumble unintelligibly.

I put on my skates, grab my hockey stick, and leave the locker room together with the rest of the team. I'm sure I won't make it out of here without tons of bruises today, but that's alright.

I'm just praying I'll still have every part of my body working by the end of today's practice.

"Colin!" Coach Carter exclaims. "Get your ass over here!" By the sound of his voice, I start to doubt this was approved by him. He's upset. I know he is.

I quickly skate over to my father, keeping some distance between us in case I have to run for my life.

"I suppose you weren't in on this then?"

"Oh, no, I was," he laughs. "Got you the wings. Eira wants a picture as proof you actually wore them."

"Of course she does."

"Colin, you need to promise you won't run away in a minute," he says in a soft tone. It's scary. My father barely ever speaks in this tone. Only when he has bad news for me.

It's not like Tobias Carter is a bad guy, he has his moments. He's a great father, and he's been my role model for as long as I can remember. At least when I was a child. But he also has his aggressive moments, though he lets his anger out on the ice, never on the people around him.

Except for his team, that is.

When Tobias Carter is in a bad mood, he tortures his hockey players. That means more intense practice.

"What happened?"

"Your mother had to take Eira to the hospital earlier," he says. "She's alright, well, as alright as it gets given her state. They let her go back home, but she can't have many visitors these days."

"So you're saying I can't come home to visit her anymore?"

"God, no. Have you met your sister? She would rip our heads off if we no longer let her favorite sibling come visit her."

"So then what are you saying?"

"She won't make it to the game on Friday."

"Jesus. You could've just started with that and then elaborate instead of giving me half a heart attack." I feel my heart thump inside of my chest at lightning speed.

"I know you hate it when she can't come to your games—"

I cut him off. "Dad. All that matters is that Eira's condition isn't getting any worse. We can't risk losing her life. It's bad enough as it is. You really think I would get upset about her missing out on my games when these are infection catchers?"

He offers me a slim smile before turning me around and slapping his hand between my shoulder blades, dismissing me.

"We're starting with warm-ups!" He blows his whistle to signal the beginning of practice.

My father urges us to do a way longer warm-up than ever before.

Usually, we do some stretches for a couple of minutes, just to get our blood flowing, maybe shooting a puck once for the sake of it. With no goalie. But not this time. Coach has us skate up and down the ice for an hour straight, as fast as we could possibly go. And if we are too slow for his liking, we have to repeat it. Over, and over again.

As two hours pass, most of the guys are sitting on the ice, protesting to go any further. We're working on shooting the puck "the correct way". For some reason, our goalies choose today to not let one in.

See, if this was a game against some other team it would be good, great even. But not letting us, their teammates, shoot these damn pucks into the net when we're already close to dying on the ice sucks balls.

And since the team fails to get even one puck into the net, Coach continues to push us. "You won't get out of here until all of you scored at least once," is what he said half an hour ago.

Another hour later, half of the team wants to escape and never step foot on this ice ever again. Or any ice.

"Fine, you go drink something, stay hydrated, and then get your lame asses back out here!" he yells, dismissing us for only five minutes at most.

I watch as my teammates skate toward the exit, running to get some water into their system. I stay on the ice. At least until I catch the same blond hair, I've seen in the very same spot five days ago.

Lily is here.

"What time is it?" I ask my father.

He checks his phone, saying, "5:42, why?"

"Permission to say hello to someone real quick?"

I watch my father look around the arena, trying to find that *someone* I want to greet. When he finally spots Lily, he chuckles, then gestures up my body. "You sure you want to say hello to *her*, dressed like *this*?"

"Lily has seen worse days," I say, giving him pleading eyes. If they work for Eira, they should work for me too.

Spoiler: They don't.

"Stop the puppy-dog eyes, kid," he laughs. "You want to go pro, Colin. You can't leave the ice for some girl."

"But she's not just *some* girl, Dad." It's the truth. Lily isn't just someone to me. She's way more than that.

"Two minutes."

I don't waste much time and immediately skate over to the exit on the other side of the ice and run toward Lily. While running, I figure it's a great idea to take off my gloves. These gloves don't allow too much movement.

She doesn't seem to notice me until I'm standing right in front of her. Again.

"Nice outfit," she compliments falsely, biting her bottom lip to stop the laughter from slipping out. "You owe me a shirt."

I suck in a sharp breath. "This is yours?"

And finally, the slightest laugh slips from Lily's throat.

She nods. "Aaron called me earlier and asked if I had a cropped top that I don't care about."

"Traitor."

"I like it. This costume suits you."

"Does it now?"

"Don't you have to be on the ice?" Lily asks. "Your teammates are gawking."

"Let them. It's not like we're doing forbidden things here."

"What would that be?"

I don't respond. Instead, I look at her. Lily is the kind of person I could look at all day and never get bored. She's unbelievably pretty, but that's not even the point. I just like looking at her for some reason.

I take Lily's hands in mine, stroke over her knuckles. She has a few bruises on them. I wonder where she got them from, but I don't ask.

"Aren't you cold?" Her green eyes stare into mine. She looks concerned for me, it melts my heart.

"Not so much. The constant moving keeps my body pretty heated."

She responds with a sigh. "Right."

I know Lily used to figure skate, but I don't understand why she stopped when she still loves it.

"I should be out in half an hour. I have to take a shower after practice, but I'll hurry up, I promise."

"You certainly need the shower, Mr. Stinky."

"I do. Practice ends in ten minutes. You will wait until I'm back, right?"

"No."

I raise my eyebrows at her. She has to wait, I won't accept anything else. Lily looks away from me, her eyes fixed on my teammates who are probably pressed against the glass to see as much as possible. *Nosy asses.*

I take off my helmet, needing to plant a kiss to Lily's forehead. It has become a move I like to do. At least when it comes to Lily.

"Colin! Get your ass back here!" I hear my father yell, but I refuse to pay him any attention just yet.

"You hear that, dumbass? Your presence is needed on the ice," Lily says.

"Too bad. I'd much rather be here with you." I place my index finger underneath her chin, rest my thumb on it at the same time as I tilt her head up for me. I lean down, and just like I've done it before, place a slow and tender kiss to her forehead. Her skin is warm against my lips, somehow filling my body with an amount of heat I've never felt before.

When I pull away, I notice Lily biting down on her bottom lip, trying to hide her smile. She fails miserably.

I slide my thumb over her lips, freeing Lily's bottom lip from her teeth. "Don't hide your smile. It's too pretty to keep it hidden," I whisper.

"You have to go. Coach Carter will get mad."

"He's my father. He'll get mad either way."

"Yeah, but this is *your* place, Colin. You belong here. In an arena, playing hockey. You do want to go pro, right?" I nod. "So you should use all the ice time you can get and improve."

"Are you saying I'm bad at what I'm doing?"

"Not at all. But there's always space to the top," she speaks softly.

"PRINCESS FAIRYTALE!" One of my teammates yells.

Lily laughs. "I love your new nickname."

"My new nickname is Fairy Godmother. I won't accept anything else," I tell her.

"That's even worse."

I grab Lily's water bottle into my hands and take a few sips. She doesn't seem to mind it, even if she did, I wouldn't care.

"Not when you call me that." I wink at her and tilt her face to the side.

I lean down just enough so I can kiss her cheek, but Lily has other plans.

My lips are an inch away from her cheek when Lily turns her head. "What are—"

Our lips meet. It's totally unwanted and accidental, but I don't want to move away. When her soft lips meet mine, I no longer think about who's around us. All that matters to me is Lily. Lily and her lips that are connected to mine. The same lips that send tingling sparks through my body, multiplying the heat that rose inside of me a minute ago by five.

This is a new feeling for me. I never felt this electricity running through my veins when I kissed someone.

I've heard this could happen. I've read about it, but never experienced it myself. Especially not with such a kindergarten kiss like this.

Yet it's more than feeling excited. It's more intense, more breathtaking in a different way.

It's *more*.

Everything around me no longer exists. We're not in an ice hockey arena. We don't have all twenty-one of my teammates, plus my father, watching us kiss.

It's just Lily and me. Two *friends* kissing by accident.

But then why don't I want to leave her lips?

Why do I want to pull her closer, taste her on my tongue? Why do I want to *feel* her closer, kiss her harder, deeper?

As much as I loathe having to pull away, I know I have to.

This was an accident. It wasn't supposed to happen. Lily and I weren't supposed to kiss. We're friends. Friends don't kiss.

Her cheeks are flushed when I look at her again. I hope this won't change anything now.

She's clearly embarrassed. I hate that she is.

A part of me hopes that she felt the same sparks run down her spine, intoxicating her body with me as mine got intoxicated with her. At the same time, I hope this meant nothing to her. Because if it did, it will complicate the dates I've planned.

Are these even considered dates?

I'm aware that I joke about all this a lot. I call her my girlfriend to her face sometimes when I know she's not.

What does this mean? Why do I even care if she dies or not?

Sure, I care now that I know her better, but why did I care right from the start?

I bet this is all because of Aiden. He made sure I cared for people, not let myself get lost in fame and money. But Aiden and Lily are two completely different people to me. She wasn't my business, Aiden was. I made her mine to care about, and now she's too important to me to stop.

I want her alive. I *need* her alive. I need her to breathe, to live. I need her to be here, with Aaron, with her family and friends.

With me.

"You'll wait, right?" I repeat my previous question, needing her to tell me she won't run away.

She clears her throat, looking down to the floor, avoiding my eyes. "I, uh, sure."

"Lily." I sigh. "We didn't mean for this to happen. Let's not make it weird, okay?"

"It's not weird. We're cool."

Something tells me she's lying. She's still avoiding my gaze.

I quickly look toward the ice, seeing my teammates mocking me for what just happened here. Griffin does the basic making-out-with-oneself move. Aaron's rolling his eyes at me. Grey's smiling at least as much as Grey can smile, knowing me only too well.

Allowing my eyes to wander over to my father, I see him looking at me knowingly. He shows the same smile Grey gives me, just that it's so much more powerful coming from the man I owe everything to.

He waves me off, telling me I'm free to go.

I grab Lily's hand and pull her off the seat. She lets out a shriek but shuts up when I drag her after me. She only starts to protest when I step on the ice.

"I'm not going on the ice," she says with a warning tone. "Colin, I will bite you."

"You do that, Lilybug." I scoop her up from the ground, holding her up shortly before throwing her over my shoulder and begin to skate over the ice.

She is screaming for me to let her down, but I'm not. Lily doesn't want to touch the ice, so I won't let her touch it. Not yet anyway.

My teammates are whistling over what's happening. The knowing "*oohs*" and "ahhs" that escape their mouths when I pass them tell me that I'll regret this sooner rather than later.

It's definitely a challenge to skate with someone hanging from my shoulder, but it's manageable. Though, if she keeps on pinching my ass, I might drop her.

I swear, Lily Reyes has some strength in her fingers. I always thought Eira was good at pinching me, but Lily tops it.

By the time I reach the other side of the ice, I swear I'll have a bruise on my ass cheek.

Aaron steps in my way, stopping me from moving. "Colin let her down." He's the only one protesting. The rest of the team is either wooing for me or ignore the fact that I've got a pretty girl swung over my shoulder altogether.

"Not going to happen."

"Let me down, Colin!" Lily screams, pinching me once again.

"Fine, you want to walk over the ice in your shoes?" I start to let her down, pulling her back over my shoulder before she eventually stops me.

"Let me down when we're back on *not-ice* territory."

"That's what I thought." I make my way to the exit closest to the locker room.

Aaron's still watching me, I can feel his eyes on me, following my every move. I can't blame him. If some guy did this to my sister, I would have beaten him up.

"No girls in the locker room, Colin!" My father yells after me. It has always been forbidden, I know that. The locker room is the teams' private space. All of our belongings are in there. And well, it's just in general for *us*, not some visitors. But regardless, there's another reason behind the "no girls" rule. It's a simple and obvious rule. No girls because every hockey player at this school is something different.

But the rule also relies on the name "Zachery Bloom".

I step off the ice, turn my attention toward my father for a slight moment. My hand stays locked in position around Lily's wrist. If I let it go now, she will run away. I won't risk that.

"No bad intentions, Dad," I say loud enough for him to hear. "I promise!"

Chapter 11

"I think I found a flower in a field of weeds"—surrender by Billy Talent

Lily Reyes

"I'm not five, Colin," I have to remind that douchebag of jock. He's dragging me into this—not at all—nasty locker room, and even worse, he pushes me into a shower cabin and locks the door so I can't get away.

For some reason, Colin believes I will run away if he lets me wait outside.

He is right, of course, but I don't want to boost his ego even more. He can't know that he's already pretty good at reading me like an open book, and it scares me that he can.

Colin strips from his clothes, then steps into a different shower cabin, the one right opposite of where he holds me captive. Thank God that the shower doors cover just the right places.

As I somewhat expected, Colin has tattoos on his chest. They're actually quite hot.

"You're not," he agrees much to my surprise, "but Lilybug, I saw the embarrassment flash in your eyes after the kiss. Knowing you, you're about to bail when I give you the chance to. I won't let that happen."

Did he have to remind me of the kiss? It's bad enough that I enjoyed that silly thing. It wasn't even a good kiss. A middle-schooler could have a better kiss if they tried.

Colin and my lips touched for about two seconds, maybe five. It wasn't some deep shit, and totally involuntary. He wanted to kiss my cheek, not my lips. If I hadn't moved my head, this wouldn't have happened.

Still, some part of me wanted it to last longer.

Now all I feel is embarrassment and regret.

"I wasn't going to bail." I cross my arms in front of my chest. "This kiss meant absolutely nothing. Yes, I *was* embarrassed, but only because I was surprised. And it was surprisingly bad, too."

"Totally agree with that one," he says. "Shared better kisses in my life before." Damned if that doesn't evoke something inside of me. It can't be jealousy, that I know for sure. Anger, maybe? Or maybe it *is* jealousy.

How would I know? The only times I've ever felt jealous were connected to anger. So I suppose it could be both after all.

"Not the worst either," Colin adds after a short while.

He looks at me over the partition door, his arms resting on the top of it with his chin lying on his arms. Colin offers me a charming smile, winks when I finally meet his gaze.

"What kiss could have possibly been any worse?"

"Middle school. My very first one."

"Oh, my God. You weren't born as the cocky asshole with an ego through the roof?" I ask, raising my eyebrows at him in a mocking surprise.

He grins at me. "Didn't say that."

"Your very first kiss was bad," I remind him. "Meaning you weren't always good at your own game."

"It's not my own game, Lilybug," he says. "Kissing was a thing way before I was born." Sometimes I really do hate him. "And I was great. She wasn't." There he is again. The asshole deep inside of him.

"Of course, it's always anyone but you."

"Precisely."

I narrow my eyes at him, about to open my mouth to talk when I hear voices. Voices that grow louder with every second. "I don't want to be here for the sausage party," I tell Colin.

Grinning, Colin grabs a towel and wraps it around his waist, then exits the shower stall. He walks over to mine and unlocks it. For some reason, this arena, locker rooms included, is the fanciest arena I've ever seen. These showers are lockable. I'm talking full-on *passcode* needing locks.

But that's not even the highlight yet. They have Wi-Fi in here, but I don't think they need it. I bet no one has access to it either, except for the hockey team, of course. But this arena still has so much more to offer, I couldn't even count it all if I wanted to.

"About time." I push his arm away as he tries to grab me and storm past him to exit this room.

"I wouldn't walk out there without me going first unless you do want to run into that, what did you call it? Sausage-party."

I sigh in defeat. He's probably right. He knows his team better than I do after all.

I'm certain these guys don't care about running around naked in front of the other. They're basically family.

Colin walks out first, I follow so close behind, he can feel my breath on his muscular back.

Is it weird that I want to touch him? That I want to trace a finger along the lines of his tattoos? Most definitely weird.

"Any of you naked yet?" Colin asks, coming to a stop. I bump into him, gasping as the cold of the water still covering his body hits me. "Lily's here."

"Put your dick away, Green!" I hear someone yell, followed by a round of laughter. I cringe. "You too, Simms!" A moment later, the same guy speaks again. "You're good, Carter."

Colin grabs my hand, turns to face me just to grin at me, then leads me back into the locker room where the guys are getting changed—or undressed.

"Would it hurt you to leave your chicks outside?" A guy with reddish hair asks, chuckling as he walks past Colin and me. "You know the rules, big guy."

"Fuck off, Simms." Colin flips Simms off. "Ignore Jackson, he's the main asshole."

"Ignore Colin," Miles shouts from the other side of the room. His hands are giving the illusion of a megaphone around his mouth. "*I'm* the main asshole!" At least he's being honest. I can't help a chuckle from slipping out.

Colin leads me to what I assume is his locker. "Take a seat," he says and motions to the bench on the opposite side of him. I do as I'm told, not feeling comfortable with at least eleven pairs of eyes staring at me.

I don't dare look around the room, so my view stays limited to the floor in front of me. That's until someone takes a seat beside me, swinging his arm around my shoulders.

"Please tell me you will continue to lead him on just a while longer," Aaron whispers into my ear. I'm sure he's eying Colin while he waits for me to answer. "He's got it bad, Lils. Everyone can see it and it's hilarious."

He does?

That's not good at all.

Unfortunately, yet also fortunately in this situation, Aaron loves to mess with me. So I refuse to believe his words. Back in high school, Aaron used to tell me a lot about some guys "having it bad" for me. It was never the truth. Turns out, Aaron went through the rebellion-puberty phase at that time. He was messing with everyone around him.

But he's not a teenager hitting puberty anymore. He's a grown man. More or less grown with his almost twenty-one years.

From the corner of my eye, I notice the towel from Colin's hips fall to the floor. I know he dropped it on purpose to get dressed, yet it's still weird.

With just one look to the side, I would catch his bare ass staring at me. A sight I'm intrigued to see, yet I'm also not really interested in that. He can show his ass to some of those puck bunnies, I'm sure they would enjoy the view.

"Anyway—" Aaron clears his throat as he stands up from the bench "—have a great evening with Carter." With that said Aaron makes his way to the shower room. So do most of the other guys.

Strange, he once mentioned hating the showers.

It's pretty scary being the only girl among twenty-two guys. If Aaron and Colin wouldn't have been here, I'm sure my mind would've played through some horror scenarios.

At least now it's only Colin and I left… and maybe one or two other guys.

My eyes stay focused on the floor again, not sure if it's safe to look up yet. It should be, Colin had enough time to at least put on some underwear. Yet my gaze remains where it's one hundred percent safe anyway.

That is until Colin kneels and his face sneaks into my vision.

"You there?" he asks bemused, waving his hands in front of my face.

I must have been in some kind of trance because I don't remember Colin speaking to me before this. At least I snapped out of it eventually.

"I am." I follow his figure up as he straightens his back. "I just don't want to be here."

"Lilybug." Colin's sigh trails off into a groan and he lifts his face to the ceiling. "Okay, this is only the second day. Give me some more credit."

"For what?" I ask. I'm pretty sure a wrinkle appears on my forehead as I frown.

"Trying. I have so much more planned. You don't even give me a chance to prove to you that you'll enjoy our time together."

"I can enjoy the time I spend with someone and still want to die," I say, whispering. "Can we talk about this elsewhere?"

He nods. "We're going to a bar tonight."

"Hell no. It's Wednesday. I have classes tomorrow," I protest.

"As do I, Lilybug. Some fun won't hurt. It's not like you have much to lose anyway."

"Fine. One hour, then you'll take me home."

♥ ♥ ♥ ♥ ♥ ♥ ♥ ♥

He tricked me. We're not going to a bar. Colin takes me home with him, which only makes this worse. I'd much rather be at a college sports bar called *Brites* than spend a whole evening at his house.

Nine Days

"You can go upstairs if you like," Colin says, walking off toward the open kitchen. "My room is the first door on the right."

"I don't want to go to your room." I tsk and follow him into the kitchen.

"Aaron's is the first door on the left, opposite of mine, maybe you want to examine his stuff instead."

"I can live without knowing his dirty secrets. Thank you," I speak dryly in response.

Colin beams an innocent smile at me, leans against the kitchen counter. "I have three options for you. Option 1: We order pizza. Option 2: We're cooking together. Or option 3: I make some sandwiches."

"I'm not hungry."

"Well, sucks for you because I am, and you haven't eaten anything today. So you will eat if you want to or not."

"Is this why I'm here?" How the hell does he know I haven't eaten anything? Is he stalking me?

No, he wouldn't. He's just attentive, I suppose.

It's weird suddenly having someone keeping an eye on you after years of not having *anyone* care one bit. I mean, sure, Aaron always cared about me, always asked how I'm doing… but he never paid too much attention to me. Not that he has to.

"You're here because I want you here, Lilybug." There is a pause like he wants to elaborate but never does. Colin changes the subject. "So, choose one."

"What kind of sandwiches?"

"I guess cream cheese with jelly. I loved it when I was little, it's one of the only things I know how to make."

"Cream cheese with jelly?" I repeat, wanting to make sure I got that right. He nods. "Why?"

"Don't tell me you've never tried it."

"I haven't, but I guess I will," I say, whining.

"So you're just hating on great food without ever having tried it before?" He fakes a gasp, holding his hand over his heart.

"I'm not a jelly fan," I admit. "I never had a peanut butter and jelly sandwich before either. I just don't like it."

"Then why would you choose the one option with jelly?" he asks, pushing himself away from the counter.

"It's the cheapest." I raise my shoulders in a shrug.

Colin exhales a long breath, kind of like he's trying not to let loose some really stupid words.

His eyes remain glued to mine, even when he walks over to me. He grabs me by my wrist, forces me to follow him upstairs.

"We're ordering pizza." We step into his bedroom. It's big, and tidier than I expected. Definitely tidier than my room.

My floor is covered with books, papers, and clothes. His is free of *stuff*.

"Colin," I start, but stop myself before continuing. How do I tell someone I barely know that I can't afford pizza anymore?

I already donated most of what I had to charities when I decided I don't want to live any longer. It's not like I was going to need it anymore.

"I'm paying, don't worry." He looks at me with a huge question mark on his head. "You're my guest."

"I don't like people paying for my food."

"So then, what is it? You don't like pizza?"

"No." I chuckle. "I do. I just can't afford it these days." An embarrassed flush spreads over my cheeks.

"How?" His eyebrows draw together. "That sounds superficial, I know. But it's pizza? And I know your family has money."

"Wrong," I tell him. "My father has money. Ergo, Aaron lives a rich life. I, on the contrary, live off of $450 a month, which is more than enough, usually. Seeing as I'm a student."

Colin looks at me in shock. He doesn't move, doesn't speak, doesn't even breathe, I think.

I get it. Colin grew up rich, he was born into a fancy life, and I guess his allowance is higher than my mother's monthly income.

"My mother's a middle school teacher. She gets like, what? $4000 a month?"

"That's not too bad." He pauses. "You're here on a

scholarship?" Another pause. "Oh, God. I sound like an arrogant jerk, don't I?"

With lips pressed together into a thin line, I nod slowly. "Pretty much."

"I'm sorry," he says. "I didn't mean to offend you or anything. I'm genuinely asking, though. Are you here on a scholarship?"

"No, Colin. I keep getting the amount I pay for tuition transferred to my bank account monthly. It's from someone I don't know, but I'm assuming it's from my mom. She used to feel bad for me taking on two jobs to pay for college myself. The next month, payments came in from a name I didn't, and still don't, recognize. I think she's working a second job to pay for it. She would never admit it, which is why I never asked. I kept one job for some money to live off of but quit the other. Now, a week ago I quit my only other job as well because I really don't need it anymore." *Oversharing much.*

"So, if $450 usually works just fine, how come you can't afford pizza?"

"Donated all I had left to a charity."

"Well, that means Aaron will pay for our food." How does this come out of whatever I just said?

I know I'm bad at math, but this equation doesn't add up.

"His credit card details are saved in my phone. He won't mind."

"Bullshit. He will. It's his money."

"Lilybug, this household here doesn't know 'it's his money'," he tells me. "I'm pretty sure Aaron once bought a whole new bed for himself using my card."

"You guys are weird." And I stand by that.

Chapter 12

"be my friend, hold me"—Breathe Me by Sia

Colin Carter

"COLIN!"

I guess I'm awake now.

"What the hell, Aaron." Aaron is standing by my bedroom door, leaning against the doorframe. I struggle to look at him as my eyes still have to get used to the light.

"It's eight in the goddamn morning!" he yells, stepping into my room. "You've missed morning practice!"

Oh shit. Not again.

"You had the chance to wake me up, you know?"

"No." He gags at whatever memory is running through his tiny brain. "I preferred not walking in on you and my sister."

"Walk in on me and Lily?" Right. She stayed the night. Took a lot of persuading, but she stayed.

It was already eleven p.m. when she wanted to leave because she was tired, but we were in the middle of a movie marathon, with that I mean she made me watch *Twilight*. Apparently, it's very educational.

It's not.

All I learned is that a way too old Vampire guy falls in love with some way younger human girl. It's not exactly what I would consider interesting, but Lily could ask me to watch *Titanic* five times in a row and I would do it.

"Dude, you know Lily and I aren't actually dating, right?"

"You're not?" Aaron takes a seat by my desk. He stares at me dumbstruck, waiting for what, confirmation?

"We're not. We're just hanging out as friends."

"Friends my ass." He lets out one loud laugh, crossing his arms over his chest. "When I came back home last night and meant to ask you something, you were all cuddled up together. That doesn't exactly scream *friends* in my book."

"Cuddled up together?" I don't recall being cuddled up to Lily.

Aaron shrugs, leaving me sort of clueless. "She's downstairs, by the way, making breakfast for all of us."

I sit up, narrowing my eyes at Aaron.

"Chill, Lily loves to cook. Neither of us asked her to." Once again, he chuckles. He turns in my chair, facing my gaming setup. I don't usually play games, I don't have much time for it, but I never got rid of it either. "I think Miles likes her."

Now that gets more of my attention than anything Aaron said before.

In less than a heartbeat, I'm standing on my feet, finding myself sprinting downstairs. There's no way that I will let Miles King get close to my girl.

She's not even *my girl*, but Lily doesn't need Miles clinging to her ass.

"MILES!" Even I'm surprised by my tone. I never yell at my friends, ever. Except on the ice, but that's a different kind of yelling. It's not filled with anger… mostly anyway.

Lily stands in front of the stove, wearing nothing but a t-shirt that's only roughly hanging over her ass. She sways her hips to some music, and, of course, Miles enjoys the show.

I love that guy, but if he dares touch what's mine, I will have to cut off some hands.

She's not yours, I have to remind myself. I ignore my own reminder though. She is mine, for as long as she is alive.

I'm about to yell at him when I notice that he isn't even actually looking at her.

"Good morning, captain never-showing-up," Miles greets me. "That's going to be another day in the fairy costume."

"Like I care," I snap.

"Someone's a bit grumpy."

"Fuck off." I make my way over to Lily. She's making pancakes and it smells delicious, but I don't care about food right now.

"Be so kind and take care of these for a moment," I tell Miles as I scoop Lily up from the floor, throwing her over my shoulder.

She yelps, hits her hands against my lower back, telling me to set her back down. But I don't. Instead, I carry her back upstairs into my bedroom.

At least I don't have to deal with Aaron right now, he was smart enough to leave.

I set Lily down once I closed the door behind us. "Stay right there," I say in a strict tone, walking toward my closet.

"You're not my father, you know."

"Aware of that." I look through my clothes, trying to find anything she could wear. "There's still no need for you to shake your ass in front of Miles. Not like that."

I take out one of my hockey jerseys, knowing it'll be way bigger on Lily than the t-shirt she's wearing.

"Jealous?"

"Furious." I put her arms up once I'm standing back in front of her, pulling the jersey over her body.

"You can't be mad at Miles for being there."

"I'm not," I tell her, still feeling my blood boil. "Miles is like a brother to me. I would share anything with him. Anything but you."

"You don't own me."

"I don't," I agree. "Doesn't mean I appreciate him gawking at you."

"He wasn't gawking," she protests. "Miles is actually fun to hang around, you know."

"Jesus, Lily!" I brush my hands through my hair in frustration. "If you want to fuck him, just ask him. Trust me, he'll be in your pants in a heartbeat." He won't. He might be able to fool everyone on campus with his wannabe fuckboy persona, but that guy is far too busy to do anything but cook, eat, sleep, play hockey, and attend classes. Especially since he's in NYC ninety percent of his free time.

I expect Lily to freak out on me. But she isn't. I know I went too far with saying what I had, yet she doesn't seem mad.

"Can you take me home?" Lily sounds… upset. Her voice trembles, and when I look at her, she's quivering.

Is she afraid of me now? *What have I done?*

Panic streams through my system. I don't want Lily to be afraid of me. "Lily." She looks at me with fear in her eyes. It breaks my fucking heart.

"Colin, please. I want to go home."

♥ ♥ ♥ ♥ ♥ ♥ ♥ ♥

I follow Lily to the dorm rooms, walking her inside. I don't want to leave her just yet. We haven't exchanged a single word after she told me she wanted to go home.

The tension between us has never been this thick, it's almost painful. At least she doesn't complain when I walk her inside.

"I'll see you in class then, huh?" I offer her an awkward smile, she returns none.

"Yup." Unlocking the room door, she steps inside but she doesn't close it yet. "Are you not coming in?"

"Do you want me to?"

"I don't know," she admits, awkwardly. It hasn't even been this awkward after our involuntary kiss.

"I should go then," I say. "You're not sure if you want me here, that's an obvious 'leave, Colin'."

"Colin, I like your company. But this is awkward, and I hate it."

"I'll see you in class," I tell her. "Oh, you like coffee, right?"

"I do," Lily answers. The confusion is written all over her face. I don't blame her, it does happen to be an odd question.

"I'm taking you coffee tasting later."

She leans her head against the door for support. "I've heard of wine tasting, cake tasting, even soup tasting. But never once did I hear someone say, 'I went coffee tasting.'"

"It will be fun, trust me."

She has a point though. Coffee tasting isn't something a lot of people do. Might as well be a one out of one thousand situation, but driving around the city, tasting every coffee a café has to offer sounds like fun. And like a lot of caffeine.

Caffeine aside, we will find the best coffee in the city. That way Lily and I can have a spot. *Our* spot, with the best coffee.

That being said, I say goodbye to Lily and leave to get back home.

I need to take a shower before classes start. And I need to call my father to beg for forgiveness. Okay, I don't have to beg for it. All I have to do is tell him why I missed morning practice.

I could so easily tell my father about Lily. Tell him what she's going through. He would excuse me for the rest of the week, maybe even the next as well.

But given that Lily is suicidal, he would try to contact her parents, he'd be forced to. And I can't let him do that. Lily would murder me.

Chapter 13

"it kills me how your mind could make you feel so worthless"—Before You Go by Lewis Capaldi

Lily Reyes

Dear whoever reads this,
Colin is taking me coffee tasting in a short while.
I don't even know what I'm supposed to wear to that.
Do I dress up? Wear sweats and a baggy shirt?
It's complicated. Frustrating even.
I still have his jersey. I might wear it. It smells like him, I like it.
To think that Colin does this to show me life is worth living is also frustrating.
Today's morning, he seemed so mad at me, or Miles, perhaps. Either way, he was jealous. I know he was.
But that's scaring me.
What if Colin likes me more than I thought? (That can't be)
This can't happen. I can't do this to Colin.
He deserves better than a suicidal girlfriend.
We're not even a couple, and I still think he deserves better than me.
He still wants to save me.
It's only day three. I should have more faith in him, but I don't even want to believe in saving.
Imagine how embarrassing it would be.
"Oh, I will stay alive, thank you, Colin."
"No worries."

Nine Days

And then we're both going separate ways.
Forever.
Awkwardly stare at the other from across the room.
Awkwardly nod a hello.
Awkwardly say congratulations at graduation.
No, thank you.
I couldn't even continue to live if I wanted to.
Even if he shows me there's more to live for, the pain would still be there.
I don't want to die because I don't think there's more to life, but it's the pain that makes me want to leave.
I don't want to continue to feel empty.
I don't want to be numb anymore.
I want to feel joy.
I want to feel love; be loved and love someone.
But I can't.
It's all... numb.
Nothing but nothingness.
I know some people love me.
Like Aaron and my dad. Even Ana and Liz.
But it's not the same love I desire.
It's not the same love that makes me giggle, feel warm inside.
It's not the same love that makes me lose my mind.
I've never felt that kind of love. I've always been too numb for it, I suppose.
And now it's too late.
No one could love me back to life. I can't even love myself back to life.
I can't expect anyone to save me when I can't even save myself.
I'm like a ticking bomb, about to explode any second, able to destroy everything and everyone around me.

Not with an outburst of emotions, with my death.
My family will be devastated, I know they will be.
But I don't care.
That's the part that annoys me the most.
I don't care that I will hurt my family with my death.
And Colin?
I bet he'll be sad. Or I kind of hope he will be.
He devoted nine days of his life to me.
Nine days of showing me why I should stay alive.
And he will lose.
He will wonder if this is his fault.
I mean, he knows it's not, but we all know what this is going to do to him.
He will wonder if he could've done one thing differently, taken me to one other location to save my life.
But he couldn't. Colin, you couldn't.
This is about me.
I want to die because I can't live with me being me.
I can't live with my emotions or the ones that are left.
I used to be so good at sleeping.
And now I can't even do that anymore.
It's tiring. Really.
My thoughts are killing me. Literally.
I can't stand this anymore.
I'm not that strong.
I fought this for so long.
I took so many medications to fight it.
Nothing helped. Nothing is helping.
I want to leave.

Nine Days

Please just let me leave.
Dying in vain doesn't sound so bad when you see the positive side.
I won't have to suffer anymore.
I will be a free soul. No more crying at night.
No more pain.
No more numbness.
I finally found a way out, I'm no longer trapped.
And I won't be gone-gone.
I will always be around, watching over the people I love.
That's what they say, right?
Spirit world sounds peaceful.
Wandering around as a spirit, doing some mischief.
That sounds lovely.
    Lily

Chapter 14

"I'll bring you coffee with a kiss on your head"—Say You Won't Let Go by James Arthur

Lily Reyes

"Nope, this one's nasty!" Colin spits his sip of coffee back into the cup.

I laugh. This is the fifth coffee he has done this to.

Since we're taking the coffees to-go, nobody ever sees Colin's hideous way of trying them. If the staff members were to see the way he spits his coffee back into the cup, he'd get banned from the stores in no time.

We've already been to six cafés. I, for my part, liked four of them. They weren't the best, but I also had worse coffees before.

Colin, on the contrary, hates every single one. Except for the very first coffee we tried.

"I like it," I tell him.

Colin made up two rules. *"Don't drink too much"* and *"we're only buying one coffee per café with the same amount of milk and sugar."*

It makes sense. We have at least ten more cafés to visit, and I would prefer not to die from too much caffeine intake. That would be a sad way to go.

It is a waste of money and coffee anyway. I hate that. Colin promised he would take the cups home and serve them to the guys though.

I wonder if he will give them the ones he spat in as well. It certainly would be hilarious to know my brother drank a coffee that contained Colin's spit.

Disgusting, but hilarious.

"How? This one's even worse than the one we had before."

"It's not," I protest.

"It is, Lilybug."

"I would try it again, but I prefer drinking coffee without saliva in it."

"I just saved your life, you're welcome."

Colin starts to drive again, making our way to the next one.

"Who's your favorite musician?" I ask in need of this silence to be gone.

I usually don't mind silence. And the one between Colin and me isn't awkward, but ever since today's morning, it's weird. So is talking.

Yet I still enjoy his company.

Although I have to admit that this coffee tasting is completely unnecessary and stupid, it's actually quite fun.

"Don't think I have a favorite. However, I do listen to *Chase Atlantic* a lot," he answers.

My eyebrows raise without me being able to control it. "I really can't picture you sitting in this car while vibing to *PLEASEXANNY*," I laugh.

Colin shakes his head and throws his phone into my lap. "Connect it with my car and open my playlist, I'll show you."

My mouth stands wide open, and for a moment I look at him dumbfounded. He tells me his passcode and eventually, I do open his music app. He has five different playlists. The very last is titled "Alone Time."

"Seriously?" I click on the playlist only to find it filled with Chase Atlantic songs.

I hit play and *Falling* starts. And so suddenly, I'm spending the next four minutes watching, laughing, while Colin is pouring his heart out, singing along to the lyrics.

At some point I join in, now going with a duet. I don't even care that I can't sing.

When the next song comes up, we're both laughing.

"Aw, shit," Colin mutters under his breath. "I could go for some McDonalds."

I look out of every window, trying to figure out how the hell he thought of food.

Turning the volume down, I say, "I don't like McDonalds."

"God dammit, Reyes!" He's shocked, much to my amusement. I'm sure if he wasn't driving, he would look at me with those huge blue eyes, boring into my soul. "Tell me you're kidding!"

"Not kidding."

"Aw, hell." He exhales a deep breath. "Like, nothing that they have on their menu?"

"Nothing at all," I admit.

"How?"

"I don't know. I personally just don't like the flavor."

"The flavor of burgers?" he asks incredulously.

"No, but their sauces. And I don't like the consistency. It's weird to me."

"McDonald's is a lifesaver," he objects. "It's affordable and good for its price."

"So is KFC."

"So, you like KFC but loathe McDonalds?"

"I've never been to KFC before." I laugh awkwardly.

The car stops at a red light. The second the car comes to a hold he turns, eyes on me, holding a gaze of irritation and uncertainty.

"Have you been living under a rock?" His mouth stands open, not for one second does he believe me telling the truth.

"Some people prefer home-cooked meals," I say, avoiding to look at him. I find it much more appealing to stare at dead trees right now.

"Alright."

♥ ♥ ♥ ♥ ♥ ♥ ♥ ♥

Colin and I are walking into the next café, diner fits it better. It has a retro touch to it, I like it. It has the typical black and white tiled floor. Red seating booths, and red chairs for normal table seats. The front bar has white tiles and red countertops, fitting the red and metal barstools.

I never even knew New City had a diner like this.

"I love this," I say under my breath. My eyes wander around the room, taking in the stereotypical movie ambiance this place brings.

And I truly feel like I'm in some kind of Hollywood romance movie. The only thing missing is the cold and rainy weather.

I certainly have the guy of someone's dreams here with me.

All this is so mesmerizing to me, I don't even realize when Colin takes a seat at one of the booths. All I do is stand in the middle of the diner, looking around like a fool.

But when I snap back to reality, I see Colin videotaping me. I don't even question it anymore because I know he needs those for our project.

"Excuse me?" A black-haired young woman taps on my shoulder. "I love your outfit."

Her hair is straight, but it's obvious she's straightened it. She has beautiful eyes, dark and mysterious. I feel like this girl right here is someone trustworthy.

But then again, I tend to trust brown-eyed people more.

"Oh, my God. Thank you." A smile appears on my lips. Compliments about outfits are the best. "I love yours, too."

The girl is wearing a white, skintight, satin dress, showing quite the amount of cleavage as well. It's beautiful, with no doubt, but I personally wouldn't wear this to a diner. A club for sure.

The white of her dress glows on her skin, and it's absolutely stunning. *She* looks absolutely stunning.

My outfit is completely boring compared to hers. I did decide to wear Colin's jersey. Why? I don't know. I was hoping he would comment on it, think it was adorable. But he didn't, much to my dismay. And I paired it with some black leggings and sneakers.

As I said, nothing fancy. I wonder why she likes it.

"You're a hockey fan?" she asks, flashing me a big white smile.

"I guess I have to be," I answer, shrugging. "My brother is one of the hockey players at St. Trewery." I've never said that out loud. Well, if you don't count telling Colin that Aaron is my brother.

"For real?" Her eyes widen with shock. "That must be exhausting."

I decide to offer her a slim smile. I never felt as though Aaron playing hockey was exhausting, then again, I didn't exactly grow up with him. Perhaps Ana thinks differently.

"What's your name?" I ask instead of answering.

"Kya Young," she says. "What's yours?" Starting a new possible friendship isn't something I should be doing.

"Lily Reyes," I answer. "Are you here all by yourself?"

She lets out a sad sigh, then plasters a smile back onto her face. "I am. I had a date, but he stood me up."

"Such a dick." *Men*. "You can eat with Colin and me if you want." I point toward Colin. I doubt he would mind.

"I prefer not to tag along on someone else's date."

"This isn't a date." I laugh. "Colin and I have a bet going. We're just friends."

"So that's why you're wearing Colin Carter's hockey jersey, huh?" She smirks, raising her eyebrows. "But... we can exchange numbers, hang some other time. I'm sure we'll see each other on campus now that we met."

"You're a St. Trewery student?"

"Yup. I study architecture," she answers. "I'm not sure why I attend some classes. Our construction technology professor only has eyes for Aaron Marsh."

These are a lot of information to give to a stranger.

"I swear, she gives him A's for his looks."

I look over to Colin, only to find him staring at me. He has this questioning look printed all over his face.

Kya and I end up exchanging numbers, then leaves after hugging me goodbye as if we've known each other for years.

"Seems like Kya likes you," Colin says as I take a seat across from him. I blink at him like I'm in some sort of trance, trying to make up a story as to how he knows her. Every single one I could think of ends up with them having dated at some point in life.

I hate that I even think about it. I shouldn't care.

Nine Days

"She's stopping by at my parents' house every other day, tutoring Eira." A smile tugs on his lips as if he knew being in the dark about their relationship bothers me.

Colin's hand reaches over the table, lying on top of mine, giving it a reassuring squeeze. A surprisingly comforting squeeze I never knew I needed.

"Lilybug." His voice is raspy, kind of as if he's fighting the urge to spit some words out. I wonder what words those would be. Then a low guttural sound comes out of his throat, and he leans his head back.

"What's wrong?"

He adjusts his head, his eyes flickering between mine, my lips, and our hands.

"What the hell are we doing?"

"You're trying to make my life less miserable for the amount of time I have left." I offer an awkward smile. Truth is, I have no idea what's going on.

Ever since that accidental kiss at the arena, there is this certain warmth in my chest whenever I look at him. I feel safe around him. I have no idea what that could mean.

His head bobs, chuckling as he tries to find words to say. He's as much at a loss for words as me.

"Maybe we should stop," I suggest, pulling my hand away from underneath his. At least I try to.

Colin's fingers wrap around my hand, digging into my skin until it's almost painful, keeping my hand from leaving his.

"Stop what?" He doesn't even acknowledge his hand squeezing mine. "Stop trying to get you to see a more colorful world? Stop trying to pretend that I don't want to kiss you? Stop trying to ignore that I'm hard as a rock right now, only because I'm touching your hand?"

I gasp. Jesus, how can he say stuff like that so casually?

"Stop playing with me. That's not funny."

"I'm not joking."

This has taken a turn I wasn't expecting.

Colin was supposed to pretend he could make me fall back in love with life. He was supposed to give me a couple more good days, not complicate it with some attraction.

"Just forget it," he says, withdrawing his hand from mine. "You're right. It was a bad joke."

Damned if that doesn't burn in my lungs as I suck in a sharp breath. He was joking, dammit. How does one joke about... *this*?

Just in time, a brunette waitress approaches us. I'm glad she does, otherwise, I would've started to cry.

"What can I get for you today?" she asks in a sweet tone, holding her notepad right in front of her. Her name tag reads "Miriam". She looks friendly, but also kind of like she's about to lose her shit.

And despite her friendly appearance, I can't help but notice the hungry look she beams at Colin. He doesn't even acknowledge it.

"Not a clue, can you recommend anything?" Colin looks up from the menu, but he doesn't look at her. Instead, his eyes are on me.

"Would you want something light, or for a bigger hunger?" She's looking at me this time. Clearly, she got the hint that Colin isn't going to pay her any more attention.

"Not sure what he prefers, but I would take something lighter."

She beams a smile. "Sure. How about the Chicken Salad Croissant?" she suggests.

"Sounds good. Also, could I get a blueberry-cheesecake muffin?" Miriam nods, writing down my order. "Colin?"

For the first time since Miriam approached us, he looks at her, allowing himself to appear friendly enough. "Do you have burgers?"

"Yes, but our menu is small. We only offer three different ones."

"What's the best one?"

"I would have to say the Hickory Burger."

"Great." Colin fake-smiles. "I'll have one of those. And a side of fries."

Miriam nods and writes it down. "Would you like something to drink?"

Colin and I are both quiet. His eyes are back on mine, boring holes into my soul. At least until he cracks a smile.

"We'll have a water each. And one coffee, two packs of sugar, and about"—he holds his thumb and index finger up to Miriam—"this much milk."

In an attempt to fight my laughter, I bite my lip. It doesn't help much because a chuckle still manages to escape from my throat.

This one little chuckle triggers Colin to the point where he breaks out in laughter as soon as Miriam leaves. Which then makes me laugh.

Chapter 15

"so go and break up my relationships and break my fucking heart"-PLEASEXANNY by Chase Atlantic

Colin Carter

"You're not coming inside?" Lily asks as I walk her to her dorm. I stand by the door, watching when she steps inside, not even attempting to follow her.

This is one of the weirdest déjà-vus I've ever had.

I shake my head. I can't go inside. If I do, I'm not sure I'll be able to control myself for much longer.

Today has been such a fun day. Tasting a million coffees doesn't sound like too much fun, but it is.

Lily and I even ended up declaring that Retro Diner as our new favorite. It may be half an hour away from campus, but their burgers are totally worth it.

We were supposed to find the best coffee in the city. And we did. Lily and I didn't even need to drive around to find a better one. We both knew the coffee we shared at the diner was a total winner.

Okay, maybe the burger was what convinced me to vote for it, doesn't mean the coffee was bad. The Retro Diner has a great coffee, it's not too watery, not too strong either. It's perfect. *So are the burgers.*

And besides, it looks pretty cool. Not only does it make you feel like you're stuck in a time machine, or as Lily would say "makes you feel like you're in a Hollywood teen romance movie," it is freaking awesome.

I don't think I will ever be able to go there without taking Lily with me. This is what "having a spot" means, right? A place you once went to with someone you love, and now you share these great memories with that person in connection to this place.

If so, then this is totally it.

I wonder if Lily will write about it in her journal. Never mind, she only writes about her bad emotions and why she wants to die. Why she *will* die, apparently.

Lily still insists on me saying "When you will die". She refuses to let me get through to her. Then again, I know nothing about dealing with suicidal thoughts, or depression. Maybe this is just what comes with it.

Anyway, after we left the diner, I convinced Lily to come back home with me. I promised to let my friends try the coffees after all, so they wouldn't go to waste, and much to our amusement, I didn't tell any of them that I spat in most of them.

They were cold, so even less enjoyable than before.

Lily had a hard time suppressing her laughter when Aaron took a sip from my least favorite coffee, the very one I spat into not once, but twice. Come on, I had to get the disgusting taste out of my mouth, so don't you judge me.

When he said, "It's not even that bad," even I lost it. Not going to lie, hearing your spit tastes "not even that bad" is pretty hilarious.

"Why not?" Lily sounds disappointed.

"I will regret it." I slide my hands into the pockets of my jeans, slightly lifting my shoulders before I let them drop down.

She cocks an eyebrow at me, not understanding.

I hate this. I hate that I can't just walk up to her like; "Hey, let's fuck" as I would with any other girl at a party. If I do this with Lily, not only would she throw me out of the window, so would Aaron.

But that's not even what scares me. What scares me is her reaction, how she'll act the next few days. I'm afraid things would get weird.

I can't help my groan as I try to come up with a good reason. "Lilybug." I run my hands through my hair, tugging at the ends, frustration streams through my veins.

"Have I done something?" Concern sweeps through her voice like wind sweeps through the air.

"It's what I haven't done," I answer, only confusing her more.

"What haven't you done?"

"Aaron warned me." My voice is soft and euphoric, yet I sound tired, uncomfortable. Even I can hear it. "I shouldn't have gotten so close to you."

"Why not?"

Maybe I should be straightforward with her. It's so early in our friendship, but I also can't lose time. Our days are numbered, at least until she comes to her senses.

"Because now I can't stop thinking about your lips." I storm past Lily, walking into her living room. I grab her wrist on my way in, pulling her after me.

I have never felt like this before. I've never been frustrated because I wanted a girl, and yet here I am. Lily is the only person running through my mind, especially in times when she shouldn't.

We're entering her room. I practically push her inside, lock the door when I follow her in.

I try to breathe like a normal person. Try to control my urge to jump her, press my lips to hers, and kiss the hell out of this woman.

I've been attracted to her from the second I saw her, but now that I'm also getting to know her…

"Are you okay?" Her sweet voice streams through my ears like classical music, flowing, easing my nerves.

I don't answer. I don't even react at all. All I do is stand, with my back pressed against her closed door, inhaling deep breaths, exhaling even deeper, longer.

I can't fucking do this anymore.

And then she steps closer. With every step she takes, I feel like the air is getting thinner. *I can't fucking breathe.*

"Take one more step toward me and I will have to pinch you up against the door."

She freezes. "Colin, what the hell is happening?" She demands an answer I cannot provide her with, sounding louder and austere.

My behavior is freaking her out and I can't even blame her. I would be freaked out as well.

Uneasiness rises inside of me. God, she's so beautiful. How have I never seen her before? We've shared some classes for years. How have I never laid eyes on her?

She takes another step closer, clearly ignoring my warning from just a second ago.

"Lily, I mean it."

"So pinch me against the goddamn door. As long as you're talking to me, I will take it." Another fucking step.

"Tell me something depressing," I beg. "Talk about your death."

Lily snorts a laugh, coming to a halt right in front of me. Her head tilts back enough so her eyes can meet mine. The hope and amusement in her green eyes have me melting on the spot.

"You think it's depressing that I want to die?" Then she corrects herself, "That I will die *next week*."

"How could I not?"

Her hands come in contact with my chest, blood rushes right to my groin. Summoning a slight gasp from me as her hands stroke deeper down, her fingers keeping track of every curve of my muscles.

"Then how come you want to talk about it now?"

I look up at the ceiling, not being able to look into her eyes any longer. She's got me trapped, and she knows she does. The grin on her lips gives it away.

I try not to concentrate on her hands that are skimming over my abdomen, finding their way to the hem of my shirt before slipping right underneath. Her skin on mine makes this room appear so much hotter than it is.

Fuck this. I'm in *hell*. This is fucking torture.

"Now, would you look at me, Colin?"

I can't. There's no way I won't just slam my lips right to hers when I look back into those breathtaking green eyes.

Ever since that accidental kiss in the arena, her lips are all I can think about, haunting me in my dreams. It's never been like this for me. I've kissed tons of girls before and never had one stupid, *accidental* kiss made me feel… *desperate.*

Just breathe, Colin.

"No?" Amusement dances on her tongue. "Would you just kiss me already?"

My head falls, my eyes land on hers, my breath officially taken away from me.

Did she just say what I think she did?

Lily bites her lip, smiling softly.

I swear, she wants me dead.

"I can't."

Disappointment draws over her face.

"I will go way beyond kissing."

"Is that a challenge?"

Nope, I'm done for.

I reach for one of her wrists, pull her hand out from underneath my shirt and place it down over the bulge in my pants.

She sucks in a sharp breath but doesn't withdraw her hand. Instead, Lily moves her fingers, adding just a slight amount of pressure as she rubs over my hardening erection.

She smirks up at me knowingly, moving her hands closer to the button of my pants.

"Unbutton my pants and I will no longer keep up the nice guy. I will have to fuck you disrespectfully," I warn.

"You can't even kiss me, Colin."

I firmly grip her nape with one hand, push her hips against my body with the other.

My lips cover hers, proving her wrong.

Her hands are warm when they press against my abdomen, once again discovering every inch of my abs. My heart beats rapidly, not wanting to realize that this is happening.

I take control of the kiss, deepen it by pressing her a bit closer to me if that's even possible.

My tongue darts across my lips, dips inside her mouth as I taste her. She tastes like coffee and pomegranate, her chapstick flavor. And so much like Lily.

I love the taste of Lily now. I could only ever downgrade from her. No one could ever measure up ever again, now that I've got a taste of heaven.

Pulling away, I push her back just enough to bring space between us. Enough space that'll keep me from doing worse, from going further than this.

Even this is a step too far. Kissing Lily, I mean. Her lips are off-limits, as is her body. *She* is off-limits.

God dammit, she wants to *die*. She's not planning some vacation for a short while.

I cannot get anywhere near more people with one foot in the grave. I've had plenty of those in my life.

And yet...

Lily grabs the chain around my neck, tugs me close to her all over again. Her lips graze mine, never quite connecting.

Honestly, *fuck it*. One night won't hurt.

"You make it so hard to breathe," I whisper. I don't let her speak and just press my mouth back against her soft lips. Her tongue brushes mine as I claim her.

She moans into my mouth, enjoying this as much as I do. *I hope*.

I slide my hands down her body until they reach her wrists. Taking them in mine, I turn us around, force Lily's back against the door. I pinch her hands over her head with one hand, using my other to hold on to her waist.

"You taste so good, you know that?" I say close to her ear. My tongue comes into contact with her skin, trailing wet kisses down her neck, sucking and biting on the tender skin until light red spots appear, not dark enough to leave marks by the end of this.

Except for one or two maybe.

Her mouth opens slightly, eyes only half-opened.

"Colin." Lily arches her back away from the door as I press my erection into her stomach.

Deep down in my mind, I know this is wrong. I know we shouldn't do this. We shouldn't cross the invisible line that neither of us ever really drew.

But for my own sanity, I need to stop this.

"Lily, we can't," I speak, my voice hoarse. "I can't do this."

"Colin, make a decision. We can either do this or watch a movie." She looks at me with disappointment, though I guess she understands my hesitation.

No, I believe Lily that this is about her, that I don't find her attractive. The truth is, I'm afraid of myself if I go too far with her.

I've never feared going too fast or too far. I've never feared sleeping with someone. But I fear sleeping with Lily.

I know myself, and I know I've never been more attached to someone like I am to her. I've known her for less than a week and I can't stop thinking about her. I can't let this happen, because otherwise, I might never be able to recover from her.

And if she does die, by then I will be so attached to her that it will rip my heart out and I'll die with her.

"Please," she begs, "make a decision."

Please, someone cut my head off with a Guillotine.

I slide a hand down my face, blowing out one quick breath.

Attaching my lips back to her skin, I kiss my way up her neck, over her jaw, right back to her lips.

Releasing Lily's hands, I pick her up. She immediately wraps her legs around my hips, her arms swing around my neck.

"You sure you want this?" I ask, pulling away from her lips for a second.

"Whatever happened to disrespect?" *Yeah, I don't think it's going to happen.*

"A guy can fuck you in all sorts of ways, and still make sure you want it."

"I want to see those 'all sorts of ways.'" She smirks.

I carry Lily over to her bed, set her down on her feet. "We might need a repetition then."

"Who said this will be a one-time thing?" *Fuck me.*

Sliding down Lily's leggings, she steps out of them and pushes me onto the bed. She sits down on my lap, cups my face as she forces her lips back to mine, kisses me passionately, her tongue tasting mine. She's revealing a new side of possessiveness to me I never thought she had.

Her hands roam over my body like she's examining me, discovering *every* inch of muscle and skin I have to offer with hot touches that send bolts of electricity down to my cock.

As her hands travel down to my pants and she's about to undo them, I have to stop her. Not because I don't want her hands on my dick, but because I fear losing myself way too quickly when she does.

For some reason, her hands are affecting me more than anyone's ever could. Just a soft and tiny touch of Lily's and I'm a goner.

I grab the hem of her—*or my*—jersey and pull over her head in a swift move.

"Aw, fuck." I move my lips over her hot skin, kissing up her cleavage, over her collarbones back to her lips.

I found a new addiction. My lips attached to hers.

Her fingers cling to the material of my shirt, tugging on it as she forces it over my head, throws it across the room. She takes a moment to look at me, skims over my upper body like she'd never seen it before.

"I think you need to work out a bit more." Lily traces the tips of her fingers down my chest, stopping at my abdomen. "Wouldn't want my new sex buddy having fewer abs than my brother."

She's joking, I know she is.

"Jesus, can we not talk about Aaron right now?"

"Only because you've asked so nicely." She beams at me while she places her hands back onto my jawline, and kisses me.

My hands reach behind her, unhooking her bra. Sliding the straps down her arms. I curse out once again. "Fuck, you're so beautiful."

Her cheeks flush. A while ago, something told me that she can't take compliments very well, but fuck it if I have to, I will tell her how beautiful she is every hour of every day until she believes me.

Because. Lily. Is. Fucking. Gorgeous.

"Quit the admiration. You promised disrespect."

"Reyes, for fuck's sake." I stroke the pads of my thumbs over her nipples, feeling as they harden. "Fuck the disrespect. You're too breathtaking."

Lily places her hands on top of mine, lays them down right onto her breasts, giving them a squeeze with my hands.

Hint taken.

I let my hands skim over her breasts, squeezing them, roll her nipples between my fingers, listen to the whimpers coming from Lily.

"Absolutely stunning," I whisper and kiss down her body until my mouth covers one of her nipples. My tongue darts out, glides across it ever so softly. She lets out a moan, hands tugging firmly on my hair.

I know this shouldn't happen because this is going to complicate the next six days. But I can't seem to help it.

Chapter 16

"she's headin' for something that she won't forget"—Night Changes by One Direction

Lily Reyes

Colin seamlessly switches our position, pulling me off his lap, and lays me down onto my bed.

He pulls out his wallet, takes out a plastic wrapper, and sets it down on my nightstand.

Colin tugs on my underwear, slides it down my legs, and leaves me completely exposed to him.

I watch as his head tilts back, facing the ceiling, letting out a long groan. "I'm going to break you."

"Don't flatter yourself, Fairy Godmother." I chuckle.

But I think he might be right. The second he pushes his pants and boxers down, standing in front of me just as naked as I am, a gasp escapes my throat, much to his delight.

He chuckles at my reaction, crawls on top of me, leaves kiss after kiss on my body, beginning at my stomach, and ending with his lips attached to mine.

His kisses are to obsess over. Hot, with passion, lust. They're seductive, possessive; not too much tongue and not too sloppy.

His hand tracing down my body feels like fiery bits from hell, stingingly hot, yet he touches me with such gentleness.

Gasps and moans escape from me when he cups my pussy, slipping his fingers between my lips.

"Ah fuck, Lilybug." He can feel how embarrassingly wet I am. "This is hot." His voice deepens so suddenly, sounding a lot raspier than usual.

Pleasure flows through me like pop rocks, prickling through my body, tickling on the surface of my skin when Colin pushes a finger inside of me.

"I need to taste you." His voice is hoarse as he speaks against my lips.

He lifts off me, and it'd be a lie if I said I don't feel lonely with some of his weight no longer pressed on top of me. But that thought quickly vanishes when Colin pushes my legs further apart, and places a kiss on my pussy.

"Oh," I gasp. "Colin."

He kisses me again, then decides to add his tongue, gliding from my core to my clit, eliciting moans from me. I feel him vibrating against my skin like he's humming something. But if he is, either I can't hear it because he's too quiet, or my head is too busy processing and savoring every touch, every stroke of his tongue, *everything*.

Just when I'm about to tangle my fingers into his hair, Colin stops and moves over to my thighs.

Colin kisses the inside of my thigh suspiciously long and only moves in a half circle, sucking, biting.

"Are you giving me hickeys?" I ask somewhat breathlessly. I wonder where my breath went.

"I might," he mutters, and I feel him smiling against my skin.

Honestly, so be it. It's not like anyone would see my inner thighs anyway.

And then, Colin lifts my hips, my fingers gripping his hair when he presses his tongue back against my pussy, pushes past my opening, lips up until he sucks on my clit again. With his tongue back inside me, he hums with satisfaction when I moan out his name.

Two of his fingers trace around my entrance before he inserts them, making it harder for me to contain myself. Groans and pleasure-filled cries travel over my lips, filling the room with sounds.

I want to kiss him, feel his lips back on mine, but I also want him to continue working my body the way he does.

"Colin." My voice is barely even a whisper anymore at this

point. I moan out louder, he mumbles something unintelligible against my skin, continuing to suck on my clit as his fingers push in and out of me repetitively.

My body feels hot, as though I was running a fever but without actually feeling bad. In fact, I feel *good*. Great even.

"You like that, sweetheart?" His voice is deep, hoarse, filled with lust.

My back arches, my head leans into the pillow, and my grip tightens in his hair, messing it up.

"*Please*," I beg, whimpering.

I pull him up by his hair, praying it's not hurting him. Luckily, he just smirks at me, hovering right back over my body.

I don't even care that his mouth and parts of his nose are covered in my wetness, I need to feel his lips on mine.

And so I do.

With my hands on his nape, I pull his face down, possessively forcing my lips to his, working my tongue against his.

Panting, I tell him, "I want you inside of me." He chuckles softly, then reaches his arm over to my nightstand.

"What if I want you to come on my tongue?"

"No."

"No?" he snickers. "But you're fucking delicious. I could eat you all night long."

"Colin," I groan, sounding desperate.

I'm not sure when or how he put the condom on, because the next thing I know, Colin strokes the tip of his cock against my pussy, magically summoning more of my moans.

He slams inside of me rapidly, causing both of us to groan out loud—though, I'm sure I'm gasping more than groaning. Him groaning from pleasure, me gasping from pain.

But I don't mind the pain. Not at all. I heard it could hurt, so I guess I was prepared. Mostly, anyway. It won't hurt forever.

Stilling for a moment, he looks into my eyes as if he could tell this hurt me, waiting for some different kind of reaction on my part.

But when I don't react, he starts to move, pulling out of me only to slam back inside just as fast as he did the first time. This time, he's rougher, pushes into me that tiny bit deeper.

"*Fuck*," he groans. "You're so tight."

Rough, deep, and fast strokes that send my body to a whole other dimension.

One after the other, Colin lifts my legs, wraps them around his waist, making me cry out in pleasure as his cock hits *the* spot

"Is this okay?" he asks, looking into my eyes. I nod, not being able to formulate logical sentences. Or a simple *yes* for that matter.

I try meeting his thrusts, lift my hips, but strength fails me when he plunges into me over and over again.

His lips are claiming mine like he's meaning to keep them to himself forever.

I don't think anyone has ever made me feel this good. It's scary. Scary how he knows exactly when to go rougher, when to go faster, when to slow down, and when to add his fingers, circling my clit.

But also so great.

When my moans grow louder, cries become more frequent, Colin never stops kissing me. He probably tries to mute me, or at least silence me a little, but I doubt that's working. I don't mind his lips on mine though.

He holds my arms above my head using one hand, not allowing me to continue touching him. It's frustrating, I *want* to touch him. I *need* to touch him. I need to roam my hands over his body, feel the curves of his muscles, feel him tense under my touch.

"Lily." He breathes shakily against my lips and pushes into me just a tiny bit harder.

I'm secretly praying Winter isn't at home. She can most definitely hear everything, not only the bedframe rocking against the wall but everything else as well. On second thought, I don't give a shit.

"That's right, sweetheart," he praises. "You're taking me so well."

Colin rubs my clit a bit faster, adding more pressure, thrusting into me faster until I reach the point of oblivion he's been working toward.

"Oh… *God*." I dig my nails into his skin, at least as much as it's possible with him still holding them up.

"No," he says in a strict tone. He grabs my chin, digs his fingers into my skin.

My eyes jump open, not knowing what the hell I did wrong.

"You're going to look me in the eyes," he demands. "I want your eyes on mine when you come, with my name rolling over your lips. I need you to see who's fucking you, sweetheart. Who's making you feel good."

So he meant *disrespect* in a hot way. All right.

He proceeds to thrust inside of me, deeply looking into my eyes, watching me as I reach my climax, reaching a state of oblivion I never thought I could.

It's so much more intense than doing it myself.

I cry out his name, seeing, but not really acknowledging, the satisfied look on his face when he gets just what he wanted.

Colin pulls out of me, turns me over, sticks my ass up only to slam back inside of me. He doesn't even give me a second to come down from my orgasm, only rocks my world right through it.

I feel him squeeze my ass cheeks, picking up the pace as he proceeds to plunge in and out of me.

His grip tightens on my ass causing me to yelp out in pain. I'm surprised when I find the pain arousing.

The longer and deeper he thrusts, the closer I get. It makes me question whether all those women claiming to fake it each time are being honest.

Or Colin just knows how to do it right.

I wonder if Colin fights back his orgasm, wanting me to come again before he does.

With his hands on my hips, forcing my body to meet his thrusts, he hits this very sensitive spot inside of me over and over again.

"Lily," he grunts, his voice raspy, his hands moving up to my waist, pushing me against him.

The sweat on my body starts to drip, rolling down my skin.

Nine Days

At this point, I'm a panting mess, barely able to breathe correctly. It truly feels like I have forgotten how breathing works.

At least I'm not the only one who feels this way.

Colin is panting as well, cursing, groaning, fingers digging deeper into my skin.

Until he stops, softly riding out our satisfaction as we both reach our orgasms.

I can feel my wetness dripping as he pulls out of me. I tip over, landing on my stomach. I don't want to move, too exhausted from Colin's godly cock.

I barely have enough brain cells left to acknowledge Colin pressing his lips to the back of my shoulder. Only when he says, "It's a heart" do I realize. "You have a heart-shaped birthmark."

That I do, apparently.

"It's cute, Lilybug. Not embarrassing."

"Wish I felt the same about it," I speak into the pillow, still not able to move.

"Get up," Colin commands, already standing next to the bed.

How the hell does he have the strength to move his body after *that*? I mean, he was here, too. He was doing more work than I did. How isn't this man exhausted?

"I don't want to."

"You do want to." In a matter of seconds, Colin pulls me off the bed, scoops me up in his arms, and carries me out of my bedroom—disposing of the used condom into my trash can on our way out—and walks us into the bathroom.

I guess Winter isn't here, it's way too quiet for her to be around. But I'm glad she isn't, because Colin fucking Carter just carried me five steps out of my bedroom and into the bathroom. Naked.

He sets me down on my feet, plants a tender kiss to my nose, then grabs one of the towels hanging by the sink.

"Do I need to tell you how to take care of *your* body?" He looks at me with sincerity in his eyes. "Go pee."

"Not with you here."

"You do remember the part, just a couple minutes ago, when I made you scream my name?"

"Hm-hmm." Still doesn't mean I can pee with *him* here.

He lets out a sigh in defeat when I don't budge, but he doesn't complain. He simply wets the towel he just ripped off the towel holder and stands back in front of me.

His eyes scan my body as if he's taking one last look, burning the image of my naked body into his brain. He then kneels in front of me, pushes one of my legs up, and rests it on his shoulder as he starts to clean me.

I guess he does have a sweet side to him after all.

How does a guy so sweet and respectful have such an awful reputation?

Not that he has a bad one, it's mostly girls complaining about the sex experience they've gotten. It's never about the sex itself, apparently, that's mind-blowingly-amazing. I can agree now. But according to half of the sorority sisters, he's never been gentle or nice to either of them afterward.

Clearly, I can't say the same.

Colin has been taking care of me ever since we started this nine-day journey three days ago. Surely in different ways, but it's still considered "taking care of someone," right?

"Can I—" He stops himself from continuing. He stands back up, walks over to the sink to rinse out the towel.

"Can you what?"

"Stay a little while longer?"

I freeze, not because I don't want him here, because I let myself believe he would stay the night.

"You can say no, Lilybug."

"Oh." I breathe softly. "I do want you here, Colin."

He smiles at me. "Good, because I wasn't planning on leaving anyway." He presses his lips to mine one last time and then walks right out of the bathroom.

When I return to my bedroom a couple of minutes later, Colin is lying on my bed. He's wearing sweatpants, a pair he wasn't wearing before, and for some unknown reasons, my bedding is changed as well.

"How long was I in the bathroom?" I ask, checking the time. It doesn't make sense since I have absolutely no idea what time it was when he carried me into the bathroom in the first place.

"I think about ten minutes." Colin holds his hand out to me, pulls me to him when I take it.

His arms wrap around me, holding me close. He brushes my hair out of my face and places a gentle kiss on my temple.

He traces his index finger along something on the crook of my neck, chuckling. "I love this," he whispers. "Guys better stay away from you now."

"You gave me a hickey?" My eyes open wide in realization. How didn't I notice that in the mirror?

He hums a yes. "You're blind."

"But I'm not."

"You are."

"Colin, people will think I'm in a relationship. This can't be happening," I tell him.

"Why not? First of all, you certainly are *mine* now. And it gives me a great excuse to drop a few assignments by throwing in the 'my girlfriend just killed herself' card."

"Gee, thanks. At least now I know you're only here to get A's more easily." I roll my eyes, trying to escape from his embrace.

"Lilybug," he chuckles and rolls us over, lying on top of me this time, hold me captive, and uses my boobs as his pillow. "In case you haven't figured it out yet, I'm here to help you stay alive. I don't want you to die."

"Well, but I do want to die."

"That's alright. I won't be selfish and tell you that 'think about your friends and family' crap. Or add 'But I'm so deeply in love with you, stay for me.' I just think it would be a shame to throw your life away."

Everything he says leaves my mind and all I remember is that one tiny part. *I'm so deeply in love with you.* I know he's joking, and still, my stomach turns upside down.

Not sure if it's because it sounds good or bad.

"I will never understand how you feel. But, Lilybug, I can try and help you understand that you're not alone. I can try and make the pain bearable. You're such a wonderful person, I couldn't live with myself knowing you've died and I didn't even try to stop you," he says, stroking his fingers through my hair.

As much as I'd love to believe him, nothing could ever change my mind. But instead of saying this all over again, I pick up our earlier conversation. "So that's why you want me to be yours?" I raise my eyebrows at him. "You want me to be your girlfriend so you can—what? Have professors grade you with more care, pity you because you've lost someone you 'love.'"

"I never declared you as my girlfriend."

"You said I'm yours. It's the same thing."

"So it appears, huh?" I can feel him smirk against my breast as he nuzzles into me. "You're mine to spend the next six days with. Mine to convince how amazing life can be if you let it."

These are going to be six very interesting days.

A sudden warmth creeps into my chest, storing the words "you're mine" scarily close to my heart. I shouldn't feel this way. I shouldn't be wanting to jump around like a toddler, screaming, laughing with happiness.

But I do want to. Because Colin calls me his, and *he*'s lying on top of *me*, his arms are wrapped around *me*, not around someone else.

I'm getting way ahead of myself. I'm more of a mission to him, a challenge if you will. Someone to play with until I die. There's no commitment.

The room quiets, heavy breathing being the only sound filling this room with noise, though neither of us seems to be falling asleep any time soon.

"Do you mind if I give my sister a call?"

I don't care, but I do wonder why Colin would want to call his sister at eleven at night.

Reaching over to the nightstand, he grabs his phone. He pulls me against him, still wanting to keep me close. Then he swipes through his phone, landing on his messenger app, allowing me to skim over his last texts. Fortunately for my own sanity, he clicks on Eira's chat and dials her number before I get to hurt my own feelings.

Not even sure why the thought of Colin messaging a couple of other girls bugs me.

"Please tell me you were awake," Colin says shortly after Eira picks up the phone. I don't hear what she answers, but I take Colin's relief as something good.

"No, *enana*, I simply didn't manage to stop by today." So, he does visit his family every single day? That's impressive. I haven't seen my mom in a month.

Though to be honest, my mother and I haven't been quite that good for one another recently anyway.

"You know I would never do that." I hate only hearing one-half of conversations. "*Uh, claro. Dame un momento, ¿sí?*"

Colin gets up from the bed in a heartbeat, the phone clamped between his shoulder and ear, walking through my room, picking up clothes.

"Are you leaving?" I ask, drawing my eyebrows together.

Colin shakes his head at me, mouthing, "Not yet."

"*No, esa era Lily.*" He walks over to me, sticking my arms up into the air, pulling the same jersey from earlier down my body.

"Give me a second, would you?" He laughs as he sits back down beside me, holding the phone in front of his face just when the camera turns on, revealing a tired-looking Eira Carter.

She shrieks in excitement when she sees my hair in one corner of the screen. "Lily!"

I sit up, leaning against my bedframe.

"Colin won't stop talking about you, you know that?"

Colin shifts awkwardly. Through the screen I see him giving Eira a warning look. She ignores it though.

"He won't?"

"Yup. Just yesterday he was all like 'She's so gorgeous'. If I recall correctly, he was drooling as well." *Drooling?* "He has like a million pictures of you on his phone."

He does? I know he takes videos of me occasionally for our project, but pictures? Maybe they're needed as well. I wouldn't know, Colin doesn't tell me anything about our project.

"Anyway"—I need this conversation to be about anything but Colin and me—"how are you feeling?"

She still doesn't look much healthier. If I'm being honest, she even looks a tad sicker now.

"Just great." She smiles wryly. "Time's just getting tougher."

And then Eira proceeds to tell us about her day. How their mother took Eira out for dinner earlier, and that she went back to school for a couple of hours. Colin doesn't seem too excited about the news, but I wouldn't know why.

School is normal, or she has to get homeschooled at her age.

Half an hour later, Colin ends the phone call and gets up from the bed.

He kisses my forehead, gathers his belongings, and marches out the door. He doesn't even say goodbye, he just leaves like the total asshole he is.

Chapter 17

"it could be nothing cause nothing lasts forever"-Like Strangers Do by AJ Mitchell

Colin Carter

"You fucked my sister!"

Everyone's head turns, pairs of eyes stare at me like I'm some kind of performer on a stage. It physically hurts to feel the eyes of my teammates on me.

I'm used to hundreds of people watching me play on the ice, but having a good number of guys from your hockey team stare at you like you've committed a crime sucks balls.

"You literally gave me the green light." I turn to face an angry-looking Aaron. He's just walking into the locker room.

Half of the guys are already on their way to the shower room, washing off the scent of victory sweat.

We had another home game up until a couple of minutes ago, and we won. I thought the team would be in a good mood after our victory, but one of us clearly isn't.

Though, why is he only yelling at me for it now? Lily has been walking around with that hickey on her neck for the entirety of the day.

Granted, she tried to cover it, not even I could see it in film directing earlier.

"I didn't think you would actually do it!" Aaron yells, not caring that the other guys are present.

Fucking your best friend's sister can never end well, despite having the go. I should have known better.

I was a dick afterward. I should've stayed the night. I should've slept next to her, woken up next to her the following morning. But I chickened out.

Common sense kicked in. Lily and I are *friends*. We aren't supposed to have sex.

It's not like I could change anything about the way I feel about Lily.

"Remember the part when you said you'd know I'd treat her right?"

I wait for Aaron to approach me properly, but he doesn't walk any closer. I guess it's because he doesn't want his fist to end up in my face.

Truthfully, I don't think I would even fight back at this point. Only thinking about one of my teammates touching Eira in the slightest has me want to vomit.

But then again, Aaron gave me the okay. I didn't go behind his back… this time.

Aaron inhales deeply, slowly calming his nerves. "Dude, she's my fucking twin sister."

"Well aware of that." If he wants to evoke some kind of guilt inside of me, he's not doing a great job. I wouldn't regret sleeping with Lily for anything. At least for his satisfaction. I don't regret it, but I kind of do anyway. It's… complicated.

"We almost have the same face. It's like you fucked me."

And now he's exaggerating, crossing an obvious line. And even if he wasn't exaggerating, given our history, it makes absolutely no sense.

"How do you know about it anyway? I doubt she walked right up to you and told you."

"She didn't," he says irritated. "She has a damn hickey on her neck, dumbass. That couldn't have been done by anyone but you." I swear, the vein on his neck is about to explode.

"I'm not even trying to deny it was me. But now that you mentioned 'others'… would you rather it be some other guy hitting it off with her? Like one of the frat guys, for example?"

"Fuck off, Carter. She's not supposed to be with any guy."

"Aaron, your sister is almost twenty-one years old. She's old enough to make decisions."

"Aaron," Grey speaks calmly, resting his hand on Aaron's shoulder. "What is your problem? I hate to take sides, but you did tell Colin it was okay. Bitching about it now is just a dick move."

Aaron exhales deeply, steadying his breath—*again*—as he tries to control his anger.

"At least tell me she's not just one of many," Aaron demands, looking into my eyes with anger burning in his. I swear, if looks could kill, I'd be lying on the floor and kissing death hello.

"She's not," I answer with no hesitation. "You really think I would do that to Lily? Fuck her for one night and then disappear?"

"Yes," he snaps. "Like you do with every other woman."

"Did you at least stay the night?" Miles asks.

I should have, but I couldn't. I'm afraid of my own feelings. Lily and I have gone way too far with this already, I can't let this go any further.

My friends know that I usually send the girls home right after doing it, or I sprint out the door without looking back. They never hear from me again.

But it's not like those girls don't know that I won't stay. I always make that clear right from the start.

However, Lily is different. She is *more*. And definitely means way more to me than I'd like.

"I didn't." I'm incapable of lying to these guys. Perhaps not incapable given that they have almost no clue what's going on in my life most of the time. "I stayed for a while and then left.

"I don't believe you," Aaron spits out with an amount of venom I've only ever witnessed on the ice.

I fucked up big time with him.

Without saying a word, I take out my phone from my cubby, unlock it then go straight to calling Lily.

She picks up on the second ring.

Aaron watches me, still having his angry eyes focused on mine. He doesn't move, doesn't even change his expression for a second.

"Colin?" Lily's sweet voice comes through the phone. Somehow just hearing her voice makes Aaron's anger seem less angry to me.

"Lilybug, where are you right now?" I know she has to be around here somewhere.

"Same bench you found me on the day we met. Why?"

"Okay, stay there, will you?"

I quickly change my footwear. Not waiting until Lily could respond, I hang up the phone and jog over to the other side of the arena, ignoring the fact that someone—most definitely Aaron—is following me.

I need to see her.

When her blonde hair comes into focus, I experience instant relief. Not even sure why.

Lily stays seated as I approach her, but when I do stand in front of her, her head lifts for her eyes to meet mine.

"Congratu—"

I guide my lips to hers, kissing her gently, yet also rough enough to draw out a soft moan from her throat.

I didn't even know I needed this kiss until my lips are covering hers.

I also didn't know I was going to kiss her until now.

"Thank you," I say as I pull away from her lips. "For the congratulations, I didn't let you finish saying aloud."

"You're welcome."

Looking over Lily's shoulder—down to the seats—I notice her mint green notebook lying on one of them. Before she has the chance to forget it again, I grab it.

"What are you doing?" she asks with confusion.

"Holding on to this in case you accidentally leave it here again."

"I won't."

"Sure, Lilybug."

She smiles lightly, carefully swings her arms around my torso, pulling me into a hug.

What I thought was going to be a cute and friendly hug, quickly turns out to be an attempted murder as her iced-cold hands find their way underneath my jersey.

But I don't budge. I don't because if I did, Lily would no longer be hugging me. I happen to enjoy her rarely happening hugs a little too much. Even more than I like her mouth pressed to mine.

Never mind. I love her lips more.

"Are you ready for day four?" I ask, swinging my arms around her as well, pressing her closer into my chest.

"Depends. Where are you taking me?"

"We'll go visit Eira for a bit and then I'll take you somewhere to let out your aggression."

"I'm not aggressive." She looks up at me, pouting.

"Alright, we'll leave that for tomorrow then." I kiss her forehead. "Rollerblading it is."

"No," a voice from behind me snaps. "She can't do that. She isn't even allowed to skate on the ice."

I look down at Lily, raising my eyebrows. I know for a fact she is allowed to but just doesn't want to. Or more like her depression won't let her.

"What if I promise that I won't let her break her bones?" I ask nicely or fake nicely.

I mean, come on, Aaron is overreacting right now. I understand that he's pissed, I would be too, but he has to get over it already. He was the one telling me to go for it. If he hadn't said it, hell, I don't think I would have continued seeing Lily for those nine days.

That's not true. I definitely would have continued to see her. Daily.

"*Her* mother is going to chop off your head."

"Oh," I gasp. "I think it's time for me to meet your mother," I say to Lily. "She will love me. I know your dad does."

"Dude, seriously?" Aaron groans, shaking his head in disapproval.

"Deadly serious," I tell him. "Your dad loves me."

Maybe it's a bit exaggerated. Not the part with Aaron's father loving me. Not to brag, but he once called me his son. But the part where I said Lily's mother would. Mothers usually hate me… except for my own.

"Aaron"—Lily's voice is harsh—"You're not seriously mad at Colin, are you?"

Aaron doesn't answer, he chooses to go with the silent treatment. *If he won't answer, she won't keep asking.*

Just that this is Lily we're talking about.

"Answer me."

"You wouldn't understand, Lily." Once again, Aaron brushes his hands through his hair. "You don't have a younger sister to protect from guys."

"Even if I did, Aaron, it wouldn't be any of my fucking business. It's not like you don't know Colin."

"Exactly!" he yells. "I know Colin. I know who he's been with before. How shitty he treated every single one of those girls before you."

I mean, he has a point. I haven't been gentle with any of those girls before. But Aaron also knows that I do treat people I like well and truly care about them.

I can't blame him for being mad. I wouldn't have hesitated to punch him in the face if he touched my sister, no matter how good I know he'd treat her.

"Cool. But you clearly don't know what he did last night. You don't know how he's treating me, Aaron. He isn't mistreating me in the slightest. If anything, I'm the one doing crap to him. I'm upsetting him, not the other way around."

I don't want her to say it like that. It's not true. Lily isn't upsetting me. In fact, Lily is breathing air into my lungs. I thought I would be the one showing her how beautiful life could be, when in reality, Lily is the one showing me what I'll miss out on once she's gone.

"You're not upsetting him." Aaron's eyes switch between Lily and me, uncertain of whom to look at. "But I'm afraid you won't be able to handle what *his* life will bring, Lily."

"What's his life going to bring?" she asks. "He's made me happier than every Sunday we've spent together on the ice, Aaron. In just three days."

I watch as Aaron's face drops. I'm not sure what it is: amusement, more anger, shock, astonishment, maybe even happiness? It's not clear. But it's something.

"Colin managed to make me feel more alive in three days than I've ever felt for almost twenty-one years. You can't seriously be mad at your best friend for making my life better."

I'm not sure if Lily is lying to Aaron, says all those things to make him feel better, or if she truly means those words. I want them to be honest words. I wish for them to be true, not because that's a damn ego boost, but because I want Lily to be happy. More than anything.

Aaron settles his eyes on me, saying, "If I hear her say anything but good stuff about your relationship—" he pauses, focusing his eyes over to Lily for a moment before they travel back to mine. "— I will have to throw my fists at you, Carter."

"Understandable." Just that Lily and I aren't even in a serious relationship. I think. I did, technically, claim her as mine, that's because she is. I'm not letting anyone touch her, but that's because I want to protect her from even more darkness.

"Now that we got that out of the way, we're celebrating our birthday at Brites."

"We are?" Lily frowns. "Does that mean I can invite people?"

"It's a bar. Anyone can come."

"You do know the more people come, the more *you* will have to pay, right?"

"I'm not paying for everyone's drinks." Aaron taps my shoulder a couple of times. "I can't afford that, unlike this guy here."

"Sorry, I'm just paying for my and your sister's drinks."

"Jackass." He starts to walk away. I did tell him I would pay for all of the drinks if that meant I wouldn't have to get him a present. God knows what I should buy a guy who already has everything.

"Love you too, bro." Aaron flips me off. Turning back to Lily, I find her laughing, muffling it down by pressing her face into my chest. "Hey, you have no right to judge."

"I'm not. But maybe you should date my brother. Seems like he got quite jealous over us 'being together.'"

"What do you mean?" She pulls away from the hug, raising her brows as though the fact that I don't understand is equal to the world ending. "Aaron and I have been in a relationship for years. We're basically married."

"Figured." Lily takes her notebook from me, sliding it into her handbag. "Do you really think you should meet my mother?"

When I said this, it was only to make my intentions clearer to Aaron. Meeting parents is a big deal, I guess.

However, Lily met my parents before as well.

She knows my father because he's the hockey Coach at our college. And my mother happened to come home when I took her to see Eira.

I never truly intended for my parents to get to know her.

"I'm your personal chauffeur, Lilybug. You said you wanted to visit your parents tomorrow, so we'll do it together," I say. "Ergo, I will meet your mother."

"Isn't that kind of weird though? I mean, meeting my mom is a big deal, sort of."

"Nothing weird about showing me off."

Lily starts to laugh, then stops and punches her fist into my arm.

Chapter 18

"I'm happy that you're here with me, I'm sorry if I tear up"— death bed (coffee for your head) by Powfu, beabadoobee

Colin Carter

"Dear Winter,

If I'm being honest, it's a miracle that you're getting a letter from me.

You've been my best friend ever since freshman year, which makes it a shame that it took me way too much time to find words to say.

You knew I wasn't doing well. You heard me cry, scream when the pain got too much, but not once did you walk into my room to ask if I needed your comfort.

I would have said no, but knowing you were there for me would've—"

"Lilybug, you can't write that," I interrupt Lily as she reads her letter to Winter out to me.

We've been on the road for twenty minutes and Lily is still figuring out what to write. I mean, from what I've witnessed, Winter cares more about herself than anyone around her. It's truly a shame that Lily doesn't know what to say to her so-called best friend.

I can't blame her though.

"I don't know what to tell her. All I've got is to tell her how much of a shitty friend she can be."

"She's been your best friend for years, there has to be something good about the time you've spent with her." I stop at a red light, finally being able to properly look at my Lilybug, even if it's just for a moment.

Lily shakes her head no. "Whenever Winter tries to listen to my complaints, she ends up down-grading me. You know those people saying 'Oh, well, my hamster died this morning' when you tell them someone close to you passed?"

"Not exactly with this example, but yes."

"Winter is one of them." Lily sighs. "She tells me to stop whining about feeling depressed because I 'cry for no reason.' She tells me to stop whining about how horrible I feel because there are people out there having it worse."

"Alright." I pinch the bridge of my nose. "How about, instead of babbling all about friendship, you just thank her for being a *great* friend and then say something like 'I just didn't feel like breathing anymore, lol,'" I suggest, knowing it's bullshit.

At least it gets me laughter from Lily. Cheerful, happy laughter fills my ears like music.

"Might just throw in a few 'lmao's' as well."

"Exactly."

"Okay, let me try this again."

Another good twenty minutes pass until Lily starts to read out what she's written, again.

"Dear Winter,
Our friendship has been all over the place, wouldn't you agree?
I don't think I've ever had a friend anything close to what you are.
You're cheerful, kind, a literal party girl; always on the move.
You showed me that spending time all by myself—at all times—isn't what life is all about."

"Hold up," I have to interject, "*she* showed you this? I'm pretty sure I did."

"It's all I could come up with, Colin." She lets out a frustrated groan, falling back into the seat like she's just been liquified.

"Alright. Proceed."

"You dragged me out into the world, showed me that there's more to life than

having my nose stuck in some textbooks.
Unfortunately, this life wasn't for me.
I'm nothing like the party person you are, Winter.
I like being on my own.
I like spending time alone, being at home, cuddled up under my blanket while watching Legally Blonde for the hundredth time.
Sometimes I wish I could be more like you.
Carefree and jumping right into another adventure. Going out to clubs and start twerking at the next best guy I come across.
Though, if I'm being honest, I probably wouldn't just start twerking at some random guy.
Let's keep this a bit more realistic, okay?
I wish I could be more outgoing and happy like you are.
You always seem to know exactly how to suppress your madness, deal with grief and sorrow.
But sadly, that's not me.
I can't deal with the pain I'm confronted with. I can't deal with the solitude, the isolation I force upon myself for the sake of others.
I withdraw myself from people so I wouldn't annoy them with my awful feelings.
And it's getting too much to take.
It got too much, Winter.
I can't do this anymore, which is why I took the precautions I did.
Taking my own life.
This has nothing to do with you, but everything to do with me and my feelings.
I hope you understand that.
I'm just writing you this letter so you can hopefully find closure, knowing this isn't about you.
Maybe we get to see each other in another life.

Until then, I wish the best for you.
I wish for you to become the greatest actress you've wanted to be for so long.
 Lily"

"I mean, it's definitely way better than your first attempt," I tell her, offering a slight shrug.

"It's awful," she groans. "Most of this is a lie."

"True, but would you rather leave with telling her how much you despise her?"

"No." Lily connects her phone to my car, allowing herself to put on some music. She doesn't even ask if that's okay with me. But let's be real, I don't care.

Lily could steal my car and drive it into the nearest lake, and I wouldn't even get mad at her. Not because she's already dealing with way too much, but because I think it's almost incapable for Lily to do anything that would truly upset me to the point where I would be mad at her.

Those feelings scare me. It scares me that one person can make me feel so many different things all at once when I've spent the last years avoiding to feel at all.

Lily makes me happy without even trying to. Seeing her smile and hearing her laughter warms my chest in all the ways I refused to believe was possible, and I don't know why.

But what scares me the most is the thought of her dying.

♥ ♥ ♥ ♥ ♥ ♥ ♥ ♥

"We're staying here tonight, if that's okay with you," I say to Lily as we walk into my childhood bedroom. She stands in the middle of the room, looking around dumbstruck.

I know I've been living in luxury all my life—and I'm grateful I never had to worry about anything.

"Do we leave early enough so that I can see my parents tomorrow?" She turns to me, the stunned expression drained from her face with nothing but Lily's typical emptiness left.

She always looks at me like all the life has been sucked out of her. Like there's not a single spark left. But that only ever happens when we're alone. Whenever we're out in the open, with people surrounding us, Lily looks the happiest of fake happy I've ever seen. Then, when she does have a great time, for instance when I took her to see the sunrise, honest euphoria takes over her.

It's like a switch sometimes. A pretty confusing construct, but I'm here to figure her out, here to find out what makes that switch turn until she gets to feel all the excitement in the world. What makes her feel more happiness than she could ever imagine.

"We're leaving at eight," I tell her. "You just need to tell me where your mother lives."

Lily falls onto my bed. "Alright." She watches me as I walk over to my desk. I can feel her eyes on me, burning into my skin. "My dad comes first. I'm sure you know where he lives. My mother lives in Wesley Hills."

"Can't believe I'm chauffeuring your ass around the whole world."

"It's not the whole world," she laughs. "And I can take the train, you know."

"Lilybug, I'd rather sit days in a car to drive you wherever the hell you want to go than have you take the train."

It's not a lie. I will gladly be her chauffeur, not only because it gives me more time with her, but because public transport seems dangerous. All those strangers and creepy people. She could get groped, or even worse. No, thank you.

Chapter 19

"but listen, pretty lady, you don't have to be alone"-Baby Don't Cut by Bmike

Lily Reyes

After spending the next two hours in Eira's room, Colin decides that we're no longer going out tonight. Which is fortunate because I don't really feel like going on any more adventures today.

I've already been at the arena watching a hockey game, and now I've spent my energy socializing with Colin's younger sister.

I'm drained. Even if I wanted to go roller skating tonight, I wouldn't have the energy for it. So I'm glad he called it off.

Eira went to sleep, or more like fell asleep mid-talking. I already thought she didn't look too well last night but seeing her now—*in person*—she still doesn't look better.

Reece, Colin's three-year-old brother, is currently waiting for Colin to read him a goodnight story. It's already ten p.m. and Reece was supposed to be asleep hours ago, but as toddlers are sometimes, he was way too energetic to fall asleep. And now that he finally grows tired, Mrs. Carter asked Colin to read him a story.

While I wait for Colin to come back to his bedroom, I continue to write in my journal. It's nothing too spectacular anymore. All I manage to talk about is how my day has been and how tired I am.

And then I suppress the urge to write about Colin. Recently he's the only thing I can think about. I always start by writing about how I feel, and then I drift off to my day and end up with how amazing Colin is. Which irks me. A lot.

I don't want to find Colin amazing.

He's a great guy, and the more I get to know him, the more he's growing on me. But I don't want him to grow on me. Even worse, I'm afraid I'm growing on him.

Colin has been looking at me all evening long, but not the same way he used to. He has never looked at me like I was some broken glass that needed some extra strong glue to be put back together. But he also never looked at me like he was… I don't know, getting used to me being in his life? The scary and exciting kind of being in someone's life. The one that fills your chest with heat and fears loss because it would end in heartbreak.

Or maybe that's just me and I'm overanalyzing again.

The door to Colin's bedroom opens hastily. "Come with me," he speaks without even stepping inside the room. I jump off the bed—not even questioning his command—and follow Colin through the mansion. He leads me to the top floor, right outside to the balcony. From there, Colin lifts me off the ground and tells me to get on the roof. Once again, I don't question him and do as he says.

Moments later, Colin and I are both on the roof, sitting on the slope as we're watching the stars.

We're sitting in silence, feeling the cold night air brush over our skins. Or at least it's cold for me. I'm freezing. Colin doesn't seem to mind the cold.

Would have been nice if he told me where we were going so I could've brought another jacket with me. I'm wearing a thin jacket, but if I had known we'd be sitting on the roof, I would've stolen one of Colin's.

As I begin to curse Colin out in my head for having me freeze to death, he suddenly lays a jacket over my shoulders. The one he has been wearing this whole time.

"Thank you," I say in a soft tone, no longer feeling the desire to cuss him out.

"Lilybug, can I ask you something?" I just shrug. "Why have you been wearing your jacket all day long?"

"Because I'm cold," I lie. Though, right now it's not a lie.

"All day long?"

"Yes."

"I don't believe you." He takes my hand in his, draws circles on my skin. "Tell me the truth."

I remain quiet. Colin might be the only person in my life knowing about my wish to die, but there's no need to let him in on any of my other problems.

"Lily, there's no reason for you to lie to me." His eyes stay locked with mine. "When did you do it?"

"What?"

"Don't play dumb, Lily." I have recently discovered that I hate it when Colin calls me Lily. Not only have I gotten used to my new nickname, but whenever he calls me Lily, it's more of a warning, a sign of strictness and seriousness.

I hate it.

Taking a deep breath, I sigh in defeat. "After you left. It's not what you think, though."

Colin feels up my arm, starting at my wrist, he slowly works his way up, pressing the tips of his fingers against every inch of clothed skin. Until he presses one wrong spot, right on the back of my arm. The spot that causes me to wince in pain when he presses into it.

He watches my face, takes in every reaction, every bit of pain that displays on my face as he rubs against it again to make sure this wasn't just a one-time reaction.

"Cold my ass," he mutters almost inaudibly, dropping my arm. "Cut or burn?"

"Does it matter?" He nods just once, continuing to look at me madly. "Burn."

He sighs, bobbing his head lightly while he processes what I said.

"Why?" is the only thing he questions. I was prepared to be yelled at, not asked for a reason why.

"I didn't know what to do, Colin." I was frustrated when he left, and I don't even know why. Colin had every right to leave after what we did. He wasn't obligated to stay all night, especially not since we're supposed to be nothing but friends. So, why is a good question.

"Okay," he says softly. "Here's what we're going to do."

Colin reaches into the pocket of his jacket that's still draped over my shoulders and pulls out a lighter. He hands it to me, not giving me a second to question him before he begins to speak again. "Whenever you feel the urge to hurt yourself, you're going to call me."

"What?"

Colin holds up his hand, stopping me from speaking. "You're going to call me, and I'll be right over." He inhales deeply, shakily. It's like he has no idea what to do. Like the thought of me hurting myself truly doesn't sit right with him at all. "You're going to hold that lighter to my arm, not yours. You're going to burn my skin instead of your own."

"Colin"—fear takes over me—"I'm not going to hurt you."

"You will," he says, covering my hand with his. He flicks on the lighter using my fingers and holds it close to his skin. Not close enough to burn himself though. "You can have a death wish all you want, but if you're going to hurt yourself, you'll hurt me too."

"I can't." Tears begin to swell in my eyes, slowly rolling down my cheeks.

"You'll hurt me either way. Might as well use my body right from the start."

"I couldn't do this to you, Colin," I cry. "I couldn't hurt you like that."

And that's when I realize.

His words linger in my head, repeating in a loop. *You'll hurt me either way.* I'm hurting him. Right this second. Right at this moment. I'm causing pain over the guy who has done nothing but provide me with happiness.

It's been four days. Four silly days and he's done nothing but bring light into my life.

And here I am hurting the guy that tries to be my savior.

I shouldn't have agreed to these nine days. I shouldn't have let him into my life. I shouldn't have allowed this to happen.

God, I'm so stupid. How could I have done this?

How could I do this to him?

Colin's the only person to ever truly care about me, and I messed it up. I'm hurting him.

"How can you say this, Colin?" I ask through tears. "Why do you do this to yourself?"

I pull my hand away from his, letting the lighter drop onto the roof. Luckily, it's not one of those that keep the flame lit even when no one's pushing the button anymore.

His hands gently caress my jawline, thumbs stroke along the skin beneath my eyes, removing the salty tears. "I'm not doing anything to myself, Lily."

"You're here with me. You're putting yourself through hell to save me. It's only going to destroy you."

"So let it destroy me."

"No." I try to slide down the slope, wanting nothing more but to go to sleep and forget this awful encounter.

It's a coping mechanism I've developed throughout the years. Whenever I want to avoid something, I go to sleep. It started when my mother began to drink. When she came home from bars late at night, barely able to make it up the stairs without passing out on them. When she got drunk throughout the daytime as well, yelling at me for not cleaning up after her.

But I can't do it now. Colin is holding on to my body, not letting me move an inch.

"I want nothing more but for you to experience less pain. I don't need you to be one hundred percent happy. No one ever is. You're already living with so much pain, one I will never understand. But I can make sure you're not adding more to it." He sounds sincere, like he actually means what he says. And I can't help but want that as well.

Colin makes everything sound easy. He makes life sound exciting, but I've seen the ugly side of life. I know that no matter how good something sounds, there's *always* an ugly side. A side that's not worth staying for the pretty one.

His hands are back on my face, cupping it, forcing our eyes to stay on the others. "I have five days left. You'll be staying those days with me."

"I'm not."

"You are. You'll be staying with me and Aaron. They agreed already, well, Aaron said he would only agree if you stayed in his bedroom and not mine."

"They?"

"Excuse me? You think I would get around moving a pretty girl into my house without asking my roommates—who aren't my roommates—for permission?"

For the first time in way too long now, I chuckle. Chuckling or laughing around Colin is almost a habit. He always manages to make me smile, so when I haven't been laughing for a while now, I began to miss it.

When did I start to miss laughing?

"I won't share a bedroom with my brother."

"Don't worry, I kicked him out."

"You did what!?" I ask a little too loudly. I'm sure Colin's parents could hear it on the patio.

"I'm kidding," he says. "I told him that I'm old enough to have my girlfriend spend the night in my bed."

"I'm not your girlfriend."

"But Aaron doesn't know that. And now all we have to do is make sure he won't find out."

"Grey knows," I let him know. "I bet he can sense it."

Colin groans, making me laugh. "He can." Another groan follows. "But Grey knows how to keep his mouth shut. How would you know Grey 'can sense it' anyway?"

"He seems like a smart guy." I lift my shoulders, shrugging. I've never really had one conversation with Grey, except for the one in the cafeteria two days ago. "And even if he can't, I'm sure Izan knows and told him."

"Who's Izan?"

"Grey's boyfriend?" I draw my brows together, not wanting to believe that Colin doesn't know about this. "He's the captain of the soccer team?"

Colin blinks at me. "No way."

"Yes way."

"How do you know that?"

"Izan told me." Colin's expression falls, I'm not quite sure why. "You do have quite the number of friends for someone who supposedly hates being around people."

"Believe it or not, I used to have a way better best friend than Winter," I tell him. "Sofia and I were inseparable. Though, perhaps not enough because after she moved away, we weren't able to stay in touch."

"Who's Sofia?" A little fold appears between his eyebrows.

I smile at the memory of her. "We used to skate together all the time. We were partners up until we were eight. After that, she had to move away as her father had to move for work. We tried to stay in touch for a month or two, but at the age of eight, you don't really have the attention span or many possibilities to stay in touch with someone that's six hours ahead of your time. I do think Aaron took her loss far worse than me though." He loved her, even at that age, even when both of them tried to hide their friendship from me.

Colin bobs his head. "I'm sorry you had to lose her."

"Besides, I don't hate being around people." I choose to avoid talking about Sofia. Even after all this time, talking about her makes me want to cry. "I just have this social battery thing going, like everyone, I guess. I can only ever spend so much time around other human beings until my battery runs out. And then I need time to recharge."

"Well, you need a better charger then, because we will be going out tomorrow. And the day after that. And the day after that."

"And apparently I will be living with two guys for the next five days."

"One of which is your brother." Colin taps my nose with his index finger. "And I have awesome plans. Like… annoy the hell out of him."

"How?"

"Easy. I just fuck you in the kitchen."

"No." Though, it might be exciting. "We can't do this again, Colin."

"¡Colin, deja de ser raro!" A voice, sounding so much like Eira's, just with a far stronger accent, yells from the patio beneath us.

"Let me have a private conversation with Lily, thank you!"

How much of this conversation did his parents hear?

"Did you tell them about…" I trail off, not wanting to continue in case they could hear me.

"No." He shakes his head before lying down on the roof, only propping his head up with his hands. "Lie down, Lilybug."

I have to be honest, lying on a rooftop has never been on my bucket list. Plus this can't be hygienic, but I've already been sitting here for almost two hours, might as well lie down then.

"Lilybug?" he speaks softly, calmly. "You know it's never too late to ask for help, right?"

I let out a deep breath.

"I don't want help, Colin. I want my pain to go away. I want nothing more but to never have to feel the way I do ever again."

"And you think committing suicide is just going to make it disappear?"

"I wouldn't know, but it's better than to stay alive and never find peace," I admit.

His head turns, now facing me and no longer the sky. "Explain it to me."

"Explain what exactly?"

"How do you come to that decision? Wanting to die, I mean. There are so many other options, yet you choose to go with death. Help me understand why."

Another wave of air escapes my lungs in a hurry. "Okay." My voice is quiet, low. "Do you remember as a little kid, when the TV wasn't playing a show or anything at all. It only had this logo move from side to side and you were desperately waiting for it to hit the corner?" He nods.

"You were getting so frustrated when it took a little too long to reach it," I say. How am I going to explain this properly, enough to make him understand?

"Now imagine being that logo. Imagine you want to hit a corner, that corner being relief, happiness, no more having to feel the pain from hurtful words, from betrayal, separation, and more. It might take a while to get there, right?" He nods again. "But what if you never get there? Imagine you're spending all day watching that logo move to reach one of those four corners and not once does it hit one. It's frustrating, and you've only been watching for one day. Now try watching it for years on end, and it never once hits the spot. The frustration never stops, it grows and gets more with every passing day it doesn't reach its target. Eventually, you're going to give up on expecting it to happen. You grow tired of it. You stop hoping, you stop wanting it because you give up. It's not happening. And that's what my life feels like, Colin. I've been waiting to hit the corner for years, it never happened. Not once. I give up."

Colin points up at the sky and speaks. "Those look like a giraffe eating a lion." *He's changing the topic*.

"What the hell?" I don't see it. How could I? There are way too many stars to make out which ones Colin has put together to get a giraffe eating a lion.

"No, seriously. Just look." Colin pulls me closer to him until my head is only a fist away from his.

With a swift move, Colin rolls me on top of him, my front pressed to his.

"Can't see the stars when I'm facing you instead of the sky."

"No need to look at the stars when you can look at the sun," he says, offering me a smug smile. I knew this guy was in love with himself, but God, someone scratch the surface of his ego just a tiny bit, *please*.

"You know, I knew Aaron had another sister, other than Ana." Oh okay, he's trying his hardest to stay away from more death-talk. "No one ever mentioned your name. All I got as information about where you were, was 'at some college,'" he says. "And they told

Nine Days

me you were like two years younger."

"More like two minutes," I mutter.

"They also said you had brown hair and blue eyes."

"Now, that's just rude. They know I hate blue eyes."

"I have blue eyes."

"Yeah, and I hate them," I lie. Somewhere along the way, I found comfort in Colin's eyes.

Colin chuckles at my unreasonable hatred for blue eyes. It is unreasonable, I know that, so I don't mind him laughing about it.

We spend a fair amount of time just looking into the other's eyes, not speaking, not even exchanging one single word.

Until a question pops up in my head.

"Colin?" He tips his head up. "Why do you call me Lilybug?"

A small grin creeps up on his lips. Colin's arms close around my waist in a hug.

"You know the meaning of ladybugs? Good fortune, true love, innocence… needing to make the right choices in life."

I know of the first three, never have I heard of the last one.

"It's said that when you encounter a ladybug something positive is about to happen. It's supposed to resemble that even the gloomiest days will be brightened. And well, your name is Lily. The lily is a beautiful flower with yet another deep meaning. Mix that with ladybug and what do we get? Lilybug."

I'm not quite sure what I'm supposed to make of that.

Thankfully I don't get to speak because Colin checks the time on his phone, then smiles.

"Happy Birthday, Lilybug."

Before I could thank him, he presses his lips to mine, allowing the unwanted butterflies in my stomach to awaken. Again.

Chapter 20

"the world would break us out, we weren't wrong"—and by EDEN

Lily Reyes

After spending the morning of my birthday with Colin's family, I'm relieved to finally be at my father's house.

I adore Colin's parents. His father's much nicer than I imagined he'd be, and his mother has such a kind soul, I adore her even more than little Reece who wouldn't stop babbling about *Paw Patrol*. That kid loves his animated animals.

And Eira, where should I begin? Eira's amazing and truly funny. Despite having caught the flu—which is supposedly not contagious—she's joking around and enjoys every bit of life she's been given. Eira is so energetic, I wonder what she's like with more strength and less flu in her body.

His family even went as far as to get me birthday presents. These people don't know me one bit and yet they all ended up having a present for me.

I didn't want to accept them at first.

Eira gifted me a designer dress. It still had the price tag attached to it.

Mrs. Carter, whom I'm supposed to call Elena, gifted me a pair of new high heels, expensive ones. Mr. Carter added a new purse, fitting to the shoes. Reece drew a couple of pictures for me. I like his pictures the most of all the presents, mainly because he didn't pay for his.

And Colin, well, he insists I get my present from him later tonight. That's totally not freaking me out.

"Good morning there, dimples," Colin greets Ana when she comes downstairs to get breakfast. Her hair's still messed up from sleeping, she's still in shorts and a tank top, indicating that she'd just woken up.

And judging by her flushed cheeks when her eyes meet Colin's, she doesn't seem pleased to see him.

"Morning," she mumbles and walks past him, heading straight to the coffee maker.

"She's always cranky in the morning," Dad tells me like I didn't know that already. To be fair, I never stop by in the morning. The only times I've come over to visit was late in the evenings. Still, I know Ana isn't a morning person at all.

"Oh, my God," Ana breathes. "Lily!" Her excitement to see me throws me off. I've never been nice to Ana, yet whenever she sees me, she acts like I'm her favorite person. "Happy Birthday!"

"Thank you." I don't offer more than a slim smile.

"Where's Aaron?" Ana eyes Colin with caution. Of course, she knows Colin as the guy who's her brother's best friend.

"Not sure, home, probably."

"Then why are you here?" I don't know whether Ana likes Colin a lot or loathes him.

"Meeting my in-laws."

My father laughs then tries to cover it up with a cough when he sees my serious face. Ana looks just as serious as I do.

She's a lot like me in some ways, always serious when she doesn't like someone's comment. She won't even act like it was funny, just like I wouldn't. My father once told me she used to say she wanted to be just like me. I always dismissed that thought. Ana couldn't possibly adore me in that sense, given how I'm treating her.

But despite me mistreating her for envious reasons, I like Ana. She's a sweetheart and a genuinely nice person, always there when someone needs her. I'm sure she's a great friend to her people. Hell, she's a great friend to me and I've never even given her one reason to like me.

"That's not funny." Ana picks up the cup from the coffee maker, taking a sip.

"It's not," Colin agrees. "I'm deadly serious. I'm getting married to my girlfriend tomorrow."

Ana's jaw drops to the floor, her eyes widen like there's a ghost right across the room. "You're shitting me."

"Watch your language, Ana." Dad always disliked mature language, cursing is a complete no-go for him.

"He's joking," I reassure Ana. "We're not getting married."

Ana visibly calms, letting out her breath in relief. I wonder why that's a relief to her. Is the thought of me marrying Colin such a bad one? Is she worried he might regret marrying me because she knows I'm a horrible person?

"Who said I was getting married to you?" Colin looks at me, smiling. "I already signed the contract to marry Ana. Right, Emerson?"

My father shakes his head in disbelief. He has never looked at me with this amount of amusement in his eyes. I wouldn't know if he ever looked at Aaron this way, I wasn't around much. But he didn't look at me like that. Not once.

My father has always been proud of me. Always. After every new stunt I've learned, Dad used to throw a tiny party for me the following Sunday. I really miss those days a lot.

Ana disappears upstairs but comes back twenty minutes later, fully dressed and with a touch of makeup on her face.

She dressed up. Not like a normal Saturday morning outfit. No, I'm saying full-on spending-a-night-out kind of outfit.

"Where are you going dressed like that?" Dad asks.

"Picking Mom up from work." Ana grabs the car keys and puts on a jacket.

"Your mother has a car, Ana."

"She didn't take it."

"She did." I'm sure he knows whether his wife needs a ride home from work. "So, where are you going dressed like that?"

"Just driving around." She sighs and drops the keys back into the bowl by the front door. "Why can't I ever spend some time out all by myself?"

"You can, but not dressed like that, Ana." I'm not blaming my father for calling Ana out on what she's wearing. Especially not when she only wants to "drive around". I mean, Ana put on a really short dress with high heels that now make her taller than me. She straightened her hair, even put on red lipstick. And the cleavage is definitely way too much for a sixteen-year-old.

This outfit seems so familiar to me. Kind of like I've seen it before. Or worn it before.

"Go upstairs and get dressed. Properly."

"Colin likes it, don't you?" Ana now looks at Colin like she's admiring him a lot.

Somehow I keep forgetting that Colin is actually attractive when he's not riding high on his ego horse.

"It's too showy," Colin says without looking at her once. His eyes remain on our intertwined hands, watching his thumb brush over my skin.

"You like showy though."

"Says who?" He finally looks at Ana.

"You're dating Lily. She always walks around dressed like this."

Colin takes in my body, frowns. He has every right to frown at me. Colin has never seen me truly dressed up since I haven't done that in two years.

These days I prefer to fade into the background instead of standing out.

Self-hatred aside, I know I'm not bad looking. I'm aware of my curves that some girls would kill to have. I used to embrace them, but then I stopped.

All I wanted was to be on my own, be forgotten so I can leave this world without anyone noticing.

"Never seen that on her." His eyes soften when he stares at me.

Ana rolls her eyes before she storms upstairs. My father is about to go after her, clearly not tolerating Ana's behavior, but I follow her instead.

It's not like I have much to lose.

I knock on her door, waiting for her to let me in, but what comes instead is a, "Go away."

"Ana? It's Lily. Can we talk?"

"You never speak to me. You can ignore my existence now as well," she snaps. I totally deserved that.

"I need some advice."

"Get it from someone else." Her voice is quiet, suppressing tears. "Or ask your *boyfriend*."

"I'd rather get some advice from my sister." I decide on cutting the word "step," knowing calling her my *sister* will have her cave.

"Come in." *Called it*. I suppose this is my time to rectify my relationship with Ana before my death. Personally, not in the form of a letter.

I walk into her bedroom, finding Ana sitting on her bed, crying. Closing the door behind me, I make my way over to her, taking a seat across from her.

"Ana," I say, almost whispering. "What's going on with you?"

"Nothing." She groans, knowing I'll continue to ask until she spills the truth. "You. That's what's wrong."

"Me?"

"Yes. You're the perfect daughter. Everyone's always praising you. I'm living in your shadow and you're not even around."

I had no idea. All this time I thought Ana is the favorite. I mean, my father loves me, I know he does, but ever since Ana was in the picture, everything has always been about her.

"And now you even got Colin." She takes a few deep breaths, toning down her anger. "You weren't even supposed to know each other. And you keep lying to me, Lily. You need my advice, on what? How to steal my whole life?"

"Actually, I wanted to say I'm sorry." Ana's eyes dart toward me in shock. There's no going back now. "I know I haven't been the nicest to you. I was jealous of you. You just came and stole what was mine. You stole my family, it wasn't your fault, but I made it yours," I speak slowly, calmly.

"You've got all the attention from my father. You got to grow up with the man who was supposed to watch me grow up. You even got to see my own brother more often than I did. I envied that. So I made it my mission to hate you."

And then we spend the next twenty minutes talking about how much I've messed up ever since Ana is here. How messed up it was of me to hate on a little girl, one who couldn't even comprehend what was happening.

I apologize a couple of times, but each time Ana tells me to stop apologizing and goes straight to hugging me.

And just like my father and Colin told me, Ana does look up to me, so she tells me. I don't quite understand why, but it feels good to know.

"So, you like Colin, huh?" I offer a slim smile. Having a crush on someone you can't have sucks. And having a crush on Colin Carter can never end well. I've witnessed more girls crying over this guy than I've seen planes in the sky.

"No." Ana denies it, but when I raise my eyebrows at her, she admits to me hitting the nail right on the head.

"You know he's a bit too old for you, right?"

"It's just five years," Ana vetoes with flushed cheeks. "Sixteen and twenty-one sounds wrong, it won't sound wrong anymore when it's twenty and twenty-five. Or even eighteen and twenty-three."

"Well, good luck stealing his heart. You will lose a lot of nerves trying to get through his ego."

She laughs, but it quickly dies down. "He loves you."

"He doesn't."

"You do see the way he looks at you, right?" Ana's eyes light up like the Eiffel Tower.

"How does he look at me?"

"The way I've wanted him to look at me for a while," she says, but I don't quite understand. "Like he's in love with you."

Chapter 21

"I've been looking for love, all I'm finding is pain"-Shawn Mendes by Seth Bishop

Lily Reyes

Dear whoever reads this,

I'm not quite sure how to feel about today.

I'm excited, but I also fear what's about to happen.

Colin is going to meet my mother, and she'll hate him. I've never admitted this before, never even thought I would have to eventually... but she hates me. She truly hates me. It's the last thing she told me a month ago when we fell out. But she hated me way before that already.

My mother always acts like she loves me so much around everyone, but when it's just the two of us... she hates me.

She's scaring me. She's hurting me.

But Colin scares me more.

Ever since that one night, we spent together when he made me feel like I could mean more to him (moments before he ruined it by leaving like I was just another woman on his list), I fear him.

He kisses me sometimes, and when he does, I feel like a kid being handed some candy. I feel every single butterfly in my stomach explode. Not even those silly butterflies can take it anymore.

You know, ever since I could comprehend words anyone said, my parents taught me a lot of things.

Like "stay away from cigarettes. There's a chance they'll kill you."

Or "don't follow strangers, you might get abducted and murdered."

Nine Days

Whatever it is, it's always the same ending. It's always ending with my death.
And that makes me wonder; why would anyone want to live when all there is, in the end, is death?
I mean, sure, we're all destined to die eventually, but why put ourselves through the pain of life when it could all end so much earlier?
But then I think about Colin...
suddenly the pain doesn't matter anymore. It's still there, I feel it, but he makes it bearable.
And I'm scared he might succeed to convince me. (Although I don't see that happening)
But my only reason to stay would be him.
Colin Carter would be the only reason for me to stay alive, and that's such a stupid reason.
I'm not alive for anyone but myself. In the end, anyone can backstab you. Anyone can crawl under your skin and cause so much more pain than you've ever felt before. And I fear Colin would be one of those kinds of pain.
He's not a bad person, but I'm sure he would leave me. And staying alive for someone who's going to leave me doesn't sound too appealing.
I will end up dead either way. Either before he has the chance to break my heart, or after he's done it.
I choose to avoid the heartbreak.
Anyway, that's not all I wanted to say today.
Although this day started quite well, I just know it'll take a drastic turn. And it frightens me.
I feel empty, yet I have to put on a smile so Colin—who's sitting right next to me as I'm writing this—won't ask about it... about me and my feelings.
I don't feel like talking about my numbness. It's stupid.

Joelina Falk

I want to cry. But I know I can't.
So I will have to put on my big-girl pants and pretend.
As I do every day.
Lily

Before we arrive at my mother's house, I need to finish writing the letter dedicated to her.

I'm not sure I have much to tell her.

I love my mother. She's been great to me. The best even. At least until she wasn't anymore.

I could never forgive her for tearing our family apart.

She knows I blame her for it. I've given her plenty of speeches about how much I hate her for bringing nothing but misery into my life.

I have only ever told her that when I was mad about something else. Like when I wanted to go out and she wouldn't allow it. I've always had the same excuse.

"*You're a horrible mother. You tore my family, my life apart, and now you won't even let me go out with my friends.*"

She hated it. I know she did. I know it was wrong, it was wrong of me to continue to throw it at her even after years. But I was mad. I *am* mad.

Yet I still have one chance to apologize to her for it.

In the form of a letter.

I can't face her and tell her any of it, I know she wouldn't let me finish talking.

I even doubt she will read the letter. My mother doesn't care about me anymore. Not one bit. And I'm only visiting her because I will be dead next Friday. No matter how this meeting will turn out, I need to see her one last time.

I love her. I do. Which makes it difficult for me to let her go. To say goodbye to her. I know she won't be too sad about my death; not even sure she'll care at all.

So I write her a letter, stating how sorry I am. How awful I feel for holding a grudge when all she wanted was to be loved just as much as my father was by Liz. Apologizing for being the brat she always said I was. Apologizing for not being good enough.

My parents both cheated on one another. They've never been in love, regardless of being married. Their marriage was nothing but platonic and only used for financial profits.

And probably because they had two children together.

By the time I finish writing the letter to my mother, Colin and I arrive at her house. Now the only letter left is Aaron's.

"She'll hate me." I notice Colin's hands shaking, so I take them in mine, kissing his knuckles.

We haven't made whatever we are official, and we aren't going to, but both of us know there's more to *us* than just friendship. Friends with benefits, perhaps? That's what it is, right? Friends who fuck and kiss occasionally? We haven't even had *that* talk.

"She'll love you," I assure him, but Colin doesn't seem too convinced. Neither am I.

"Did you take a look at me?" *I have.* "Every mother on this planet tells their daughter*s* to stay away from me."

He's got a point. Colin doesn't look like he has any good intentions with anyone. And before I knew him that tiny bit better, even I thought he was a bad guy.

Not like in a sexy way. Well, he's handsome, but I mean, a genuinely bad person.

And I know my mother will judge him for his tattoo, probably won't even give him a chance to prove that he's a great guy.

"We'll only stay for an hour. I can't be around her for too long anyway," I tell him as we approach the front door. We stop and Colin's eyes are on mine almost instantly.

I wish I could describe the way he looks at me. It's sweet and I feel the respect he has for me portrayed through his eyes. But there's something else to it. Something I can't name. Words are failing me.

"Why is that?"

I sigh, debating whether he should know the cold and naked

truth. "My mom doesn't like me very much." It's not like he won't witness her hatred in less than two minutes.

Colin studies me, studies my words like he's trying to find one bit of false information in them. But he can't, my mother truly doesn't like me.

"Colin, she's the only person I had. She was an okay mother, but she wasn't always nice to me. I wasn't nice to her either. We've had our difficulties, a lot of arguments, and hatred. She was relieved when I moved out for college."

Technically, I could've stayed home for college. I could've taken the bus or my mother's car to get to my classes since our house isn't too far away from campus. But I wanted out.

He blinks. Once. Twice. Never says a word. He just stares at me and blinks like he's waiting for me to continue, as though he's expecting me to say that it's all better now. But it's not.

"She is slobby," I tell him. "I've been handling the household most of the time. I cleaned after her. I was more of a mother to her than she was to me. Not right from the start, it started when I was around ten." Colin remains silent. "I said a lot of hurtful things to her back then, so she started to dislike me, I guess. She would have never said it to my face, but I could feel the gap extent between us."

"Alright," he says, almost whispering.

Moments later we're seated at the kitchen table. My mother is smoking her cigarette while she looks at Colin like she's never seen another human before. She eyes him with disgust.

I knew I'd be wrong about my mother liking Colin. She doesn't even like me, so how is she supposed to like him?

I feel Colin stiffen, especially now that our fingers are tangled. He doesn't say a word, only looks between my mother and me.

My mother didn't bother wishing me a happy birthday when we came inside, nor does she make any attempts to do so now.

I could swear she was about to… until she noticed Colin next to me. Then Mom turned into a brick—emotionless and cold.

"So that's your boyfriend?" she speaks with revulsion.

"Yes." *No.*

"I see." She blows smoke out into my direction, knowing very well that I hate it when she does that.

I don't care about her smoking. It's her own body, she can do whatever the hell she wants. But that doesn't give her the right to force me to passively smoke along with her.

At least Colin seems to feel just as disgusted by the smoke. He tries not to let it show though. I, on the other hand, I'm coughing, waving my hands around to free, not only my sight but the air I'm inhaling, from smoke.

"And you're an athlete?"

"I am," Colin answers, offering my mother an awkward smile. I bet he wishes he stayed away.

Now that Colin met my mother, I'm sure he'll tell Aaron that it's not worth getting to know her. It'll make it easier on my part because then I won't have to talk too much about our mother in his letter.

"Like Aaron then," my mother says. I almost choke on the air and Colin gasps.

She hasn't mentioned Aaron's name in sixteen years. Never said it once. Whenever I tried to speak about him, my mother would dismiss the topic and tell me to stop thinking about him.

So how the hell does she know Aaron is an athlete? And why would she connect Colin to Aaron?

Colin looks at me, eyes filled with fear. He has no idea what to say, and neither do I. I have so many questions, yet I don't know where to start asking.

"I know you'll be together tonight." Now it's my time to stiffen up. "Celebrating your big birthday together."

"Mom, how would you know that?"

"Don't be silly, Lily," she chuckles. "You've been seeing him for way too long. I know you have. Why do you think I started to dislike you?"

"Because I was misbehaving?" It stings in my heart to hear this. I mean, she said it before... a month ago, but I thought that was the heat of the moment and it just slipped out.

She ignores me. "Your father knew what he signed you up for when he kept in touch with you. We had very few rules, and here he was breaking every single one of them."

I'm not sure if my mom mentions all this now to scare Colin off, or if she's just fed up with me. Either way, I'm kind of glad she finally says it, meaning it. Hating me. It will make leaving this fucked up life a ton easier.

"You're so much like him," she says, smiling. It's a devilish smile. If Colin wouldn't be here with me, I'm sure I would be running out of the door right now. "And your brother, he's just as arrogant as I imagined he would be. With his rich father, the rich stuck-up stepmother. You're both little shits."

I want to cry. I want to rip my heart out of my chest, tear every organ out of my body until I pass on to another dimension.

My mother has officially ruined my birthday for me.

"With all due respect, Mrs. Reyes, Lily is amazing. She's a really great person, and so is Aaron, by the way. Maybe you should try to find flaws in yourself and not the children you've abandoned." I only roughly pay attention. I'm more focused on suppressing my tears. I won't cry in front of my mother. I won't.

"I didn't abandon Lily. I'm a great mother. I've always been good to her. I let her live here for many years."

"That doesn't make you a great mother. In fact, it makes you an even worse one. You've had no intentions of keeping Lily close to you, so I would assume by the way you're talking about her. The best thing you could've done was to give her away to her father. To someone who would've made sure she was happy."

Colin stands up from his chair, pulling me up to my feet as well. He tightens the grip around my hand as he looks at me. His other hand places down onto my cheek, wipes underneath my eye. *A tear must have slipped. Dammit.*

"Lily is suffering from what you've caused her. She's handling so many things, stuff you would know about if only you paid a little more attention to your own daughter. And yet here you are, telling her that you dislike her. On her birthday."

"It's not my fault she can't care for herself," she snaps.

Words could never express what it's like to admire the woman who gave birth to you and treats you like a waste of space.

She hasn't always been like this, maybe that's why I'm still holding on to her. Even now.

"I gave her everything and she threw it away for a guy who cheated on me."

"It's not like you didn't cheat on Dad!" Dear God, please stop these tears from wanting to roll down my cheeks. I can't do this today.

"Your father is a piece of shit. Just like you and your brother!" She slams her hands onto the kitchen table.

Colin and I haven't even been here for fifteen minutes and she's already about to break the next window. I can sense it.

It certainly wouldn't be the first time. I know if this doesn't stop soon, she will throw something at the kitchen window until it breaks. And for what? So she can run after me with one of the shards and threaten to kill me with it.

Colin takes a deep breath as he pulls me out of the kitchen, forcing me to leave this house.

I'm glad we're leaving. I don't want to be here for another minute.

"You shouldn't have been born, Lily!" My mother yells right before the front door slams close. I can still hear her scream and throw things around, breaking furniture, even through the closed door.

She doesn't come outside. She doesn't want to make this right. She won't apologize, I know she won't. I also know that this is the last thing my mother will have said to me before I died.

You shouldn't have been born, Lily.

How much hatred does a mother need to have inside of her to yell this at her child? How much pain does she have to be in, to make her daughter feel this miserable?

She's not feeling any better than I do, I know that for sure. Only a broken soul can react this way. I don't blame her for wanting to hurt me. She's trying to deal with her own problems. She's trying to deal with her own pain.

That doesn't mean it hurts any less.

But now that the door is closed and it's just Colin and me, I let the tears go. I allow myself to break, allow my tears to run down my cheeks, allow my pain to take over my body.

No matter how shitty my mother treats me, I will never stop craving her love. I'll never stop wanting her to be in my life. She's my mother. I know that sometimes relatives can cause more harm than anyone, but I still love her. She hurts me like no one ever could, and I still love her with all that I have.

"I'm sorry you had to witness that," I mumble and tug on Colin's shirt. He doesn't answer. All he does is wrap his arms around my body, holds me.

He doesn't care when my tears wet his shirt. He doesn't care when some of my mascara stains it, or when I start to cry so much, I can barely breathe.

He just stands there with me, hugging me so tightly that I almost feel okay. Almost like my mother didn't just tell me that she wishes I was dead.

But she did say that. And he heard it. And he now knows where I get these thoughts from.

"Lilybug." His voice is a whisper, filled with concern and sympathy. I can hear how sorry he is for me. But I don't want him to feel sorry for me, I don't want his pity.

"Can you just drive me home?"

"Can I take you somewhere else first?" Colin pulls away from the hug, looking at me.

His hands remain on my body. He's holding me by my waist, gently moves his thumbs over my body, looking so deeply into my eyes, I could melt. I *would* melt if I didn't believe there was almost nothing left of me.

"I'm tired, Colin. I don't want any more adventures today."

He nods, but then lifts his shoulders as he shrugs at me. "It will be good for you, I promise." I don't get to answer because Colin lifts me and carries me over to his car, sits me inside like I'm unable to do that myself.

My eyes follow him as he jogs over to the driver's side and slips into the car, starting the engine faster than I could blink. And just like that, we're back on the road, leaving my mother behind like nothing happened.

Fifteen minutes later, Colin stops in front of an older-looking building. It doesn't have any signs, no indications that anyone lives there, but it doesn't look like an abandoned house either.

We get out of the car, his hand intertwines with mine the second we're back next to one another. I like his hand in mine, or mine in his. It's a simple gesture, yet offers more intimacy than I would've ever thought.

The longer Colin holds my hand, the more it starts to burn. Not that I feel any physical pain, but it burns in my heart. It burns like a lit torch is being held right underneath me. The flame isn't hitting my skin, but the hot air still touches me.

If his touch was a color, it'd be yellow. It's the heat you feel when you rub your palms together. This kind of warmth floods through my veins when our hands link together. It's as joyful as seeing the little drop of water on top of grass, so simple yet so beautiful.

And that's what I feel in my heart when Colin is with me. It's what I feel when his hand holds mine. Happiness. Warmth. He makes me *feel*, banishes my numbness for a short while.

Chapter 22

"When your eyes can't see, take your eyes from me. When you're lost and losing faith, I will be your saving grace"-Saving Grace by Kodaline

Colin Carter

I believe Lily needs this. She needs to let out her negative feelings, her anger, her frustration. Especially after what just happened back at her mother's house.

Lily doesn't speak when we're inside the building. She looks quite irritated even, like she doesn't know why I took her here. Plate smashing.

I think it's self-explanatory, she doesn't seem to agree.

"Take this sharpie," I say, handing her a black one. She hesitates at first, only furrows her eyebrows at me. Eventually, she takes it.

I tell her to wait right where she's at, then walk off toward the reception to pay for a couple of plates. I make sure it's alright that we'll be writing on them. All the guy sitting at the front desk says is, "They'll break anyway. Do as you please."

He has a point. Still, I wanted to make sure it was okay.

I pay for a total of twenty-two plates, carry eleven plates over to Lily, then go back to get the rest.

Lily doesn't help, but I also don't want her to.

Once all of the twenty-two plates are placed on the table nine feet away from a huge target sign, I only walk back to the reception one last time to get two helmets and safety glasses.

I put one of the helmets on my head, as well as the glasses, then go back to Lily and put the other one on hers. She's confused, but I guess she has assumptions as to what this is about.

"You got the sharpie?" Lily nods once, holds it up. "Good."

I hand her an empty plate and take one for myself. She watches me as I write something down on mine.

Forgive me, Aiden.

"Who's Aiden?" Lily cocks her head.

"Not important." I offer a slim smile. I didn't tell her everything there is to know about me. Actually, I don't think I've ever truly told Lily anything about me.

And with no further explanation, I throw the plate at the huge red target sign with all of the anger I feel inside. It smashes, splinters into tons of tiny pieces when it hits the wall.

It's a relief. I know this doesn't take away the vicious truth and the fact that the problem is still present, but it does offer some temporary relief.

I turn to Lily, nod for her to do the same. She thinks it's silly, so she doesn't want to do it.

"Do it anyway."

Lily shakes her head. "I won't write something down and smash a perfectly fine plate."

"They're all malfunctions, have a few cracks already. They would have gotten thrown out anyway. You'll feel better."

Lily sighs, knowing I'm right. I wouldn't go as far as to say I'm always right… but I kind of am.

"Just throw one and see if it does something," I tell her.

Lily nods carefully then pulls the cap off the sharpie before writing something down. I would love to know what she's writing, but I'm not going to ask her about it. If she wants me to know, she'll tell me.

Before I know it, Lily throws the plate across the room, watches as it shatters into pieces. She falls to her knees, sobs again.

She's been crying ever since we stepped out of her mother's house, and it's breaking my heart. I don't want to see her tear-stained face anymore. It hurts me.

I don't dare touch Lily, not right now. I want her to deal with her pain, feel the relief as the emotions she wrote onto that plate shatter.

So I'm waiting. Waiting for Lily to react. Waiting for her to say something, move, do literally anything. But it doesn't come. Not for the next two minutes at least.

"Why'd you get so many?" she asks, her voice so quiet, I barely hear it.

"Twenty-two, for twenty-one years of bullshit. And one for me, because I had to demonstrate how to do this safely."

She turns her head to look at me. A soft smile tugs on her lips, her eyes hopeful and filled with appreciation.

God, she's so cute.

"That must've been expensive."

I shrug. "It was a dollar for each plate, $8 for extra time."

"I'll pay you back."

"You will," I say, "by throwing those plates against the wall."

"Thank you, Colin." Lily stands back up on her feet, so I hand her another plate. She takes it and starts to scribble down another word, or a couple more.

She throws it against the wall with all of her strength, letting her tears roll down her face as she momentarily lets go of her pain.

"*I've never been more disappointed in you, Liliana.*" Her tenth plate reads. I wonder if her mother said this to her.

Liliana?

Why did she keep this from me?

I want to ask Lily about it, but I don't think this is the right time to ask if her first name isn't Lily but Liliana.

Maybe I'm imagining things. I mean, my heart is still aching for this beautiful blonde girl in front of me. It's still hurting from the tears that I see on her cheeks whenever she turns around and smiles at me. It still hurts when I see her red puffy eyes and her reddened nose. It still hurts every time I hear her voice break when she screams as she throws the plate.

It still hurts to know that she's in pain.

"*Maybe I should have kept the other disappointment instead of you, Liliana.*"

Lily isn't writing down what she feels. She writes down hurtful memories. Memories she wished she didn't have. Sentences that broke her world, ones she's now shattering, banishing from her life. Maybe just for a moment, maybe forever. Who knows?

"I don't want to see you anymore. Just leave. Leave or die. I don't care."

Lily is down to two plates. Her eyes lock with mine for a second when she takes one from my hands. She looks happier. Maybe not happy, but definitely lighter.

Like throwing these words against a wall and seeing her connected emotions burst into pieces lifted some of the weight she's been carrying.

"Can I write down wishes?"

I nod. She can do whatever the hell she wants with those plates. She could have thrown them all at once for all I care. As long as it's helping, even just for a little while, I'm fine with it.

"Good." She smiles and turns away from me. She won't let me read what she writes before throwing the plate against the target sign.

This time she's not crying when it shatters. Lily turns around, scrunches up her nose as she beams at me. "One more," she says as she takes the plate from my hands. But before she turns back around, Lily tugs at my collar, pulls me down to her enough to brush her lips against mine. "Thank you," she whispers and turns back around.

Kissing Lily is starting to feel natural. I could never get bored of it, and it's not like I fear kissing her anymore. If I want to kiss her, I do and I will.

She may think I'm only trying to protect her from more pain when I said she was mine, but that's not what I was talking about.

She is mine. Even if she dies, she's always going to be mine. I know this girl is special. She has a huge heart, loves with so much brightness. It's so sad that she can't see it.

So I'll be loving her. I'll love her until her last breath, and even after that, I'll continue to love her with every breath I take. Even if I have to breathe for the both of us.

"This plate feels different." *Different*? How is that even

possible?

She throws it anyway.

It doesn't break.

The both of us look at the plate a little flabbergasted.

Lily just threw a plate against a brick wall from a nine feet distance, and it didn't break. What kind of dark magic is that?

Maybe it was plastic?

"What the hell?" Lily laughs. "It was the most important wish." Her hands fall to her sides, her body sags with frustration.

"What did you wish for?" I ask. I would get the plate for her if the area wasn't closed off to anyone but employees.

I see Lily's brain work like she's contemplating telling me. It can't possibly be that big of a secret.

"Your happiness."

"What?" I almost start to cough from surprise.

"I wished for you to find a girlfriend who loves you unconditionally. Someone to be alongside you when I can't do that anymore."

I gulp, swallowing hard. Once. Twice. Probably a couple more times before I find my voice. "Why?" is all I can come up with. It's all I can get myself to say. My mouth is far too dry to bring words across my lips.

"Because I need you to be happy, even after my death. I need you to be okay. I want to know you found your happiness, Colin."

I inhale deeply. How do I tell someone who's suicidal that I've already found my happiness, and it will leave right when she does? How do I tell her that she is my happiness, that she is bringing light to my life? How do I tell her that she is my joy, everything that brings me satisfaction, that she is my euphoria… without sounding like I want her to stay alive for me?

"Better luck next time," I say, grabbing her hand in mine.

We return our helmets and glasses and say goodbye. The guy, whose name I think is Jeff—at least that's what his nametag says—seems a bit confused.

Can't blame him. He's watched Lily have a whole mental

breakdown over plates and then she leaves with a huge grin on her lips while half of her face is still covered in mascara smudges.

She still looks pretty though.

♥ ♥ ♥ ♥ ♥ ♥ ♥ ♥

"I just don't get it," I say, munching on some popcorn.

When Lily and I got home, she asked me to watch a movie before we eventually have to get going for the bar. Of course I agreed.

I wouldn't have if she told me *she* was picking the movie.

Okay, I still would've agreed.

But now I'm stuck here, watching *Legally Blonde* because it's Lily's favorite movie. And I don't get it.

"What's there not to understand?" She laughs at me. I don't like that she thinks I'm stupid, but at least she's laughing.

Luckily, it's the end of the movie now, meaning I no longer have to sit through an overly sexist representation of a rich girl who lives off of Daddy's money.

Seriously, why do these older movies always have the rich teenage female main character dressed in pink? And only pink, like it's some sort of character trait of theirs. What if they wanted to wear blue? Not every rich girl loves pink.

"The ending," I say. "Emmet totally should've gotten with Elle."

Lily laughs… again. "Did you not read what it said on the screen by the end?"

"It's a movie. You don't do reading while watching a movie, Lilybug."

Lily rolls her eyes at me. "It literally said they've been dating for two years."

"Liar." I don't believe Lily. Okay, I do, but I know if I rewind the part now, she will laugh again, so pretending to not believe her seems like a great choice.

I rewind the movie until the beginning of their graduation. We watch until—*who would have guessed it*—it says just what Lily told me.

"Oh, fuck me."

"Like, right now?"

My eyes shoot toward Lily with shock in them. I was expecting another round of laughter. Maybe even her making fun of me, but I never saw *that* coming.

I feel my dick harden instantly.

In not even a heartbeat, I tip Lily over, her back meets the sitting space from the sofa and hover right over her. She lets out a breathless shriek as I press my weight onto her, though I make sure she can still breathe properly. Lily is a tad dramatic sometimes.

"I'm always down to have sex with you, Lilybug." I grin. "But are you down for it?"

Lily smiles at me mischievously, shrugging, not saying a word.

She's trying to kill me.

"I'll find out myself then." That said, I trace my hand down her body, cursing her out in my head for deciding to wear jeans today. If she'd be wearing leggings it would be a lot easier. But I'm not going to complain… to her at least. In my head, I'm complaining.

I unbutton her pants and sneak my hand inside, watching her gaze change from pure sweetness to pure lust. The way she looks at me, the need, wanting me to get her off almost makes me come in my pants.

Cupping my hand over her pussy, just slightly brushing over her underwear has Lily's breath shaking. I'm absolutely digging it.

She doesn't tell me what to do. She isn't telling me to stop, but she also isn't begging me to touch her, *yet*. She's just letting me do what I think is right, knowing it will get her out of here satisfied.

I'm not saying my finger game is mind-blowing, but I'm pretty confident with what I do.

I add pressure against her entrance, press her underwear slightly against her core, feeling the wetness slowly soak through the fabric.

Lily lifts her hips, silently urging me to go further than that.

So I slip my hand underneath her underwear, slide my finger

through her lips, coating them in her wetness. I dip one finger into her core before pulling it out to spread the evidence of her arousal.

She moans, wraps her arms around my neck, and pulls me down until her lips connect with mine. I'm not fighting the kiss. In fact, I'm glad she kisses me. I was craving to feel that sweet mouth of hers pressed to mine again.

Dipping fingers back inside of her, Lily's breath hitches, her hips shift into my touch.

"Aw, fuck." The feeling of Lily causes my head to spin—A good kind of spinning.

All I want to do is rip off her clothes and fuck her right here on the sofa. I want—*need*—to feel her. I need to be inside of her. Right. Now.

But there's one thing I want even more. To please her. To listen to her whimpers, begging me to make her come. To hear her moan out my name when she does.

My fingers curl up inside her as I stroke the pad of my thumb over her clit, slowly drawing circles.

What I'd do to taste her right now. Taste her when I suck on that clit of hers instead of massaging it with my thumb. Taste her on my tongue when I dip into her core, lick her.

But instead, I have her lips pressed to mine. More or less so. Lily barely manages to kiss back, instead of finding that annoying, it's a great way to tell that she's enjoying this. That *I'm* making her feel good.

And then, she starts to beg. "*Please.*" Her mouth is open against mine.

It brings a chuckle to my throat, but I don't let it slip.

I could continue to tease her, pull out my fingers and stop stimulating her. I can decide to be a tease or give her what she wants: an orgasm.

Since it's Lily's birthday, I choose the latter, be nice.

Lily pants, tries to steady her breath, my hand still inside her jeans when gags appear from somewhere by the door.

I don't budge, knowing that's Aaron. Lily, however, is

panicking.

She pulls my hand out of her pants, quickly zips them up before hiding her face in her palms. She doesn't sit up, doesn't move at all. All Lily does is lie there, hiding.

It's amusing, but I know I shouldn't find this funny. Lily is embarrassed, mortified probably.

I sit up and look into Aaron's eyes as I slowly suck off Lily's wetness from my fingers. He watches me with disgust written all over his face.

If it wasn't Lily lying on the sofa next to—*or behind*—me, Aaron wouldn't care. Truth is, I once fucked a girl right next to him. Like the good best friend he is, he pretended to be asleep until she left. He didn't care one bit. But this is Lily, of course, he cares now.

"Did you just finger fuck my sister on our sofa?" It's a rhetorical question, I realize.

Lily squeals at his words, not wanting to hear him say this. Then she finally sits up, having found enough courage to face her brother.

Or not. Instead of facing him, Lily moves right behind me and wraps her arms and legs around my torso, and hides her face in my back. It's like she's using me as her own personal armor.

"No," Lily mumbles, yet at the same time I voice a "Yes." Lily slaps me for it, but I don't understand why. It's not like Aaron is stupid. He knows what he's seen.

"That's disgusting." And once more, he gags. "Can you at least try to keep this away from my eyes? Otherwise, I'll move out."

"Even better. Gives Lilybug and me more privacy."

Lily slaps her palm to my chest once more, hitting her forehead against my back a couple of times with a desperate groan escaping her.

"Wait, you said Lily would stay for five days only."

"Yup. Still only five days."

"I don't want to be here," Lily groans out. Aaron laughs, shaking his head.

Even when Aaron stops to laugh, he still has a gentle smile on his lips. I'm not sure if it's there because he's happy for Lily that she found someone to use as her shield, or if he's just bemused by all this and plans on killing me tonight.

I'll go with the latter, taking a mental note to lock my bedroom door when we get back home from the bar.

"I'm so glad it's my birthday and we're going to Brites. I really need a drink after *that*. Or ten." Aaron makes his way upstairs, but I stop him, calling out his name. "What is it?"

"Happy birthday."

"Fuck off. But thanks."

Chapter 23

"even when it's do or die, we could do it, baby, simple and plain, cause this love is a sure thing"—Sure Thing by Miguel

Lily Reyes

I hate bars.

I hate that wherever I look, there's always some guy hitting on a girl, being just a bit too touchy.

And I hate that I'm seated at a booth with five hockey players, one soccer player, and only one other woman.

But what's worse, Aaron won't stop looking at me with this weird look on his face. Like he's traumatized. I'm sure he is, I know I am. If I had walked in on him doing something remotely close to that, I would have to go straight back to therapy.

"I thought you would bring your friends, Lily." Miles smiles at me with a little more than admiration in his eyes.

If I wasn't somewhat engaged with Colin, perhaps I would find that charming. A bit disrespectful, but at least I'd feel attractive.

This guy could have anyone. He just has to look in some girl's direction, and he'd find her in his bed less than an hour later, according to the rumors about him. So why is he looking at me like he wants to undress me?

"Stop gawking and drooling over my girlfriend," Colin snaps at Miles. I like that he calls me his girlfriend, but it's bad for my health, then again, my mental health isn't really alive anyway, so what does it matter?

Izan, however, looks at Colin with suspicion. I knew this guy would look right through him. Izan is smart, and he's good at analyzing people.

He's the only other person who figured out I'm not doing too well mentally.

We had one class together back in freshman year and immediately became good friends. We don't speak too often anymore as he's busy with his soccer team, and I'm busy with Colin, apparently.

Anyway, Izan figured out my desire to die way before I was sure of it. He provided some help for me, asked his mother to become my therapist. And it helped, for a short while at least.

Fast forward three years, I no longer go to therapy because "I'm doing better", and now I plan to die in a week.

Aaron is on his third beer, he hasn't been drinking anything else since we've gotten here. The *stronger drinks* will get into his system after midnight. Up until then, he'll stick to beer.

Colin isn't drinking anything alcoholic, neither am I. Colin's reason to stay sober is that he has to drive, which is true. He has to get us home, and probably drag Aaron away from some girl's ass.

I, on the other hand, just never had the desire to drink alcohol. I've always been too afraid that I would start babbling about myself and my feelings.

Actually, I know I'd do that. I was drunk once in my life, and all I did was cry and whine about everything.

Nothing I'd like to repeat.

"Since when are you guys a thing?" Izan asks, confusion visible on his face. He crosses his arms in front of his chest, impatiently waiting for an answer that confirms his suspicion.

"Couple of days. Aaron wouldn't let me—"

"Nope," Aaron interrupts, holding up a hand. "I don't need a reminder of what I've witnessed earlier."

Colin starts to laugh like getting caught in the act is completely normal to him.

"Excuse me, what did *we* witness?" Miles asks. For a second I'm mortified, thinking Grey and Miles were there as well, but turns out, these guys just tell the other every little detail. So if Aaron knows something, the rest does as well. With the same amount of knowledge.

I think it's great that they have such a deep bond, yet I feel miserable. I feel bad because Colin keeps secrets from them. That secret is me and my situation.

And then I realize. When I die next week, Aaron will find out Colin knew. Colin will lose his best friend and he knows that's what's going to happen to his friendship after my death.

And yet he stays with you, Lily.

"I will not recall that, Miles." Aaron brings his glass to his mouth, chugging down his entire drink at once.

"But some hot information about Lily won't hurt anyone," Miles protests, teasing. I think his behavior is only to fuck with Colin.

Colin warned me about Miles not having a filter. He warned me about Miles being the best at saying stupid things without comprehending what they might do to others.

Supposedly, it's never meant in a bad way.

I want to believe Colin. Miles seems like a nice person, but he certainly acts like a teenager hitting puberty.

As I stare at him for a little while, I notice something odd about Miles. He gets nervous. It's as though the nasty guy he pretends to be is just a barrier to hide whatever lies beneath.

"I will hurt you when you continue to speak about Lily like she isn't here," Colin says. His hands ball into fists but he loosens them shortly after. "Don't be like that Miles. Lily isn't some toy. She means a lot to me, and I promise you, I will break your nose if you continue that behavior around her or me. I'm not sure Brooke would like to see that."

And the butterflies are back. *Stupid butterflies*. Maybe I should refer to them as dragonflies because nothing about this is good.

It stings in my stomach like fire burns skin.

From the corner of my eye, I catch Aaron's grin. I'm not sure what that smile is about, nothing funny happened, but it also doesn't seem like an amused smile. It's genuine, soft... a happy smile, perhaps?

Colin leans closer to me, his mouth close to my ear as he

whispers, "Let's go dancing, Lilybug."

I shake my head. If there's something I can't do, it's dancing. I can move on the ice, but dancing in high heels is impossible. It's impossible in sneakers already.

He presses his lips to my temple, slides out of the booth, and pulls me after him.

I guess I'm going on that tiny dance floor after all.

"Colin, I can't dance," I tell him, but he shrugs his shoulders at me. I'm not sure he heard me. The music is quite loud, and I wasn't speaking loudly.

"They're not even playing a good song, Colin." If he hears that, he heard what I've said before as well.

"What do you mean?" He wraps his arms around my body from behind, resting his chin on my shoulder. "They're playing *Sure Thing*."

"That's not a song to dance to." Clearly, his ears aren't working, neither are his eyes. "No one is dancing anymore."

"So what?" He chuckles and pulls me right into the outlined dance area.

Colin's hands remain on my body, along with tons of eyes that are staring at Colin and me. I mean, who's crazy enough to dance to a song that can't be danced to?

But what I've come to learn, Colin doesn't care what other people think about him. He doesn't care who's staring at him. He just does what he wants and enjoys it with every beat of his heart.

I close my eyes, terrified to accidentally lock them with some stranger who's laughing at us. Though it doesn't sound like anyone's laughing. In my head, they're all laughing anyway.

With Colin's hands on my hips, I start to sway to the rather slow rhythm.

Once the chorus comes around, Colin leans in closer to me, whisper-singing the lyrics into my ear. And once his voice streams through my ears, I no longer hear the whistles from his friends. I no longer feel the gazes of strangers on me.

All there is is Colin.

He's all over my skin, under my skin. He is in me, intoxicating every piece of my body.

Colin has become my addiction. He's like a drug. I told myself "Just this once," one kiss wouldn't hurt. One kiss wouldn't mean anything. And then we kissed. And we did it again. *One more time*, it wouldn't hurt.

And now this *one more time* has turned into a constant repetition.

So as soon as the song ends, I tug on Colin's necklace, pull him down until our lips meet.

My tongue slips into his mouth, not caring that people are watching us. Not caring that Aaron is watching us.

Colin tastes like Coca-Cola and Colin, but fuck do I love it.

And—who would have thought—the butterflies are back.

The way his lips move over mine, how his tongue tastes mine, how his fingers press into the skin by my waist, it all has me melt into him.

In the moment of our kiss, all of my feelings for him sneak out, pouring all the attraction into it. I fear bursting into flames, that's how heated it gets when our lips lock.

I want nothing more but to give him my heart. I want more time with him. But it's impossible. My time is running out, we both know that. We both know that I only have six days left, five if you don't count the day I die.

Suicidal thoughts aside for a moment, I do wonder if there's a chance for me. If there's a chance for Colin and me *together*.

But I shouldn't stay alive for someone. I should be wanting to live because I want to, not because I seem to be attracted to a guy.

I love Aaron, and yet I don't want to stay alive for him. I should feel the same about Colin, given that I'm only attracted to him and don't love him.

The next song starts to play and suddenly more people make their way onto the dance floor. It's getting a little crowded, but I don't mind because Colin's lips are still pressed to mine.

I found peace in his kisses. It's like when my lips are attached to Colin's, I'm home. It feels right.

We might need to pause for air sometime soon, but I really don't want to. Yet, we're both pulling away anyway.

His forehead comes down to mine and he stares into my eyes. His have nothing but absolute admiration in them, and if there was more to it, he's good at hiding it.

"I love that dress on you," he whispers into my ear, then leaves a kiss right behind it.

I was going to wear jeans and a sweatshirt but changed my mind and ended up wearing a red, skin-tight dress. It shows off my shoulders and collarbones, and I guess I look good in it.

"Do you know the song?" I ask. Colin shakes his head no. "Me neither."

"You want to go sit back down?"

"No." I grin, intertwining our hands. Spanish songs always have the best beats to dance to. Or most of them do, anyway. "Can you translate it?"

Colin cocks his head, smiling just a little bit, yet I can tell he's confused.

"I know you speak Spanish."

He laughs, then shakes his head. "Someone's a bit of a stalker," he says. "I've never told you."

"You call your mother *Mamá*." I raise my eyebrows at him. "And if that wasn't already a dead giveaway, you occasionally switch to Spanish when you're on the phone with your sister."

Something happens inside of him, like a thought that doesn't quite want to settle passing through. "I do?" I nod. "Really? I don't usually switch between languages in front of anyone but my family."

How did he not notice?

"Why?" I find myself asking, but either he doesn't want to answer me or he's refusing to do so.

His eyes narrow at me, one side of his lips tipping up. "You don't want to understand the lyrics to *Rechazame, mi sol*," He laughs and pulls me off the dance floor.

He leads me back to the booth, but we're not sitting down.

"We're leaving, sweetheart," he whispers into my ear.

Instead of replying, I voice, "What does it mean?"

"What does what mean?"

"Whatever you just called me. I know you've called me something."

Colin turns to my brother. "You better not lose it." His voice is strict as he lays his credit card on the table in front of Aaron. "I need it tomorrow."

Surely that's because of me. Because tomorrow is another day he'll take me somewhere. I hate that. Well, I hate that he's spending so much money on me, not that we're spending time together.

He hasn't spent too much yet, I think. The sunrise didn't cost anything. The coffees were expensive. God, it doesn't matter what he spent, he spent money on me, and I hate that.

"Why? Going on a date?" Aaron speaks with a sarcastic undertone. I'm still not too sure if he's happy or if he wants to strangle Colin.

Aaron has a glass of whiskey standing in front of him, which tells me that it's after midnight by now.

"Got to spoil your sister." That said, Colin turns back to me, smiling tenderly.

I lean in closer to his ear, saying, "I don't want to leave yet." I'm not even surprised when his eyes widen in shock and a spark of concern shines through.

Colin knows I'd much rather be at home these days instead of with a crowd. Although I appreciate his concerns and the fact that he wants me to be comfortable, I do want to stay this time.

"You sure?" His hand places down on my lower back, a bit too low for Aaron's liking.

"God, would you stop this already?" Aaron groans, taking a sip from his drink. "I want to enjoy this night and not be reminded of what I've seen."

"Just grow up and you'll be fine." Colin slides into the booth, seating himself next to Grey. I slide in beside him.

Nine Days

Izan watches us with knitted eyebrows. Only then do I realize that Aaron might've told his hockey team we're twins, but that doesn't mean Izan knows. I assumed Grey told him.

"Aaron is my twin brother," I enlighten Izan, not wanting him to remain clueless.

Instead of being surprised, Izan covers his mouth in horror when his eyes travel from Aaron to Colin and back. *Does he know something I don't?*

"You broke the bro- *and* team code?" Izan utters, aiming his question at Colin. His sudden courage aside, Izan still appears horrified.

"Not so much to break it. I asked for permission and still got some beating." Colin shrugs like it's nothing.

"I didn't hit you."

"Guys, I have an idea." Miles sets his drink down on the table, bringing a much-needed end to this conversation.

I already saw the red and blue lights from police cars flash in front of my eyes. Seeing how I have to explain to an officer why my not-really-boyfriend and my brother started to beat the shit out of the other.

"Let's see who'd cave first, Colin or Aaron." *Excuse me?* "I bet Lily could never get Archer Kingston's phone number," he voices a bet.

Miles certainly has all of the guys' attention now. Every ear and pair of eyes are on him as he explains his "*amazing*" bet in detail.

I'm saying, me flirting with some guy named Archer and what exactly I should get from him. Apparently, Archer is hard to get.

It is the stupidest bet I have ever heard and a dangerous one with Colin and Aaron around.

If the guy I'm being dared to approach so much to looks at me the wrong way, Aaron will have his fists in the guy's face. If he so much to breathes in my direction, Aaron will freak out. But so will Colin, I think.

I'm not sure Colin cares much about me flirting with other guys. However, I'm certain he might act as though it bothers him a lot.

Next thing I know, Miles points toward a really handsome guy, telling me to get started. I don't usually walk up to random bar guys, nor did I ever even try to flirt with one before. But I guess this is my time to learn.

I don't have much to lose anyway. Worst case scenario, the guy hates me and gets beaten up for it. Well, or he breathes and still gets beaten up... *He will get beaten up.*

Making my way over to the hot-looking redheaded Archer Kingston, I take a seat at his table without asking. He blinks at me as if to ask why the hell I'm being so disrespectful and just take a seat at a stranger's table.

"Hello"—my voice is thin and lacks confidence—"I'm Lily."

"Archer." He raises one eyebrow at me. "You need anything?"

"*You.*" I cringe at myself for this one. Feeling at least seven pairs of eyes on me, two pretty intensely staring ones, I decide to shake off my fear and proceed to speak. "I was kind of hoping…"

"Cupcake, who are you trying to impress?" He barks a laugh, looking around the bar. "Your friends sent you over here?"

I shake my head no. *Not friends, my brother's friend.* "It's my birthday and I figured spending it alone would be a shame."

"Your birthday?" Archer doesn't buy it, so I take out my ID to show him my birthdate.

"Liliana," he says.

I roll my eyes. "Lily."

"Technically, your birthday is over by now," he says, pointing at his phone screen that says it's 12:23 a.m.

"Well, as long as I haven't slept, it's still Saturday."

Archer takes my hand and kisses the back of it. "It's nice to meet you, birthday girl." *Not so difficult after all.*

"It's certainly an adventure knowing me."

He chuckles, yet he doesn't know what I was referring to.

"How old are you?" I find myself asking, even begin to get touchier. I slide my hand up his muscular arm and back down, offering him a smile.

"Thirty-two." My face must have turned completely pale

Nine Days

because Archer starts to laugh like I've bathed my face in baby powder. "I'm twenty."

I want to speak, but when I feel Archer's arm wrap around my waist, pulling me closer to him, my voice leaves my body. It just packed a suitcase in a whole second and left me.

He slides his hand up my side, then guides it deeper down until it's almost touching my butt. I don't say anything, I still can't. My voice still moved over to Australia. Maybe my voice bought a one-way ticket.

"Are you more of a one-night kind of girl, or do I need to take you out on dates before you'd let me in your pants?"

Now that's straightforward.

I find my voice, which is surprising because I had all my money bet on it never coming back. "Let's discuss this after you gave me your phone number."

"She's got her eyes on someone." The deep voice appearing from behind me speaks madly.

"Carter." Archer nods up at Colin. "Don't think she's much into you when Lily here came to speak to me."

"You will have four fists in your face in about two seconds if you don't remove your hand from my girl."

Archer looks at Colin's hands, saying, "You only have two," in the cockiest way I've ever heard.

"So it appears." Hands are being shoved off my body, I'm being scooped up from my seat, put back down onto my feet a second later. "But she has a twin brother with another pair of fists."

"You're babysitting for the bro?"

"Close," Colin says, sliding his hand down my body before it lands on my butt, squeezing it. "She's my girl. Not just a date. My *girlfriend*." My stomach makes a little flip, tickling in excitement.

"And yet she started to flirt with me."

"Had a bet going." Colin steps behind me and loops his arms around me, then his lips press to the heart-shaped birthmark on the back of my shoulder. "Totally adored the way she was looking at you. With so much disgust, it almost made me hard."

"You're such a dick," Archer says, yet Colin understands something else… or just makes it something else.

"You're right, I have a great dick. And it'll be inside my girlfriend in about twenty minutes."

"Didn't need to know that," Archer speaks in an irritated tone. His eyes meet mine, but this time they're not friendly and welcoming at all.

Congratulations, Lily, you've just earned yourself your first enemy for life.

Colin pulls me away from Archer's table, but he doesn't lead me back to our booth. He leads me out of Brites entirely.

"We're leaving," he tells me in a harsh tone. There's no arguing. Even if I wanted to, I wouldn't stand a chance.

"You're jealous," I note. The little glimpse of green in his eyes gives it away.

"Heck yes, I am, *mi sol*." Oh, okay. Let's make this easy then.

Colin escorts me to his car, opens the passenger door for me, waiting until I'm seated before he slams it shut. He jogs over to the other side of the car, and I watch him through the window. He looks pissed.

For a moment I wonder how the hell Colin is so effortlessly hot. He isn't even trying to be, and yet he's the hottest guy I've ever laid eyes on.

And why would he be jealous when he could have anyone?

"Clearly, you weren't aware of it, but you're mine, Lily." Colin takes a seat inside the car, not yet looking at me. "I won't put a label on whatever we are because you'd run for the hills if I did. But if I see you flirt with another guy ever again, I will make sure he experiences afterlife earlier than you do."

Not sure if I should find that charming or if I should be afraid.

"Besides, I don't think any other guy would like to put up with a girl who has one foot in the grave. One who *plans* to be dead in less than a week."

Okay, ouch.

Colin is right though. I have my death planned out. I know how

Nine Days

I will die when I will die, and who will find my body when I'm passed. It's all planned out. Nobody would put up with it.

Nobody but Colin.

Chapter 24

"cause you're the reason I believe in fate, you're my paradise" –Infinity by Jaymes Young

Lily Reyes

"Close your eyes," Colin orders as I sit down on his bed. "You're still getting your present, Lilybug. Even if it's technically not your birthday anymore."

"I don't want a present. It's not worth it."

"Shut up and close your eyes." So I do. It's not like I have much of a choice anyway.

Hearing as Colin rummages through his closet, the anticipation rises. I really don't want any presents, but somehow I'm still excited to find out what Colin got me.

The sounds stop and I feel Colin's presence in front of me. "Okay, you can open your eyes."

And with his go, I do. I open my eyes, only to find Colin kneeling in front of me. For a moment I want to run out of this room. I want to leave and never return, but then Colin starts to laugh hysterically.

He laughs so much, he tips over and lies on the floor, holding his stomach as he proceeds to laugh to the point where no sounds come out anymore. I suppose he figured out what his position looked like.

It wouldn't have scared me as much if I didn't know Colin is the type of guy who'd totally propose to someone for the hell of it.

"Okay, I'm sorry," he finally speaks, slowly sitting back up. "The look on your face, sweetheart… I should've taken a picture."

I debate slapping him. Maybe I should, he deserves it right now. But I don't. I don't because when I'm about to, Colin holds out a small gift bag for me. I watch him with suspicion as I take it.

Though, besides my suspicions, Colin watches me with more intensity than I could offer. As though he's more excited for me to open this bag than I am.

Not being able to wait any longer, I open the bag and take out a small stuffed animal. It's a replica of the frog stuffed animal I have back at the dorms. But not only that, it has a chain attached to it.

Colin got me a keychain. A *frog* keychain.

And I absolutely love it.

"Kermit will love this," I say, beaming a smile.

"Who the hell is Kermit? I thought we agreed on Sergeant Froggo."

"I never agreed to that."

"But I did." He takes one of my hands in his and a second later, Colin pulls a small box out of his jeans pocket. "Don't think I just got you the mini Sergeant Froggo."

Before I know it, Colin has put a bracelet around my wrist. It's a thin silver bracelet, no charms, just one thin continuous chain. It's simple and perfect.

"Colin," I say in one exhalation, feeling tears building up. I'm not sure if they're happy or sad tears. Actually, I'm not quite sure what I'm feeling at all.

I want to be happy. I'm happy, I think.

Yet at the same time, I want to cry because my heart aches. Not the good kind of aching, like when it's aching from love. It hurts from emotional pain. Possibly because this one goddamn bracelet reminds me that I will lose Colin very soon. Forever.

"It's perfect." I inhale a deep breath, looking up as I blink my tears away. "Thank you."

Silence falls over us, but it's not the uncomfortable kind. Colin is looking at me, watching me as I inspect his gift. I come to think it's the best gift I've ever received. Plain, modest, and just perfect.

I mean, it's a simple bracelet, but *Colin* gave it to me, which makes this bracelet a million times more special.

"Lilybug?" I look up from the bracelet, meeting Colin's gaze. "Is Lily a nickname?"

I freeze for a moment, unsure why. I'm not ashamed of my full name, I just don't like being called by it. The only person to ever call me Liliana is my mother, and she ruined it for me.

Colin seems to notice my hesitation, so he takes that as an answer. "Your full name is Liliana?" Not sure if it's a question or a stated fact.

I nod, feeling my body start to shake. I *really* don't like being called Liliana. Yet when Colin says it, it doesn't sound half as bad anymore. In fact, it feels welcoming.

"It's beautiful."

"You think so?"

He nods. "So, who started to call you Lily first?"

I chuckle at that, the story behind how Liliana turned into Lily connects with Aaron's incapability to pronounce words the right way.

"Aaron," I say. "He couldn't pronounce Liliana, for God knows what reasons. I bet he was just too lazy to say it, instead, he called me Lily."

"He should've given you a better one."

"Thank you." I roll my eyes at him.

"Lilybug?" Colin gets up on his feet only to take a seat next to me on the bed. He lays a hand down on my thigh, giving it a slight squeeze. "Tell me something I didn't know."

Again? I thought I'd already done that before. Like, all the time, actually. I believe Colin knows me the best out of all the people knowing me. He definitely knows the more horrible things about me.

"I was a virgin."

His eyebrows draw together, head slightly tilting as he waits for me to say I'm joking. At least that's what I assume he's waiting for.

When he says, "Before what happened?" I realize he's thinking completely differently from what I meant. His tone is serious, with no indications of amusement whatsoever.

Suddenly I feel stupid.

"Two, or now three, days ago, I mean."

He visibly calms, yet he still seems uncomfortable. His hand leaves my thigh, no longer touching me.

Colin stands up from the bed, walking up and down his bedroom while repetitively running his hands through his hair. I think I might have broken him.

He isn't saying one word, nor does he react when I call his name to get his attention.

Colin continues to pace around his room for approximately the next five minutes, ignoring my presence up until he finally turns to look at me again. "Why didn't you tell me earlier?"

"Because I wanted to avoid *this* reaction." And besides, it's not like what we've done wasn't consensual. I wanted to sleep with him as much as he wanted to sleep with me.

"*Fuck*, Lily." Another hand slides through his already messed-up hair, tugging at the ends as he lets out a frustrated groan.

Different from what I'm expecting, Colin stays in the room and doesn't run away.

In fact, he walks over to me, picks me up from the bed. My legs wrap around his hips almost instantly.

A cloud of his scent fills my nostrils. He smells nice, like rosewood and fresh laundry. I think I might've found my favorite scent after all. *Colin*.

That's what it is, right? When a scent fills you up with warmth and increases the feeling of well-being, makes you addicted, wanting to smell it again, and again. That's when it becomes an ultimate favorite.

His hands lie on my ass, underneath the skirt of my dress, as he holds me up, his mouth capturing mine immediately. His tongue darts across the seam of his lips, dipping into my mouth.

My hands grip his hair, stroking through his soft strands. Gently, I scrap his scalp with my fingernails until Colin releases a throaty noise.

"I'm going to give you a better 'first time,' sweetheart. Okay?" he speaks between slow pecks, carefully laying me down on the bed.

Colin hovers over me, kissing my lips, then down my neck. When he reaches my cleavage, Colin sits up, slides down enough to reach for my ankles. He undoes the strings from my high heels, one after the other he sets them down next to his bed.

Then he starts to kiss his way up my legs, whispers compliments every time his lips burn into my skin. With every kiss, my body heats up. With every kiss, a wave of anticipation gets send right between my legs.

When he's kissing up my thigh, Colin halts for a second, pushing up my dress enough to free my body up to my ribs. He doesn't remove it completely, so I take it upon myself to do it.

Since the dress is meant to be shoulder-free and my breasts aren't all too big, I'm not wearing a bra, meaning my chest is now completely exposed to him.

"You're trying to kill me, Lilybug," he says, looking into my eyes as he licks his lips like I'm the most delicious thing he's ever seen.

He tugs on my panties, slides them down my legs, and leaves me naked for him.

"Aw, fuck," he groans. His head tilts back into his neck just before he lets out a short blow of air, then looks at me again. "Are you on birth control?"

I shake my head, not as an answer, but because his question catches me off guard. "Why?"

"Was hoping I could feel you without latex between us," he answers. "It's alright though. We'll stick to condoms."

He lowers his body over mine, reconnecting our lips. His lips are soft, and he doesn't taste like Coca-Cola anymore. His mouth is claiming me so possessively, if he weren't Colin, I would back off. But he *is* Colin, and he is claiming *me*.

"I am, Colin." He looks at me with uncertainty, so I elaborate. "On birth control."

"Then why'd you shake your head?"

"I was confused as to why you're asking. But I promise you, I am."

Flashing me a cocky smile, Colin gets off the bed and strips off his clothes fast enough to be back on top of me in no time.

Regardless of my arousal and how desperate I am for Colin, I can't shake the feeling that he only wants to sleep with me to feel better. His reaction when I told him I was a virgin still doesn't sit right with me. So I ask, "Do you feel guilty?"

Colin sits up. "Why would I feel guilty?"

"Because you took my virginity and weren't exactly gentle with me."

"Sweetheart, if I wanted vanilla sex then, I would have given you nothing but that. If you wanted it, you should've told me. And besides, you took it well. So, no, I don't feel even one bit guilty."

I want to speak and ask about his reaction, but all that comes out is a slight gasp when Colin plants a kiss to my pussy.

He hugs my hips, holds me down as his tongue explores the spot between my legs slowly. One of his hands glides up, rests on my breast, fingers pinching my nipple.

I love that he's so touchy. I love that Colin doesn't care for one part of my body only, instead, he makes sure to work all of it.

Feeling his tongue dip inside of me, I can't help the moan from slipping out. I cover my mouth with my arm, muffling my sounds. But when I do, Colin stops to please me and says, "No, stop covering your mouth. I want to hear how good I make you feel."

I don't think I've ever blushed more in my life. I'm literally lying buck naked in front of Colin, and yet this comment makes me blush.

Once he sees my arm is no longer covering my mouth, he sucks on my clit, groans when he hears my whimpers. My hips keep shifting until Colin digs his fingers into my skin to hold me in place.

"Please," I beg. All this tension is too much. I'm in desperate need to feel relief.

I can feel Colin smile against my skin, and for a short moment I want him to suffocate for it, but a breathing Colin sounds better than a dead one.

"I need you inside of me," I say with a husky voice, hands tugging at his hair in an attempt to pull him up. He doesn't budge though. All Colin does is chuckle and continue to work miracles with his tongue.

Not that I'm complaining.

As much as I love his tongue on my clit, I do want to feel him inside of me. "I want to come around your dick, not on your tongue," I say, hoping so desperately that it'll change Colin's mind.

"Aw, fuck, Lily," he curses. "This is going to be over way too soon if you keep saying things like that."

"Colin, please."

He pushes two of his fingers inside of me while continuing to lick and suckle on my swollen clit.

His fingers push in and out, the tips pressing against my walls, eliciting cries from my throat. Loud moans I didn't even know were possible to come out of me.

"You're going to come on my tongue, even if it takes us hours to get there. You got your way last time, I'm not missing out on it again."

His tongue licks me while his fingers continue to thrust inside of me, curling up and then pulling back out in a repetitive pattern.

I can feel my orgasm build with every thrust.

Just when the tension inside of me gets so intense and I'm forced to let go, Colin removes his fingers from me completely, sticking his tongue inside of me instead.

With his thumb on my clit, pressing, circling, I finally feel relief as I cry out in pleasure. Euphoria shoots through my body, tickling my skin.

Colin reaches over to his nightstand, takes out a condom wrapper, and opens it.

In a matter of seconds, Colin has rolled the condom down his erection. He then grabs a pillow from beside my head and lifts my hips like I weigh nothing, putting the pillow beneath me.

"Thought you wanted to feel me?"

"I do, but I'm not quite sure if you're lying to me or not. I won't risk anything." That being said, Colin adjusts his cock to my entrance.

Risk what? It's not like I'd turn him into a father as I'll be dead by next week.

"I'm not..." I gasp, not being able to continue my sentence when Colin slowly sinks inside me. With each light push, as he eases deeper inside, I feel fuller. And once his full erection is inside of me, my body suddenly feels as though I'm completely filled up.

"Is that a promise?"

I only manage to nod my head when Colin starts to move his hips and his pubic bone rubs against my clit.

"I've never had sex without a condom before," he admits, easing out of me completely. He removes the condom, tosses it to the floor, and slowly sinks back inside of me.

That must mean something to him, right? *I* must mean something.

"Ah, shit." His mouth is back on mine, kissing me without moving his hips. Not being able to wait any longer, I lift my legs and wrap them around his hips, forcing him to be closer, deeper.

A moan breaks out of me when he moves. Feeling his cock slide in and out of me sends my senses flying through the roof. I feel the urge to dig my nails into his skin as he makes love to me so fervently, I barely have anything left in me to function properly.

Cries of pleasure elicit from my throat with every thrust.

"Fuck, sweetheart," he moans into my mouth, breathlessly. Doubt I've ever heard anything sexier. "You're going to be the death of me, *mi sol*." He thrusts into me.

Colin doesn't go rough with me this time. He keeps it all passionate and sweet, yet still hot and steamy. He has completely fogged up my mind, pleasuring me in every sense of way. Making parts of my body feel things, I didn't even know were possible.

"Oh, God," I cry out, moaning.

His lips crash down onto mine, biting my bottom lip. His hips still, looking into my eyes with a stern look. "Say my name."

I blink. "What?"

"Say. *My*. Name."

"Colin, I—" He pulls out of me and slams back inside so hard, I gasp.

"You see God around here somewhere?" I shake my head. "Exactly." He kisses me. Deeply. Possessively. "You're mine, Lily. I'm not even sharing you with God."

His lips claim mine like he means every word. And I believe him. I believe his words, his mouth.

Sweat appears on both of our bodies and pleasure rises deep within mine when Colin brings his hand between my legs. Fingers rub my clit, causing my vision to go dark.

And then, when he steals yet another orgasm from me, Colin kisses me as he comes inside of me, mumbling the word *Fuck* under his breath.

His forehead rests against mine, panting as we're both calming down from our orgasm.

I can smell him on me, his scent colliding with mine. I send out a silent prayer, hoping I'll get to smell his scent wherever I'll end up after death.

His soft, yet swollen lips press to mine as he eases out of me. Lying down next to me, Colin pulls me close to him, resting my head on his chest. I can hear his heart beating; fast and strong. His breathing is quick as well, but it calms with every breath he takes.

"I'm never going to do this with anyone else ever again," Colin speaks into the silent room. "It's only going to be you."

"Poor you."

"Indeed." Neither of us has to address this with more words. We're both aware of what we're talking about.

"Let's get you cleaned up and ready for bed, okay?" Colin says softly, lifting us both to sit. "See, this time, we're even sleeping in one bed after. No more doing this all wrong." He stands, pulling me up to my feet right after.

As I stand, I feel something run down my thigh. "Colin." My voice is completely gone again. "I think your cum is running down my leg."

He snickers, then tilts his head back in his neck and groans. When his eyes are back on mine, with a gentle touch, his arm traces down my body, bringing his hand to my thighs. With a bit of pressure against my skin, Colin slides his fingers up my thigh until he's touching my pussy. I spread my legs, letting out a gasp when his finger dip inside of me.

He leans down, mouth to my ear, whispering, "I might just do that again in the bathroom… but with my cock."

Chapter 25

"hearts break and hell's a place that everyone knows"—Don't Be so Hard on Yourself by Jess Glynne

Colin Carter

I'm not sure how I've noticed that Lily isn't asleep, but I did.

We *both* went to bed shortly after we came back from the bathroom and now I'm pretending to be asleep while Lily is writing something into her notebook.

She's crying, and that's the only reason why I don't take that notebook away from her. Maybe she needs to write her feelings down on paper to cope. Or maybe not. But she certainly wants to write something into it, so who am I to keep her from it?

It also takes all of my willpower not to wrap my arms around her right now.

All I want to do is press her against my body and hug the pain out of her. But I can't. Not because a simple hug won't put her back together, but because I think crying is good. As much as it wounds me, I think she needs to cry sometimes.

I think it might make her feel a little less heavy in her chest.

At least now that she's busy writing, it gives me another look into her thoughts.

I know I shouldn't look, shouldn't read what's going on in her head. But how else am I supposed to figure out what's happening?

So I read.

Dear whoever reads this,

I'm a mess.

A complete goddamn mess.

Nine Days

It's Sunday, October 3rd—5:30 in the morning—and I'm sitting on Colin Carter's bed, crying, while he's sound asleep next to me.

This time it's not about him. It's all about me. My least favorite topic.

As soon as he fell asleep, I felt it all.

The pain.

The solitude.

The numbness.

I felt numbness.

How is that even possible? How can I feel something that's not supposed to be felt, because... it's numbness?

How do I feel my heart break, and yet I feel nothing at all?

My mother wants me dead.

I knew she disliked me for a while now. But never did I think she'd tell me to die. I thought, maybe she hates me, but she's my mother, she must still love me.

I was wrong. So awfully wrong.

And it hurts. It hurts so much more than I thought it would.

I've been wanting to die for quite a while. Turns out she wanted the same ending for me.

It's one thing when you want to die, but another when your own mother wants you dead.

But aside from my mother's wish for my death... it's Sunday.

I loathe the Sundays.

And yet today, I will have to plaster a smile onto my face and pretend I have fun all day long.

Maybe I will have fun because I always do with Colin. For some reason, he affects me like that.

He makes me smile randomly. He makes me forget my pain.

Joelina Falk

But then he's not with me and I feel it all again.
Today will be torture.
I used to hate Saturdays just as much. You know why?
September 24th, 2005, the day my parents decided they'll get a divorce. It was Saturday. The worst day of my life.
It's the day my mother pushed Aaron out of her life forever. The day my mother took my brother from me.
My parents' announcement to get a divorce was only half as bad. But what followed was the worst.
Ever since then... my depression got and still gets the better of me with every new day.
I was born with a genetic makeup, prone to depression. My parents knew that. And they've done everything to prevent it from developing.
At least until they split up and made all my happiness go away.
The doctors said it's possible that I'd never end up developing a mood disorder such as depression. But I did.
Because my mother tore my family apart.
And now she wants me dead. And I want me dead as well.
If it weren't for Colin, I'd probably be hiding in my room right about now. I wouldn't have set one foot out the door, wouldn't have done anything but look at my ceiling, and wish for the days to pass faster.
That's what I used to do a lot.
Spend time on my floor, looking at the ceiling for hours on end. The only other occupation was the music streaming into my ears. So loud, it probably could've led to hearing problems.
I really don't feel like going out today. But I will. For Colin.
Because seeing him smile warms my heart. And seeing him happy... it makes me happy.

Nine Days

I think he doesn't notice me watching him when he watches me.

Like on day one. When he was watching me instead of the sunrise.

I felt his eyes on my skin. It prickled everywhere.

He wanted to watch the sunrise and ended up watching me. It was one of the most magical sunrises I've ever seen, and yet I couldn't concentrate because his eyes were on me.

And when I screamed my lungs out, he didn't seem to find that weird. He didn't seem to be less intrigued to spend more time with me.

He watched me, filmed me for our project—whatever that is about—and smiled when I turned around to look at him.

He. Smiled.

He smiled like he knew I felt lighter.

God, please someone press my off button; I need to stop writing about Colin.

This is my unalive journey 101. Not a "Colin Carter is such a great and freakishly hot guy" fan book.

And now that I've mentioned him, I might as well add another thing.

He is a nosy pain in the ass. Thinking I don't know he's awake and reads this right now.

  Lily

I can't hold back my chuckle at that last sentence. "You think I'm hot," I note, now being able to speak since she obviously knows I'm awake.

"You know you are," is all I get in return.

"But freakishly hot?" I take Lily's notebook from her, not to read more pages, but to put it away. She tries to protest until I have it in my hands. She stops trying to reach for it, kind of like she knows she doesn't stand a chance. "Today's going to be a rainy day."

"Seriously?" She chuckles. "You're talking about the weather?"

Yes, because the only other thing on my mind would be her tears and how I'm supposed to get rid of them.

I nod and pull Lily closer to me. "We're staying home today."

A quiet gasp leaves her throat. She stiffens up when she tries to come up with a reason as to why I wouldn't just take her somewhere indoors.

Which would be a great question if she asked.

After what she wrote, how she's too exhausted to leave the house… I figured it might be best to stay home—just the two of us—for a day.

I'm glad she's not asking. Telling her I want to stay home because she feels too exhausted to go feels like the wrong thing to say.

"Nothing planned?" Lily narrows her eyes at me. I don't think she's trying to come off as annoyed. I think she's trying to look into my eyes through the dark. I mean, it's not too dark, otherwise, I wouldn't have been able to read her notebook entry.

"Before you agreed on these nine days, you said you'd need a day off… so this is it. It's going to rain all day and it's Sunday. You hate Sundays. So might as well spend it here and do jigsaw puzzles." If Lily was anyone but her, I'd probably have forgotten this minor information already, but for some reason, my brain just saves anything that has to do with Lily.

"Puzzle?" Her forehead creases—*I think*.

"Yup."

"Why?"

"Don't tell me you don't like puzzling, Lilybug." I pretend to be offended by that. "I have this amazing frog jigsaw puzzle, you know."

"A *frog* jigsaw puzzle?" She shifts, rolling right on top of me. Not that I care. "You do know I'm not into frogs, right?"

A shocked gasp comes from the depth of my throat. "You aren't?" Lily shakes her head. "Well, then why did I get you a frog keychain if you don't even like them? You're totally digging frogs."

"Colin," she laughs, "*You* got it for me. I didn't ask for it."

"You had Sergeant Froggo and many others before I got you the mini version of him. By the way, we need a better name for him."

"Kermit," says Lily with no hesitation.

"Still too boring, Lilybug. And I'm talking about Corporal Froggo." A few seconds of silence falls between us. "That's it: Corporal Froggo."

"I thought Sergeant?"

"God dammit, Lilybug. We're talking about the mini Froggo. You've got to pay more attention to me." I stroke my hand from the small of her back deeper down, resting them right on her butt. She doesn't tell me to remove it, so I keep it there, giving her butt a slight squeeze.

"You'd like that, wouldn't you?" My eyebrows rise. "More attention from me," she declares, tilting her head up just enough for her lips to collide with mine... well, almost. She's not kissing me, not even touching my lips with hers, but she's awfully close.

"Hm-mmm." I slide my hand up enough to trace along the outline of her panties.

Lily isn't wearing any pants, only underwear and a shirt of mine. And I don't think I ever want her wearing anything else ever again—when it's just Lily and me, that is.

I can feel her breath hitch when one of my fingers slides beneath the fabric, so I pull on it before letting it snap back into place.

"Can I ask you something?"

She rolls her eyes. "Like you wouldn't, even if I said no."

"Okay, it might be a bit too deep given how early it is... but, how come you're good to have sex? I always kind of thought people with depression don't feel the desire to get intimate."

Her eyes widen instantly. I'm even sure Lily has a slight blush on her cheeks. It's adorable, the tint to her cheeks, I mean.

"Well, it's not the same for everyone. It can affect one person but the other doesn't have to show this kind of symptom. Depression in men, for instance, a sign *could* be self-medicating with sex and alcohol," she explains roughly. Though, I think I understand anyway.

Joelina Falk

"And to be fair, I didn't have the desire to sleep with anyone before you came along and were all kissy with me."

"I wasn't all kissy with you. I kissed your breath away," I object. "It was hot and steamy, and the best kiss you've ever experienced."

"It wasn't all too bad, but whatever helps you sleep at night." I swear, if she keeps downgrading our first—*real*—kiss, she might hurt my ego. "Anyway, Grandpa, you think we could actually have fun today with all the puzzling you've planned?"

"Depends. Will that include a great breakfast together?" I ask in all seriousness.

"You're hungry?" I nod, about to return the question when she gets up. "What do you want?"

"What do you mean?"

"I'll make breakfast. It's the least I can do for you, considering you're letting me stay here and all."

"Lilybug, you had no other choice. I wasn't letting you stay at your dorm with all the shit going on. Even if you were to protest, you would still be here right now," I remind her. "You didn't ask to stay here, I made you."

She lifts her shoulders, shrugging. "You're fine with pancakes?"

"I would eat anything you made, simply because *you* made it."

"It could taste disgusting." Her eyebrows lift. "Maybe you're allergic. Speaking of allergies, do you have any?"

"Coconut, why?"

"Interesting," she says, rubbing her chin like she is coming up with a plan to kill me. "I happen to have this amazing shower gel. It's tropical. I think it's coconut scented."

"You think?" I laugh, now being sure she's trying to murder me. "I've never smelled it on you before then."

"That's because I didn't buy it yet. But I will."

"So you do want me dead, huh?"

She shrugs again, but this time she walks out of my room right after, leaving the door open.

I can hear her talk as she walks down the stairs, but I can't quite

Nine Days

make out what she's saying.

I feel the sudden urge to check out who she's talking to.

Doubting it's Aaron, I get up from my bed, throw on some sweatpants that I find in the depth of my closet, and follow Lily downstairs.

"Good morning, Princess," Grey greets me as I come down the stairs. He sits at the kitchen island, holding some sports magazine in his hands. He's not even reading the damn thing.

"What are you doing here, Grey?" I ask like I wouldn't already know the answer.

"Grabbing something to eat, like I do every morning." His eyes move over to Lily, standing by the refrigerator, looking through it. "Turns out I'll be getting it served today."

And so suddenly another déjà vu pops up. Lily, half naked in my kitchen. At least this time it's not Miles gawking at her. Grey doesn't care one bit about Lily, and he'd never have any intentions of getting into her pants. So I'm not worried about that.

"Where's Miles?" I find myself asking. I have to be sure he won't march in here and drool all over Lily's perfect ass.

He wouldn't do that, and if he does, it's just to mess with me, which, frankly, would work quite well.

Taking a seat right next to Grey, I rest my elbows on the island top and hold my head up with my hands, watching Lily.

"He's not in New City. Kya, Izan's sister, bumped into him last night and I think they drove down to Manhattan half an hour later. They also had some other girl with them," Grey says. Man, this guy knows exactly why I've been asking. He knows I wouldn't care one bit if Miles was around or not—if it weren't for my half-naked girlfriend in the kitchen.

She's not your girlfriend, Colin.

"Kya is Izan's sister?" Lily turns around, her mouth wide open.

"Very much so. She's a year younger, so it's quite a miracle Miles wanted to tag along with her."

"I thought she's a senior." Lily turns back around and starts to mix up some ingredients that end up being a pancake batter.

"She is," Grey confirms, "I think she skipped sophomore year in high school."

"Seriously? I wish I was that smart."

I snicker but try to cover it with a cough. Lily notices it anyway and shoots me her own perfectionated death glare.

"Why wouldn't Miles go for younger girls?"

Grey and I sigh both at the same time. "He says he's afraid they might be too immature," I tell her, though that's not the truth.

To that, Lily says Miles is the immature one. Grey and I both neither agree nor disagree.

Even though Miles is Grey's best friend, Grey knows how much of a pain in the ass our teammate can be. He experiences Miles's more-or-less immaturity more often than anyone else does, given that they've been sharing a house for three years.

Grey's words speak volume when it comes to Miles.

But to be fair, Miles was thrown into being an adult instead of maturing into one.

"According to Miles, every woman who's younger than him wants nothing but a diamond ring and his babies before they'd even gotten to know each other." Grey looks at me, eyes narrowing as if to say I shall go along with it. "Or something like that," he mumbles, but Lily hears it.

"Maybe he's bonding with Kya to get your man, Grey." Lily turns to him, cocking her eyebrows with a devilish smile on her lips. "I mean, Izan would definitely be Miles's type."

Grey laughs, shaking his head. "Wouldn't even be surprised."

"However, I don't think Miles would be Izan's type. Izan has a way better taste." Lily's voice is soft, sweet. I love when she speaks… if it's not about some other guy, that is.

Grey's laughter grows more hysterical and Lily joins in. I have no idea what is happening, but I don't like where this is going. Not at fucking all.

"I thought you'd have better taste than sir moody here, darling," Grey utters, speaking of me like I'm not even here.

I growl quietly, mentally planning how I'm going to murder him later tonight without getting caught. I'm sure Lily knows some ways. She seems like one of those girls listening to True Crime podcasts while getting ready for the day.

Grey sighs. "I doubt he left to actually get to know Kya though. He's most likely visiting Brooklyn. Kya was probably just driving him."

The sound of her name makes me wince. We don't talk about Brooke. Not to anyone but *us*.

"I heard that name before… Who is Brooklyn or Brooke, and why wouldn't Miles drive himself?" Lily asks. Of course she would ask who Brooke is.

Grey shrugs, his eyes on mine like he knows he just fucked up. *He did*. "Miles had a beer or two. He doesn't drive with *any* alcohol intake. Not even half a beer, or just the teeniest sip."

Lily nods then turns over to me to get the rest of her question answered. I can't look at her. If I do, I'll spill things out like throwing up my guts after a drink too much.

I look at Grey in defeat. He shouldn't have fucking mentioned Brooke.

This is a test on his part, isn't it? Like "Would this dumbass keep quiet even when he's falling for a girl he's not supposed to fall for, and she's asking questions?"

No. No, I would *not* keep quiet.

Grey looks at me with a warning in his eyes, but I ignore it. "Brooke is Miles's daughter."

Lily gasps, her eyes widen drastically. "Daughter?"

I nod. "She's four years old. They faced a few complications during Millie's c-section that ended her up in a coma. Millie died a couple of days later."

Grey's eyes close as he takes a deep breath.

"Millie Scott?" Lily asks. I nod, though I do wonder how she knows her. "Seriously? She promised me she'd come to Trewery once we finished high school. She didn't even attend classes the last few months of junior year, and she never returned for senior year either. Her mother told me she decided against college and that she transferred to Emory's school. I always wondered why her mother reached out to me and not Millie herself."

That's what everyone thinks. Neither her family nor Miles wanted the school, or anyone, to know as they all wanted to grieve in peace. And since Millie didn't want anyone to know she got pregnant at the age of seventeen, she stopped going to school. At least that's what Miles had told us.

And her transferring to Emory's school? Yeah, no, I would've known of that. Emory, Miles, and I attended the same high school in New York City, though Miles was a grade above mine, so we didn't talk until we found ourselves on the same hockey team in college. And Emory? Well, we shared some classes, but I didn't care about her one bit either. I was too focused on ice hockey and passing high school at the same time.

"So where does Brooklyn stay when Miles is here all day?"

Grey licks his lips then says, "She's usually with Maeve, Miles's older sister, but stays here on the weekends. I told Miles I don't mind Brooke staying with us all week, but since he's still in college and plays hockey, he figured it was better for her. He also doesn't want to force her to his classes."

We all believe Brooke would much rather be with her father, but it's his decision to make, not ours.

"You can't tell anyone, Lily," Grey adds, the same look of seriousness he gave me before back on his face. To be fair, ninety percent of the day, that's his normal face. "The only people who know of Brooke's existence are the team." *And I suppose Kya now that Miles allegedly took her to see Brooke. Plus Miles' and Millie's family.*

I always wondered what I would've done if I was in Miles's position. What I would've done if the woman I loved died a couple of days after giving birth to our child.

How Miles managed to somehow live through the death of his child's mother, and handle being a single father at the age of eighteen… I will never understand.

And to make matters worse, Brooke looks so much like her

mother, and therefore Emory as well.

"Princess, you're not getting your girl off enough." Grey taps his hand on my back.

"Huh?" I'm not quite sure what I've missed, and I'm also not sure I want to be enlightened either.

"That's not the problem, Grey." Lily sighs, setting down a plate right in front of him. "Colin is just… too extra."

"Excuse me?"

She ignores me. "He doesn't even know what he's doing."

Watching as Grey takes a bite from the strawberry banana pancake, snickering. I almost lose my temper. *What the hell is going on?*

And since when do we have strawberries here? Aaron and I barely buy them because of Brooke.

Swallowing, Grey says, "I mean… did you look at him?" His head turns, facing me.

"I'm fucking gorgeous, thank you very much."

When Lily sets another plate down—this time meant for me—I grab her wrist in my hand and pull her around the island. She ends up standing between my legs, facing me. She might be a bit surprised, but she's not complaining.

"*Mi sol*, you're going to have to enlighten me." Brushing my nose along her neck, I feel her shiver under my touch. Not a cold-shiver, a goosebumps kind of shiver. "What were you talking about?"

With my hands on her waist, I push her a tad closer to me, brushing my lips against hers.

"You guys are bullshitting yourselves," Grey says. Shooting Grey a stern and bewildered look, he cares to explain himself before I have to ask. "You may be able to fool Aaron into thinking you guys are a thing, but you can't fool me." A dirty snicker comes from deep within his throat.

"I told you," Lily shrieks, hitting her palm to my chest.

Knowing Grey—and judging by the nasty grin on his lips—I know he knows better than to open his mouth about it. Especially because I know that he knows more about my feelings toward Lily than *she* does.

"Why's she staying here, Princess?"

For a moment I'm debating on telling Grey the truth. The whole truth. Not in front of Lily, obviously, but when I get a moment with him alone.

Grey would never run to Aaron and tell him all about this, though he probably should. He also isn't the judgmental kind of guy. If anything, Grey would offer to help. Help me help her. He wouldn't go behind my back and get Lily the help she clearly needs.

Though, I'm sure he would ask why I'm not going behind her back and do so myself.

And if I had to answer that question… I wouldn't know what to tell him. Why *aren't* I doing that? Why aren't I dropping her off at some hospital, tell them what's wrong, and let them help me get her the help she needs?

Maybe because I feel like I'd be betraying her if I did?

But that's alright because I *will* get her some help once our nine days are over.

"Sex," I finally answer, slipping my hands underneath the white shirt Lily is wearing. Grey cocks his head, his eyes boring into mine as if to call me out on even more of my bullshit. "I just want more time with her."

"You have all the time you need, even if she's not living with you." *If only you knew*.

"I wanted to stay, actually," Lily blurts out. I think she can sense my uncertainty. If she hadn't opened her mouth and spoken for me, I think I would've told Grey the truth right here, right now.

Maybe I do need someone I can talk to about her. About this. About Lily's situation. That person certainly can't be Aaron.

"I have a few problems with Winter. She's a pain in the ass sometimes. I'm sure you've heard of her. Aaron's ex-girlfriend." Grey nods. "Yeah, she's a lot. And we just had this big fight recently. I don't want to be around her for a while."

Nine Days

I'm fascinated by how easily these lies roll over her tongue. Not only this one with Winter. Everything. Her pretending to be alright all day long, plastering smiles onto her face, faking happiness.

In desperate need to change the topic, I pick up where we left off. "Anyway, tell me what you were talking about."

"You sat right here, didn't you listen?"

I shake my head no. "I was too busy planning Grey's death, Lilybug."

"Why?"

Grey's eyes shoot toward me like he'd love to hear the answer. I'm sure he knows why, yet I tell *Lily* anyway. "He thinks I'm a bad guy."

"I did not say that," Grey defends himself. He did, though not using those exact words.

"You thought my Lilybug had better taste in men, meaning you think I either look bad, which we all know would be a lie, or I'm a bad person."

Lily smiles softly, her eyes never leaving mine even when Grey speaks. "I said you're moody."

I don't look away from her either. "I'm not." Not when Lily's here. "I answered your question… now answer mine."

"I told Grey we're having a jigsaw puzzle day."

"And you think that makes me 'too extra?'"

She snorts a laugh, shaking her head before pressing her lips to the corner of my mouth.

"No, but your bet to show her 'the world' in nine days does," Grey answers for Lily when she wouldn't.

I freeze, not knowing how to react. Did Lily tell Grey about her death wish? She didn't, right? She wouldn't do that.

A bet.

She said we were having a bet going.

How long was I in my head for that I didn't hear a word they said?

"I'm sure you can join us?" Lily says her invitation as a question. I don't want anyone to be around us today. I told myself

254

Joelina Falk

I would keep other people away from Lily for the day, and here I'm failing before breakfast even really started.

"Maybe I'll join in later. I have plans with Izan." Grey winks at Lily, and for some reason it makes my stomach turn. *Get your shit together, Colin.*

I shrug him off, turning my attention back to my girl just when she starts to yawn. Maybe she's more exhausted than I thought. Or maybe she just didn't get enough sleep.

"You didn't sleep much," I note, brushing Lily's hair out of her face. "If I recall correctly, not at all. What's going on, sweetheart?"

Her cheeks flush like she's embarrassed. Drawing my eyebrows together, I wait for an explanation that doesn't seem to come.

I hold her face in place with my hands, having both my hands on her jawline, thumbs gently caressing her heated cheeks. "Talk to me, Lilybug."

She sighs and proceeds to remain silent. It annoys me. Why wouldn't she just tell me what's going on? Is it because Grey is here? Insomnia maybe? But that wouldn't be embarrassing, would it?

Her eyes wander over to Grey, where she sees that he most likely doesn't even care about her presence.

"I, uh"—once again her eyes drift over to Grey—"I can't sleep without Kermit," she admits. It's adorable, and definitely nothing she should be embarrassed about. Now I'm wondering if Sergeant Froggo isn't as new of a stuffed animal as I thought he was.

"You're so cute, you know that?" My expression softens as a smile creeps onto my face. I plant a chaste kiss to her lips before whispering, "I'll get him for you."

What have I turned into?

Never in my life would I have gone to get a stuffed animal from a girl's house just so she could sleep in peace—or at all.

What the hell are you doing to me, Lily?

Grey clears his throat and gets up from his seat. He takes his plate, thanks Lily for the pancakes, and leaves the house. I suppose he figured he shouldn't be around.

Nine Days

At least I'm alone with my Lilybug now.

"You really want to stay home all day?"

I nod, pulling her closer to me again. She had moved a bit while saying goodbye to Grey.

Only now do I notice that Lily smells like roses and sex. That brings a smile to my lips because I know exactly how that happened. I consider telling Lily about it, but I also don't want to freak her out.

"What are your favorite flowers?" I ask, surprised by my sudden interest in it. I've never really cared about giving anyone flowers, and I don't think I'll get some for Lily, yet I'm still interested to hear her answer. Not sure if that's because her name is Lily, and lilies are some type of flowers—and the fact I find it hilarious that she smells like a mix of roses and vanilla at all times—or if it's just pure interest in general.

"You're not getting me flowers." Well, now I have to.

"Wasn't planning to get you some. Just wondering."

"Don't laugh," she says, holding out her pinky finger. I give her a quick frown of confusion before eventually hooking my pinky to hers and pinky promise not to laugh. "I think lilies."

"You think?"

"I think I know so. I'm not sure. I don't know a lot about flowers, I just know my name is a flower, and I know roses. I know of dandelions, though I'm not sure if they count as a flower or weeds. And sunflowers, of course."

I listen to her babble about different flower types for the next following ten minutes. Every now and then I get a bite from my now completely cold pancake, while also making sure she eats some herself.

"What's your favorite color?" I then ask.

Lily lifts her shoulders. "Mint green, I guess."

"Makes sense. I'll get you a mint green frog." I won't, but I might do something really stupid anyway.

"Colin?" Her voice is so soft, loving. I think her voice is the sweetest of sounds I've ever heard. Seriously, just listening to Lily talk brightens my mood. "Tell me something I didn't know."

"Playing my game now, are we?" I chuckle, then kiss her one more time. *Did I mention that I'm addicted to her lips?*

Feeling Lily smile against my mouth, I slide my hands down to her ass, squeezing it. She yelps, laughing, slapping my chest just once.

"I had an older brother," I admit. I don't think I've ever truly talked about him before. Never wanted to either. I didn't even tell Aaron about Aiden. I've done well hiding my pain, hide the hole he'd left in my chest when he died.

But maybe it's time for Lily to understand why I'm doing this, why I want her to stay alive. Though this might be a huge mistake to let her in. Maybe the biggest even.

"Had?" she repeats back to me.

I attempt to nod. "He died when I was nineteen. Around the time when Eira got diagnosed with leukemia."

And then the fearful reaction I expected happens. Lily's eyes fill up with so much pity and horror, it wounds me.

"You once asked why I'm doing this," I say, hoping she might remember her question. "I never answered your question." She nods. "I let him slip away, Lily."

Her eyes widen, beautiful green eyes filled with nothing but sadness. Somehow, I know this would happen if she ever were to find out about Aiden.

She takes a step back or tries to. Fortunately, I still have my hands on her ass, so I can force her to stay in place.

"Aiden couldn't take it. He said he couldn't watch Eira die, couldn't have her be the first one of us to go down." Lily stays quiet, listening only. I guess her mind is blocking me out, seeing me as nothing but a blur and some background music. But I started already, so I will continue. "He would leave hints, tell me how fucked up all this is. How weird it is that he's the oldest and yet our younger sister is about to die from cancer."

Lily shakes her head, not believing a word I just said. I can't blame her, not even I wanted to believe it two years ago.

"But she survived. She's all right, isn't she?"

I nod, though hesitantly. "But two years ago it looked a lot like she wouldn't make it. Doctors kept saying there was nothing they could do. And as painful as it might've been to my entire family, it hit Aiden the hardest." Looking away from Lily, I continue, "He has always been protective of Eira, and to think that his fourteen years old sister will die before him, he couldn't take it, Lily." I can feel old wounds reopen, tearing at the seams in my heart.

"He told me he wasn't going to let her down like that. He kept telling me that he won't let her be the first to die. I didn't think he would kill himself, but he did."

She gasps but still doesn't comment on it.

"I could've prevented it. If only I had taken him more seriously. If I had told our parents what he told me. If I had spoken to him about it... anything. It doesn't matter, but I know I could've prevented it if I had opened my mouth to my family. Yet I didn't take him seriously enough."

"You couldn't have known."

"I did know. Tell me how 'if one of us is going to die first, it is going to be me' isn't a clear indication."

Chapter 26

"if I can't be close to you, I'll settle for the ghost of you"—Ghost by Justin Bieber

Lily Reyes

Hours have passed since Colin told me about Aiden. I'm still in shock, but it all makes sense now.

It makes sense why Colin sticks around.

He doesn't want to help me out of this hole of darkness for my sake, but because he thinks it might cleanse his soul. That it might cleanse his subconscious for letting his brother commit suicide when he could've prevented it.

Forgive me, Aiden. It makes sense now.

I still don't think Colin could've kept Aiden from committing. I understand he might feel guilty for not opening his mouth about it, for not taking his brother's words more seriously.

But this is just one more reason why Colin shouldn't stick around me much longer.

He will fail again.

He will feel like he failed me, Aiden, himself all over again when I die.

I can't allow Colin to destroy himself like that. I can't keep being around him, allow him to show me a good time.

I don't want to see Colin hurting. And he will get hurt.

Yet at the same time, I can't stay away from him. I want him around at all times. I want to be with him, be in his presence. I want to talk to him all day long, even when I don't have the strength to speak anymore.

With Colin, I don't even have to speak. He's great at creating this comfortable silence to give me space.

And he makes me feel safe. He makes me feel good, gives me

hope again.

Regardless, it won't last. The happiness, the feeling of safety… it won't last. He won't stick around forever. He'll leave as soon as he successfully convinced me to stay alive.

And yet I'm thinking what if not? What if he'll stay? What if all those kisses he's given me recently mean more than just… kisses? What if there could be more to us, and we never got to explore it because I died?

Fuck you, Colin. Fuck you for fucking with my head.

"*Mi sol*," Colin's voice comes through to me, so gentle and sweet. My heart smiles. "The puzzle's not done yet." *Right.*

I still have no idea what my new nickname means. He could be insulting me for all I know.

"Why did you want me to stay here?" I look through the tons of green puzzle pieces.

"Had to keep an eye on you."

"I would've been fine at the dorms."

"No, you wouldn't have been, Lilybug." He sighs heavily. "At least here I can look out for you. I can make sure you're not hurting yourself. And I get to kiss you all the time, so that's a bonus as well."

"You can stop doing that. The kissing, I mean." *Please don't.*

"No can do, *mi sol*. I'm addicted." Colin falls back against the sofa, holding his hand to his heart. He's looking at me with those mesmerizing blue eyes with nothing but happiness in them. There's a warmth in his eyes, a spark.

And then, as if the thought of my lips goes off like a bomb in his mind, Colin sits back up and pulls me in. His hands are on my jaw, cupping my face as his lips press to mine.

It's nothing heated. No tongue. No lust. But it's sweet, sensual, loving. It's passionate, yet soft and gentle.

His kisses feel like feathers, but they weigh so much more.

His kisses warm up my chest, make my stomach fill with *dragonflies*. It's the best, yet also the worst feeling in the world.

The best because I love feeling his lips on mine. I love the effect it has on my heart, even if it scares me. It feels natural. It feels like this is supposed to be. It feels right.

The worst because it scares me. His kisses scare me. I get lost in them because they're captivating. Mesmerizing, powerful, strong. He's got me hooked, making me lose my sanity.

And just like that, like my body is being controlled by a switch, I no longer have the strength to even puzzle.

Once the thought of Colin being heartbroken over my loss—*not because he lost me but because he failed again*—settles in, and the anxiety I get from his kisses… I'm no longer even remotely strong enough to do a simple task.

I can feel my heart break. I can feel the strength leave my body. I can feel the emptiness creep up on me once again.

My hands begin to shake, dropping the puzzle piece I used to hold between my fingers.

Everything turns gray. The puzzle no longer has color to it. It's now gray and empty. Colin's blue eyes, the ones I've learned to love, they're gray and empty. His cheeks no longer have a slight touch of pink to them. No, he's pale. He's as dull as my world. Everything is painted gray. Like an old—*mute*—black and white movie.

"Lily?" I can see his mouth moving, but I don't hear a sound. He repeats it, again and again. But I don't hear him.

His hands take mine. His heat rolls over my skin, spreading through my body. He's warming me. His touch is comforting, but it's not repainting my world with colors.

It stays gray. Everything stays gray.

"What's happening?" His voice is muffled. He is so far away. endlessly far gone. Yet I see him sitting in front of me. His face so pale, so lifeless, so worried. *He is worried.*

He speaks again but I can't hear it. He envelopes my face with his hands again, forcing my eyes to look into his. *I'm looking at you, Colin.*

I can feel his touch. I can feel every part of my body his hands come in contact with. It sings. Burns. Everything is burning.

Nine Days

My heart hurts. It's hurting so much. Why does everything always have to be so painful?

"Lily." I still hear no sounds, only muffles. It's so quiet. But he speaks. I can *feel* my name roll over his lips. I can feel everything. Feel his worry, his angst. I feel his hands shake when they're touching me. I feel his eyes on me. I feel his breath on my skin when he moves his face closer to mine.

Chapter 27

"she has the power to save you, the only one who's got enough of you to break you"—She by Jake Scott

Colin Carter

Her body is shaking. It's even worse than it was when she was late for class. She doesn't listen to me. I think she's trying to, but it's like Lily isn't even inside her own body right now.

"Lily," I repeat for the fifth time. Still no reaction. Her eyes are on mine, but she doesn't respond.

Her breathing seems to be normal, maybe a bit faster than usual but not as bad as it was the other day.

Lily's hands are cold when I hold them—she is cold. It's like holding the hands of a corpse in mine. If she wasn't breathing, I would assume she just died on me.

"I'm taking you upstairs, okay?" I feel the need to tell her what I'm doing. I don't want her to panic just because I'm picking her up. If she's conscious, I think she will appreciate me talking to her. "You're okay, sweetheart."

I don't know if she really is. I'm not sure if I told her she is for her, or for my sake.

She has to be okay. I can't lose her. Not yet, not this Friday, not ever.

Lifting Lily off the sofa, I carry her upstairs, calling out for Aaron in hopes he might know what the hell is going on. Maybe this happened before, and he was around when it did.

"Aaron!" I repeat half-way up the stairs. It's only ten in the morning, he's still asleep but I don't care. I believe he won't care either once he sees his sister motionless in my arms.

Though, she's not too motionless. I can feel her fingers pressing into my nape. Additionally, her head isn't hanging low, so she does still have some kind of control over her body.

Aaron's room door swings open. The angry look on his face quickly vanishes when he sees Lily in my arms. "What… what is going on?"

He holds his bedroom door open, indicating for me to carry her inside. I would've preferred to take her to *my* room, but his will do.

"I don't know what happened," I say, my voice filled with concern. "She just started trembling and stopped acknowledging her surroundings. I'm not even sure if she can hear us. She's not responding, not reacting. She's not doing anything." Gently easing Lily into Aaron's bed, I allow myself a second to panic before snapping back into protection mode.

"Has this ever happened before?" I ask, coming off a little snappier than intended.

"I don't know."

"What do you mean you don't know?!"

"I'm not exactly familiar with her condition. I've never asked if she takes any medication. She's depressed, that much I know. So I always assumed she's taking antidepressants, but how the hell would I know if she's ever done… *this*?" He points over to his sister, who's currently lying on his bed. Her eyes are still on me, which tells me that she's here with us.

Groaning, I rake my hands through my hair. *What do I do?*

"Does your father know?" I ask in a rush. Aaron shrugs. "Call him." It's not a question, it's a command.

"Maybe we should take her to a hospital?"

I look over to Lily. Her eyes are wider than before. She's scared. It breaks my fucking heart. I know she doesn't want to go to a hospital. They would figure out what this is about faster than anything, especially with Aaron there.

Aaron would tell the doctors that his sister is depressed and now "she's doing this". Maybe that would be the right thing to do. Perhaps even the only thing we should be doing. But I can't betray Lily like that. Can I?

But what if her condition has nothing to do with her mental health? What if this is some kind of other illness that hasn't been diagnosed yet?

"She doesn't like hospitals," I inform Aaron. Not sure if that's a lie or not. "She's afraid of them. You can't do that to her."

"Are you kidding me?" He laughs, once. "Fucking look at her!" I regret calling for his help.

I'm looking at her.

I can't blame Aaron for freaking out on me. This is his sister. She looks pale. Emotionless. *Dead.* She's even as cold as a corpse. But I know she's alive. She's breathing, and she can hear us talking, I suppose.

"Carter, she can't die on me," Aaron says, his voice breaking. It's barely a whisper. I don't think I've ever heard him speak with so much pain in his voice.

He takes a seat on the bed, right next to Lily. Looking down at her pale face, he brushes a few strands of hair out of it, tugging them behind her ear.

I'm filled with guilt. Aaron should know about Lily's plans, he should know she's not doing alright at all.

"She can't die, Colin," he repeats. "I've never been the best brother, but she's all I have left from my mother. And even if that wasn't a reason, she's the other half of me. If she dies, I don't think I could get through this."

For some reasons, I know exactly how he feels. I felt the same when Aiden died. Or when I had to learn that my sister is dying. I didn't want to accept it. I felt as though the whole world was crashing down on me.

I still feel like that sometimes, but Lily makes it better.

And Aaron's her twin… that's a whole different kind of bond. A whole other pain.

"She's not dying."

"She looks dead." Normally I would hit him for saying that, but she does look exhausted. I think dead fits it pretty well.

Though I'm not sure what the hell is happening to Lily, I feel

Nine Days

like she just needs some rest. She did say she was exhausted. I didn't think it would ever get to this point of exhaustion, but what do I know?

"I'm calling an ambulance." Aaron is about to get up from the bed when Lily wraps her hand around his wrist. She shakes her head ever so slightly when he looks at her. It's so weak—she is so weak. "Lily..." before he gets to finish his sentence, Lily's eyes fall shut.

Another wave of panic streams through me. With her eyes no longer open, it's way harder to figure out if she's here with us. The only source Aaron and I have is her breathing, the way her chest lifts and falls with every single inhale and exhale.

"Colin," Aaron speaks, "it did happen before. She was fourteen then. It was the scariest day of my life." His eyes remain on Lily, and yet I can tell he's serious. "At least I think that's what it is."

"How did... *this* come to an end?"

"I'm not sure, our father made me stay with Ana. An hour later he came back from my room, where he kept Lily, and told me she'll be fine and that she's just in shock." *Shock?*

Suddenly I'm wondering if I'm the cause of this, of her unconsciousness.

"I'll call my father. Will you stay with her?"

"I wouldn't move a muscle, Aaron."

The second Aaron walks out of the room, I'm next to Lily again, holding her hand in mine. She's not opening her eyes, doesn't even react one bit to my touch.

For my own sanity I'm telling myself that she's asleep. I keep telling myself that she's alright. She's just exhausted, needs a good, refreshing, and long sleep.

I'm not sure how much time passes until Aaron comes back. He's still on the phone, talking to his father. At least Aaron looks... relieved?

"I'll put you on speaker, Dad. Lily's asleep, as far as I can tell." Removing the phone from his ear, Aaron presses the speaker button. "Colin is here as well."

"Colin?" Emerson's voice comes through the phone. "What did you do to my daughter?"

I'm a bit startled. "Nothing. We were puzzling and then—"

"I'm kidding, son." A slight chuckle comes through. "Lily will be alright," he reassures me, I think. "It's a temporary reaction caused by anxiety. Just, at least one of you, stay with her for a little while so she's not alone. Let her sleep it off, and don't let her attend classes tomorrow. I think she should take a day off to regain strength."

"Dad, I don't think either of us is going to leave her," Aaron responds with no hesitation whatsoever.

"Good," Emerson says, sighing. "If either of you boys hurts my Lily..."

"Dad, have I ever intentionally hurt Lily?"

"You best believe you did."

With a dropped jaw, Aaron's eyes meet mine like he expects me to disagree.

"And Colin? I didn't get to threaten you yesterday, but I think you might have a second for me to do so, am I right?" I'm not even sure that's a real question at this point.

With Aaron's eyes still on me, I say, "Sure, go ahead."

Emerson snickers, kind of like he wasn't expecting me to let him.

I used to be so rude at all times, not to him but almost to everyone else. I never would've let anyone threaten me.

But I guess ever since Lily came along, it all doesn't matter anymore. Suddenly a father threatening me seems about right.

♥ ♥ ♥ ♥ ♥ ♥ ♥ ♥

"What are you doing here?" Grey asks when I storm into his bedroom only an hour after Emerson Marsh threatened to murder me if I let anything happen to his precious daughter. I would've gotten here earlier but I had to get Sergeant Froggo from Lily's dorm room and give it to her.

Not going to lie, I was about to tell Emerson that I would protect Lily with all that I have, but I'm not going to risk this family hating me any more than they will—that is *if* Lily will die. Though I doubt that'll happen.

Once they figure out, I knew about it, and I didn't open my mouth… even Aaron will hate me.

"We need to talk," I tell Grey. Yes, I did come back here for advice. Grey is the safest person to speak to. "Like, in private. It's important."

It's not that I don't trust Aaron. I would give my life for my best friend, but Grey is easier to talk to. He has a clearer head, doesn't judge, come to think it's good that he's a psych major.

And Miles… well, he has plenty problems of his own. No need for me to add more to it.

"You do see Izan here, right?" Grey asks.

I nod. "It's about Lily. I wouldn't come and interrupt if it wasn't important, Grey. I guess it could wait another day, but then, I really don't have much time left."

Izan's attention is suddenly on me. I don't know him very well, but what I do know is that his mother is a shrink. Maybe letting him hear all this isn't too much of a good idea.

"Is it life-threatening?"

Is it? I chuckle to myself. "I'd say so, yes."

"I'll leave." Izan gets up from the bed.

"I'm really sorry, Izan. I promise I'll cook for you on, I don't know, Saturday?"

That earns me, not only one but two snorts. "I'll hold you up for it once you've learned how to cook."

Fair enough. The only one of us who can cook is Miles.

He walks over to Grey to kiss him goodbye, and then I watch him leave, closing the door behind him.

Once the door is closed, I climb onto Grey's bed—like we're some teenage girls at a slumber party, about to reveal some deep dark secrets.

He laughs and lifts the blanket, offering me to slip underneath.

And since he offers it so nicely, I do.

"You're so weird sometimes." Grey shakes his head.

"That's alright with me," I say. "I need momma Grey for a moment."

"Oh, that serious, huh?" All of his amusement gone.

As much as I hate that I left Lily back at home with Aaron, I really need some advice. And since she's asleep, I might as well go and get it now.

"It's about Lily." *Okay, this is harder than I thought it would be*. Also, I mentioned this about.

"Look, you've only known each other for a little while. Maybe you shouldn't propose yet. I know you've never been in love—"

I cut him off before this gets silly. "She wants to die."

Grey inhales sharply, blinking a couple of times, waiting for me to say that I'm kidding. I wish I was, but unfortunately, it's the truth.

It does feel good to say it though. It feels good to finally tell someone about that one thing that has been killing me for nine days now.

"Colin, I'll need more information than that."

I know he does, but it's really difficult to speak about her when I promised I wouldn't say a word to anyone.

"I've known for a while…" and then I tell him everything. I tell him what I've read her notebook when I found it. I tell him the reason why I needed to give it back to her so desperately. Why I'm actually spending nine days showing her "the world"—that not being bet reasons. Why I can't let her live on her own right now. How I promised her I wouldn't say a word, as well as the reason why I *need* her to stay alive.

"Well, fuck." He's in shock, still processing all the information I've just given him. I wish I could say this feeling of shock will get lighter, but it won't. Not for me anyway.

I bob my head.

"You need to tell Aaron."

"I can't, Grey." Desperation rushes through my body. *That's*

Nine Days

why I came to talk to you. "I promised I wouldn't."

"So you're going to see what happens?" Even though Grey doesn't know Lily very well—or at all really—he seems to be concerned about her. "You have what, three days left? You said she's in some kind of shock right now, what the hell do you think will change?"

And there is it; One question I have no answer to.

What *am* I expecting to change? I can't just magically erase suicidal thoughts from someone's mind, no matter how much time I spend with her. No matter what I'm showing her, how much fun she might have. I can't *heal* her.

Lily needs to *want* to be alive. If she doesn't want to be alive, there's no way I could ever keep her.

"You're not a therapist, Colin. You can't fix her. No one can fix her. You can't just take her on some fun dates and expect her to feel alive, not to the point where she magically *wants* to *be* alive."

I guess he's right. *What was I thinking?*

But I will get her help in about three days.

"She's depressed. Lily is *suicidal*. Get her the goddamn help she needs. She might not want it, hell, she might hate you for betraying her, but what would you rather be the outcome? The girl you so clearly adore and obsess over being dead, or her getting better thanks to professional help?"

"She can't hate me, Grey."

He sighs and puts his hand on mine. I really do feel like some teenager talking to his mother about his first love and some broken hearts. It's ridiculous, really. I wish this was about some heartbreak and not Lily's death.

"She will hate you," he says, straight forward, no soothingly removing the band-aid. "But she'll get the help she needs. She might even start to realize you've done it for her own good. And then, if you're lucky, maybe she won't hate you as much as you might think."

"Lily would cut me off completely," I say, feeling my throat clog up. I feel like I can't breathe, but I know air is getting into my lungs.

"She might. But at least she would be alive."

"It's not that easy, Grey." I know Grey is right. I know I should get her help. It doesn't matter that Lily will hate me for getting her help, she needs it. Providing Lily with help is more important than avoiding her hatred. *She would be alive… but she would hate me.*

I want her alive, but I also want her to like me.

And in three days, I can always say Aaron somehow found out and got her the help. I'm planning on telling him in three days anyway, and then…

God, it'll all end with Lily hating me.

Chapter 28

"there were fires burnin' and my hands learning to paint with passion"—Charing Stars by Alesso, Marshmello, James Bay

Colin Carter

It's officially day seven, which means I only have two more days left... and today. But that doesn't matter, not right now at least.

Lily is much stronger today. Not one hundred percent back to her (more or less) joyful self, but she's doing better.

After my talk with Grey yesterday, I decided to do something really, *really* stupid. Maybe it's not that stupid. I don't think it is.

Okay, maybe it is. Doesn't mean I regret it though. Now I'm just hoping Lily won't see it earlier than necessary.

"How are you feeling?" I ask when I walk into my bedroom, carrying a tray with food and a glass of water. Miles cooked, not me.

Lily starts to laugh when she sees me, or the tray, or both combined. "That's sweet, but I'm not hungry."

I bet she just doesn't want to let go of her precious frog. She snuggled up to Sergeant Froggo all night, when instead she could have snuggled up to me. *Can't believe that frog is better than me.*

"That wasn't my question, Lilybug." I set the tray down on the nightstand, taking the glass of water and handing it to her. "Drink," I order.

She hasn't been getting much liquid into her body yesterday. She's been asleep all day and night, mostly anyway. I woke her up a couple of times so she would take at least one sip of water... and eat a piece of bread for that matter. I couldn't let her eat and drink nothing at all, not all day long. So despite hating to wake her up for that, I've done it anyway.

Nine Days

She seemed glad about it. At least she didn't wake up with a major headache this morning. Though, she was starving.

"How was your day?" she asks, still ignoring my previous question.

"Without you? Lonely," I answer. "But now that we're reunited, I'm feeling much better."

"You're so weird sometimes." Chuckling, Lily takes the glass, taking a couple of sips before she hands it back to me. "Your hair is wet."

"It's still raining," I let her know. "Just hope my hair will dry before I have to leave for practice. I'd rather not have frozen hair."

"I don't think your hair would freeze, but just in case, why don't you blow-dry it?"

"I don't even know if I own a hair dryer. And if I do, I'm sure I have no idea how to work it."

Next thing I know, we're in my en-suite bathroom and Lily is blow-drying my hair. Usually I'd find it weird if someone were to do anything to my hair, but it's different with Lily. Every single touch of hers is wanted—even if she's just blow-drying my hair.

But of course I can't let her dry my hair without messing with her. I have to sit on a closed toilet so that she can reach the top of my head properly, so might as well mess with her a tiny bit.

Tracing my fingers up her smooth legs, I can feel her shiver. She tries to hide her goosebumps by moving around, avoiding my touch, but she's always near me, right there for me to touch her.

I love that she's not wearing any pants, thinking the t-shirt she's wearing would be enough. It's more than enough for spending her day in my bed, I would prefer her naked with me buried deep inside of her, but I'll take half-naked, hair-drying Lily as well.

Actually, I'll take any Liliana Heaven Reyes.

Well, if it's my Lilybug. I only want—*need*—this one. The one who's currently laughing at my hands on her ass while she stands between my legs, drying the front of my hair.

"Lilybug?"

She hums, showing me that she's paying attention.

I know this is a bad idea and I know how displeased my father will be with me when he sees her, but I just can't hold myself back. "Come to practice with me."

It's not that anyone would really care about Lily being around during practice. My whole team keeps mocking me about her living here already, so might as well give them something else to bully me with. Though, I know they're all glad to see I have a heart, I guess.

My father, he's a difficult guy when it comes to hockey— especially when it comes to *his* team. It was a miracle that he gave me five minutes to go talk to Lily the other day. Having her around, distracting me, won't be on the good page of his likes and dislikes.

I know he likes Lily, he told me so himself when we left the house the morning of her birthday.

According to my father, bringing the girl you kind of have a thing for to hockey practice will complicate a lot. I don't see much of a difference to bringing her to a game or bringing her to watch the team practice.

Perhaps he just sees practice as something… private?

Hell, what do I know? I wouldn't even care if he saw it as such.

I can't leave Lily alone for much longer. She's been at the house by herself all day long already. I had a few classes to attend, and neither Aaron nor I allowed her to attend hers today.

Have some mercy on me.

This is a serious situation. I've already had to deal with Grey's disapproving looks when I told him I couldn't tell Aaron. And then when I told him Lily was all by herself back at the house. Surely I won't spend another two hours away from her, leaving her all alone.

"Can't," she says, "I've a lot to do."

"That's a lie and we both know that."

Lily shrugs, smiling. "I didn't attend any of my classes today, I can't just show up at the arena to watch your team practice when I'm 'sick', Colin."

I suppose she has a point.

But my team won't rat her out, so she's fine. And it's not like any professor cares anyway. As long as she hands in her assignments and knows her stuff for tests, she'll be fine.

"I'm taking you to a pumpkin patch after practice," I inform her. "And when we're back home, we'll do some chocolate tasting." She never asked for information about what we're doing today, but I figured telling her is better than continuing to pretend that she wouldn't be spending the next two hours at the arena.

"To how many more weird tastings are you going to drag me to?"

"I bought a bunch of different chocolate bars, even ordered some from different countries. The guys are beyond excited for it."

Another laughter from her follows. "You've invited them?"

"Excuse me?" Aaron's voice comes from the bathroom door. "He didn't need to invite the team, it's an open invitation. Always."

"Shut up, Aaron."

"Is that true?" Lily unplugs the hairdryer and sets it down onto the counter to let it cool.

We're in my en-suite bathroom, not the one down the hall that's accessible for everyone, and yet Lily doesn't question Aaron's presence.

"Kind of," I answer. "We have this group chat. The guys always know exactly where the others are. Plans don't really go lost on each other. They know what we're doing today, so if they want to tag along, they most likely will."

Lily looks at me through the mirror, her mouth standing open in either surprise or shock. Maybe both. "That's like the ultimate stalking."

"Not really. It's voluntary, not a rule or anything. If plans are supposed to stay unsaid, they will," Aaron explains. "The guys always knew when I went off to see Winter."

"Gross."

"Hm… It's weirder when *your* boyfriend sends a text saying he's about to get laid by you and I have to read that text."

And that's my cue to get up and punch Aaron.

Before I can do that, Lily shoots me a warning look. I'm not sure if it's because she knows I'm about to murder her brother, or because she's asking me what the hell this is about. I'm not so good with reading minds.

"Not once did I text that."

And like Lily is waiting for more information, her eyebrows rise as her arms cross over her chest. It's cute when she does that. As though she believes she has some more power when her arms are crossed. It's like an armor.

She doesn't need that armor. This woman could ask me to rob a bank and I would do it for her.

Most likely my father's bank account, but same thing.

"Lily, it's not that deep. We're just having the other's location at all times. You know in case someone sends an *SOS* and doesn't have time to send their location. And the plans just kind of became a thing we do."

"And besides, most of the team knows when tagging along is okay and when it's an absolute dick-move to do," Aaron adds, crossing his arms in front of his chest just like Lily. "Chocolate sounds amazing though, and I bet at least forty percent of the team is in."

I bet so, too.

"I know Grey and Miles are," I say. "Maybe even Brooke."

"Obviously," Aaron responds, chuckling. "It's free chocolate, and a good show because Lily will make you carve a pumpkin and put it on your head."

I eye Lily, waiting for her to laugh and tell me Aaron is kidding. But instead she shrugs pitifully.

He's not fucking joking.

But you know what? Fine. I'll do it. I've survived a fairy costume on ice, I'll survive turning into a pumpkin. I hope.

Chapter 29

"lately I've been feeling not alive but you bring me back to life"-Cloud 9 by Beach Bunny

Lily Reyes

"I have good and bad news," Colin says when he comes walking into the locker room where he left me behind to take a shower.

I could've easily waited outside, but no, Colin refuses to let me do that. So instead, he forced me into the locker room, while his teammates were also present. At least he made them march into the shower room together with him.

The sight of naked Colin—completely naked except for that white towel wrapped around his waist—makes me a little nervous. Though, not as nervous as knowing that when Colin just got out of the shower, twenty-one other hockey players are about to follow.

Colin lets his towel drop to the floor right in front of me, pretending I'm not even here. And the fact that a really hot and very naked hockey player is standing in front of me only makes things worse, makes it feel like it's a million degrees in here.

At least his back is toward me. I don't think I would've survived looking at his chest. More like, his tattoos. Who would have thought I'd ever be into tattoos? Certainly not me.

Oh, the sight of his ass is quite the show as well. Not as intriguing as his bare chest covered in tattoos though.

"We don't have to carry twenty-three pumpkins on our own," he tells me while drying his body. "However, we do need about twelve." That can only mean that more of his teammates decided to tag along for today's plans.

As much as I'd rather spend time with Colin alone, I begin to think that maybe today could be fun. I mean, as far as I know, the guys are fun to have around. Not once did I hear someone complain about spending time with one of the hockey players—well apart from sex rumors about Colin, which also aren't true at all.

"We'll be thirteen in total. Is that okay with you?" Colin turns his head to meet my eyes, yet his body stays in the same position, almost. It has a slight turn to it now, but not enough for me to view his abs. He refuses to turn all the way around, not sure why though. I've seen him naked before, technically there's nothing more to hide from me. Unless he isn't trying to hide his body parts, but something that is on his body... like a tattoo. Or maybe he just thinks it's inappropriate right now—which it is.

"Thirteen of your teammates just so decided to tag along to a pumpkin patch?" I ask. It's amusing, really. I never would've thought thirteen super attractive, massive and... *tough* guys between the ages of eighteen to twenty-two would even consider going to a pumpkin patch. Voluntarily.

"Nine, plus Izan, you, and I, which brings it up to twelve people in total. And Miles asked to bring Brooke, as predicted. So thirteen. They're sharing a pumpkin though."

"So, who are the other six guys?" I'm assuming three of the tag-alongs are Aaron, Miles, and Grey.

"Kaiden, Zac and a bunch of guys you probably never even heard of. They're all nice, have fucked up brains though. Don't worry, you won't even notice they're with us."

I snort a laugh, watching as Colin finally finishes getting dressed and turns to face me.

"That seems unlikely."

"They'll probably challenge you to do dumb stuff, but they know how to have a good time. If you want them to stop annoying you, just threaten them with me. Is that okay?"

"I don't mind. Sounds like a fun evening."

"Are you sure?" Colin sits down beside met. "If you'd rather do something alone with me, I'm happy to ban them from joining."

"I think this is more about you wanting to be alone with me than the other way around."

"Obviously. I'd rather stick my dick inside you without people watching, but I can work with some viewers." I slap him about three times before he starts to laugh. I'm sure me hitting him hurts about not at all. "Seriously, I'm talking about whether or not you have the strength to socialize today."

I want to roll my eyes and scream. Not because Colin cares about me, but because these few words cause my heart to skip a beat. Or two. Or a hundred. I don't know, I feel like this is a dream.

Maybe I'm already dead and Colin is my afterlife.

♥ ♥ ♥ ♥ ♥ ♥ ♥ ♥

"Your head doesn't even fit into it," Wees, so I've heard Colin call him, yells from across the pumpkin patch. Colin holds up his middle finger, flipping Wees off.

We've been here for good an hour and we're still looking for pumpkins. Colin pays. He voted for everyone paying for their own pumpkin, except for me, of course. Colin would never let me pay, even now that it's a new month and I have some extra money.

But because Colin is rather unlucky with Aaron around, he will have to pay for every single pumpkin since going to a pumpkin patch was his idea.

When Colin said he'd pay for mine, he earned a few slaps from his teammates, or friends… and Izan. Not sure why, but I suppose that's what guys do?

From what I've heard from Winter, guys aren't too good with that whole feelings stuff. And often times, if one guy develops feelings for someone, their friends will try to humiliate or make fun of them.

It's sad, truly sad. Love is supposed to be something good, something relieving to know there's this one person that loves you for who you are. That there's a person to call home and be yourself with.

So why would anyone make fun of it?

I don't see anyone making fun of Izan and Grey for being together. Come to think it's a male-female-relationship thing only.

Well, or this team is just afraid of Grey or Izan. I know I am.

Grey hasn't stopped eyeing me every now and then ever since he spotted me at the arena earlier. I know he's aware of Colin and my fake-relationship thing. But it's still odd, the way he watches me, I mean.

"Stop ogling my best friend," Colin whispers as his arms wrap around me from behind. I could swear right before he rests his head on mine, he placed a kiss on top of my head. "You should be in love with me, not Grey."

I chuckle. "Grey has a boyfriend."

"So do you," Colin says. Before I would get the chance to protest, Colin twirls me around, cups my face with his big hands and presses his lips to mine, shutting me up.

This guy does want me dead after all.

"No face eating in public, Cap," speaks Kaiden, tapping his hand to Colin's shoulder a couple of times.

Something seems odd the second Colin looks up and his eyes meet Kaiden's. Suddenly, all of Kaiden's courage leaves his body.

I've seen that happening a few times when someone spoke to Colin—with people that aren't his three idiotic best friends, that is.

"No one ever cared when you did that," Colin utters, his hands sliding down my body until they come to a stop by my waist.

"Yeah, but you should spare Aaron the show. He's about to cry and vomit at the same time."

Trying to hold in my chuckle is almost impossible. The thought of my brother crying because his best friend kisses me occasionally is pretty hilarious.

But then another thought crosses my mind. What if Aaron has other reasons to dislike Colin and me together?

I excuse myself and walk across the pumpkin patch to get to my brother. He's comparing pumpkin sizes together with Grey, Izan, and Miles. Though, Miles barely pays attention as his daughter clings on to him like a tiny monkey.

Brooklyn looks so much like Millie, it's kind of scary. She even wears her blonde hair the same way Millie always used to. In two braids. Though, I suppose that's more an adult's doing than her own. And by the looks of it, most likely Miles's.

When I approach the guys, all of their heads turn to face me at the same time. And Brooklyn, she smiles up at me, yet keeps on hiding behind her father's leg.

"Can we talk for a second?" I ask Aaron. I'm solely speaking to him, yet Grey is watching me with suspicion.

Something in Grey's aura has shifted since the last time he'd seen me. Yesterday morning, Grey was nice, calm, and fun to be around. And today… he seems cold, and as if he's judging me. It's weird.

"Sure." Aaron lays the pumpkin in his hands down before taking a few steps to get away from the other two guys. "What's up?"

Now, how do I phrase this? "I need to ask you something." *That's not the way to go, Lily.*

"Alright?" I can tell he's confused by the way his forehead wrinkles slightly. "Something happened?"

I shake my head. "Why do you hate the idea of Colin and me so much?"

He laughs, just once, one loud *Ha!* "Lily, I don't hate you together," is what I get in response.

"Then why are you so tense all the time? Kaiden said you're about to vomit and cry at the same time just looking at us."

Aaron lays his hand on my shoulder, smiling at me softly.

"I'm happy for you," he says in the softest voice I've ever heard him speak in. "You deserve some happiness, Lily. And it's pretty obvious that this big guy over there is head over heels for you."

Lies, I want to say, luckily, I can stop myself before it slips out.

"How would you know?"

"Are you serious?" He laughs again. "Lily, I know Colin. He's an asshole to everyone that isn't Grey, Miles or me… and you, apparently. It worries me that he might start to cut you off like the dick he is. I don't want to see you hurting, not over some guy. And especially not over my best friend. If he hurts you, I will have to cut him off as well. That would be such a shame. However, I've also never seen him happier this whole time I've known him. I've never witnessed Colin seeing one girl for longer than one night, that is *if* it lasted a night. He moved you in with us in a heartbeat, only because you can't deal with Winter at the moment."

A smile tugs at the corners of my lips. *Stop smiling, Lily.* I hate that my body betrays my head. And I hate that my heart does little jumps.

"He didn't even ask if I was okay with it. He just informed me you'd be staying with us, said if I had any complaints about it, I could move in with Grey and Miles."

Another jump. And those goddamn *dragonflies* in my stomach.

Didn't Colin tell me he *asked* all three of them? It doesn't matter.

"He cried, you know," Aaron says, lowering his tone. I furrow my eyebrows, not understanding what he's talking about. "When he got Kermit—"

"His name is Sergeant Froggo now," I correct. I don't even know why I correct him, I just do.

Aaron's jaw drops slightly, but his open mouth quickly forms into a soft smile. I understand the jaw-drop. It was Aaron naming him after all, and for all those years I've had him, I've never changed the frog's name.

"I see." He presses his lips together, inhaling deeply. "When he got that frog and came back, seeing you half dead lying in his bed—after I figured that's where you'd rather be—I heard him sniffing and saw him wiping away some tears. Not that he'd ever admit it, so I never brought it up. But I know what I saw, and I heard what he said to you. Not a clue what it meant, but you know, probably something lovey-dovey."

Probably something like: "I should have let you go."

Wrapping an arm around my neck, Aaron asks, "What's the actual reason you came to ask me?"

I hate that he knows me well enough to know when I had other intentions. Luckily, he doesn't know me enough to see through my skull and read my mind.

"I thought that maybe…" I trail off, not knowing how to phrase it without making it awkward.

"Finish your sentence, Lily." Bemused, he looks at me with that nasty grin. He knows my assumption; I don't have to phrase it.

"I thought you might… you know… like him."

Aaron laughs, rubbing his knuckles over the top of my head like our dad used to do when we were younger. "I've seen enough of this guy to know I'm not, in *any* possible way, attracted to your boyfriend."

"Too bad." I shrug. "Colin knows how to work… bodies."

Gagging, yet also laughing, Aaron pushes me away, holding his hand to his stomach. "I don't need reminders of what I've seen, Lily. I'm good with fake sleeping while he fucks some chick next to me, if that chick isn't you."

"Wait, what?"

"Can I get my *girlfriend* back?" Colin's voice comes from behind me at the same time as arms wrap around my chest.

♥ ♥ ♥ ♥ ♥ ♥ ♥ ♥

It starts to rain just as we're on our way back to the cars. It's not a light rainfall. No, it's pouring. All of us are soaking wet in seconds. Not a clue where that came from so suddenly, but I like rain.

Maybe I like it a little too much because I stop walking without even noticing. I look at the sky as I let the cold water run down my body.

Something about rain is freeing. Something about the cold water washes away some stress and anxiety of mine. It truly is the most relaxing thing ever. It's easy to tip your head toward the sky and let the raindrops hit your face, shoulders, arms, chest, and heart. And the feeling it comes with—the feeling of relief—it's unimaginably easy to accomplish with some rain.

But what's more of a benefit, tears are almost invisible in it.

I stand in the middle of the parking lot, head held up toward the sky that's crying on me.

Maybe that's why I find rain freeing? It looks like the sky is crying. If the sky can cry and let its frustration out, so can I.

The sky can look so dull, so sad for a moment, and then the next thing you know, the sun is shining in all its glory. Everything is happy and sunny, and so bright. But even the sky has moments of sadness and anger.

Ignoring every single one of the guys as they walk past me, carrying some pretty heavy pumpkins to the cars.

I feel their looks, but I ignore them. Because what matters is that the sky is upset and cries. And although I don't have a particular reason to be upset right now, nor do I feel any kind of sadness for a moment, I still want to feel the cold drops on my skin, savor them.

Headlights turn on, but I ignore those as well. I just want to stand here for a minute, let the rain drop against my chest, open my heart.

"I haven't seen her do this in years," I hear Aaron say. He's watching me, probably with that same soft smile he used to give me back when we were kids and I stopped walking to look at the rain.

"She's done this before?" I think Zac asks.

There's no response, so I'm guess Aaron nods as an answer. But a second later I feel a presence right next to me. At first I assume it's Colin because he's always right beside me, but it's not.

It's Grey.

"Is this any good?" he asks, his tone calming.

"The best feeling in the world." I don't look at him, but I know he's copying the way I stand. His arms open to the sky as he looks up.

When I feel another presence next to me, I'm certain it's Colin. So when I look up and find him standing there, doing the exact same thing Grey and I are doing, I can't help but smile.

Not sure if I should be happy or mad when Colin intertwines our hands and pulls me to him until my back hits his front.

"Lily," he whispers, sounding almost out of breath. It still feels weird when he says my name.

He turns me to face him. My hands find his shoulders almost instantly.

"Tell me what you said to me when I was asleep," I demand, not caring that Grey is still beside us. Colin seems to care though. He eyes Grey, who nods and makes his way over to the other guys. The ones that are waiting inside of the cars because it's pouring.

Colin knows what I'm talking about, and judging by the horror in his eyes, I'm assuming he thinks I've heard him talk. *I wish I did.*

"I didn't hear it, but Aaron did. He told me." He sighs in relief. "Tell me what you said."

He shakes his head, closing his eyes like he's dismissing his own thoughts, his own words.

"Lilybug, you won't understand it."

"Tell me anyway, I want to know."

"*Eres el amor de mi vida, mi sol.*"

Now I'll forever wonder what he said. I bet he won't give me a translation when saying it to my face—in a language I don't even understand—is so difficult for him.

"*Siempre te amaré.*"

I'm not quite sure if that should make me nervous.

"What does it mean?" I find myself asking, leaning my forehead to his as he leans down.

"Can't tell you. At least not yet."

Chapter 30

"wise men say only fools rush in, but I can't help falling in love with you" -Can't Help Falling In Love by Elvis Presley

Lily Reyes

"I have no idea what flavors these are." Colin places a box down onto the coffee table.

The living room is a bit small for ten huge hockey players, and one massive soccer player... and me. Well, maybe the living room itself isn't, but the sofa most definitely is.

We're only five people (Wees, Aaron, Zac, Miles, and I) sitting on the sofa while the others seated themselves on the floor, and it's getting a bit crowded. And well, Brooklyn is fast asleep behind her father.

Colin is still standing, as of now. I'm sure in less than a minute I'm going to be sitting on him instead of a comfortable sofa.

"Chocolate, obviously," Miles states the obvious with some great sarcasm.

"Duh," Kaiden adds to the conversation.

Colin rolls his eyes and takes a deep breath, trying hard not to make some comment about his friends' stupidity.

He takes my hands from my lap, pulling me up to my feet. When I'm about to protest, Colin sits down and as predicted, seats me on his lap.

His arms wrap around my stomach, holding me close to him. "You okay?" he asks quietly so only I can hear.

I yawn, then voice a quick, "Yes."

"Tired?"

I am. I really am. It's only eleven, yet I'm exhausted. If I wasn't excited to see some hockey guys rate chocolate, I for sure would've gone upstairs already. I don't even know what's so exciting about jocks tasting chocolate, but it just is.

"I'm not," I lie, "but thank you for asking."

"Come on, does anyone not know what Hershey's tastes like?" Wees, I'm still not sure if that's his actual name, asks, chuckling. He pulls out a box filled with Hershey bars and sets it down on the coffee table.

"This is a chocolate tasting, Ezra"—I guess it's Ezra then—"we'll try *different* ones. Hershey's should be on the list," one of the other guys says. I have absolutely no idea who's talking. Maybe I should've asked Colin for their names.

Miles rips open the box and then opens up one bar, handing one piece to each person. To our luck, we're exactly twelve people and this Hershey bar contains twelve pieces, so there's no waste at all. Except for the rest of the box, but we're not talking about that. They're closed and will be eaten eventually, I'm sure of it.

On the count of three, we're all eating this one piece. It's nothing new to either of us.

Some of those guys take the tasting part really seriously, savoring the flavor, opening another bar to get yet another try.

"I'll rate it two out of five Oompa Loompa's," I say, starting the rating. If only I had known my rating would have about nine heads from turn toward me like I've insulted someone.

"What the hell is an Oompa-Padoompa?" Zac looks at me with wide eyes, impatiently waiting for an explanation.

"Oompa Loompa," I correct. "From Charlie and the Chocolate Factory?"

"Do we have a chocolate bar from there, too?"

Miles laughs and then covers his mouth. "It's a movie."

"As if none of you have seen it?" I look at Colin, praying he's seen the movie, but when he shrugs instead, I almost fall off him and to the floor. "We'll change that once we're done here."

After the guys rank the chocolate, we move on to the next one. It takes us good thirty minutes to get through the next three options, simply because Colin, Ezra, and Zac take the rating a bit too seriously. They're analyzing each piece to the gods, comparing them to previous ones. If they were only comparing tastes, it would be understandable, but no, they're comparing price to volume and all that.

It's ridiculous but fun... in some ways. I assume Colin does this mainly to make me laugh, and it does make me laugh.

Every time he reaches for another piece and makes those tasting sounds—which, by the way, annoy the hell out of me—I can't help but laugh.

Another half an hour passes, and we're finally down to the last bar. My stomach hurts, protests to try the last bar that's being handed out right now.

I feel like if I were to eat one more piece, I'll explode. The guys seem less like it. In fact, I think they could go on for another hour. I'd love to see how that'd play out.

Something about this last piece of chocolate seems off though. Well, not that it's expired or poisoned... but something tells me that trying this is a bad idea.

When Parker, apparently Wees's best friend, counts down from three, telling us to hurry up because he wants to try it oh so badly, my brain suddenly starts working, trying to figure out what's wrong with this piece of chocolate in my hands.

It isn't until Parker reaches the number three that I realize why this is a bad idea.

"Wait." I wrap my hand around Colin's wrist, stopping him from plopping his piece into his mouth.

His eyebrows draw together, eyes locked on mine as he waits. I'm sure there's even some concern for me drawn over his face, but I ignore that. He should be concerned for himself.

"Lily, this is just the same piece of chocolate we've tried before. Almost the same taste, different brand, but still just chocolate," Zac says. I'm sure he's making fun of me in some ways, but I couldn't care less right now. Especially not when Colin glares at Zac with heat in his eyes, as if he's telling Zac to fuck off.

Taking the piece of chocolate from Colin, I turn to Miles. "Give me the wrapper," I demand, holding my hand out. He picks it up and hands it to me, watching me with as much confusion as everyone else.

I check the wrapper, reading every single word until I find what I'm looking for. It takes me a hot second, but then on the back, written in the tiniest font size I could think of.

"It contains coconut," I mumble, mostly to myself. "Why didn't they write that information right on the front?"

Maybe it's unreasonable to get angry at this, but I do get angry. I know allergies, especially nut allergies, can turn into a matter-of-seconds kind of situation.

How many people with allergies must have eaten this, thinking it's milk chocolate because that's what it says on the front of the wrapper?

And the worst bit, you can't even smell the coconut. Maybe that's also good? Considering that some people just have to smell the product they're allergic to and trigger their allergy.

"You don't like that?"

Ignoring whoever just asked that, I look at Colin, seeing his dumbstruck expression. I want to touch his face, but I doubt that's such a great idea, so instead I stand up, take his hand, and force him to the next bathroom with me.

He doesn't talk, which is unusual because Colin usually speaks a ton when he's around me.

"Are you okay?" I ask, starting to panic. What if it's already too late and his airways are about to clog up and he's going to die? "Can you breathe?"

He nods lightly, so lightly I barely see it.

"Colin, you need to speak to me, please." I don't think I've ever begged someone to speak to me. "Should I call an ambulance?" Fuck it, I might do it anyway, just to be sure he's completely okay.

"You—"

I grab my phone from my back pocket, struggling to unlock it with my Face-ID. Why is it that whenever you're in a rush your phone just doesn't want to cooperate?

"Lily," I hear Colin say, at the same time as water starts running. I think he's washing his hands. Typing in the emergency numbers, I'm about to dial when Colin takes the phone from me. "I'm fine," he says, lifting my chin up so our eyes meet.

A light breeze of air hits my face as he sighs. When he lays his other hand on my face, tracing his thumbs underneath my eyes, only then do I notice tears running down my face.

Why am I crying? *Lord*, what's happening?

"Sweetheart, I'm alright," he speaks softly, calmly. His voice is flat and low but reassuring. "I'm alright," he repeats. I'm not sure if he's trying to convince me or himself.

"You could have died," I mumble, once again, to myself, but of course, he hears it.

Tears continue to slip past my eyes, running down my cheeks. The thought of Colin dying is too absurd, too much to think about, too *painful* to think about.

What would I have done if he ate it? What if he would have died?

The only source of light in my life can't die on me. Colin can't die even if he wanted to. Not ever. Okay, maybe of old age, but even that is almost crossing the line.

I need to get a grip. I can't feel the way I do about Colin, it's not fair to him.

Sure, Colin didn't want me to die right from the start, but this is not about him dying that's bugging me so much. I mean, I don't want him to die, but the pain I feel just thinking about his death… that's what's bugging me.

The way my heart shrinks and my lungs tighten when I think about losing this guy. The way my head starts to hurt, and my eyes begin to water when I think about never seeing him ever again.

"Colin?" I sniff.

"Please stop the tears, *mi sol*, my heart can't take them." He wipes the couple of drops away as quickly as they come, but they keep on coming. "You're breaking my heart, Lilybug. I can't stand to see you cry."

Nine Days

You're breaking my heart by saying these words, Colin.

A knock appears on the door, followed by someone asking, "Everything alright?" I don't recognize the voice, but I'm sure Colin does.

"Yup, all good." Colin talks a bit louder than did before.

"I'll call an ambulance," the guy informs Colin, I guess.

Colin shakes his head but of course his friend can't see through the door. "No, it's alright. I don't need one, Wees."

Oh, Wees, aka Ezra.

"You sure?"

Colin sighs, chuckling slightly. He seems annoyed by people caring about him. That's quite ironic given that this guy cared, and still cares more about me than my mother ever truly has.

As he walks off to open the door and speak to Ezra face-to-face, I use that time to wash my hands, freeing myself from any kind of coconut remains.

"The guys have cleared the room from everything coconut, so you're safe to come out," I hear Wees say, followed by a quiet chuckle from Colin.

"I figured you'd call some more people in and ask them to bring coconuts."

"I was thinking about it," Wees laughs, "just to mess with you. But the risk wasn't worth it."

"I'm alright, Wees, I promise. I didn't smell it, and even if I did, I don't think it would've caused me to die. I don't react to smell, just the intake."

"That means, hottie saved your life." I bet Wees is smiling cockily.

"Her name is Lily."

"Everyone deserves a nickname."

Drying off my hands as a distraction, I try to stay calm before I'd punch Wees in his average-looking face. Okay, who am I kidding? This guy is handsome, and I thought he was nice… before those words left his mouth.

"Lily has one. In fact, I have a few for her. She doesn't need any more, especially none that are based off on her appearance."

In a matter of seconds, Colin reaches out for my hand and pulls me to his side, wrapping an arm around me like he just offered himself to be my own personal shield. Which he is. I know he is. Colin wouldn't let anyone do me wrong.

"Could you tell everyone to go home. I think I need some alone-time. You know, dealing with the fact that I almost died." Colin's grip on my waist tightens, but not in an uncomfortable way, quite the opposite. It's comforting.

Ezra nods. "On your own, with your girl."

"Yeah, she doesn't bother me. Like you said, *my* girl."

My cheeks heat up, feeling as though fire is tingling on my skin. For some reasons my body loves that feeling of fire on my skin now. It happens a lot with Colin around.

As much as I keep telling myself that I can't let Colin get this close to me, that I can't keep hurting him any more than I already did, I can't seem to stop it.

It's like this man is giving me some kind of strength that I never knew was possible to receive. He's not only a light bulb, shining some brightness into the clouded space that is my life. No, he's the whole sun. Giving me light, warmth, helping flowers grow through rainy days.

I don't even notice when Ezra leaves and Colin leads me upstairs into his bedroom. Or I subconsciously crawl into his bed and throw the covers over my body. I'm not even tired.

"*Mi sol*, you should probably change into something more comfortable before going to sleep." I hear him rummage through his closet.

Sending a silent prayer that Colin is about to hand me one of his shirts to sleep in, I allow myself to watch him look through his clothes.

I love his scent. Colin smells like rosewood, and yet the scent that is *Colin* never passes me. He always smells nice, warm, and comforting. I never even knew someone could smell *comforting* until I met him.

Nine Days

Maybe it's some broken piece in my brain that says he smells comforting, but then again, I don't mind it. Colin gives me comfort at all times, even when I don't want him to. Just knowing he is here, not letting me go without a fight, feels right, peaceful.

And as if my prayer has been heard, Colin throws a shirt right in my direction, landing on my head. He laughs, filling my chest with something so familiar with, yet strangely unknown.

I pull it off my head, and the smell of him brings an immediate smile to my face, to my broken and shaken soul.

Not caring that Colin's eyes are on my body, I lay the shirt down in front of me and start to strip off my own. The gasp that rolls over Colin's soft lips when I sit on his bed in just my bra and jeans quickly turns into a low toned groan when my hands reach behind my back, unclasping my bra.

To put up a show for Colin—pretending I'd have no idea he's staring—I stretch. My back arches, my breasts press into the air.

Avoiding Colin's eyes, which I'm sure are more focused on my breasts than my eyes, I pull his shirt over my head, slowly lowering it over my boobs, then pull it down over my stomach a bit quicker.

I wouldn't want to make him believe I did this on purpose.

My eyes follow his body as he walks over to my side of the bed, coming to a halt next to me. Colin removes the blanket from my legs, then gently, yet firmly, tugs on them, causing me to lie on my back.

I don't question him. I wouldn't dare to do so. Colin could do whatever he wanted with me for all I care. Okay, maybe that's a bit exaggerated. But right now, I would let him do anything. Except for maybe bad stuff, like… drug me.

Feeling his warm hands on my body sends another wave of comfort through my veins, just like his laughter had before. To my displeasure, it also leaves me craving him.

My breathing quickens when Colin pushes my shirt up until my stomach is freed again. Anticipating his touch, I'm disappointed when he leans over and plants a kiss to my stomach, then undoes the button of my jeans, pulls down the zipper only to remove my pants from my body. The second my jeans are no longer on me, he tugs on the shirt, covering me up.

Grunting, I roll my eyes at him when I realize he only wants to get my clothes off the bed and isn't about to jump me.

Why do I even care? We're supposed to be friends, and nothing more than that.

He's supposed to try and convince me that I want to stay alive—which we all know won't really work anyway.

We're not supposed to have some kind of friends with benefits arrangement. And yet I'm longing for his touch. Longing for the sweet relief I know he would give me.

"What's that movie called again?" I hear him say but my mind is still elsewhere.

My mind is still focusing on his hands on my body, skimming, gliding, caressing every inch. His lips on mine when our tongues collide. His hips pressing against mine, his erection rubbing against my core right before he leaves me breathless.

"Lilybug?" He sounds amused. *Oh God, have I said all those things out loud?* My eyes meet his and I'm sure my face is turning red when he grins at me knowingly. "The movie? With these chocolate figures."

I can't help my chuckle. "They're not chocolate figures. They're Oompa Loompa's."

"Oompa Loompa, Hoompa Poompa, Chocolate Shooter. It's all the same thing. What's the movie called?"

"Did you just say, 'Chocolate Shooter'?" I laugh, genuinely laugh.

He shrugs. "I might have. Name?"

"Charlie and the Chocolate Factory."

Less than a few minutes later, Colin is in bed with me, holding me close to him when the movie starts to play on his TV.

Chapter 31

"we're on the right side of bad karma"–Rock Bottom by Hailee Steinfeld, DNCE

Colin Carter

Stepping into the kitchen at six in the morning is something I never learned to like.

Until I figured that it can be pleasing.

The second I walk down the stairs, the kitchen coming into view, my eyes land on Lily standing in front of the stove.

She's making breakfast. Again.

I don't remember one day this house smelled like fresh strawberries or bananas, or even just pancakes. But ever since Lily is forced to stay here, she's been making breakfast every morning.

And I'm quick to learn that she loves pancakes. Not the normal ones. No, Lily puts strawberries and bananas in the batter. I think these have become my new favorite kind of pancakes.

To be fair, I didn't even know this was a thing. Apparently it is, but I'm not mad about it.

Though, I might have to tell her she can't make them should Brooke ever be around in the morning.

"Good morning," says Lily in a sleepy tone. I don't think she's been awake for long yet, at least according to her sleepy voice.

She doesn't look at me, just continues to cook as I make my way over to her.

Standing right behind her, I slowly, and ever so gently wrap my arms around her, lowering my head until my mouth is at the same height as her ear. "Good morning, *mi sol*," I whisper, then leave a tender kiss on her temple.

She shivers, but I don't think it's because of my touch. Her skin is cold, she's freezing.

"You should've put on some more clothes before getting down here." Rubbing my hands up and down her arms to bring some warmth to her, she giggles.

"Maybe I wanted you to warm me."

Before I get the chance to answer, my phone vibrates. As much as I hate checking my phone with Lily around, I know I have to.

I pull away from the comfort of Lily and grab my phone from my pocket as I walk over to the kitchen island, taking a seat.

Eira: What are you up to?

Whatever Eira is planning (at six in the morning), it can't be anything good. She never asks what I'm up to.

Colin: About to eat breakfast. ¿Por qué?

Eira: You didn't come home yesterday. Can we do something fun today? I know you have classes and practice, Papá told me. But Colin, I really need you today.

How could I say no to her? Ever.

Eira: And bring Lily. ¡Te quiero, Colin!

Sighing, I fight the urge to groan. Telling Eira that Lily is my girlfriend—which is a total lie, sort of—was the worst thing I've ever done.

Lily doesn't know it yet, but she totally is my girlfriend.

Instead of continuing to text my sister, I decide to call her. It's not only easier, but also, I need to hear her voice before it's too late.

She picks up right away. "*¡Ay, Colin! Es bueno que llames.*" Of course it's good I'm calling. I know Eira prefers calls over texts as well.

"What do you want to do, *enana*?" I ask, having not only Eira's but also Lily's attention.

Joelina Falk

"Does Lily skate? We could go to an ice rink, *quizás*? Oh, we can teach her if she can't skate. That would be fun too!"

Eira's way too excited for someone who's supposed to be bed-bound and can barely even stand on her own anymore. Especially too excited about possibly going skating.

"Hate to burst your bubble, *enana*, she can. But I don't think she'd go. I'll ask her though."

I know for a fact that Lily will turn her head, then frown at me the second the question leaves my mouth. But for Eira's sake, I have to ask.

"Lilybug?" She hums, showing me she's listening. "Eira asked if we could go skating together. Now, I know you don't step on the ice, but—"

"I can't," she interrupts, turning toward me, frowning. A cute, little, and irritated frown. "You know I can't. I know I'll love it, and I can't find back to something I used to love only to leave it behind again in a couple of days."

And those couple of days are less than I'd like. It's the fifth of October today, meaning there are only three days left. Two dedicated to me.

I hear Eira gasp through the phone. She must've heard Lily.

What Lily doesn't know yet; she will step on the ice again. I wouldn't let her die without at least feeling the freedom of what she once loved one last time.

I'm sure if I told Lily why it's so important to me that we go with Eira—*hold on.*

"Can you even go? Eira, you're not that strong anymore," I ask in Spanish, not wanting Lily to ask questions afterward.

"I'm fine, Mr. Nurse. I know you'll hold me up. Mamá doesn't like the idea of me going, but she certainly isn't going to stop me."

She's right and I hate it.

"Lily, I really have to go with her. I have to give Eira that much. I already didn't see her yesterday, so it's the least I could do." *And maybe I should tell you the whole truth… but I can't.*

"You can go, I have classes anyway. Also, it gives me some

time to annoy Aaron for a while, tease him about liking some girl or something."

As intriguing as that sounds, I need Lily to come with me. I know she'll have questions—ones I can't give her answers to—but I need Lily around.

"She has to come, *gigante*. *Please*." Even my sister wants Lily around.

"I need you, Lily." Running my hands through my hair, I let out a soft sigh. "If anything happens, I need you to call 911 for me."

She shoots me a *what-the-fuck* kind of look, silently asking me what that's about. I wish I could tell her, but it would only guilt trip her.

"Eira is a bit clumsy, and she has thin skin, easily breakable bones," I explain, lying. But maybe it's not too much of a lie. She can get hurt so easily.

Eira snorts, knowing very well that I'm not being honest.

"You're such a liar," she blurts out in Spanish. "No cancer talk, got it. Bring her, *por favor*."

♥ ♥ ♥ ♥ ♥ ♥ ♥ ♥

It took a lot of persuading and promises—*and a couple of milkshakes afterward*—but I got Lily to come with me.

Eira is sitting on the stairs to the entrance of the ice rink in New York City. It looks like it's closed today, probably my father's doing. My mother's standing next to Eira, handing her probably six different gloves and a million scarfs.

We all know Eira is easy to break these days, but come on, seriously?

"*¡Ay, hijo!*" my mother shouts when she sees Lily and me exiting the car. "*¡Y sus novia, Lily!*" Suddenly I'm wondering how I was so confused when Lily found out I speak Spanish. My mother doesn't exactly try to hide her Spanish genes.

I suppose neither should I, but I've always found it difficult not to feel judged for it. It's like that one single incident—back in middle school when I used to have an accent and other kids would make fun of me—just completely ruined it for me.

Okay, and apparently, I switch between languages on the phone, even in front of her. Which, not going to lie, threw me off track when Lily told me.

I barely notice when I switch languages. But I do, however, know I don't go around showing off my Spanish genes.

"Take care of your sister, will you?" The concern in her voice doesn't stay unnoticed. I can't blame her, Eira shouldn't be outside anymore. I get that she loves it, that she wants to live but it's simply not possible anymore.

"I wouldn't let anything happen to her, Mamá."

"Good, good. Make sure Eira wears her gloves and stockings, and a helmet, and scarves and—"

"Estaré bien, Mamá," my sister reassures. *"Estoy enferma, no muerta."*

My mother glances at her, as do I. It wasn't funny the first time Eira said this, and it isn't now. It *especially* isn't now.

I hold my hand out for Eira, helping her up. "I can walk, Colin," she says, knowing I would very well carry her inside.

"That's good, otherwise I wouldn't know how you'd want to skate."

As we're standing in front of the ice, Eira can barely wait to get on it. She used to love skating, just like Lily. The difference is, Lily stopped skating because she didn't have the motivation to do it anymore, Eira was forced to by her doctors.

I got Eira one of those cute penguins, little kids use when they learn how to skate. I have no idea why, but this ice rink just loves being extra. So instead of those normal skate helpers, they have penguins.

It doesn't even matter what they look like, it's only for some support. Eira isn't able to skate all she wants; she'll need the help.

"You're a figure skater?" Eira asks, taking in Lily's outfit.

Despite Lily not wanting to come here in the first place, she refused to possibly go skating without wearing one of her costumes. She said something about, if she is going to do this, she'll do it the right way.

I don't really care if she's wearing shorts or jeans… or a figure skating costume. As long as Lily will step on the ice, I will throw a party, silently, anyway.

The smile Lily offers doesn't quite reach her eyes. The sweetest green eyes are filled with pain as she nods just as softly. "Former figure skater. I haven't been skating in years."

"Like me," Eira cheers, grabbing Lily's hand. "I never skated professionally, my father wouldn't let me. But Colin and Aiden used to take me skating a lot."

"My brother used to sneak me into the rink when I wasn't allowed to be there because of hockey practice," Lily says, smiling at the memory.

Eira grins brightly. One of her many talents is bringing smiles to people's faces. Genuine and shiny smiles. Somehow Eira has always managed to grow flowers even when it's storming.

"So come on, Lily, let's skate." Eira pulls on her hand, but Lily doesn't budge. She slightly narrows her eyes and then let's go off of Lily's hand, taking a step back. "Maybe Colin can change your mind more easily than I can."

I place the penguin onto the ice for Eira, helping her get on to it. When I'm sure she's all good, I smile at her warmly and watch as she—slowly and carefully—skates away.

I'd be lying if I said I'm completely chill about it. I'm truly afraid something will happen to Eira in the next couple of *minutes*.

"I can't do this, Colin," I hear Lily whisper.

I turn to look at her, taking her face into my hands, looking deeply into her green eyes.

Chapter 32

"he's gonna save my life like superman"—Hide Away by Daya

Lily Reyes

"Step on the ice, Lilybug," Colin says, never moving his eyes away from me. His voice is strict, demanding.

I don't think he will stop demanding me to start skating until I finally do.

As much as I want to, I just can't. So I tell him. Again.

He's aware that skating played a huge role in my life once upon a time. He doesn't know how big of a role, but I guess he has an idea. However, I put skating to ice when my motivation froze. There's no way I can get back out there without drawing a panic attack out of me.

Skating doesn't scare me. It's merely the fact that I'm afraid I won't like it anymore, or I might like it too much.

I'm afraid skating will come back into my life like I've never put it in the freezer to rot there until I die.

"I can't force you," he says softly. "Do it for yourself, Lilybug. For the little girl that used to love standing on the ice, feeling like she's floating, jumping from cloud to cloud. I know that's what it used to feel like. Freeing. Like you're floating through the sky, above the clouds, reaching for the stars. Do it for the little girl that had big dreams, dreams she shared with her favorite person in the universe. *The* dream that had you on the ice between hockey halves to show the audience—with a huge smile—that skating doesn't require a puck and sticks, goals, and massive guys that try their hardest not to send their opponent into a long-lasting sleep. Think about the little girl that couldn't wait to get back on the ice the second she stepped off of it. The same little girl that would hate herself right about now if she knew her older self put her dreams to rest, buried it under tons of layers of regret, blood, and tears. Make her happy, just this one last time."

I hate him. I do. Why does he have to say smart things when I need him to be stupid?

I'm sure Colin knows this would somehow get to me.

He doesn't even stay for me to yell at him. Colin is running away, skating over to his sister.

The same girl that would hate herself right about now if she knew her older self put her dreams to rest.

He's not wrong.

I hate that he's not wrong. If ten-year-old me learned I would stop skating at the age of nineteen, never starting again either, I would've thrown a tantrum.

I wouldn't have believed it for a second.

Skating was my life. It was what breathed air into my lungs, what would let me forget pain, let me forget that my family wasn't one anymore. It would make me happy, make me smile, laugh.

Apart from bringing out the competitive side in me, skating has taught me how to release frustration. Maybe my coach caused most of the frustration by pushing me over my limits, but that doesn't matter right now.

I'm standing right in front of the ice. It takes one tiny step, and I would be on it. I would feel my feet slip, the blades of my skates glide over the ice in a smooth motion.

Is it possible to forget how to do what you once loved?

What if I forgot how to skate?

That's unlikely, right? My muscles must remember how to do it. They have to. It's all I have left.

Eira is laughing, causing my head to jerk up, my eyes following Colin and Eira as he pulls her after him, skating over the ice so effortlessly.

She says something in Spanish while laughing. And when a cough follows, Colin immediately halts and turns to her, puts his hands on her shoulders, watching her face.

I still don't understand what all this is about, but I no longer think this is just a flu. It has to be something more, otherwise neither Colin nor their mother would react the way they do. Parents and siblings don't usually get so worried about skating unless there is a serious issue.

As much as I want to know the real reason, I won't push Colin to tell me. If he wants me to know, he'll enlighten me.

Then Colin's words come back into my head. *Make her happy, just this one last time.*

Something's seriously wrong with Eira, and I'm here whining about my passion possibly no longer being my passion.

Even if it's not, what do I have to lose? Nothing. And it sure would make child-me a whole lot happier, knowing I died and still did what I loved at least one last time before my death.

Taking a deep breath and clenching my hands into fists, I carefully set one foot onto the slippery ice. My breath is shaky, my heart pounds like I've been running a marathon. I can feel the *thump-thump* through my entire body, being awfully aware of every inch of myself.

I know better than to step on the ice without doing a little push before coming to a stop, but I can't help it right now. I need to do this slowly, ignoring that I might fall right away.

Inhaling one more deep breath and exhaling, my brain turns off, muscle memories activate themselves. And before I even realize it, my left foot—the one that's not on the ice—pushes me away from solid, non-slippery ground, causing both of my feet to glide over the ice.

I don't trip, don't fall. I just glide over the ice. I don't move though, just allow this one push to come to a natural stop.

And when it does, my eyes open slowly, my breathing still shaky, still weak.

I can't feel Colin's eyes on me, but he must've noticed me stepping on here. I'm glad he knows better than to approach me and leave a comment.

When the feeling of me being back on the ice finally settles in, it's like the sunrise I've watched with Colin.

Something inside of me rises, shines, and glows, brings warmth to my chest in the way only Colin ever managed to. It's this kind of warmth that screams comfort, passion, *love*. It's as though my body knows this is what I was supposed to do, where I'm supposed to be.

The feeling of something missing I felt in my heart just a few moments ago completely vanishes. I know I've missed skating. Ever since I gave up on it, I knew I would miss it more than anything. And now that I'm back on it, I realize just how much I've actually missed it.

I wonder how I ever thought that giving up on what I love would help get me through dark times?

How could my body, my own mind, betray me like this?

How could my own thoughts tell me that I didn't want this anymore? That I didn't want to skate anymore, didn't want to pursue my dreams when clearly it's still a part of me?

How could my own mind betray me, when all I ever did was listen and act in its favor? Not once have I done something my head told me not to do.

We were in for a long run with skating until my brain wasn't anymore.

My heart kept yelling for me to go back, put those skates on, and do what I love, but my brain tuned those cries down, left me thinking I didn't want it.

When did I stop listening to what my heart wanted? When did I allow awful thoughts, an *illness*, to come between me and my passion?

I know this is temporary thinking. I know that by the time tomorrow arrives, maybe even in an hour, my depression will get to me again. It will rip me to pieces, *again*. Throw me under the bus like it always has.

But until then... I will—*have to*—make this time count.

With a smile on my face, I allow myself to skate, skate as though I've never once stopped. As though I haven't laid my dreams to ice and let them rot together with my will to live.

It gets even more magical when I remember that I used to be a figure skater, being able to ace jumps and spins. I'm not quite sure I could still pull them off, especially without any warm-ups, but I can try.

Of course, I wouldn't be me if I'd choose the easiest jump I know, or just normal jumping up and seeing if I could even still catch myself. No, instead I decide to go for the Lutz. Skating backward has always been my favorite—it's more exciting, at least to me.

I'm just going to pretend the Lutz isn't one of the hardest jumps for a lot of skaters, and yet I choose to go with it for my first jump after years.

I will break some bones.

Taking off from the back outside edge, I do as I'm supposed to; perform a long glide in a long arc right into the corner of the rink, do everything to get ready to shoot up into the air. I've never been one to take the easy way out—apart from my plan to end my life in a couple of days—so counterrotation it is. I mean, otherwise, it would be more of a Flutz and not a Lutz, anyway.

The jump works out better than expected. I thought I'd end up with broken bones, but I land pretty safely, a bit wobbly maybe, and definitely not as professional-looking as it used to, but at least it felt good.

What I realize now, one only ever starts missing something when you no longer have it. Eventually, that can turn into your new "normal". A life without that one thing, but it's never going to be the same again. You start to forget what it was like, what it felt like with your passion still being in your life. You learn to live without it, and it becomes natural. And then you get it back—if you're lucky enough, that is—and only then do you realize how much you've missed it.

I never want to let skating go ever again.

That's what I was afraid of. Love skating again. Having skating to hold on to. Having skating become a life-savor, again.

Nine Days

Well, at least until my depression makes a reappearance.

It will return. Depression doesn't just leave because you actually do what you used to love for once.

If it was that easy… there's no use talking about it, it's not.

Overcoming depression will never be easy: if overcoming is even a thing. Lord knows it might stay forever.

Turning around, I find Colin and Eira watching me. Eira has a huge grin on her face, as does Colin.

For two whole different reasons.

Eira's smile looks more like an amazed smile. Kind of as if she is fascinated by my jump. Colin, on the contrary, looks proud.

I'm proud of myself. Colin might have given me the push, but I did it. I stepped on the ice because I wanted to.

Hell does that feel good.

"*¡Dios mío!*" Eira shrieks as I skate over to them, approaching her and her brother. "I've never seen someone pull that off in person!"

"I didn't think I could still do it," I reply in all honesty.

As much as I will hate myself for doing this afterward, I fall into Colin's arms, in desperate need of a hug. Not because I sort of pulled off this jump, but because I'm skating.

My eyes want to tear up, but I suppress the urge to cry.

His arms wrap around me immediately. "I'm so proud of you, *mi sol*." I can feel him plant an ever-so-soft kiss on the top of my head. So soft and gentle, it tightens my chest.

"What did you call her?" Eira asks Colin.

I look at her, seeing that her eyes are widened with something that I can't put a label on sparkling in them.

"*Mi sol*," answers Colin with a rather shy but happy smile, cheeks slightly flushed.

"I still have no idea what it means," I tell her. "Care to enlighten me?"

Eira shakes her head. As soon as Colin's words seem to settle in, her jaw drops and only a second later, the corners of her mouth tug into a wide and joyful smile. "Oh, Aiden would love that! He has to be so damn pleased with himself right now. And he'd be proud of you, obviously."

"I suppose."

"Colin, if Aiden was here and he would've heard you say that, he'd be flashing a smile as bright as the Eiffel Tower when it's doing this sparkly thing."

Chapter 33

"I'll take your bad days with your good, walk through the storm, I would. I do it all because I love you" – Unconditionally by Katy Perry

Colin Carter

"Colin always called shotgun, totally forgetting that both of our parents are in the car. He'd get so mad, then refuse to get a milkshake from McDonald's by the end of the day."

Eira is laughing. I don't think she stopped laughing once since we walked into The Retro Diner.

Neither has Lily.

And as it turns out, Lily loves listening to the embarrassing stories my sister keeps telling her about me.

"When we'd be back home, he would throw a tantrum, cry, and throw pillows, breaking anything only because he didn't get a milkshake. You know, the very one *he* refused to get because he was mad for not sitting in the front seat."

Lily continues to laugh with such delight, I kind of wish Eira wasn't here. I want to keep Lily's laughter for myself, and I want to be the reason she's laughing. At least I get to hear it, I guess.

"You okay, *enana*?" I ask when Eira starts to cough from drinking her milkshake way too fast. I'm pretty sure she's not even supposed to drink it. But how could anyone say no to her?

Eira nods. "I'm a bit tired."

"I'm sure you are. We'll take you home after this, or do you want to leave now?"

"No thank you. I'd rather spend more time with you and your *fake* girlfriend."

Lily gasps but doesn't speak.

Before speaking, I take Lily's hand in mine, laying them both down on one of my thighs. "She's not my fake girlfriend. Lily and I are a real couple. She doesn't know it yet, doesn't want to accept it yet, but we are." My eyes find Lily's. Her cheeks are flushed. "Wouldn't you agree, *mi sol*?"

Lily rolls her eyes, but she can't hide that slim smile of hers. I know she wouldn't admit it, but if she wasn't so keen on dying in three days, we would totally have put a label on *us* by now.

Eira winks, her whole face shining brighter than the sun. "You're certainly sure about it." She only says that because of the nickname. "So when you lied to me, you weren't lying?"

"Lily has been mine from the second we met. There were no lies in me telling you she's my girlfriend."

Eira shrieks excitedly. "Yeah, '*mi sol*' doesn't sound like something *not* serious."

I swear, Eira is planning my death as well. Lily has been doing it right from the start, and now Eira is giving her even more fuel.

"Can someone please tell me what that means?" Lily's forehead creases and a groan slips from her throat.

"My sun," Eira translates for me. To my luck, she doesn't tell her the *meaning*.

The meaning is connected to Aiden. To twenty years old Aiden, only one month before he died.

"*If you ever find someone that makes you want to rip your heart out and hand it to that person on a silver platter. If you ever find someone that warms not only your bed but also your heart and soul... hold on to them forever. They're your sun. They're what's bringing light into your life. If they can ease your pain by just being there, lighten your mood, brighten up your days by simply being in your life. Colin, Eira, el o ella es tu sol.*"—he or she is your sun.

"*La amas, ¿verdad?*" Eira asks, clearly aiming her question at me since Lily doesn't speak one bit of Spanish.

I exhale deeply, feeling terribly sorry for Lily because she probably feels completely left out. I'm glad she doesn't understand a thing though. If she did, this would be embarrassing for me.

"Hm-hmm," I hum as a quick response. Eira's smile widens.

"Now, could we stop talking in Spanish? I don't want Lily thinking we're talking about her." But we are… in some ways.

"You know, I can repeat it in English if you'd like?" Eira cocks a brow at me, grinning. Mischievous, that's what she is.

"Drink your milkshake or I'll do it."

Eira grabs her glass in a matter of seconds, shaking her head at me. "You refused to get one. Get yourself a brand new one and don't come for mine."

I could let her have it that way, order myself a milkshake—which I most definitely wouldn't finish because I just don't like them that much anymore—or I could steal my sister's.

Instead of stealing my sister's milkshake, I go with Lily's. Personally, I always preferred strawberry milkshake to chocolate milkshake anyway. It's only convenient to steal hers instead.

Unlike my sister, Lily doesn't complain, much to my displeasure. I kind of like it when she acts all feisty, probably because anything's better than seeing her sad. Not that she's sad right this moment. Lily looks happy… but I know she's pretty good at faking it.

Eira yawns, which tells me that it's about time we leave. She needs the rest. But Eira wouldn't be Eira if she didn't try to pretend as though she's not tired.

"I swear, Colin, it's not even that bad. Just thirty more minutes, then you can take me home."

I hate to say no to her, especially these days, but I'm also aware that she needs to get the rest her body clearly requests. "Fifteen," I offer.

"*Bien. Quince minutos.*"

Eira doesn't fight for another fifteen minutes once the time is over. I don't think I could've said no.

So once those fifteen minutes pass, I pay for the drinks and fries my sister so desperately wanted, and we leave.

♥ ♥ ♥ ♥ ♥ ♥ ♥ ♥

Nine Days

"Okay, you took me skating today, what are we doing tomorrow?" Lily asks just when I walk into my bedroom. She's lying on my bed, reading a book. She doesn't even look up when she speaks.

"Are you cold?" I voice instead of answering her question. Truth is, I have absolutely nothing planned for tomorrow. Tomorrow is day nine, the last day I get with her before I'll find out if she wants to live or if she's going to stick to her plan. Well, I doubt I'll find out tomorrow, probably Friday morning.

Butttt we're not getting there anyway because once tomorrow is over, I will talk to Aaron, and I'm sure Aaron will help me get her some help.

"No, why?"

"You're wearing a skirt and a baggy sweatshirt."

She lowers her book. "It's called fashion, look it up."

"You know what I'd rather do?" I walk over to the bed. Without waiting for an answer, I crawl onto the bed, making my way up until I reach Lily's legs.

In order to watch me, Lily spreads her legs, offering me a view I'd normally enjoy if I didn't have other plans.

"What are you doing?" I can hear her ask when I spread her legs a little further apart and lie down. A gasp that turns into a soft chuckle draws out of her throat when I lift her sweatshirt enough for my head to fit underneath. "Colin?"

Once my head is under her shirt, my head lies on her stomach, pressing my ear to it. "What does it look like I'm doing?" I wrap my arms around her hips, which must be a bit uncomfortable for her to lie on, but that's not my problem.

"You're so weird." She laughs, her hands tracing over my head that's covered with her sweatshirt. Then she shrieks. "Did you just lick my stomach?"

"Yeah. I had to make sure you still taste like mine."

I remove my arms from underneath her, realizing it's even uncomfortable for me. So instead I rest them right under her boobs, just above my head.

"Taste like yours?" She lays her book aside, at least that's what it sounds like. "How does that even make sense?"

I don't provide her with an answer, instead, I hope to distract her by planting some kisses along her stomach and ribs.

"Colin," she speaks. Her back arches the lower I kiss. The second I reach the hem of her skirt, I stop and lift her shirt, crawling out from underneath.

She giggles. "You're crazy."

"Crazy about you, *mi sol*."

She freezes as I crawl up her body until our eyes meet. I can feel her hot breath roll over my skin. Our lips are almost so close together, I can taste her on my tongue.

"Colin," she sighs. "You're not supposed to say things like that, let alone feel that way about me."

Chapter 34

"I fell for you all the way to rock bottom" - 24 Hours by Alexander Stewart

Colin Carter

"We're going to be late for our classes."

Today's classes aren't on my mind at all.

Lily is sitting on the kitchen counter right next to the stove, while I—for once—make breakfast. It's not as fancy as Lily's fruity pancakes, but I'd say it's edible. Don't think there's much to mess up by pouring cereal into a bowl.

"Seriously, Colin. You know what happened the last time I was late. I refuse to have another panic attack."

I set the cereal box down, walk over to Lily, stand between her legs, and lay my hands down on her waist.

"We're not attending today." We're not. I figured since it's the last day I have with her, we'll stay here. I have plans.

Besides, it's not like Lily really needs those classes anymore. I truly doubt she'll change her mind at this point, so it doesn't matter whether or not she's attending. And she'll probably spend the next couple of weeks in a mental hospital, so I'm not even sure she'll graduate even though she *will* be alive.

"I have to. What about my grades?"

I narrow my eyes at her, trying to make sense of her caring about her grades when they won't really matter.

Lily places her hands on my shoulders, one of them slides down over my chest. "Maybe it's good we're staying home. We can do… other stuff."

Smirking, I take her hand from my chest, kiss her knuckles before pressing her hand right against my crotch. "All in for 'other stuff.'"

Nine Days

I'm expecting Lily to make fun of me because she's definitely not good for a man's ego, but she surprises me when instead she traces her fingers along the outlines of my cock, rubbing me through my boxers.

"Are you cold, Colin?" she asks, smirking. "You're not wearing any pants, but you're wearing a shirt."

"It's fashion, look it up," I repeat her answer from yesterday.

"You're hiding something, Carter." Lily reaches for the hem of my shirt, lifting it. I stop her the second she's about to pass my abs. "So I'm right. What are you hiding?"

I choose to remain silent, but I should know better. Lily will find a way to get the truth out of me.

"I love your dress, where did you get it?" I ask, sliding my hands up her thighs, hooking my fingers into the elastic of her panties. With a bit of a strengthened pull, I manage to remove them, sliding them down her silky soft legs.

I keep her panties tugged in my fist, using my other hand to trace along the inside of her thigh.

She gasps, but she knows this is me trying to distract her. As an attempt to distract me just as much, her hand slips into my boxers, wrapping around the length of my dick. Her thumb glides over the tip of my cock, eliciting a groan from my throat.

"Tell me, Carter, what are you hiding?" she says while her lips almost brush mine. "Or do you want me to suck an answer out of you." Her mouth is so close to mine, if I moved even the tiniest bit I'd feel her soft lips, get a taste of the fuel to my addiction.

She strokes me in my boxers, making it harder to breathe. "What's wrong, *baby*? Not so mouthy anymore, are we?"

I want her mouth on mine, shut her up, and fuck her until she forgets her own name. Right. Fucking. Now.

But I won't be the first one to cave.

"You want to kiss me, don't you?" A tease, that's what she is. She moves in closer, but her lips never touch mine. Lily kisses the corner of my mouth, then plants a couple more kisses along my jawline and down my neck.

Her hand pulls away from my cock. With a soft *thud* on the floor, Lily slides off the counter, kneels in front of me. She looks up at me, her gaze filled with lust and something dangerous for me—mischief.

"Where's Aaron?" she asks, hooking her fingers into the elastic of my underwear.

"Early practice," I say in one exhalation.

Grinning, she pulls down my boxers until my erection springs free, her soft hand instantly wraps itself back around my cock.

I inhale sharply when her tongue darts out, past her lips, licking along my dick.

Hissing, my free hand finds her soft blond hair, gripping it firmly, but not to the point where it would hurt.

Lily's still looking up at me, and if I didn't know any better, I'd say she's asking me what to do next.

Then she plants a kiss to my dick before opening her mouth and wraps her lips around the tip of my cock, sucking.

My head tilts back into my neck, my breath growing heavier the deeper Lily takes me.

"Fuck, Lily," I rasp, savoring the warmth of her mouth wrapped around my dick.

She moves so teasingly slow, it's torture. The part of my cock that doesn't fit into her mouth, Lily pumps with her hand, using slow and gentle strokes.

After a couple of torturously slow strokes, Lily moves quicker, her grip around my cock tightens just enough for her touch alone to send me off to see stars.

Pretty sure my groans and grunts get louder when Lily forces as much of my dick into her mouth as possible.

When I think she couldn't surprise me anymore, she does.

Knowing that she's not wearing panties at the moment doesn't exactly help my urge to come.

The last time I felt like coming after a couple of moments when receiving a blowjob, was back in high school. Lily has managed to make me lose my mind.

Nine Days

"Lily, you have to stop," I grit out, pushing her away from my cock and pulling her up onto her feet.

My mouth immediately slams against hers, I'm no longer able to stay away from her lips. With no hesitation, I push my tongue into her mouth, waiting for that all too familiar tiny whispery moan to elicit from her.

And when it comes, that soft sound shoots right into my balls.

"I need you, Colin," she speaks against my lips, her voice hoarse. "I need you inside of me, right now," Lily corrects when I reach my hand down to her pussy, gliding a finger through her folds.

"So impatient, Lilybug." Giving Lily as she wishes, I lift her up and carry her to the kitchen island, sitting her down. She spreads her legs, allowing me to stand in between her thighs.

I grab my erection, stroke the tip of my cock through her folds, to coat my dick in her wetness.

With her lips on mine, my hands on her ass, I gently ease inside of her, pushing in piece by piece, watching her face for signs that it hurts. When nothing comes, I feel somewhat relieved.

If there's one thing I refuse to do, it would be hurting Lily. In any possible way.

Once I'm completely inside of her, Lily clutches my shirt in her hands, lifting it up. And although that's the last thing I want right now, I'm not fighting it. I help her take off my shirt, but to my luck, Lily doesn't pay much attention to my body when I start to thrust in and out of her.

She moans my name, leans back on the island, and holds herself up by her arms. "More," she demands, and so she gets what she wants.

Digging the tips of my fingers into the skin over her hips as I hold on to her tightly. I move faster, push into her deeper, rougher.

"Fuck, yeah," she cries out, lying down on the counter, her arms no longer keeping her up.

"You like that?"

She moans out loud in response, bringing a grin to my lips.

One of her hands traces down her body, her fingers finding her clit, rubbing it. Her other hand rests on her covered breast, giving it a squeeze. She's doing all the things I want to do.

But it's hot watching her. Watching as her fingers get covered in her own wetness when she circles her clit just the way it's the most pleasurable for her.

Yet as much as I enjoy watching her, I take over, using my thumb to rub the pad of it over the clit.

I can feel her walls tighten, clenching around my dick. "Let go, sweetheart," I order, looking into her eyes.

She's staring back at me, her mouth forming the perfect "O" as more moans roll over her lips.

"I want you to come with me."

She's panting heavily, so am I. Drops of sweat rolling down our bodies, making it appear as if neither of us took a shower just an hour ago. But fuck it, I'd take a shower every other hour if that meant Lily would blow my mind like this in between.

I only manage to nod, pushing into Lily a bit deeper. And when she comes with my name leaving her mouth, I come inside her, marking her even more as mine as she already is.

♥ ♥ ♥ ♥ ♥ ♥ ♥ ♥

Lily takes a lot longer to shower than I did, so by the time she's coming downstairs, freshly showered, I've already finished my breakfast.

After my shower, I threw on some underwear and sweatpants, which means I'm still shirtless. But it's not like Lily didn't see my new tattoo before.

I know she has, just refused to ask me about it... until now.

"Why did you get a lily tattooed on your chest, right over your heart?" She takes a seat on the barstool next to me.

"I like the meaning, Lilybug."

Lily snorts, not believing me. "What meaning? Purity?"

"Not purity."

Her arms cross. "What kind of other meaning is there?"

"Devotion."

I can hear the sharp intake of breath, but instead of losing her shit like I'm expecting her to, she says, "It doesn't fit your other tattoos."

I shrug. She's right. All of my tattoos lack color, simply because black ink seems to fit me better.

Except for my new one.

It has a couple of green strokes along the petals. The same color of green that I see when I look into Lily's eyes.

All of my tattoos have important meanings though. Important to me, at least. Lily's isn't too unique on that part, and yet somehow it's still the one that means the most to me.

"It fits the mark I have on my heart."

A bit startled, Lily hops off the barstool and stands in front of me, tracing her index finger along the outlines of the lily on my chest.

"We both know you got this tattoo because of me."

"Not even trying to deny that."

"Devotion, huh?" She pauses, inhales deeply before she continues, "You'll regret it, Colin. I mean, you've already committed to it, so there's not much you can do about it anymore. But why did you get it in the first place?"

I blow out some air in a rough sigh.

"I want the truth."

"Cause, *mi sol*, even if you're going to die, I'll always remember you. You'll always be a part of my life, of my heart. Even if *this* ends in pieces of glass, shattered. You've made my life better in a couple of days. You've shone through the layers of fog that clouded me. You *do* have my ultimate loyalty, even after you've died. I couldn't move on from you. I don't even want to. You're all that I am, Lily. I feel like I'm suffocating when you're not around. And when I do breathe, you're in every breath I take. You're everywhere I look, everywhere I go. You're everywhere. And that's how I want it to be."

I add, "I didn't want to get this tattoo after you've already passed. I wanted—needed—you to know that you've got me. You'll always have me."

A tear rolls down her face, one I want to wipe away, but Lily isn't letting me.

"This is crazy," she says, crying. "*You* are crazy."

"Perhaps it is. Perhaps I am. But that doesn't mean you mean any less to me."

"This wasn't supposed to happen!" She takes a couple of steps back. "You weren't supposed to… do this, *feel* this! You were supposed to show me beautiful places, get a couple of good, glowing memories into my head before it's all black for all of eternity."

"Life doesn't always play out the way you want it to. Guess you should know that."

Lily rolls her eyes at me, turning away. She starts to walk toward the stairs, probably to get her stuff and run away. Then she turns around again and starts to speak, "I can't do this, Colin. I can't do *this*—*us* anymore." She takes a deep, shaky breath. "You're hurting the both of us. Unnecessarily."

"It wouldn't hurt you if you didn't feel the same way about me."

My phone chimes just as Lily storms off, muttering something about life and the world being cruel.

I check my phone just in case it's about Eira before I run after Lily.

As I read the message on my screen, my whole world stops for an entire second. I push whatever I feel in my heart aside. Taking a deep breath, I shove my phone into my pocket and run after the woman who owns my heart.

She's in my room, sitting on my bed as she holds her legs tightly to her chest.

"Lily," I say calmly. My eyes wander to my window, watching for a moment as it's pouring. My room is dark from the lack of sun, but it fits everything going on inside of me right now.

"Stop," she cries. "I can't deal with any more cruelty."

Nine Days

I'm two seconds away from losing my shit. And when Lily mutters something under her breath, I can't hold it back any longer.

"Yes, Lily, the world is fucking cruel. It's breaking you down, taking away every good thing you have. It's painful. It's dark. It's making you lose your goddamn mind."

I shake my head and press my lips together. "But it's also bright and filled with joy. It has good things to offer if you fucking let them in." I let out a disbelieving chuckle. "You're living on a floating rock filled with water and you're expecting life to make sense. Well, breaking news: It doesn't make any fucking sense to anyone. Your whole existence doesn't make sense. For all we know, we could be a part of someone's imagination and wouldn't even know it because *this*, our current life, is all we're familiar with. Yet you're here. You're here for a reason, regardless of it maybe not making sense at all. Your reason to be here certainly isn't to die earlier than you're destined to. You have so much more to experience, so much more to see. And you're wanting to throw it away.

"I showed you the world. I threw the fucking world to your feet and you're still complaining about it not being a happy place. It's not a fucking happy place, but you *can* get life to suck a little less if you'd only tried to."

She's crying more than before, and it breaks my heart. Perhaps all I'm saying is all the wrong things, but at this point, it's all I have left to offer.

"I can't get through life on my own, Colin. I can't. I'm not that strong. I'm falling apart at every single *tiny* thing that fights back. I can't keep living, feeling like a broken piece that's never going to be whole again."

"For fuck's sake, Lily!" I say louder than intended, being seconds away from hitting something—*not Lily*—with my fists. "You are not alone!"

"I am."

"Say that again, I dare you."

"I'm alo—"

"YOU HAVE ME!" I yell from the top of my lungs. "You have me. You'll always have me, Liliana Heaven Reyes. You've had me since the day I found you crying in the arena. I've done nothing but to love you all these days. I took you on silly dates. The happiness you've experienced all this time, it wasn't because the places were oh-so magical. You felt alive. You felt *loved*."

"So what? You just played with my heart?" Her eyes are red from crying, her nose too. She sniffles, wiping away tears that I swore I'd never be the reason for.

I run my fingers through my hair in frustration, inhaling a deep breath while looking at the ceiling. For someone who's naturally smart, she comes off as pretty stupid right now. "To hell with that, Lily." My eyes meet hers.

I hate that she's crying. And I hate it even more that I'll have to leave in a few moments. My phone keeps vibrating, and I know that whatever my mother is trying to tell me, it's nothing good anymore.

"I fell in love with you, Lily. I spent eight, or seven, however many days I've actually had with you, trying to make you fall in love with me too."

She opens her mouth to speak but I cut her off before she gets to do so.

"I know I'm fucking selfish. But yeah, there you have it. I love you. Now, go on, break my heart, Lily. I don't care what you do with it, you have it all. Throw it on the streets and let a car run it over, step on it, I really don't care, as long as you're the one breaking me." This time she's not even trying to say something anymore, probably because she's sobbing too much to do so—or because she just refuses to say anything. "Look, I have a second car parked down the road. It's a black BMW, you can use it to get away if you want to. The keys are downstairs. I have to cancel today, not sure if you'd even want to go out anymore anyway. This is going to be so shitty of me, but I have to go."

Chapter 35

"and you don't know how you feel but you're getting real close"—I Need You to Hate Me by JC Stewart

Lily Reyes

It's been hours since Colin left me here all by myself.

He didn't send a single text, didn't care to call me, not that he has to. Yet a quick notice that he's okay, that he reached his destination in one piece would've been nice.

But I can't blame him.

He loves me. That's what he said, straight into my face.

And what did I do? I cried.

No one's ever openly admitted to loving me. Never have I thought my first reaction to that kind of confession would be to cry.

And yet here I am. Hours later and still crying.

Although technically I still had enough time to get ready and attend at least my last few classes for the day, I decided against it. I didn't feel like listening to my professors talking about the film industry—I still don't.

Aaron hasn't come home yet either. It's past four and I know his classes—*at least today's classes*—end shortly after two. So now I'm wondering if they have hockey practice, even though they had one this morning.

Also, why haven't I gone back to the dorms yet? Colin did say I'm free to go. So why do I stick around?

The texts I've allowed myself to send him have stayed unanswered, so I'm not even sure he truly wants me around still.

I go downstairs, Sergeant Froggo tugged in my arms, to get something to eat. My stomach has been growling for something to get inside of it for the past two and a half hours, I just never had the strength to get up.

Just when I reach the last step, the front door opens and Aaron marches inside. He's alone, no signs of Colin whatsoever.

"Are you okay?" he asks when he spots me. His brows draw together, his head tilting slightly as his eyes follow my figure from head to toe and back up. "You look like you haven't slept in days."

I feel like I haven't.

After Colin left, I'm pretty sure I did nothing but roll over in his bed, crying, screaming, messing up my hair.

My eyes must still be puffy from all the crying, not that I ever truly stopped.

"Doing just fine," I lie. It's a really bad lie. I don't even sound convincing, nor do I look like I'm close to being alright.

"Lily, what the hell happened?" Aaron doesn't give me a chance to avoid him. He grabs my wrist, pulls me into the living room where we both take a seat on the couch.

I really don't feel like talking, especially not to Aaron, not about Colin. But maybe Aaron knows more about where Colin's at than I do.

It's truly a surprise to me. I've never been the one to care if someone doesn't respond to my texts, but Colin ignoring each and every single one of them is so… unlike him.

I'm worried. Worried that something happened to him.

Maybe he's gotten in an accident, being too much in his head to concentrate on the road.

"Did you have hockey practice?"

Aaron shakes his head no. "Was out with someone, getting lunch. Practice had been called off a couple of hours ago."

"But you had practice this morning?"

"Nah," he laughs. "I was home for most of it. Didn't leave until nine, when you were in the shower."

Oh, so Colin lied to me about Aaron being at hockey practice. What else did he lie to me about?

"Coach sent a message early this morning, maybe at six, told us we're off for the day—and the rest of the week—because of something going on at home. The guys think it's a divorce, I highly doubt it. I think it's Eira," he tells me. I stare at him with confusion. "Didn't Colin tell you any of this?"

It's my time to shake my head.

"I wasn't sure he would, to be honest. He's definitely at home now. I mean, when it's about Eira, he wouldn't stay away."

"I have no idea where he's at, Ron." I sigh. At least I now know he should be home with his parents and siblings. Still doesn't help the fact that I'm not quite sure if he's okay or not.

"Fight with the boyfriend, huh?" He nudges my side with his elbow. "How bad is it? Do you need me to call your mother?"

I chuckle ironically, almost like a really soft snort. "Aaron, this woman, the one you rarely refer to as *your* mother, she hates me just as much as she hates you."

He freezes. Aaron looks so lost like he has no idea what I'm talking about. And he doesn't because I've never told him any of this.

And so I spend the next thirty minutes telling Aaron every single thing about our birth mother, everything about when she started to dislike me to the last encounter I had with her. He doesn't seem too surprised about it though.

"Dad kept in touch with her, you know."

He did what?

"No, he didn't." There's no way he did.

"He did. Every Sunday, Mom knew you were with us. Remember that day at court when we were asked whom we wanted to stay with? I chose Dad, hoping you would, too. You didn't even choose one, you said both. Dad won custody over me because I said I never wanted to stay with our mother again, but they had shared custody over you."

Does that even make sense? The judge could've chosen for me to stay with my father as well, no?

"I could have chosen both as well, but I didn't. I used to hear our mother talk on the phone, and whenever it was about you, she only ever said cruel things, complaining about your obsession with figure skating when you should be into princesses and whatever she considered girly. I was so mad at her. I've never been surprised that she didn't want to reach out to me."

Why am I just learning about all this now?

"I don't remember a lot from when we were four or five, or younger, but I do remember our mother saying those things in connection with your name. Every single skating lesson you've taken was paid for by Dad. Competition fees, Mom didn't even pay one dollar. Your college tuition, it's all paid by Dad, not one dollar comes from her. Even the private high school we went to, she didn't pay for it. Dad tried to get you out of there for so long, but you always said you liked having both parents in your life. If you had, even just once, said you'd rather stay with Dad, you would have been out of there."

And like I haven't just stopped crying twenty minutes ago, the tears are back.

At least my skin stays hydrated. More or less.

"Lily, you've always been that kind of person to make their life more complicated. I'm not sure why that is, but you have that talent. You come up with the most complex plans instead of just letting life take you where you belong. You came up with a plan to hide the fact that we're twins because God forbid our mother finds out you're in touch with your own brother. When, by the way, by the time you turned eighteen, she couldn't have told you to quit contact with me even if she wanted to. You also tend to think you have to go through life on your own and refuse to get help." *Did Colin mention something?*

"I know you're allowed to skate," he tells me. "I didn't question it when you told me you'd quit skating with a lie. I did question why you'd want to stop though. I was certain it was about your mental health. I don't know what it's like to live with depression. I have no way of knowing what it does to you. I also didn't want to force you to speak about it, so I just let it be and accepted your excuse."

He takes my hand, gives it a light, comforting squeeze. "I know it's getting worse; you're getting worse. No idea how bad, but I know you're not okay. Colin knows, too, otherwise, he wouldn't have insisted on you staying here."

"Wait, did Colin mention something?" I ask, feeling a wave of panic rush through my veins.

"He didn't have to, Lily. I'm disappointed he didn't say anything, but I'm almost ninety-nine percent sure he didn't because you forced him not to."

When I meet his eyes, his are filled with pain, something I've never truly witnessed before. Whenever I thought he was hurt… this tops it.

"I've read your notebook," he admits. Maybe my death will come earlier than expected. "You know when you so desperately wanted it back."

I nod, knowing exactly what he's talking about. which few pages he's talking about.

"At first, I thought it's some kind of writing for a short movie you're working on in class, a screenwriting practice perhaps. It didn't look like one of those scripts though, yet I still didn't think much of it. Until I've come to read the '*Dear Ana*' pages. After we met up, and I was back home, I would start throwing pillows around the house in anger, frustration. I tried to come up with anything that would save you. For the next couple of days, I would still try to figure out how to keep you alive. My only thought was to send you off to a mental hospital and get you the help you need. But I knew that's something you'd hate me for, even if it would possibly save your life," he tells me.

"It wasn't until I noticed Colin getting closer to you, and you guys hanging out daily, Colin skipping practice, that I would finally shove the thought aside. He took you out to try and save your life, didn't he?"

I nod, not being able to speak through my tears.

God, Aaron knew this whole time?

"How many days do you have left?"

"One and a half." My voice is a whisper, weak and broken. I

don't even recognize my own voice.

He closes his eyes, exhales in defeat.

"There's nothing I can do, is there?" he asks with pain in his eyes, even in his voice.

I shake my head, seeing as tears swell in his eyes.

For once I don't feel an ounce of pain.

I should be crying. I should be begging him to help me. I should be feeling bad for him.

But I don't.

All I can feel is… nothing. I feel absolutely nothing at all.

Chapter 36

"and I didn't think it'd go this way; can I please have one more minute"—Heaven's Not Too Far by We Three

Colin Carter

My parents are both seated on Eira's bed as I walk into the room.

My mother holds her hand, her eyes barely open. She's trying her hardest not to cry.

It's what Eira wanted.

"I don't want to die watching you all cry, ¿vale?" Eira said so many times, it's carved right into my brain.

I lied. I lied to Lily when I said my sister is cancer free. She never was. She never had a chance to survive this.

My family knew it though. We had years to prepare for Eira's death. Years to make more memories with her and say goodbye.

But no matter how much time you have to prepare, losing someone you love to death is never not going to hurt.

Eira gives me a weak smile as she spots me by her door. She blinks so slowly, she might as well keep her eyes closed forever any second.

She tries to reach a hand up but is too weak to do so.

I walk over to her, take a seat next to her on the bed as my father frees some space.

Taking Eira's hand in mine, I can feel how close she is to leaving us. She's cold, colder than her hands were yesterday after skating for hours.

"*Gigante*," she says, her voice so weak, so quiet... I barely recognize her.

I wonder if she could already feel it yesterday, that she leaving sooner than we thought.

Nine Days

"*Enana.*"

She giggles, though it's less of a giggle and more of a really heavy breath.

"I printed out a picture for you," she says weakly. "Of me."

I chuckle. "Of course you did."

"You're going to take care of Lily for me, won't you?" She attempts to squeeze my hand.

I shake my head. "I think you're more likely going to have to do that for me."

Eira shakes her head *very* softly. "She'll live."

With a soft smile on her lips, Eira looks at our parents, her breath getting weaker with every second.

I can feel my fucking heartbreaking. I'm so not ready to say goodbye to my sister. I don't think I'll ever be.

I knew this was going to happen. I knew Eira was going to die. But it's only now getting… real.

"*Sin lágrimas.*"

My mother rolls her eyes. "*Vale, lo prometimos, nada de lágrimas.*"

No tears.

The room quiets down just as Eira whispers, "I love you." She takes her last breath, eyes closing… and they never open up again.

♥ ♥ ♥ ♥ ♥ ♥ ♥ ♥ ♥

It's been two days since I've been at home, my childhood home. Two days since I've left Lily in my own house, all by herself.

But two days later also means… it's October 8th. Lily's death day.

I'm certain after what went down on Wednesday, Lily will go through with her original plan, that being her death. And due to the… uh, situation at home, I didn't manage to tell Aaron yet, let alone call someone to get Lily some fucking help.

I haven't answered any of her texts or picked up her calls. To be fair, I also didn't see them until right now, when I finally pick up my phone and see I'm left with only one percent battery.

Truthfully, I had my bets on it being completely dead at this point. How the hell did it last two whole days?

"You're leaving?" My father stands by my bedroom just when I finish getting dressed. He leans against one side of the doorframe, crossing his arms over his chest.

"What else am I supposed to do here? Watch Mamá cry? Listen to another round of you trying to explain to Reece why Eira isn't coming back home anymore?"

My father shakes his head slowly, sighing as he does.

"We knew Eira was going to die, and we all knew it would be pretty soon. Eira wouldn't want me putting my life on hold over her death, not when she was way too excited to go on a new adventure. So staying here for the next week until her funeral is no option," I say.

"The team's been asking why practice is off since Wednesday. I know you didn't tell them about Aiden, but you'll have to say something about Eira. As far as I'm concerned, they all adored her."

I chuckle. "Dad, they loved her. You remember Eira's quinceañera? They went nuts planning it for her." I pause, letting the memory of that day play out in my head. "I'll tell them, just not over the phone."

"I'll keep coaching the team for the rest of the school year. You don't have to be alone when you tell them. That is if you want me to be there with you."

I nod, appreciating his offer.

"Did something happen between you and Lily? The whole hour before you arrived Eira has been hoping you would bring her."

I take a seat on my bed, looking down at the floor. "Dad, Lily is suicidal. She didn't even know Eira was about to die. I felt bad about telling her, was worried that it would somehow guilt trip her."

"I understand," he says as he walks into my room and takes a seat next to me. "You've spent a suspicious amount of time with this girl. I figured something must have been up. Well, either that or you fell in love."

Without having to look up for confirmation, I know my father has a slight smile on his lips. I also don't have to say the word, he knows option two is also the reason.

"I have no idea what to do. Aaron doesn't know about it. I couldn't bring myself to tell him, which is so stupid, I know. I've done the same mistake with Aiden. And now I'm not even sure Lily will be alive when I get back home."

"Colin, Aiden's death wasn't your fault. You were nineteen. Kids that age often joke about death, even when they shouldn't. Of course, you didn't take it seriously, especially knowing that Aiden was the type to say, 'might just die instead of doing this assignment' every time he was doing homework."

I don't answer. Dad has been trying to tell me this for two whole years.

Plugging my phone into my charger, only long enough for me to be able to call someone in case of an emergency on my way home, I skim over a few messages Lily sent me yesterday and the day before.

Lily: Are you okay? You haven't been answering me all day. Please just give me one sign that you're alive. I'm really worried.

Lily: Okay, it's the next morning. Aaron said you'd be with your parents. He mentioned something about Eira. Colin, I'm so sorry…

Lily: I tried calling your house telephone, your dad picked up. He said you made it home in one piece. At least now I know you're alright, physically. My deepest condolences to you and your family. If you need anything… I'm here for you.

"You didn't tell me Lily called yesterday?"

"Well, your sister died, so forgive me for that." I don't think he meant to come across that harsh. "You also didn't tell her you were here, or even just let her know you didn't get into an accident on the road."

He's right. I had plenty of free moments to send her a quick text. But then again, I didn't really think Lily cared, not after the way I left.

"Do you want me to take Reece with me? Give Mamá and you some space?"

Given that my mother hasn't stopped crying since Wednesday, I figured maybe taking Reece home with me will give her at least something less to worry about.

Dad stands up from my bed, taking a few steps toward my door before saying, "No, I think it's good that at least one of your mother's kids is still at home."

He might have a point.

"Colin—" he pauses and turns around "—give Aaron a call and tell him everything there is to know about Lily. You won't be home for another hour. One hour can change everything. Even if you risk losing your best friend, and possibly the woman you love for opening your mouth. Saving her life is more important than risking some hatred."

My father disappears just as quickly as he appeared.

Once he's no longer in sight, I make my way down the hall as well, right to my little brother's room. The only sibling I have left.

His room door is open, it always is. I mean, he is only three.

Reece smiles at me brightly when he spots me watching him from his door. He always smiles. I know eventually his smiles will get less the older he gets, that's how life goes. But for now, his smiles are still present and never seem to run out.

"Eira went to the beach," he tells me, giggling. "Mamá is sad because *enana* left, *gigante*."

Stepping into his room, I sit down beside him on the floor, offering a half-smile. "Very sad."

"Daddy said she visits Aiden now."

I nod, pulling Reece in for a much-needed hug. He doesn't

understand any of what happened yet, nor does he know what happened to Aiden or why he never truly got to know him.

He has only ever seen Aiden in pictures and heard stories.

Again, Reece is three years old, though he turns four very soon, anyway, of course, he doesn't have a clue of what's going on.

"But Eira comes back like you do."

Sighing, I press a kiss to his head, holding him against me just a tiny bit tighter. "Yeah, bud, she'll come back eventually."

Is it cruel to tell a three-year-old his sister died and will never come back again? I think so.

He will understand it eventually, once he's a bit older. But for now, Reece doesn't understand the whole concept of death, so why take his still present happiness from him earlier than necessary?

"Can we go to the park?" he asks, pushing himself out of my grip.

"Tomorrow, alright? I have to go, but I'll be back tomorrow and then we'll spend all day at the park, okay?"

He nods quickly. "And Lilybug?"

If Reece wasn't my younger brother, I'd probably be pissed at him for using the same nickname as me, but I actually find it adorable.

"I'll ask her to come."

Chapter 37

"I'll remind you of the world and it's wonder"-Wait for you by Tom Walker

Colin Carter

Because I'm so good with taking advice, I didn't call Aaron.

Calling him seemed unfitting. Sure, I could've asked where Lily was, if she's still staying at our house, or if she went back to her dorm. But I feared that'd bring up more questions.

At least I sent him a text saying I'd be home in approximately an hour... but that was seventy minutes ago.

I'm standing in front of our house, too anxious to walk inside.

As of now, I have no idea whether Lily is still alive. The second I walk in there, I'll receive an answer to a question I'm not sure I'm ready to get.

When I walk in there and Aaron is devastated, Lily has died. If he's unbothered, she might still be alive, or she hasn't been found yet.

Great, either I'll know she's dead for sure or I'll still be in the dark about it.

After a short moment of hesitation, I take a deep breath, unlock the door, and walk inside.

I can barely keep the air inside my lungs when I notice the wrecked-up state our house is in.

The barstools are lying on the floor in various positions, none of them standing by the kitchen island. Our sofa isn't in its usual position either. It's turned upside down and looks like someone took a hell of a lot of anger out on it. The TV is broken. The screen is now covered with what looks like two to three punch holes. Counter decorations, papers, shards of broken glass are splattered all over the floor. It genuinely looks like this house has been met with a tornado.

"Aaron?" I yell out when I don't see him in the living room.

Silence.

Maybe he didn't hear me, so I call out for him again. This time I hear his bedroom door open, shortly before footsteps sound through the house as he makes his way downstairs.

The second I can get a glimpse of him, my heart shatters.

He looks awful. His shirt is ripped from what looks like being pulled too strongly. His hair is messy and standing in various directions. His eyes are red and puffy, just like his nose and cheeks, his face tear-stained.

I can see his hands ball into fists as he sees me, but he loosens them up soon enough and starts to sob.

His legs begin to tremble, a shaking hand finding to his mouth as he falls to his knees. His shoulders shake as he lets out painful cries.

"She's gone, Colin." His voice is nothing but a whisper.

My heart breaks for the second time in a couple of days, and as shitty as it sounds, this time it hurts even more as to when I watched Eira take her last breath and close her eyes for all of eternity.

"I couldn't keep her," he cries.

I would make my way over to him, but I can't. I'm frozen on the spot. I can't seem to find the strength to move one bit.

"I had this whole plan and she looked right through it," he hiccups. "She left a note for you… it's in your room."

Once the words leave his mouth, I sprint upstairs, leaving Aaron by himself. I'm such a shitty best friend, but I also don't really care at this moment.

My room is just as wretched as the rest of the house. Everything looks upside down. Aaron has been in here, throwing stuff around, breaking my own personal belongings. And the worst bit, I can't even blame him for it.

I find a piece of paper lying on my desk, the only part of my room that doesn't look like I've thrown ten parties in one day.

I pick it up, finding Lily's handwriting.

Joelina Falk

> *I'm so sorry we didn't see each other again.*
> *I'll be where it all started.*
> *Make of it what you will.*
> *Lily*

Great. Not only did I lose Lily as well, but she also made a fucking riddle for me to find her dead body… because seeing her dead body is exactly what I need.

I know I've promised I'd take care of the letters, but never did I truly believe it would come this far. And never did I allow myself to think I'd be the one to make the call.

I don't know what I imagined it would be like, but it wasn't that. Not at all.

I'll be where it all started.

What the hell does that even mean?

There are at least ten different places.

The hospital she was born in (I doubt it's that one); her childhood home, the place where she had to say goodbye to Aaron and her father; the ice rink…

The. Ice. Rink.

The hockey arena is the only place near that would truly connect to anything to her life.

The ice. The place where her passion began. The place where she'll end her life.

I run downstairs. Maybe she isn't dead yet. Maybe if I hurry up and by the time I get there, she's still breathing. I only have to call an ambulance, get her help, pray to God she'll survive.

"What time did Lily leave?" Words rush out of me, faster than ever before. Aaron is still on his knees, crying.

He barely acknowledges me, but I can't blame him for that either.

"I couldn't solve that riddle, Colin," he speaks through sobs.

"I have my bets on the hockey arena. When did she leave?"

Nine Days

His eyes meet mine, breaking my heart all over again. I never thought seeing my best friend heartbroken would hurt me the way it does. I never thought it could punch me in the guts and force me to swallow my own vomit.

"During the night," he says quietly. "We talked and she promised we would get her help first thing this morning. I made her stay in my room with me... but when I woke up, she was gone."

"What the *fuck*, dude!" I have no right to yell, I'm fully aware of it. Yet I can't suppress my urge to do so anyway. "Why didn't you get her help right when you found out!"

I'm praying he doesn't know I knew about her condition. But of course he does. "Because you have room to talk." He scoffs, chuckling ironically. "Why didn't *you*?"

"I had no right to," I answer truthfully. It doesn't even matter if I had the right to or not, I still should've done it. "She was no one to me. I couldn't have cared less if she died or not. I didn't even know she was related to you."

"Well, you got to know her, and you still didn't get her the help she needed."

Fighting about this now won't bring her back either, so instead of saying anything, I walk out the door, sprint to my car, and probably drive like a maniac toward the arena.

I don't look back.

♥ ♥ ♥ ♥ ♥ ♥ ♥ ♥ ♥

The parking lot is empty, completely empty. Except for one car. My BMW. *She's here.*

This is a big arena, she could be anywhere. By the time I find her, she's probably already dead... if she isn't already.

She's not on the ice itself, that much I can tell by just walking inside and having a great view of the ice. It's empty.

This whole arena seems empty, and so much colder than usual.

I go to check the locker room next when it's empty, I check the shower room—also empty. So is the other locker room.

Before I go to check the upper half of the arena, I have one more *seat* to check.

I didn't see blond hair anywhere before, but that doesn't mean she's not lying on the floor somewhere.

Running to the other side of the arena, to the seat I first found Lily two weeks ago, I'm more or less surprised to find a mint green notebook lying on the seat.

The notebook of horror.

The very same that's going to make my heart ache a million times more.

She planted it here. That means I'm too late. Lily just placed the notebook down to keep me occupied so her death is even more guaranteed.

I mean, God forbid me to find her still breathing.

This girl had her death planned out for weeks, I never stood a chance.

I drop myself down on the seat beside the notebook, sliding my hands down my face while letting out a long, pain-filled groan.

Grabbing the notebook, I take a deep breath, slowly opening it. *This book is all I have left of her.*

I wouldn't even be surprised if she didn't leave a letter for me.

Oh God, the letters. I promised I would make sure they'll get to everyone.

That's not what I should worry about right now. I have to read it. Everything.

I have to understand why her mind didn't change… and maybe I'll come across a glimpse of hope she had at least once.

I don't skim over the pages. I read every single one with care.

My heart breaks just a little more with every page I turn, finding out how much pain this woman truly carried inside of her.

By the time I come to the more recent ones, I notice a lack of something.

Letters.

The last one I've come across was dedicated to her mother. That one is good twenty pages back now. Judging from her previous

pattern, she had a new letter every ten to twelve pages.
So where the hell is Aaron's letter?

Dear Colin Baby,

That's new.

they say time heals all wounds...
they were wrong.
As you already know, this is my unalive journey 101.
The book that will break a couple of people's hearts.
At least that's what I told myself.
I told myself that there are at least three people out there who truly love me.
You want to know who these people are?
Yeah, I'm sure you do. But I'm not in a rush right now, so I'll keep you waiting and take my sweet time before telling you.
By the way, no, this isn't your letter. You deserve a better one than this. I still wanted to address this to you.
You left me today.
I'm not sure why, and you're not answering any of my texts or calls.
I'm worried about you.
I'm worried you've gotten into an accident and you're lying somewhere on the side of the road, dying.
I'm worried you'll never come back to me.
I'm worried I'll never see you again.
I was mad when you left me, at least for a short while.
I was so mad because you dropped this huge "I'm in love with you" bomb and then you ran away before I had the chance to respond.

Joelina Falk

I couldn't even say goodbye or tell you to drive safely.

Aaron told me something happened back home, which only increased my worry level.

You didn't tell me what was going on, where you had to go, or why you had to leave in the first place.

It's not that you have to tell me anything, but right in this moment, right after you dropped that bomb on me... I felt like I deserved at least that much of an insight into your head.

Anyway, I can't be mad at you.

A couple of hours after you left, Aaron got home. I was still crying, the very same as I did when you left me.

Of course I couldn't hide my tears from my brother, so we talked.

Or he talked.

You know Aaron, he loves to talk.

My talkative brother has of no importance right now.

Actually, he does.

He knows.

He knew from the day he gave me back this notebook. He read it, just like you did.

Aaron knows of my desire to die.

Now you may think "then why the hell wasn't he trying to get you some help?!"

The same question aims at you, Colin.

Why the hell didn't you get me some help?

I know I made you promise not to.

But you said you loved me, yet you still risked my death so you wouldn't break a promise.

You had the chance to give this book to the counselor anonymously. He would've been forced to speak to me and get me some help. And all that before you

Nine Days

offered those nine days to me.

Before you devoted nine days of your life to me.

Maybe this is wishful thinking...

but I'd like to think you're a little bit selfish when it comes to me.

I'd like to think that you'd rather have me all to yourself or nobody's allowed to have me at all.

That means, if I don't fall in love with you, the way you fell in love with me... you don't want me to be alive, so I don't get the chance to fall in love with anyone else. Anyone who isn't you.

But that'd also mean you fell in love with me way before we even truly knew one another.

Maybe it was love at first sight on your part, but we all know it really wasn't.

Anyway, that might also seem a bit... asshole-like.

You're not an asshole.

You did nothing wrong, Colin.

You did as I asked you to. You didn't get me the help I didn't want. And I'm grateful for that.

Although you might have lost me in exchange for your silence.

Aaron also knew of my depression going deeper than... surface level.

Just like you, he had no idea how to deal with it.

Unlike you, he had no idea how to approach me and ask me what he could do to help me.

You helped me. Or at least tried to.

The past seven days were the most fun days I've had in a very long time.

I'm saying seven days because I'm not sure we can count day one as day one.

Day one: The day I had a panic attack in one of our school's hallways.

You took me home with you, let me meet your siblings, your mother.

Joelina Falk

I have to admit, that was weird for me.
A guy, the hockey team captain, taking me home when he didn't even know me. And I didn't know him either, not in the slightest.
Yet even that day was fun.
Day two: You took me to watch the sunrise. I never liked sunrises, never thought they'd be anything close to miraculously beautiful. Yet you proved me wrong.
Sunrises are amazing.
Day three: Coffee tasting. Hell, that was some fun.
Especially the part when you let your teammates, and friends, drink the cold coffees that you spat in to.
Not only did we find a place, our place, we had tons of fun together. Driving around and tasting coffees.
I never would've thought tasting coffees would be enjoyable.
Day four: we stayed at your parents' house. Over night. I was scared shitless. It was weird, but I was still so excited. After the night before...
I felt like our relationship had shifted.
And you only proved it when you told me to harm you if I felt like harming myself.
The words you said to me... Colin, they were the most pain-filled and most loving words I've ever heard.
"You can have a death wish all you want, but if you're going to hurt yourself, you'll hurt me too."
I hurt you. With every new day.
I didn't know friends wouldn't say things like that. Not a normal friend would offer their skin in exchange for your own.
And you also tried to understand me... You could never imagine how much that meant to me.

Nine Days

Day five: My birthday. You met my mother. You were there when she told me to die.

And what did you make of it?

You took me to a plate-smashing place.

You gave me the chance to let go of my anger, let go of words that hurt me.

When I wished for you to be happy, to find a girlfriend who loves you unconditionally. Someone to be alongside you when I can't be there anymore.

The plate didn't break.

Colin, do you believe in miracles? In the universe sending signs?

What if the plate didn't break because the wish wasn't supposed to be granted?

What if you're not supposed to find a new girlfriend.

Now that sounds awful. I'm sorry.

What if the plate didn't break because the universe was trying to tell me, or us, that there won't be any unconditional love when it's not with me?

Wishful thinking round two?

Also... you were right. I'm totally digging frogs.

Day six: We stayed home because of my panic attack that paralyzed me for a short while.

You know what you did?

You went to get Sergeant Froggo for me, because earlier that day I told you I couldn't sleep without him.

You drove a whole fifteen minutes to the dorms, broke into mine, only to get a stuffed animal for me to be able to sleep.

Day seven: The pumpkin patch. That was something. Not that it was very interesting, but watching a couple of tall as fuck hockey players walk through a pumpkin patch, trying not to step on the tinier ones... it was art. I wish I videotaped that.

Joelina Falk

Carving those pumpkins and rating each one... the laughs that came out of me were unbelievable. God, when Miles almost cried because I rated Eira's mouth better than his. It was incredible.

We don't talk about the chocolate tasting. I refuse to think about almost losing you.

Day eight: Ice skating.

Is there any more to add to this?

I loved it. Every single part of it. The whole three hours the three of us spent playing some games on the ice. Even the part when Eira made me teach you how to do a "not awful-looking" jump.

I'll never forget it.

Thank you for giving this to me.

Day nine: You told me you loved me.

Do we finally get to the three people that I think truly love me?

One being my father. You can imagine why. He's my father, the man who paid for my dreams, my education. He took care of me even when my mother was supposed to do that.

Then there is Aaron. It's self-explanatory. He's my brother. The guy who stuck with me when I thought we weren't allowed to.

The very guy who held my hand when I was too afraid to go to the toilet late at night because it was dark, and we were eight years old.

Yup, I'd say he has some love for me after doing that.

And the third person is you, Colin.

Not only were you the first and only guy to ever say those words to me (apart from Aaron and my father, but you know, it's a different kind of love). You were also the first guy I felt something back for.

You didn't give me the chance to reply, but honestly, even if you had, I probably wouldn't have known what to say.

Nine Days

Colin, you said it yourself. You took me on dates. You loved me in an attempt to save me.

Not saying your love is platonic and solely based on whether or not you managed to keep me alive.

You showed me what love is.

You showed me that I don't have to be alone. That I'm not alone.

Now, I think love needs more time than nine days to properly develop... but our hearts were in a rush. Our days were numbered.

Of course, the love part would try and sneak in way faster.

I'm glad it did.

At least now I've heard it before.

Also, I'm sorry. I'm sorry for leaving the way I did. You deserve better than that.

Colin, I'm not here. I'm not at the arena where you found this notebook (hopefully this is you reading).

Go back home. My body has been taken care of already.

   Lily

How could I possibly not cry after the woman I love basically told me all about how she feels the same in form of a diary entry, without even directly saying it?

And all that while I know this is her goodbye.

Fighting against the urge to skip right to the end to hopefully find the letter that's truly meant for me only, I turn to the next page.

It's empty.

Maybe she just missed a page, it happens.

Not thinking much of it, I turn to the next page.

Empty.

So I turn another, and another, and probably another couple of pages. All of them empty.

I skip to the last page and my heart skips a beat… or two.

Joelina Falk

    Dear Colin Baby,

I told you to go home. There's nothing more to find here.
I never managed to continue writing after day six.
Somewhere along the way you had me thinking I could actually do it. You had me thinking I could live, that maybe life doesn't need to be painless.
When you gave me time to truly think about everything... I concluded that life doesn't have to be perfect, that it doesn't have to be painless...
but I've been too burnt to continue to live anyway.

    Lily

Chapter 38

"What you did boy, I'll never forget"—Wasting All These Tears by Cassadee Pope

Colin Carter

Upon Lily's suggestion—or plea, demand, or whatever else you'd like to call it—I leave.

My BMW is still parked outside of the arena, but I don't care enough to even try to find out why that is. I guess Lily left it here as a sign.

But I can't help thinking about where she died. How she died. Was it painful? Did she jump off a bridge? A building? Did she overdose?

Was she scared?

Not sure why I feel the need to know all that, but I do. And for some reasons my brain has a hard time believing she's truly gone.

For every person who died in my life, I've seen evidence. I've seen their lifeless bodies, I *watched* my sister die.

I watched as Eira's weak smile slowly faded and her last breath drew out of her lungs. I could feel her muscles loosen up. I witnessed the moment she left us.

I may not have seen Aiden die, but I saw his lifeless body. I had proof of his death.

It sort of makes sense that my brain refuses to believe the only woman I've ever loved, the only woman to ever bring light into my life, died.

I drive around the city for a while, not sure how long but probably a few hours. Home is the last place I want to be right now.

When I do finally get back, I'm startled for a second.

The living room, the same that looked like a complete mess a couple of hours ago, is completely tidied up.

Nine Days

The couch is back in its usual place. The floor is cleaner as it has ever been. The barstools are by the kitchen island. Though the TV is still broken. But it's as if the mess I've seen before never happened.

Was I hallucinating? Is that a thing? Hallucinating from anxiety? Hallucinating from fear of having lost the most important person in one's life?

This time I don't call out for Aaron. I can't face him right now. I can't tell him his sister has died. My presence without her would be the confirmation.

Her body wasn't there. She's been taken care of already.

Did Aaron find her? No, that can't be. He would've told me she's dead, right?

What do I know?

I don't care enough to think about this any longer. I'll just be waiting for an announcement from the school that states a student has passed away, and we're all invited to a ceremony to say goodbye, a get-together to grieve.

Can't wait.

Neither of those people deserve to grieve her. Lily's mine, and I was the only one to truly care about her. The only one who valued her life, wanted her.

I head upstairs, needing nothing more but to take a long shower and… cross that. Needing nothing but to crawl into my bed and cry to the smell of Lily that is hopefully still on my bedsheets.

My bedroom is completely tidied up… and some of the clothes Lily left on my floor when I left two days ago are in my laundry basket. This means, either Lily put them away before she passed, or the mess I've seen before wasn't me hallucinating after all.

Either way, that's not of much importance right now.

To my surprise, when I inhale, I'm greeted with a *strong* scent of Lily. It's not even faded. She sure has a strong perfume.

Or she was in here shortly before she left, and her scent just didn't escape this room yet.

But I could swear I didn't smell her this heavily when I entered this room earlier. To be fair, I also didn't pay much attention to the way my room smelled in the hurry I was in.

I look at my perfectly made bed, feeling the sting in my heart, even more so when I see that damn frog on my bed.

Staring at it for a moment, I sigh deeply and walk over to Sergeant Froggo. Although that frog creeps me out, I grab him and press him to my chest as I take a seat on my bed.

God, this frog smells so much like her. I miss her. I miss her so much, it's ridiculous.

When I cross my legs and stare at my door, I notice something on my bed. Something that I'm sure wasn't here before.

My eyebrows draw together as I look at the green envelope with a frog face on it.

In a matter of seconds, I have the envelope in my hands, open it carefully so I wouldn't ruin it. I'll keep this stupid envelope forever.

Taking out a couple of papers, I stare at them for a short while before I find the courage to read.

Dear Colin Baby,

they say time heals all wounds...

they were wrong.

But you know what they don't tell you?

You don't need wounds to heal right away when there's tape.

You didn't heal me, Colin... but you sure held—hold—me together.

You're the medicine that's making pain disappear. You're the antidote to the poison in my life.

I get it, Colin. I finally understand.

Everyone fights demons.

Everyone struggles in their own ways.

When I hit rock bottom, on the verge of giving up... I've been sent someone to—not to show me the most beautiful places—but to remind me that I

Nine Days

don't have to fight my demons on my own.

You know how people tend to give advice but don't practice what they preach? I figured out why that is.

We think we have to fight on our own. That we're a burden to anyone we ask for help.

And yet, we don't think of someone as a burden when we're asked for advice.

In fact, we always give the best advice, yet never find the courage to get some ourselves.

They got their advice, their help. And we're still struggling, thinking we're not worthy of help.

But we are.

My past will always be my past. But that's just where it is.

I will always carry the scars, they'll never fade. But that doesn't mean I have to keep the wounds open.

I have the choice to put some tape over it.

Sure, tape eventually opens back up, but there's always more tape.

Maybe it's not the healthiest way to deal with pain, but it still seals the wound. And who knows, maybe with time they will heal after all.

The kind of wounds I have... they won't disappear.

It's always going to be a part of me, but it's in my hands how much tape I use to cover those open wounds.

Maybe I'll get some stitches, they'll heal eventually.

I want to heal.

I want to tape my past away and move on, become the happiest version of myself as I can be.

I don't have to be happy at all times, I get that now.

I want to be alive, Colin.

Even if you won't stay in my life after this day...

you'll always be the person who saved me. The person who loved me back to life.

The person who showed me that there's happiness in cruelty, that there's light in the darkness.

No matter what will happen between the both of us, please know:

I'll always think highly of you.

You're the only person who ever tried to understand me. The only person who dug deeper and tried to make me happy.

You wanted to understand how I felt, and you tried your very best to accept my feelings rather than tell me they're not valid because I have no reason to feel the way I do.

So, thank you, Colin. For Trying. For being there. For understanding.

Thank. You.

    Lily

I hastily turn each page to hopefully find more. But there's nothing.

"So, they say time heals all wounds, Colin…"—I look up, my breath getting caught in my lungs—"maybe they were right. You taught me that wounds can't heal when I keep stabbing them. Maybe it'll leave a scar, reopen at some point… but all that doesn't matter. It doesn't matter because life is too precious to give it up too early. Just when I thought I've been through with it, when I gave up on life… *you* happened. You threw my whole world upside down and for what? Apparently there's always at least one thing to hold on to. You happen to be mine."

"Lily," I breathe out shakily. I remain seated on the bed, frozen, not knowing whether she's truly here or not.

Lily has a fainted smile on her lips as she walks closer to me. With every step she takes, I stiffen more and more. If this is a dream, I'll hate myself the second I wake up.

Then my mattress dips slightly as she takes a seat right next to me. *This is a very realistic dream.*

Her hands brush my skin, wiping away some of my tears. Her touch is so gentle, it's like this is only the ghost of her. *What if it is?*

Chapter 39

"if I was dying on my knees, you would be the one to rescue me"—Brother by Kodaline

Lily Reyes

Colin is breathing heavily. His hands are shaking and I'm sure he can't figure out if I'm really here or not.

I can't even take it badly. I don't think I would react much differently if I found out the person I loved died and then suddenly they're standing right in front of me.

His eyes are locked with mine, and his muscles tense when I touch him, but he doesn't speak.

It's not very healthy to hold on to a person, to allow one single person to keep you alive, but for now, that's far better than the alternative. I will learn to choose myself as motivation to live. I'll learn that life is more than dark clouds and empty alleys.

Life is… it's snuck-in glances at the people you adore. It's finding the perfect coffee place. It's watching the sun rise in the cold. It's finding sparks in the dark.

Life is finding yang in yin.

"Colin," I finally say. "You can believe this. It's really me."

I'm sure that in about five minutes, maybe ten, I'll have to explain why I let him—unintentionally—believe I've died, but that's not what I should be focusing on right now.

"Lily," he whispers. His voice is filled with so much pain, I could actually start to cry from hearing it.

Then his forehead leans against mine and his eyes close. Colin's arms slowly sneak around my waist, and he pulls me into him. I sit on his lap, straddling him.

His grip tightens, holding me closer, and we stay like this for a short while.

Nine Days

"I need to be able to breathe if you want me alive," I remind him. And the second those words leave my mouth, his arms loosen around my body, and he slowly inches his head away from mine.

"You're here," he says as if he's just realizing it.

Colin takes a deep breath, exhaling shakily but definitely steadier than before.

"You didn't leave, *mi sol*." I'm sure at this point he's more talking to himself than to me, but that's alright.

"I didn't."

Although he's heard me talk, felt me on his skin, his palms find my face again, enveloping it as if to make sure I'm really present.

"You're alive?" he asks, still looking at me as if he doesn't trust himself right now.

"I am, Colin. I'm alive, and I don't plan on dying today, or tomorrow, or for the next years."

A tear slips from his eyes and I quickly wipe it away. He lets out another deep breath then lightly nods his head a couple of times as the realization finally settles in.

"I'm so sorry about Eira, Colin," I say. "If I had known—"

He smiles at me softly, or tries to, then shakes his head. "I knew she would die. It's alright. Eira would kill me if I wasted more tears on her. She was excited to start a new adventure."

"This is a stupid question, but are you okay?"

He looks up at the ceiling for a second, then back into my eyes. "I will be." Then his hands leave my face, but he's not pushing me away. *That's a good sign.* "Why did you let me believe you've died?"

"I didn't know when you'd be back. As much as I love Aaron, we both know he couldn't have convinced me to stay if my mind changed again. When I woke up this morning and I was still going strong with wanting to stay alive, I needed to see my mother. I needed to tell her that she drove me this far. That because of her, because of her actions, I'm way too close to make her wish come true. She didn't even flinch when I told her I wanted to die as much as she wanted me to. All she did was stare at me with this emptiness in her eyes, the same I'm sure I've shown you plenty of times," I tell him.

"Colin, I wasn't sure if I'd come back. I wasn't sure if I'd still be alive after I witnessed my mother still not giving a fuck about me. I could've called Aaron, probably even should have. I should've given him a sign that I'm still alive when he texted and called me a million times after he woke up. But I didn't want to give him hopes that I'd still be alive five minutes later.

"When I left my mother's house, I was mad. I wasn't sad that she didn't care one bit about me. I was *angry*. I went to the arena and planted the notebook there, still unsure of what my outcome would be. I guess, something inside of me knew hesitation was a clear indication for one answer only, so the next thing I know, I found myself in front of a mental hospital. I was sitting on the concrete in front of the building, crying, trying to find the courage to walk inside. And when it finally came… I wanted nothing more but for you to be there with me. For you to hold my hand while these people talked to me and admitted me. They asked me if I wanted to call someone, I said yes, ready to call you. I looked at my phone and saw Aaron was calling, so I picked up. He was yelling at me, but I cut him off and told him where I was," I explain. Colin doesn't react much, all he does is look at me with the tiniest attempt of smile on his lips. A smile I believe to be pride *and* relief.

"I asked one of the women who work there if I could go home today and come back tomorrow because I wanted to be home so I could proudly tell you I'm getting the help I now *want* face-to-face. Of course she said no, granted, she kind of had to be worried given my state so I wasn't too surprised. Aaron told me you were out looking for me, and that's when I panicked because I knew you're not okay, thinking I'm dead and all. After we ended the call I wanted to shoot you a text or call you, but the fucking second I hit call, my battery ran out and I don't have your number memorized, but I thought Aaron would tell you. It took me a while to convince those people to let me go just for a few hours. One of them drove me home to make sure I wouldn't kill myself on my way back, she also talked to Aaron then. Anyway, when I got here, you were still gone and so I wrote that extra letter."

There could've been an easier way, I admit. But I never took the easy way out. "I tried calling you from Aaron's phone, but it went straight to voicemail, even my texts didn't go through, so I'm guessing your phone was dead, too? Anyway, my only other option was to wait here until you finally showed up. I'm sorry." A sob breaks free. "I'm so sorry I made you think I've died. It wasn't my intention, Colin."

Colin wraps his arms back around me, pulling me in for a much-needed hug. I wrap mine around his body as well, lean the side of my head against his.

My heart aches for this man.

"All I've ever wanted was to tell you that I'm getting help. In person. But if my stupid phone hadn't run out, and yours, too, I would've told you a whole lot earlier."

I kind of expect Colin to give me a speech about how fucked up my way of thinking was, but he's not doing that. "I'm so proud of you, my Lilybug." He holds me just that tiny bit closer. "But I have to warn you, you're stuck with me now, *mi sol*. For as long as you'll have me," he whispers and pulls away from the hug.

Tilting my head back for his lips to easily meet with mine, he eases us into a powerful kiss that's still gentle and loving. A kiss so good, it leaves me breathless.

When I pull back, in desperate need for some air, it's my turn to lay my hands on his jawline. Looking deeply into his eyes, I begin to speak again. "I love you, Colin Carter. Truth be told, if it weren't for you, I wouldn't be standing here anymore. You saved me, Colin."

"Sweetheart, I'll save you a million times more if that keeps you by my side." His lips brush mine again, softly. "I'd burn the whole world down if that saved your life." He pauses for a second, then speaks again. "But Lilybug, this wasn't my doing. This was all *you*."

I guess… but for now I'd rather not take the credit.

"Okay, how about we try not to put our lives anywhere near the death-line? I don't think you would survive another heart attack."

He chuckles and presses his lips to my forehead. "Lilybug, we both know I'll have to survive tons of those when I'm with you. Especially with your judgmental Sergeant Froggo in my bed. That frog creeps me out when I wake up at night. I swear he stares right into my soul and debates on murdering me right there."

I laugh. "He's a stuffed animal, dumbass. He won't murder you."

"Did you look at that thing? He's so totally murderous. But if you promise to tell him to let me live, he can stay."

"Deal." When I press my head into the front of his shoulder, Colin rests his chin on the top of my head, caressing my back.

I'm not quite sure when my head started to tell me this is where I'm supposed to be, right in Colin's arms. But I'm glad I finally listened.

I'm glad I finally realized that I don't have to be alone. That there are people willingly holding their hands out to me for support, even if they can't help.

Knowing that I don't have to go through a dark period of time on my own is as much help as I could ever ask for.

Pain comes in all sorts of ways. Some might get hit worse, some less, but there's always pain in life.

The amount of pain doesn't matter, pain stays pain, and it sucks. It will never leave, will always be present.

But it's on us to decide whether or not we'll let it consume us.

Epilogue

"I wouldn't have made it if I didn't have you holding my hand" –Control by Zoe Wees

Colin Carter

Two weeks later

"Five more minutes!" my father yells as I skate past him. It's not like I don't have eyes and couldn't read the scoreboard myself. I guess he just has a great time reminding me of the pressure I'm supposed to be under.

St. Trewery University and Princeton University are playing for a win. As of now the board reads 3-3. However, five minutes can change a lot. In only five minutes, if it goes smoothly, we could possibly score at least one more goal, if extra smoothly, even two or three. *Maybe not three*.

Parker, our goalie, does his best trying to keep the puck away from our net, but Princeton players are ruthless. They play with much more body than any of us.

Hockey is known for its brutality, but these guys are cruel, not brutal.

Parker came in as exchange for Kaiden two minutes ago. Only because Nico Cams, one player of the opponents, decided to almost break Kaiden's arm.

The puck is currently in Grey' possession, and he appears to be winging it.

My guys try to keep the Princeton guys away from Grey as good as only possible. However, their goalie is great. Getting past him turned out to be harder than we have practiced for. It appears Beck got quite the amount of practice in before facing us.

Nine Days

Grey is so close to the goal, almost ready to shoot when one of the Princeton players comes up from behind and presses Grey up against the boards, the puck glides over the ice like it's dancing to a classical song.

Time seems to be frozen when a few players, me included, make their way over to the puck in no time.

Since we're so much closer to the enemy's goal and I made sure to stay close to Grey, it's easy for me to reach the puck first.

Not wasting any more time, I turn to the goal, pick up my pace and shoot for a win.

Thinking back to time freezing when players run up to the puck, it's nothing compared to what I feel now that the puck is so close to a win.

Ten seconds left.

Everything moves in slow-motion. And then finally, *finally*, the puck hits the net, the sound of sirens ringing as a point for St. Trewery adds to the scoreboard.

Another loud siren goes off when the time runs out.

St. Trewery U wins.

I spend a quick moment saying a few words to the other team captain, and then my very cheery team skates off the ice and runs toward the locker room to get ready for interviews.

Everyone but me.

When I exit the ice, I'm greeted by two lovingly green eyes and blond hair. The one person I grew so close to in a matter of no time at all.

She smiles at me so brightly, I can feel heat rushing to my heart.

"Congratulations, dumbass!" Lily screams all excitedly while jumping into my arms. Mind you, I'm still in skates, but I'd gladly fall to the floor for this woman. Even in front of a crowd.

I spin her around as much as I can before setting her down to the floor, then take off my helmet to kiss her. I deserve that.

Lily's lips are still my obsession, my addiction. I'm addicted to her. Maybe that's not too healthy, but I don't give any fucks. This woman owns my body, heart, and soul.

"What are you doing here, *mi sol*?" I ask, completely dumbfounded by her presence when I thought she was at the mental hospital.

I missed her so much. I haven't seen Lily in three whole days. Haven't really touched and kissed her in two weeks.

It was torture. But at least I've got her back now.

"You weren't supposed to get out until later today. I thought I were to pick you up," I say, stealing yet another kiss of hers.

"I wanted to watch your game, so my dad picked me up and drove me here. He should be around still."

I want to get out of my clothes, at least the hockey gear. I want to feel Lily against me, body to body. Hug her without any of my protective gear in between.

"Dad invited you for dinner in a couple of hours. Well, he asked if *we* would like to go out for dinner with him." She takes my hockey stick from me as we walk toward the locker room.

"Sure, just let me take a shower first, okay?"

She laughs, nodding. "Of course. You stink."

"I don't stink."

"You're right. You just smell like sweat and old, stinky equipment on a daily." Lily smiles, then gets onto her tiptoes before planting a chaste kiss to my lips right when we stop in front of the locker room doors.

"Sweetheart, where do you think you're going? You belong inside this locker room. Now, close your eyes and get your cute butt inside."

She obeys and holds on to my arm, her eyes closed as I lead her inside the locker room.

Nine Days

Lily Reyes

We lie in bed, my head rests on his shoulder and his arm is wrapped around me.

Colin's laptop is set down on his legs to makes sure we both have a good view.

I was supposed to spend another few weeks at the mental hospital, but upon my request, my therapist agreed that I could go home early *if* I come see her at least five times a week. I'm doing okay-ish enough that she trust me I wouldn't do anything to myself, so I'm calling this a win.

"Okay, Lilybug, our topic was life's beauty," he says as he presses the play button and our film directing project begins to play.

Videos of me crying start to show, only seconds of my body shaking, my hands covering my face, me screaming by the hill he took me to when we watched the sunset.

Pain. He is portraying pain.

"Life's beauty isn't about the magical and perfect side of life."

His hand reaches out to grab mine as we walk toward his car. I turn to look at him. My eyes are red and puffy from crying, but a smile appears when our hands touch.

"Truth is, there wouldn't be one beautiful thing if there wasn't anything bad."

We're at The Retro Diner. I'm laughing at Colin because only two seconds ago he was trying to push the whole burger into his mouth, but it didn't fit. Instead, the sauce dripped onto his shirt, ruining it.

"We wouldn't know how to cherish what we call 'beautiful moments' when there weren't any bad ones."

Another video of me crying, sitting on Colin's bed with my notebook in my hands.

The next clip shows me in the rain, spinning with my head held high, letting the cold raindrops hit my skin.

I didn't even know he filmed that.

"Life's beauty isn't about happiness only. It's not sunshine and flowers. It's the pain, scars that tell a story. It's about darkness and the tiny source of light shining into the depth of the forest."

More clips of me struggling appear, but they all fade into other clips of me smiling, laughing.

One clip shows the moment when I step on to the ice, my face lights up like fireworks, a big smile spreads across my face.

"Life might seem warm and bright for one moment, and the next it's all back to gray, back to darkness and freezing temperatures. It beats you down after rewarding you, then rewards you again only to get another hit from it. The true art in life is to see beyond the pain. See that there is a source of light in everything."

It cuts to videos of Colin and me.

Colin running up to me in a fairy costume, making me laugh.

Colin smiling when I try to lift a way too heavy pumpkin.

Us, dancing in the middle of a bar with tons of eyes on us, ignoring every single one of them because what truly matters is Colin and I being there together.

"Love," he says. *"Life's beauty is connected to the one thing we all seek. The one thing that brings people together, splits them apart. Pain wouldn't exist without love, and love wouldn't exist without pain. Whether it's family, friends, a pet, sports, a significant other, anything, or anyone. Loss is the pain that comes with love. The true criminal, but without it, beautiful things wouldn't exist. If you don't fear losing it if you don't fear it leaving you… it's not on the side of beauty it should be on."*

More videos of Colin and me together, hugging, laughing, videos of the ways we look at one another when the other isn't looking.

"Love and loss are life's beauty. Both comes unexpectedly. It can destroy you, but it can also be a savior. Whatever it is, it comes together. One follows the other. They'll keep on coming to remind us to cherish even the smallest number of times we get to have with Love. But it's there, and if it's not yet, it will come when it's least

expected."

I sniffle, wiping away some tears.

Colin closes his laptop, a second later I'm completely cuddled up to him, wetting his t-shirt with my tears.

He chuckles, but he pulls me into his embrace and plants a kiss to the top of my head.

"That was beautiful," I tell him between sobs.

"I will deny making this. I'll say you had me say a couple of words and mixed them all together."

I look up, finding his eyes. Colin wears a smile on his face, one that says he's proud of himself for creating something so beautiful. And maybe also a bit of "I regret this more than anything."

"I'm not that talented, dumbass."

"Hm, they don't know that." He puts a chaste kiss on my lips. "Professor Meisner said he won't show it in class because he doesn't want to humiliate you and your 'crazily good acting' because it 'might seem too realistic.'"

At least that's something. I don't think having a couple of hundred other students see me cry is something I ever want to experience.

♥ ♥ ♥ ♥ ♥ ♥ ♥ ♥

"No, dad, do you know what your daughter is capable of? She's been home for a whole two hours and then... the whole goddamn *living room* looked like the decoration section of an IKEA." Aaron slides his hands down his face and lets out a desperate groan.

"I thought you guys needed a bit more color in there. Your whole house is made of white and gray's," I defend myself.

"Sweetheart, mint green is not a color that fits inside our house." How dare he be on Aaron's side instead of mine? "And your frog obsession still creeps me out."

"Thank you! These tiny frog statues are everywhere." Another groan comes from Aaron.

Honestly, if they didn't want me "girl up" their house, they shouldn't have offered me to stay. Well, it's not like I have any other choice. Colin insists I stay so he can have an eye on me, and Aaron… doesn't have much to say when it comes to me. Not when Colin already decided.

I do have a choice to stay at the dorms, but why would I when I get to annoy my brother with my presence at all times instead?

I didn't get to do that when we were younger, so I have some making up to do.

Plus, my therapist thought this is a good idea as well, mainly so the chances are lower I'd disappear as there'll be two guys looking out for me now.

"Guys, you leave Lily alone, otherwise you'll find killer frogs in your bed, and I doubt that's what you want," Ana says. At least someone's on my side.

"Thank you, Annie."

"Not another one of those Sergeant Froggo's, *por favor*," Colin begs, making a face that looks like he's in pain. "It's bad enough that Lily loves that frog more than me. I don't need more of those in my life."

I roll my eyes, trying to appear annoyed but my lips betray me as they stay stuck in a smile.

"Ladies,"—my father motions his hand around the table then stops when it's in front of me—"and frog lovers." Everyone chuckles. "If mint green decoration and frogs make the woman happy, then you all will have to make some sacrifices."

"But Dad, I can't," Aaron growls. "You don't live with us. You don't have to see those creepy creatures all day, every day. I, however, do."

"Sucks for you, Ron." Colin shrugs while winking at me.

Aaron grunts, disapproving. But just like it was for me, his mouth is betraying his annoyance.

Then the question I've been waiting for drops. Not that I was looking forward to answering it, but I knew it would come eventually.

"Will you have to go back?" Ana asks. "To the mental hospital,

I mean.",

There wasn't any need for clarification, but I'll give her an A for effort.

"Not for now. Before they released me, I talked with a psychologist. She said I'm making great progress. Sure, I won't magically get better from one day to another, but she's positive that with some more work, I can live almost to a 'normal' life," I say, probably explaining it worse than the psychologist did.

"It's going to be a hell of a lot of work to get near 'normality', whatever that shall be. I honestly don't think there's a thing such as 'normal', but whatever, that's not the point. I'll still struggle sometimes, just like everyone else. Though, if I continue to take my meds, see my therapist, and stick around the people I love, even I'm certain I can get through this without keeping up the desire to die. It's not gone yet, sometimes I still think it would be better if I did die, but you know, it's not like I think it's the only solution anymore. But apart from that, if my condition doesn't get any worse again, I'm good to stay away."

Colin squeezes my hand. He is proud of me.

No matter how small my victories might be, Colin makes sure to tell—or show—me how proud he is.

He couldn't visit me daily, the visiting hours wouldn't allow him to, neither would his schedule… but whenever he did visit me in the last two weeks, Colin listened to me telling him all about what I've learned. But most importantly, he always smiled at me like I was making him proud.

It felt and still does feel, good to know I'm not the kind of disappointment I thought I was for years.

Colin makes me feel better. And with the help of my family, I do feel as though I'm doing better.

Of course, I still have a long way to go, and I'm sure my depression will never go away, I do feel like I can conquer so much more with love in my life than I could when I was all by myself.

♥ ♥ ♥ ♥ ♥ ♥ ♥ ♥

Hours later we're finally back at home and I'm all cuddled up in Colin's bed. He's still in the bathroom, so in the meantime, I figure it would be fun to hide something under his tiny part of the blanket.

Yup, about three-quarters of the blanket is mine. There is no discussion needed. Even if Colin wanted to argue with me, he'd lose.

"What movie are we watching?" Colin asks just when the bathroom door opens.

He's only wearing some sweatpants, granting me the sight of his bare chest. Ever since I know of his not-so-new-anymore tattoo, his chest seems so much more interesting.

"The Princess and the Frog, obviously."

He groans, causing me to laugh.

"Listen, *mi sol*, you can torture me with that movie for the rest of our lives, but not tonight. It's your first day back home, let's watch something… good."

He walks over to his side of the bed, looking down at me with pleading eyes, he even adds the pouty lips.

"Are you saying this movie is bad?" I'm totally not offended by that. Nope. All good.

"No, I'm saying I want to watch something like a Marvel movie. Or some horror movie, like paranormal activities."

I hum, pretending to think about it. "Alright. *The Notebook* then."

Colin narrows his eyes, slowly lifting the blanket. "That doesn't sound like anything *action*."

"Oh, it has quite the action in it. Like… love."

Thankfully, my words go lost on him when he flinches from the stuffed animal under his side of the blanket. The one that lost an eye from Colin's last fight with it.

I can't help the horribly loud laughter spilling out of me when Colin holds his hand to his heart, breathing heavily as he tries to come back to life.

"Oh, you're so done, Liliana," he speaks through gritted teeth.

Nine Days

Colin throws the frog across the room, gets onto the bed, and hovers right over me. His face is so close to mine, I can feel his breath fanning over my skin. His chest presses against me, so close, I can feel his heart beating against mine.

He lowers his face, his nose gently touches mine before his lips connect with my lips in an ever so heart-exploding kiss.

My tongue pushes past his lips, dips into his mouth to deepen the kiss. And because I get way too touchy with this man, my hands automatically reach up to caress his back, scratching his skin with my fingernails.

"I love you, *mi sol*," Colin whispers like he only wants me to hear. "I finally have my sun back."

"I love you too, dumbass." I kiss him.

"What's the notebook about?" he asks, now lying next to me, keeping me in his arms.

"It's about the power of love and—"

"Mi sol, I mean the one on my nightstand, not the movie." He picks up the mint green notebook and brings it into my view.

"Oh." I grin, scrunching up my nose. "I have a few letters to write. They'll be about how much I'll miss you when Sergeant Froggo has murdered you."

Colin snatches the stuffed animal from me and throws it to the other side of the room. When I'm about to run after it, he holds me tighter, peppering my lips with kisses.

"He can try, but I'm pretty much invulnerable, immortal even. For as long as you're with me, my Lilybug."

The End

Acknowledgements

This book would not have been possible without those people back in school that decided to make my life a living hell. So thank you so very much for the experience. You helped me grow, realize who I definitely don't want to be, and see how not to raise my future children. I really hope that *if* you ever have children, you'll raise them better than whatever went through your heads back in the day.

I'd like to thank Joel Böhm for answering my very stupid questions about ice hockey. You kind of saved my ass here.

A big thank you to Sofía Elizabeth Cortés for letting me bug you for Spanish translations, without context or anything. I couldn't have done it without you, honestly. I wouldn't have been able to scratch up my little knowledge of Spanish to make it work myself. So, thank you, so, so much!

Also, thank you to my parents and grandparents for believing in me, celebrating every other chapter with me, even though you had absolutely no clue what I was writing.

To my mom, thank you so much for always believing in me, even when my plans seem absolutely ridiculous and completely unrealistic.

Thanks to my best friend "What-is-a-Laur," aka my TikTok account manager (who never got to the managing part) for…well, doing nothing really. But you are emotional support, you know? Having you in my life stresses me out but it's also a blessing. Seriously, I couldn't go through life without you by my side. Thank you for all the unpaid therapy sessions in the middle of the night because we're both a little too stupid to function as humans.

Because I know the two of you won't read this, which means I won't have a talk with you about this; thank you to my brothers, Tim, and Noel, for… I'm not quite sure yet, but I felt like you should get a line or two as well. Let's be honest, my life would be a lot more boring without the two of you in it.

To everyone out there struggling, I promise better times are coming. I didn't believe so myself, but for whatever reason, the universe decides to throw good and bad things around like money was free. They're both coming, always. But know, good things *are* coming your way.

ALSO BY JOELINA FALK

Unfrozen Four Series:

Nine Days #1

Eight Weeks #2

Seven Months #3

Six Years #4

Tartarus Club Series:
(Coming Soon)

A Taste Of Light #1

A Taste Of Darkness #2

Printed in Great Britain
by Amazon